Bless Her Heart

Hickory Flat Public Library
2740 East Cherokee Drive
Canton, Georgia 30115

Other books by Debby Mayne

Sweet Baklava

The Class Reunion Series

Pretty Is as Pretty Does

Bless Her Heart

Tickled Pink

BLESS HER HEART

The Class Reunion Series

Book 2

Debby Mayne

Abingdon fiction™
a novel approach to faith

Bless Her Heart

Copyright © 2013 by Debby Mayne

ISBN-13: 978-1-4267-3359-8

Published by Abingdon Press, P.O. Box 801, Nashville, TN 37202

www.abingdonpress.com

The persons and events portrayed in this work of fiction
are the creations of the author, and any resemblance
to persons living or dead is purely coincidental.

Published in association with the Hartline Literary Agency.

Library of Congress Cataloging-in-Publication Data

Mayne, Debby.
  Bless her heart / Debby Mayne.
      pages cm. — (The Class Reunion Series ; Book 2)
  ISBN 978-1-4267-3359-8 (binding: soft black : alk. paper)
  I. Title.
  PS3563.A963877B53   2013
  813'.54—dc23
                                                        2013008276

Printed in the United States of America

1 2 3 4 5 6 7 8 9 10 / 18 17 16 15 14 13

To Georgette Ingraham and Terri Carrol.
Y'all raised some awesome men,
and I'm thankful to have them as sons-in-law.

Acknowledgments

Thanks for the Abingdon marketing and sales team for embracing this series and working so hard to get it out there.

Thanks to Julie Pollitt and Paige Dooly for reading this book and offering suggestions. I'd also like to thank Rachel Overton for editing the first several chapters of the series.

For you have been my hope, O Sovereign LORD, my
confidence since my youth.

Psalm 71:5

1

Priscilla Slater

Come One, Come All
to
Piney Point High School's
Fifteen-year Reunion
June 14, 2008, at 7:00 PM
Piney Point High's Cafeteria.

Attire: Business Casual
RSVP: Laura Moss 601-555-1515 or
Celeste Boudreaux 601-555-4854

PS: The preparty will be at Pete and Laura's house,
starting at 5:00 PM.
Setups will be provided. Bring a dish to share.

I hold the invitation with one hand while unlocking the door to my townhouse with the other. The delicious sounds of silence fill my ears as I close the door behind me and make my way to my bedroom to get ready for my night out with the girls while trying to wrap my mind around the fifteen-year reunion. So they decided to go ahead with it. I warned

Laura we might not have enough people who'd want to attend so soon after everything that happened during the last one. The memory is still pretty fresh—at least in my mind. But her response insinuated that I spend too much time here in Jackson and points beyond to know what's happening with folks in Piney Point. Right. Like I don't still have a salon there.

We nearly didn't have a reunion last time because Laura was so disorganized. Her husband, Pete, wound up in the hospital from alcohol poisoning. Trudy passed out from extreme dieting while her ex-husband played the jerk. And I nearly missed the whole thing from fussing with my mother.

At least Laura has the sense to let someone else have a piece of the responsibility this time, but knowing her, I question how much control she's willing to give up—especially to Celeste. According to some of the people in my Piney Point salon, the two of them are firmly established in a *frenemy* relationship.

I was tempted not to attend five years ago, but not so this time. There's nothing that will make me happier than to off-handedly mention the fact that I've expanded my business, and I now own at least one salon in every major southeastern city. I close my eyes and envision my classmates' expressions as I explain that my next goal is to grow my business up the east coast and then to be accepted on the TV Network Shopping channel. This is my ultimate dream, and it looks like I'm getting very close to realizing it. They do a bazillion dollars' worth of business every year, and I'd love to have a slice of that pie. In fact, I've been getting some interest from some of the bigwigs about a system I designed to help women have the coveted big hair without all the teasing that damages the hair shaft. Apparently the rest of the country has finally acknowledged what Southern women have always known—big hair is hot.

Yeah, I'm totally going to this reunion.

Rather than wait to hear from Mother or Dad about the reunion they've probably known about since Laura made the decision to have it, I grab the phone and punch in their number. "I wondered how long it would take you to call," Mother says.

"I just got the invitation in today's mail."

She sighs. "You know you're always welcome to stay here. I'll have Teresa get your room ready." After a brief pause, she asks, "How long do you think you'll be here?" There's a tightening in her voice that always worries me.

"I haven't really thought about it."

"You were here an awful long time for the tenth . . . not that I mind, but you know how busy I am . . . I mean your dad and I are, and . . . " Her voice trails off, but I know that what comes after the dot-dot-dot is probably what I need to know.

"Tell you what, Mother, if I decide to hang around more than a week, I'll make other arrangements."

"No, Priscilla, that's not what I'm saying. It's just that, well . . . " Her voice cracks, so she stops and clears her throat. "You know you don't have to limit your stay here to a week. A couple weeks will be just fine."

At least I know what I'm working with. "Thanks, Mother. I'm sure that'll be plenty of time to help Laura and Celeste and maybe even work in a few appointments."

"Oh, that's another thing. We're already getting calls from people who want you to make them over after what you did for Celeste last time."

She's right. I did a wonderful job of taking Celeste from dowdy to desirable, and I hear she's actually dating now. Jimmy Shackleford and Celeste—not the ideal match in my mind, but it is what it is.

"You still there, Priscilla?"

13

"Yes, I was just thinking. Please just tell people to call the salon and book with Sheila. I don't want you to have to worry about my schedule."

"When should I tell Teresa to have your room ready?"

I look at my calendar and give Mother a date before we finally hang up. As I get ready for a girls' birthday night out with my office manager, Mandy, and salon manager, Rosemary, I find myself wondering how Dad managed to talk Mother into hiring someone to help out around the house. My parents have certainly always had the money to hire domestic help, but Mother resisted, using the argument that she'd have to clean before the cleaning lady came, so there was no point. Yeah, she's a control freak.

The rest of the evening, the phone call with Mother plays through my head. She seems vulnerable and . . . scared. I've heard that at some point in almost everyone's life, the child-parent role reverses. I hope that's not what's happening, but I put it on my mental list to consider, along with something even worse. Divorce. They've had problems in the past, but I thought they had worked them out. Even if I didn't want to go to the reunion, being there for a couple weeks will give me some time to figure out what's really going on with Mother and Dad. I know divorce is more common than staying together these days, but it's not like either of them has actually done anything that they can't fix. Plus—and I know this may sound selfish—I've always seen them as my safety net, a place to fall if things go bad. No matter how well things have gone for me, I still wanted to have that. Problem is, between reunions, I can never think of an excuse to stick around Piney Point more than a day or two—not nearly enough time to evaluate my parents. I just wish I could figure out what went wrong after the last reunion, when things started looking up between Mother and me as well as in their relationship.

"Happy birthday, Mandy," I say as I lean in for a hug and air kiss. Five years ago when I met this girl, I wasn't so sure she would work out, but I was desperate for someone to answer the phones, and now she's my office manager.

She flicks her hand from the wrist and rolls her eyes. "Don't remind me. Let's just party and forget it's my birthday."

I laugh. Mandy isn't even thirty yet, but I play along. "You don't look a day older than when I first hired you."

She starts to comment, but Rosemary breezes into the restaurant looking harried as usual. "Sorry, but my client needed extra TLC, and you know how I am."

"Boy howdy, do we ever," Mandy says. "C'mon, let's get a seat. I'm starvin'."

Rosemary billows her top. "It sure is hot out there, and it isn't even summer yet."

"That reminds me," Mandy says. "I better eat a salad, or I won't be able to wear my bikini when I go to Biloxi with Mama in a couple of weeks."

"I don't remember the last time I was able to wear a bikini," Rosemary says. "In fact, I don't even own a swimsuit."

Mandy tilts her head toward Rosemary. "So what do you wear to lay out?"

"Lay out?" Rosemary and I exchange a glance and grin as we follow Mandy to the hostess stand. "Girl, you better quit doin' that, or you'll wind up with alligator hide, or worse."

When I first hired Mandy, she and Rosemary were avid turf defenders, but over time, they've developed an understanding and affection for each other that I never saw coming. I'm relieved I stopped getting phone calls from one or the other of them tattling like a three-year-old. Now when I go out of town, the only thing I have to worry about is Mandy keeping an assistant. From what I understand, she's quite the taskmaster.

"So how's, um . . . what's the new girl's name?" I ask. Mandy struggles to keep assistants, but when I talk to her about it, she says it's the nature of hiring people for their first job.

"Clarissa," Mandy says with a shrug. "She's okay so far, but time will tell. I don't know what's up with some people. Doesn't anyone have a work ethic anymore?"

Out of the corner of my eye, I see Rosemary fighting a case of the giggles, but I nod my agreement with Mandy. "Let's hope Clarissa works out."

She lifts her hand to get the waitress's attention. "I haven't eaten since breakfast, so let's order."

After we place our order, Rosemary turns to me. "So I hear you're having another class reunion."

I grunt. "Word sure does get around."

"According to Sheila, the appointment book is already filling up," Mandy says. "Chester will have his hands full, since he's the only aesthetician in the salon . . . unless, of course, you do what you did last time and go early."

After Chester realized how much business I got from facials, he didn't hesitate to take classes so he could make his clients *Hollywood glam*. "I think I will go early."

"Then we need to move the closing date up for that salon in Raleigh," Mandy reminds me. "I don't think that'll be a problem since the current owners are so eager to get out of it."

Rosemary chuckles. "I have to hand it to ya, Priscilla. You have a knack for sniffin' out opportunities."

I smile but keep my mouth shut. My knack has more to do with Tim knowing the heartbeat of practically every privately owned hair salon between Florida and New York. The one in Raleigh came on the market when the couple who owned it decided they couldn't continue co-owning a business after their divorce.

"I've been thinking . . ." Rosemary slowly looks at me then averts her gaze. "Never mind."

I frown. "You know you have to tell me now."

"It's nothing." She nervously glances over her shoulder and turns back to face me. "Promise you won't be mad?"

"You know I can't make that kind of promise. What is it?"

"I have a cousin in Apex, one of the little towns near Raleigh. Her husband's been sick, and well . . . " Her shoulders sag as she contorts her mouth.

"What?"

"How about if I transfer to the new salon in Raleigh?"

Rosemary's husband passed away a couple of years ago, and she's been visiting her cousin every chance she gets, so I shouldn't be surprised. But I am.

"They already have a manager." I lean back and study Rosemary's face for a reaction. "You know I don't like to go into a new salon and make too many changes too quickly."

"Yeah, I know, and that's fine. I don't have to be the manager." She shrugs. "In fact, I'd sort of like a little less responsibility."

When I turn to see Mandy's reaction, I realize she already knows. I feel left out of the loop, and to my surprise, it bugs me. But I can't let on, so I fold my hands and force a smile.

"Okay, let's do whatever we need to do to make this happen as smoothly as possible. Who do you think would be a good candidate to promote in Jackson?"

"Vanessa's pretty good with the other hairdressers, and she could use the extra money."

Mandy nods. "I agree."

"Okay, then I'll have a chat with her to see if she's interested."

Mandy and Rosemary look at each other before Mandy speaks up. "She's definitely interested."

My insides suddenly feel as though someone has pulled a plug and drained all my blood. At some point along the way, these two very fine women have learned to run my business without me, which should make me pleased as punch, but that's not happening. Still, they're just *feelings*, and this is *business*, so I can't let on. ·

"So when do y'all propose the changes take place?" I speak slowly and pray my shaky voice is only obvious to me.

Rosemary places her hand on mine. "Everything will be okay, Sweetie. You've done a good job with the salon."

Mandy nods. "Rosemary has already started working with Vanessa, and the salon in Raleigh has an open station."

Whoa. "So it's already in the works?"

"No, of course it isn't," Rosemary says. "We would never take action on something so important until talking to you. After all, you're still the boss."

I take a sip of water to calm down and moisten my dry lips. Finally, I nod. "Sounds like y'all have everything under control, so go ahead with your plans. What's next?"

The server takes our order and brings our food, and as we eat, Mandy and Rosemary tag team the details of what is about to transpire. I straddle the fence of being proud and feeling left out, but I'm pretty sure I do a good job of showing a positive attitude—at least until we step outside. Rosemary places her arm around my shoulders and gives me a squeeze.

Mandy takes my hand and looks me in the eyes that have begun to sting. "We are so proud of working for the Cut 'n Curl we could pop. There's no stoppin' you, Priscilla, and we want you to know you don't have to worry about a thing. Keep that forward momentum going and know we've got your back."

I close my eyes, nod, and fill my lungs with air. As I exhale, I open my eyes and see the concern on Mandy and Rosemary's faces. Again, I force a smile, hoping they can't see the insecurity that's behind it but realizing they probably do. "I know that, and I'm proud of you too."

"Then stop worryin' and enjoy the journey," Mandy says, stealing the words from the self-help CD I gave her last Christmas. "I have no doubt your big-hair system will catch on big-time, and every woman east of the Mississippi will have one."

"Oh, I think every woman in *America* will have one by the time it's all said and done," Rosemary corrects. "I can't imagine anyone not seeing the value of a poof without the messy teasing."

I laugh. These two are working hard at making me feel better, and I can't let them down. "Let's hope y'all are right."

"Oh, Honey, when it comes to you and your career, I know I'm right. From the moment I met you, I've known you're a force to be reckoned with. Matter of fact . . . " Rosemary takes a moment to sniffle. "I even told Ted you were gonna be a big name in hair some day, God rest his soul." She glances at her watch. "I need to run home and call my cousin to let her know she needs to start looking for a place for me to stay. She offered to let me live with her, but you know what they say about fish and company: more than two or three days, and they begin to stink."

We hug good-bye and walk to our cars. All the way home I reflect on the conversation and think about how I have a choice of seeing it as an ambush or an opportunity. Change is good, right? I've always thought that, but at the moment it's rather unsettling.

I met Rosemary's husband, Ted, shortly after she joined my salon in Jackson, and I have to admit I was surprised to see a man old enough to be her father. In fact, she later confided that he was two years older than her father, but he was young at heart. She's always known that she was statistically likely to outlive Ted, but the reality when it actually happened hit her hard. I can't blame her for wanting to leave Jackson for a new start. At least I'll still have her working for me, and I'll do whatever I can to make the transition as smooth as possible.

My cell phone rings as I pull into the driveway of my town-house. I look down and see Tim Puckett's name and number. It took him a while to start calling again after the ten-year reunion, but now we have a more defined relationship that I wouldn't trade for anything. Every once in a while I get the impression he'd pick up right where we left off, but then I occasionally hear about some girl he's dating. I have to admit to an occasional twinge of jealousy, but I know that's only my ego tugging at me. I've relinquished all rights to romance with this very sweet man, and he's entitled to see whomever he wants.

2
Tim Puckett

I'm a little surprised when she answers on the third ring. Most of the time Priscilla's so busy she lets the calls go and gets back with me later . . . much later—sometimes several days or a week. But I clear my throat and jump right in.

"Hey, Priscilla, I was just wonderin'—"

I hear her sigh. "Yes, Tim, I'm going to the class reunion, and if you still want to go with me, that's fine."

"Don't give yourself a heart attack from excitement."

"Sorry, Tim, but I just got some unsettling news, and I haven't had time to process it all yet."

"About the reunion?" I think back to her last one and try to figure out which of the many crazy people might have upset my favorite girl on the planet. Of course we're just friends now, but stranger things have happened, and . . . well, you know.

"No, it's Rosemary. She's leaving."

"Well, it's not like she's leaving the Cut 'n Curl altogether," I remind her. "She's just going to Raleigh."

"You *knew*?" Priscilla's high-pitched voice lets me know she's not happy. "Why didn't you say something?"

"Because it's not my place?" With anyone else, that would be a statement, but with Priscilla, I tend to have more questions than answers. That girl sure does keep me on my toes.

"I understand. Anyway, if you don't mind putting yourself through it again, I'd love for you to go to the reunion with me."

"My pleasure." I lean back in the recliner as relief floods me from head to toe. After seeing Priscilla get all gooey-eyed over that Maurice fella and knowing she wished she was with him instead of me, I wasn't so sure about where I stood with her. Even after it was all over, and she gave him the heave-ho for trying to take advantage of her, she pretty much let me know she wasn't feeling for me what I felt for her, and I've finally come to terms with the fact that we're not likely to ever become a couple. But I still enjoy her company when we have time to get together.

"I don't want you taking all your vacation time this year," she says. "Why don't you just plan to come the night before the reunion?"

"Uncle Hugh gave me an extra week of vacation on account of he can't give me a raise this year."

"So you don't mind wasting . . . I mean spending that time in Piney Point in the midst of all that drama?" she asks.

"I don't mind at all. In fact, I rather enjoyed the drama."

This might come across as silly, but the sound of her laughter is how I imagine harp music in heaven. I used to fantasize about her laughter with our young'uns. "Tim, you are definitely a glutton for punishment."

She might call it punishment, but as long as I can hang out with Priscilla Slater, I know I'm gonna have a good time. "You didn't seem to mind having me there last time."

"You were mighty helpful."

"And I will be this time too. At least now I know what to expect. Maybe I can dodge Pete Moss's fist a little better next time he tries to deck me."

"That was crazy," she says. "According to Sheila, he's still drinking, so maybe you better try to avoid him completely."

Sheila is the manager of Prissy's Cut 'n Curl in Piney Point, and she knows more about what's going on in town than the mayor. "I'll just try to stay in his good graces."

After we get off the phone, I get up from my recliner and carry my empty chip bowl to the kitchen. Seems no matter how much I eat I can't seem to put on weight. Mama used to tell me she thought I swallowed a tapeworm, but I think it's because I'm in and out of the car all day, and it can get mighty hot in Mississippi, Alabama, Georgia, Tennessee, Kentucky, the Carolinas, and the Florida panhandle, my territory with Uncle Hugh's beauty supply company. By noon, I'm always sweatin' bullets, and by the end of the day, I look like a drowned rat that couldn't find the cheese. That's why I try to stop by Prissy's Cut 'n Curl office first thing in the morning. I like to smell nice for Priscilla.

I go to bed with happy thoughts, hoping to dream about Priscilla. Only problem is I can't get her last class reunion out of my mind, and I wind up dreaming about Pete Moss and the flask he keeps in the back of his pickup.

Early the next morning, I give up trying to sleep. I get up before the alarm goes off, and I trudge toward the bathroom. A look in the mirror has me groaning. For the past year I've been trying to grow some facial hair, but it don't come in nice like Justin Timberlake's. Instead, I look like one of them guys who keeps trying to break into MacCaulay Culkin's house in *Home Alone.*

Since I'm grooming for someone else, I make the decision to get rid of the uneven stubble. After all, I wouldn't want to embarrass my favorite girl—especially since I'm fully aware of how important it is for her to keep up her image, even though I reckon she'd say it isn't so. But I'm not blind. I saw her in action with all her classmates, and I can tell she still has something to prove.

And that reminds me. I haven't been too good about learning a new word every day. I make a mental note to pick up the book she gave me when she first found out I wanted to learn to talk as good as her—the one called *A Hundred Days to a Smarter Vocabulary.* I was actually moving along at a decent clip, back before Priscilla's last class reunion. But I got so perturbed I figured there wasn't any use in filling my brain with words longer than my forearm if she still had a hankering for that bozo Maurice. In my book, he's got two things wrong with him: he's a pretty boy who looks in the mirror more than he'll look at any girl, and his muscles bulge in all the wrong places, which tells me he's a gym rat. Everyone knows those are fake muscles and not all that useful in the real world. I might look scrawny, but I can lift my share of grocery bags and rearrange my mama's furniture when she gets in one of her moods. I reckon some girls don't realize guys like Maurice don't wanna get their hands dirty doing actual men's work.

After I shower, I down a cup of coffee before going out on my beauty supply route for the day. As I head toward Birmingham, I call Priscilla to find out the exact dates of the events so I can let Uncle Hugh know when I'm taking off.

"If at any point you change your mind and decide to back out, I promise I won't think any less of you," she says. "I mean, I appreciate your loyalty and everything, but—"

"Relax. I don't have anything better to do. In fact, I been lookin' forward to it . . . and hopin' you'd want me to go with you." I actually got a kick outta seeing some of those people misbehaving and carrying on like they didn't know their mamas would find out. Plus Aunt Tammy told me she thinks I'm one of them people who like to feel needed. I don't see nothin' wrong with that."

"If you're sure . . ."

I laugh. "I like helpin' out."

"Okay," she says. "Just remember it's never too late to back out."

"Priscilla." I clear my throat, wondering if what I'm about to ask is just downright stupid, but I can't help wondering. "You had a rough time at the last reunion. Why do *you* wanna go?"

I hear her sigh. "Good question. Maybe I'm just a glutton for punishment."

"Naw, I don't think that's the case. I think you really do like your old friends, and deep down, you enjoy bein' there."

"I think you're right."

We hang up, and my day looks brighter already. My chin feels smooth, and I realize I never really liked the prickly feeling from my feeble attempt at facial hair, so I make a deal with myself. No more trying to be something I'm not . . . and I'm definitely not a pop star.

The drive to Birmingham is long and boring. I listen to the contemporary Christian music station, but then I'm out of range, and I still have a way to go. I try talk radio, but the guy gets on my nerves. Sometimes I think those folks just love the sound of their voices because it don't sound to me like he's saying much—just the same thing over and over.

I grip the steering wheel with both hands and stare at the road ahead, trying to project myself into the future. My daydream starts out all nice and rosy, with me and Priscilla walking into the reunion arm in arm, but then the image gets hazy. I blink and turn my thoughts over to something I can predict. I bet Mama would appreciate a call. I haven't talked to her in a while.

"Hey, Timothy. I was about to head on out to yoga class. Is everything all right?"

"Yes, Mama. Just wanted to check up on you and let you know I'm goin' to Priscilla's fifteen-year high-school reunion."

Mama makes a clucking sound. "You're not still holding onto the notion that you and Priscilla are—"

"No, Mama, it's just that she needs a date and we're good friends and I'm available."

"That's your own fault. Listen, Timothy, you're a good-lookin' boy who has a lot to offer some worthy woman. I like Priscilla, but I don't think she's the one the good Lord meant for you to spend the rest of your life with."

I disagree, but I don't say it. Arguing with Mama is like getting in the ring with a bull and telling him not to charge.

She goes on and on about my heart getting tromped on, but I focus on my driving. What was I thinking when I told her about the reunion?

I zone back into the conversation when I hear her winding down. "So when was the last time you had a date with Priscilla?"

It's been almost a year since me and Priscilla hung out, but I wouldn't exactly call it a date. I sigh. "This isn't a date, Mama. I'm just goin' with her to show my support."

"Don't get your heart broken again, Timothy. No girl—not even Priscilla Slater—is worth losin' sleep over. Besides, you need to stay away from those career-type gals and get yourself someone who dotes on you." She pauses. "I gotta get outta here. My yoga instructor says part of people's problems today is we wait 'til the last minute, and that stresses us out."

I'm relieved to be let off the hook. "Okay, Mama, love you."

There's nothing worse than a mama trying to protect her grown son's heart. Mama and Daddy split up when I was little, so I was all Mama had. We moved in with Granny, and Mama got herself a job. Them two women would've spoiled me rotten if I hadn't been so caught up in trying to act like a man—even at the young age of three. When I started school, Mama and I moved into an apartment nearby.

Daddy's brother, Uncle Hugh, was just getting his beauty supply business going then, but he got all ticked off at Daddy for leaving and found time for me. He taught me the manly stuff like fishing and hunting and how to fix a toilet when it wouldn't stop running, but he couldn't grow his business and stay in Mississippi, so he moved to the Big Apple. I sure did miss him, but every now and then he'd send a plane ticket for me to come up and visit. Once when I got upset with Mama, I threatened to move north. That was when Uncle Hugh promised to hire me if I stayed put and went to college. My daddy never came around much throughout my childhood, but Uncle Hugh more than made up for it. I reckon Uncle Hugh wanted to be the father figure in my life, and I'm happy he did. Working as a beauty supply sales rep is perfect for me. It pays real good, and I have more freedom than I'd have at a desk job.

Once I get to Birmingham, time goes by fast. The salons are scattered all over town and in the suburbs, but I have them all lined up in a route. Some of the folks I do business with have their orders ready for me when I walk in. Others want to spend a little time with me going over the new products and chatting my ear off about this and that. Before I even step foot in each salon, I know about how long I'll be there, and I save my favorite for last. Angela Stanton, senior hairdresser and proprietor of Making Waves, greets me with an ear-to-ear grin and hearty, "Come on back to the break room and let's catch up."

Uncle Hugh warned me early in my career that hairdressers like to get to know people real well. "Don't tell them nothin' you don't want comin' back at ya later," he said. That's easier said than done. What I've discovered is that hairdressers have a knack for getting folks to talk. I'm thinking they'd make excellent government interrogators.

"So how's your love life?" Angela asks. "Seen that girl at the Cut 'n Curl lately?"

"Not much." I rub my chin, trying to decide whether or not she needs to know about the class reunion. "She's been busy."

"So I hear. Word out there is she's about to acquire every available salon east of the Mississippi."

I laugh. "I'm not sure how accurate that is, but she's ambitious."

"Ambition is a good thing as long as it doesn't get in the way of a happy life. I don't mean to tell you what to do or who to fall in love with, but be careful not to lose your heart to a woman who's all wrapped up in her work."

I shift uncomfortably in my seat. "I'll try to remember that."

Her eyes narrow as she tilts her head before taking a sip of coffee. "So are you seein' anyone else? I'm sure you meet enough women in your line of work to have your pick."

"Speaking of work, I've been pretty busy myself. My uncle is about to expand, and he's all but promised me a promotion." The instant those words leave my mouth I wish I'd kept it shut. Uncle Hugh once told me if he promoted me it'd likely involve relocating to New York City. That's a great place to visit, but even with a raise, my salary wouldn't be high enough to cover an apartment near as nice as the one I have in Mississippi.

"Is that so?" Angela lifts one of the hairstyle magazines and flips through it without looking at the pages. "What kind of expansion?"

When she looks me in the eye, I see something I can't quite put my finger on. "We're addin' more products and movin' west of the Mississippi."

She clears her throat as she puts the magazine on the stand behind her, then she leans forward on her elbows. "Tim, I need to share something with you, but you have to promise not to breathe a word of it to anyone." Her forehead crinkles. "Okay?"

I nod. "Of course."

"Business isn't so good lately, with all the folks cuttin' back and all. Those cheap salons in the suburbs are thrivin', making things tough for beauticians in the better salons. I been thinkin' . . . you know, what with all the experience I have . . . well, I might want to see what Priscilla Slater is willing to give me for this place."

"Really?" I never saw this coming. I try to recover by clearing my throat and straightening up in my chair. "What will you do?"

She grins. "If I get enough money, I'll probably take a cruise, but I can't be a lady of leisure forever, so I thought maybe I could do what you do." She gives me a puppy-dog look. "Think you might be able to help me out? Put in a good word?"

Wow. Double whammy. She wants me to help her find a job, and she wants me to use my influence on Priscilla. "I reckon I can try, but I can't promise anything."

"I wouldn't have mentioned any of this if you hadn't said your uncle was wanting to expand."

"I reckon I can talk to him," I tell her for lack of something better to say.

She lifts her eyebrows into a pleading expression and nods. "Do you mind?"

"I'll ask if he's planning to add more sales reps."

"Oh, and don't forget to talk to Priscilla. Let her know I might consider selling this place if the offer is right. I don't want her to think I'm desperate or nothin' . . . 'cause I'm not, ya know?"

"Sure, I'll see what her plans are." I stand. "I best be gettin' outta here. I have a busy day tomorrow."

Angela walks me to the door, chattering about unimportant things. I'm out on the sidewalk when she winks and grins. "Thanks, Tim. You're a sweetie pie."

3

Laura Moss

Mama, when am I gonna get my period? Bonnie Sue done started hers, and that ain't fair."

I turn around to face my second-born child and firstborn daughter Renee. "Only God knows. And stop using *ain't*. People will think you're stupid."

"I'm the only girl in my homeroom who never had a period."

"Oh, Renee, I'm sure you're not the *only* girl."

She rolls her eyes in a way I suspect all thirteen-year-old divas do when they think their mama is dumb as a sack of rocks. "The only girl except Myra, and she don't count. She's gross."

"She *doesn't* count." What's up with my young'uns who know how to talk but insist on sounding like a bunch of hicks?

"See? Even you know what I'm talkin' about."

"Renee, Honey, just stop worryin' about gettin' your period. It'll happen when it's supposed to." And once it starts, she'll regret wishing for it, but I don't say that. I've learned to say as little as possible to my preteen and teen children 'cause everything that comes out of my mouth comes back to bite me on the backside later.

"Laura!"

One thing I'll never have to worry about is my husband sneakin' up on me. When he comes home from work, everyone in the house knows about it.

"I'm in the kitchen." As usual.

He walks through the door and casts a curious glance at Renee before turning to me, waving an envelope in the air. "What's up with this?"

"If you're talkin' about the class reunion invitation, I sent them out last week."

"You told me we wasn't havin' a preparty."

I turn around to face him, plant my fist on my hip, and stare him straight in the face. "And you told me we were."

He snickers as he crosses the room, opens the fridge, pulls out a can of beer and pops the top. Ever since we caught our oldest child, Bubba, sneaking a smoke in the backyard, I've worried that Pete might be a bad influence. He claims drinkin' and smokin' have nothing to do with each other, but I beg to differ.

"So we're havin' the preparty here, huh?"

I nod. "I figured that would be easiest."

"What're we gonna do with the young'uns?"

I glance over at Renee. "Why don't you go on up and see what Bonnie Sue is doin'?"

Her look of pure horror brings back memories of my own attempts to be cool. "She kicked me out of her room. Says I'm too nerdy to hang out with her and her stupid friends."

I jab my finger toward the door leading to the stairs. "You go right back up there and tell her that's not okay with me."

She lifts her hands and backs out of the kitchen. "Okay, I get it. You don't want me around either. I guess I'm not good enough for this family."

After she leaves, Pete takes another swig and tilts his head. "What's that all about?"

"Ever since Bonnie Sue made the cheerleading squad at the early tryouts for middle school for next year, she thinks she's too cool for her britches." My heart aches for Renee who has never been popular. It's gotta be tough watching your younger sister grow more popular by the day, while you sit there counting flowers on the wall and then realize you're one of 'em.

Pete takes a long swig of his beer, makes a face as he swallows it, and slams the can down on the table. "If Bonnie Sue don't get over herself, I got a good mind to yank her right out of cheerleading."

As annoyed as I've been with the snobbery that comes with Bonnie Sue's newfound popularity, I know that's not the answer. That would only anger her and drive the wedge even deeper between them.

"You tell her she better straighten up and start treatin' her sister right," Pete says as he picks up his beer can and leaves the kitchen, half the words coming out on belches. I don't know how he does that. Practice, I suppose.

Once I'm alone, I shove my latest concoction into the oven, set the timer, and pick up one of the reunion invitations. I'm surprised Pete didn't mention the fact that I included Celeste's name as a co-coordinator. Back in high school, she had the biggest crush on him, and they even had a few dates. These days, she's too busy flaunting her plucked and microderm-abrased face around town, but Pete still thinks she's making eyes and winking at him. I know better. It's those contacts she hasn't gotten used to yet, and they make her blink. I've been trying to talk her into getting some eye drops, but she's afraid it'll make her mascara run, and heaven forbid that should happen. Oh, another thing. I'm pretty sure she got a nose job, but it's hard to tell with all that other stuff going on with her face. She never had a bad nose, but it does look a bit perkier than before.

At any rate, I'm just happy to share the burden . . . and the blame for the reunion. The last one took every bit of energy out of me and nearly killed my husband 'cause I couldn't give him the attention he needs. Even though Celeste helped me more than I'll ever let on, no one held her personally responsible for anything.

Tacky as she is, Celeste can be a hard worker, and I reckon she's sort of amusing. The only thing I have to worry about is that she might go back to crushing on Pete, and then I'll have to smack her. Not literally, of course, but with some words that remind her that he's mine. She might be dating Jimmy, but he's not near as cute as Pete, and I have to admit, I'm still a little insecure about it. Celeste really looks fantastic.

"Hey, Miss Pudge, what time's supper gonna be ready?" Pete leans against the doorjamb looking all wore out. Too much beer'll do that to a man.

"Don't call me that," I say. "You know how much I hate it."

He laughs as he pulls away from the door and comes toward me, his arms extended. "You know that's my way of sayin' I love ya, Honey."

I relax just enough to snuggle deeper into his arms. "I still don't like it." There's something about this man, beer belly and all, that I can't get enough of. I've thought off and on about leaving, but he's loyal and cares about his family. Besides, where would I go with four kids? Besides, I really truly love Pete Moss, and I don't think that'll ever change.

He gently brushes a few loose strands from my face, drops a kiss on my forehead, and then pushes me away. "I told Bubba and little Jack I'd toss the baseball with 'em before supper."

I lift an eyebrow. "They want to toss a ball with their daddy?"

He shrugs. "They didn't say they didn't, so I reckon they do."

They're at an age when I never know what they want, and Pete is trying to be a good daddy, so I decide to cut him a little slack. I glance over at the timer that shows we have about twenty minutes. "You have time so long as you don't let the boys get too dirty."

"You know how our boys are. They can look outside and wind up with dirt on 'em."

"Then come inside in fifteen minutes so they can wash up."

Pete lifts his head and sniffs the air. "Watcha cookin'? Smells like one of your fancy dishes."

It's just chicken, noodles, and vegetables from a can that I tossed with cheese, but to Pete who grew up thinkin' all hot meals come from the school cafeteria, it's about as fancy as it gets. "It is," I say. "And I made some grape Kool-Aid to go with it."

He wiggles his eyebrows up and down as he rubs his tummy. "That sounds mighty good, Honey. Where's the baseball gloves?"

I start to ask why he thinks I would know when I see his gaze settle on the mudroom shelf behind me.

"Oh, there they are. We'll be back in to wash up in just a few minutes."

The screen door slams behind them followed by the sound of Renee and Bonnie Sue arguing as they enter the kitchen. "Don't you dare wear that hideous T-shirt to school tomorrow," Bonnie Sue says. "It's bad enough you hang out with all the dorkiest kids. You don't have to dress like 'em."

"So what's it to you?" Renee stops at the snack basket and inspects the contents.

"Why are you rummaging around that junk food? Aren't you fat enough?"

Renee pulls her hand out of the basket and slowly turns around to face her younger sister, her nostrils flaring and her eyes all squinty and mad. "You are the meanest girl I know." Her chin quivers as she looks over at me. "Mama, make Bonnie

Sue quit bein' a cheerleader. She's startin' to act just like the rest of 'em."

"Girls." I point to the table. "Sit down. Now. We need to talk."

"But—" Bonnie Sue frowns but clamps her jaw shut when she looks at me.

"We are family, and I will not have y'all actin' like this. Renee, I think it's just a matter of time before you get your period 'cause you're already PMSing." I pause to let it sink in before I light into my younger daughter. "And Bonnie Sue, stop acting too big for your britches. One of these days you'll wish you were nicer to your family, like when one of those girls you been hangin' out with says something that hurts your feelings."

She bobs her head like the diva teen actresses do on those TV reality shows. "My friends will never do anything to hurt my feelings."

"Maybe not, but if they ever say or do anything to your sister or brothers, they are not welcome in our home." I lean over until she makes eye contact with me in order to drive my point home. I can tell when it works because she jumps up from her chair and runs from the kitchen.

Renee starts to say something, but I shut her up with one of my trademark growls. "You are so mean!" Next thing I know she's taking off just like her sister did.

Anyone without a trained parent's eye might think I'm making a bigger mess of things, but I know what I'm doing. I've always known the best way to bring people closer together is to give them a common enemy, and as someone who was snubbed and mistreated throughout my childhood and teenage years, I don't mind being that person.

Once the girls are out of the kitchen, I lean over and glance out at the backyard, where Pete is staggering around, trying to catch the ball one of the boys obviously just threw at him.

36

Bubba and Jack look disgusted, but Pete is mighty proud of himself when he gets control of the ball after it wobbles a bit. He holds it up and says something I can't quite hear, but both boys remove their gloves and throw them on the ground. Pete takes his off and throws it at Bubba, who turns on Jack. I stand there wishing things could be different for my family. Even when Pete tries to be a good daddy, he falls short, and I wind up having to come up with a way to make things better. One of these days, I won't be able to, and I fear something really awful might happen. In fact, something did happen during the ten-year reunion, which is why I need this one to redeem myself and Pete.

I'm about to open the back door and holler that supper's ready, but before I put down my oven mitt, the boys come tromping in, grumbling about their daddy being too drunk to play ball and Pete raking his fingers through his hair like he doesn't know what they're talking about. I feel sorry for all three of 'em, but I have the sense to keep my mouth shut and let them work through things without my interference. I've learned to only stick my nose into matters when I can actually make a difference, and it's obvious there's not a single solitary thing I can do for them now. After Pete's court-ordered therapy, I assumed he was cured, but apparently, it's pretty common for folks to fall off the wagon over time. I've tried dragging him back to counseling, but he says he can stop drinking when-ever he wants, and no amount of nagging I do will make him go when he's not ready. I hate for the kids to keep on seeing him like this, but the only solution now would be for me to leave and take 'em with me. And I'm not about to go off on my own. First of all, in spite of his misbehaving ways, Pete loves his family, and we love him. Second, I don't know what I'd do to support us, and without me around, I'm not so sure Pete would survive. I've got plenty of folks praying for us, though, and maybe one of these days, Pete will see the light and snap out of his addiction.

"Where's the girls?" Pete asks.

"Upstairs."

"Why haven't you called them down for supper?"

I glare at him. "Because I haven't. Why don't you do it for me?"

Pete licks the front of his teeth, which is a sign he's already getting the dry mouth from too much beer. "Okay." Next thing I know, he's hollering at the top of his lungs, ordering the girls to come down right this minute, or they'll miss supper.

"I coulda done that."

He shrugs and pulls out a chair. "I didn't mind. Don't say I never do nothin' for ya."

Renee shows up at the kitchen door. Alone. And with a scowl.

"Where's Bonnie Sue?" Pete asks.

She lifts her top lip in a snarl and shakes her head. "How would I know? I'm not her keeper."

Pete frowns as he meets my gaze. "Did something happen I need to know about?"

"Not really," I say. "Just the normal PMS stuff."

"That is so mean!" Renee hollers as she takes off running back to her room.

"What?" Pete's clueless-man expression is so sweet I want to give him a hug, but I force myself to stay in front of the stove, dishing up some heaping servings.

"It's a girl thing," I reply.

"Girls are stupid," Jack says.

Bubba dances around behind his chair as he mocks Jack. "You don't think Mackenzie's stupid. I saw you—"

"Boys!" Pete's sly grin lets me know he's in on something.

"Is there something I need to know about?" I ask as I put a plate down in front of my husband.

"Mama, I'm starvin'." Bubba gives up his brotherly taunting and plops down in his chair.

"We need to say the blessin' first," I say. I finish scooping food onto the plates and carry them to the table. "Bow your head. Bubba, it's your turn." I figure Renee and Bonnie Sue can eat later, after they've had some time to cool off. No point in giving everyone else a tummy ache from their bellyaching.

Bubba mumbles a few words, followed by "Amen." I say my "amen," and by the time I move back toward the stove, I hear forks clinking against plates.

No matter how dysfunctional we are as a family, I reckon the Lord will grant us some grace and mercy as long as we give him a nod every now and then. Suppertime blessings are the least we can do. I used to insist on bedtime prayers, but try forcing an adolescent girl to kneel beside her bed. It's not gonna happen unless she wants it to.

"Looky who the cat drug in," Bubba says, imitating his daddy.

I glance over my shoulder and see that Renee has shown up again. "Want me to fix your plate, or do you wanna do it yourself?"

She grunts as she stomps past me. "I'm not an invalid, like some people I know."

Pete has been perplexed by our daughters from the moment they grew past his belly button. He pulls out the chair next to him. "Have a seat, Princess."

She plops down with her plate that's heaping with vegetables, chicken, and gooey cheese. "You got the wrong daughter. The princess is still up in her room, talking on the phone to one of her stupid friends."

Pete pushes back from the table but stops and looks at me. "Want me to go up and get her?"

I think for a second before shaking my head. I'd like to eat my supper in peace. "She can have leftovers when she's ready to come down and be nice."

He scoots back into position and picks up his fork. "Just say the word, and I'll take care of things."

Little Jack has scraped as much supper as he can get with his fork, and now he lifts his plate and sticks out his tongue. I slam my palm on the table. He jumps. "What did you do that for, Mama?"

"You will not lick your plate like a dog."

"But Mama . . . " He turns to get help from Pete, who shakes his head, grinning.

"You heard your mama. It's bad manners to lick your plate clean."

"But you do it."

Pete laughs. "Just when it's us guys. Ya gotta learn things is different when you got women around, watchin' your every move."

Bubba rolls his eyes. "Ain't that the truth. Not a one of 'em laughed at my monkey imitation in the cafeteria."

"No wonder the girls think you're such a dweeb," Renee says as she scoots her chair closer to the table. .

"They do not." Bubba scrunches up his face, reminding me he's still my little boy.

"Who does monkey imitations?" Renee asks, her mouth full. "This is good, Mama."

I jerk my head around to see if she's being a smart aleck and see that she's serious. She's already shoveling another bite of food into her mouth. Her mood swings have me spinning in circles. One minute she's spewing venom, and the next, she's sweet as sugar pie.

4

Trudy Baynard

I've barely come to terms with my size eight thighs, when bam! The button pops, and I've moved up to a size ten. That just beats all.

Mama told me I needed to consider wearing Spanx last time I went to Piney Point, but until now, I've been determined not to. It's obvious I need some help to smooth out these bulges, or I'll have to resort to elastic-waist knits. The very thought sends a shiver down my spine.

I flop down onto the bed and call Mama. "I can't believe I'm resorting to buying a girdle. I've even been working out at the gym, eating diet food, and nothing I do seems to help."

"You're in your thirties now," Mama says. "As you get older, you need all the extra help you can get. Patty's been wearin' Spanx for a while."

I hate when Mama brings up either of my sisters—both of them obviously more together than I'll ever be. "That's 'cause she has kids."

"I'm sure you'll meet someone nice one of these days . . . that is, if you ever get past the fact that you and Michael will never be a couple again—"

"Don't start in on me about that." Even after all these years of being divorced from my childhood sweetheart, Michael, my eyes still sting with tears when his name comes up. I've had dates, but not one of them was a good candidate. It never fails that if I want to pursue a relationship, the guy doesn't, or the other way around.

"I'm just sayin'—"

"I gotta run now, Mama. Good-bye."

"Trudy, before we hang up, I got something to tell you."

I let out a sigh. "What?"

"Amy is engaged."

My heart skips a beat. I'm happy for my baby sister, in spite of what other people might think. She's the only one of us three girls who stuck around and made sure Mama and Daddy got the attention they need. "To Derek?"

"No, he took off with one of the Stafford girls. She met Tyler Patterson at a church retreat. I have to admit I thought it was a rebound romance, but your daddy and I actually like him. He comes from a good family over in Hattiesburg."

Good family means everything to Mama, but this is quite a surprise, since Amy's been dating Derek for the past three years. "I hope she's happy."

"Oh, I'm sure she's very happy. She's always wanted to get married and have a bunch of young'uns."

I'm not so sure about that. From what I remember, it was Mama who wanted us to get married and have families. Don't get me wrong. I wanted a family, too, as long as it was with Michael. The two of us were always the beautiful couple in town, so there was never any doubt we'd have beautiful children who could carry on the tradition of Piney Point royalty. The problem is he went and messed things up by finding himself a pretty young thing . . . and then another and another.

Once girls hit their mid-twenties, he considers them over the hill. I used to be shallow too, but at least I've matured.

"Ooh, gotta run," Mama says. "Don't forget to let me know if you need some Spanx. I'll need to get them soon, since with the reunion comin' up, there'll probably be a run on 'em."

"Okay, Mama." I'd rather get them myself than have Mama do it for me. If I resort to wearin' that stuff, I certainly don't want everyone to know. Mama said people talked about me, saying I had anorexia, but I really don't, even though I did starve myself before the last reunion.

I'm just about done getting ready for work when my phone rings. "Hey, Ms. Baynard, this is Marlene Vanderford."

No matter how many times I tell her to call me Trudy, she continues to say Ms. Baynard. "Hey Marlene. How are you?"

"Still a little sad, but I'm sure everything happens for the best. The Lord knows what I need more than I do."

"Why are you sad?" I ask as I rummage through my purse to make sure I have everything.

"Well, considering the situation, I probably shouldn't tell you this, but if I were you, I'd want to know."

Alarm bells ring in my head. "Tell me."

She sighs. "I guess you know how much I liked Hank Starkey. He broke up with me a couple of weeks ago, saying he just wasn't feeling it."

I know how she feels after my broken marriage, but I don't get why she thinks I would want to know this. "I'm so sorry, Marlene, but that happens to the best of relationships."

"I know. He told me he's always had a thing for you, and nothing I do can change that."

Whoa, wait a minute. Hank Starkey has always had a thing for me? I knew he had a crush on me back in high school, but fifteen years have passed, and he had a gorgeous—even prettier than me, I'm now willing to admit—woman falling all over him. I mean, why would he have a "thing" for me when he could have Marlene Vanderford, second runner-up for Miss Mississippi?

"Ms. Baynard, are you still there?"

"Y-yes, I'm here."

"Please be good to Hank. He's a wonderful man with a lot of love to give. I've never met a smarter, kinder, committed Christian person who lives his faith."

"Will you be at the reunion?" I ask.

She lets out a soft, sweet laugh. "No, I'm afraid not. After Hank broke up with me, I joined a mission group that's going to Brazil next week. I have a lot to do before we leave." She pauses. "Please pray for us. The conditions are terrible. There's no running water or electricity to parts of the village, and the people are suffering."

I can't imagine intentionally putting myself in the kind of conditions she's talking about, but I know she loves doing stuff like that. "I'll pray for you." And I will when I have time later today.

"Thank you, Ms. Baynard. I also want you to know I don't hold any bad feelings toward you because I know you didn't do anything to lead him on."

"Enjoy your trip, Marlene." After we hang up, I realize how trite my closing words are, but there's nothing I can do about it now.

I have to think about Hank Starkey's admission to Marlene. It never even dawned on me that he'd still hold a torch for me. And to think he'd let someone like Marlene go just because his feelings for her aren't as strong as what he's always felt for me. Maybe I should give him a chance. He was geeky back in high school, but according to all my magazines, geeky is the new "cool." And if Marlene saw something special in him, maybe I haven't looked hard enough.

Of course, a lot of people liked me when I was Miss Piney Point. How can a person be so on top of the world and sought after and then fall into anonymous oblivion so fast? Oh, sure, the people I went to school with remember me and who I was, but even they aren't as impressed as they used to be. Can't say I blame 'em, since every time I think about the way I used act, I cringe.

Crowds parted and chins dropped as Michael and I made our way toward our next class. I close my eyes and sigh.

The soft ticking of the clock on my dresser reminds me I need to finish getting ready for work. It's prom season, and we've been slammed. At least my customers know I'm the go-to person for formalwear. Mamas and older sisters refer daughters, siblings, and friends to me, knowing they'll be in the best hands for style. I'd never put a fair-skinned girl in a cream-colored dress or a brunette with olive skin in peach. And since there will be pictures, I advise my customers to stay away from lemon yellow. It might look great in person, but it makes people look sickly in photos. Pictures are the highlight of every prom because they last forever. I understand the value of finding the perfect dress for each occasion—from proms to Junior League events. Then I send them over to the cosmetics counter to learn the fine art of hiding zits, dark circles, and under-eye bags.

"It's all smoke and mirrors," I tell them, leaving out the fact that until the past few years, everything came natural to me. Now I have to resort to taking my own beauty advice.

As soon as I walk into my area in one of the anchor department stores at the mall, my supervisor, Cynthia, approaches me. "Hey, Trudy, I know you're busy today, but the regional manager is here, and she wants to have a talk with you."

I can't read her face, so I ask, "Any idea what she wants?"

She averts her gaze. "You better talk to her."

"When?"

Cynthia glances at her watch. "In about fifteen minutes. I told her you're expecting a crowd after school, so she said she'll be brief."

"Okay." I pause a moment, willing away the flood of worry, but I can't stand it any longer. "Did I do something wrong?"

"No," she replies with a chuckle. "She's just doing her regular one-on-ones with all the department managers."

I blow out a sigh of relief. "I hope she doesn't mind that I'll have to keep my meetin' short."

Cynthia nods. "She understands. I'll be back in about ten minutes to relieve you while you're gone."

I go to the backroom and line up the boxes I need to empty. Then I roll the rack over to the steamer to get it ready. Before I started working in retail, I had no idea what all was involved in selling clothes, but now I pride myself in mastering every aspect, from merchandising to putting the right outfit on each girl or woman.

"You're so organized," Cynthia says from the doorway, startling me. "Why don't you go on up to the administrative offices now? I'll keep an eye on the sales floor."

"Thanks," I say as I move the rack another few inches.

All the way up the elevator to the office, I think about things I can report on. Whenever anyone from the home office comes to visit, they generally like to hear what we've done to improve the bottom line and what we plan to do to make it even better. I've managed to increase business every quarter since I started, but I'm still concerned because there have been some rumblings about the economy lately. Even though I've been in my position more than six years, other managers have way more seniority and would likely be the last to lose their jobs.

The door to the office is open, and I see the administrative assistant talking to someone on the phone. She glances up at me, smiles, and gestures to go on back. The sound of my heels clip-clopping on the tile floor echoes in my head, making me nervous. I take a deep breath and knock on the very last door on the right.

"Come on in," Sandy says. She smiles as I open the door and step inside. "I hear you've been a busy lady."

"Yes, very busy. But I like it." I have to throw that in for good measure to make sure she knows I want to keep my job.

She points to the chair closest to me. "Have a seat."

As I sit, she stands, and this confuses me. Then she goes behind me and closes the door. In the past, my meetings with regional people have been open door. My palms start to sweat, and my pulse quickens.

"I told Cynthia we might be a while, so don't worry about time."

That's not what Cynthia said. "I have an appointment with the mother of twin girls going to the prom," I say. "She wants to help pick out some appropriate dresses before she brings them in."

Sandy smiles. "That's a very smart mom."

"I started doing that the second season I was in this position. It averts a lot of sales floor disasters."

"And you are a very smart saleswoman, which is why I want to talk to you about something."

In spite of my nerves practically screaming from their roots, I'm curious. I swallow hard, nod, and look at her.

"We've been looking for ways to increase our bottom line throughout this store as well as others in the region. What we've decided to do is choose the manager in each department who is thriving to go around and visit other stores in the region and show them how to improve their business."

I blink. I'm slightly confused. "So what does this mean for me?"

Debby Mayne

"As soon as prom season is over, I would like to send you out to Macon, Chattanooga, Jackson, Hattiesburg, Birmingham, Montgomery, Raleigh, Charleston, and maybe even Charlotte to teach your techniques to other managers and their sales staff." She glances down at something on the desk before looking back up at me with a smile. "All expenses paid, of course."

That sounds like fun, but I try not to show my excitement. "Who'll be in charge of my area while I'm gone?"

"Cynthia and I have been discussing it, and she thinks Darlene would be able to handle her department and yours quite nicely."

I can't think of a worse person to take over my department. Darlene is the manager of plus-size women's ready-to-wear, and she used to be in charge of formal wear before I came along. Ever since I got promoted and turned the department around, she's held a grudge against me, even though she has less work for the same amount of money.

"So I'm thinking we can start this thing in the smallest store first so you can get used to working with people you don't know." She studies a list of stores. "Hattiesburg, Mississippi, has a tremendous amount of potential, with the University of Southern Mississippi right there. Just the sororities alone should bring in double what they're seeing. The manager is willing, but she doesn't have your skills."

"Wh-when would you like me to go to Hattiesburg?"

"How does the second week of June sound?"

I glance up at the calendar on the wall and see that my class reunion is at the end of the second week of June. Since they're paying for all my expenses, I can stay in a nice hotel in Hattiesburg and not have to face my family more than I want to. "That's doable," I say, trying to hold back my excitement.

"Cynthia reminded me that your family is in that area, and we really need to be cautious with the bottom line. If it's not

48

too much trouble, maybe you can stay with your family . . . of course it would only be for that week."

There go my plans. "I'm sure they won't mind."

"Good." She stands. "That didn't take long." She walks me to the door. "Oh, and I almost forgot to tell you. We're working up a compensation package for this new position. I'll e-mail it to you after we have everything calculated."

"Compensation package? New position?"

"Of course. This is a promotion, and we wouldn't expect you to have all the added responsibility without being compensated. Of course, with the economy being what it is, the extra pay isn't what we think you're worth. Our goal is to increase that once the sales go up."

I shake her hand and thank her for her time. All the way back to my area on the sales floor, I hear the words to "Moving on Up" playing in my head. I might not still be with the high-school hero, but at least my career is doing just fine. The timing is good, too, because I'll have something to brag about at the class reunion.

Cynthia gives me a handshake and a hug when I join her. "Why didn't you say something?" I ask.

"Oh, trust me, I wanted to, but Sandy insisted on making it a formal offer. I hope you're okay with Darlene filling in for you while you're gone."

"Of course I am," I say as I cross my fingers behind my back. I'm not about to ruin my happy day by grousing about how Darlene has tried to sabotage everything I've done since I started. It must really get her goat that I'm better with customers than she'll ever be. I've tried to help her, but she just pushes me away, saying she has more experience than I have. "Does anyone else know?"

"No, but I'm going to take care of that right now." She takes a step back, waves, turns, and heads toward the women's department.

A few Junior Leaguers walk up, and I show them some dresses they might want to consider for their next function. One of them is the emcee at a charity auction, and the other is hosting a dinner party for the board. They both leave with smiles on their faces, and I feel good about being such an integral part of a good cause.

I've just cleared a rolling rack to pull some prom dresses for the twins when I spot Darlene coming toward me. When I turn to face her, I see her nostrils flaring, reminding me of an angry bull.

"So you've managed to fool the higher-ups into thinking you know what you're doing? Well, I got your number, girl-friend, and it won't be long before everyone else does too."

My chin drops, and my eyebrows shoot up, until I spot Cynthia coming around the corner looking madder than a hornet. "Darlene," she says. "You and I need to have a talk."

I stand there dumbfounded—first from the fact that Darlene dared come at me in such a confrontational manner in the middle of the store and second from having Cynthia catch her in the act. Today is full of surprises.

A sense of satisfaction washes over me as I watch them walk away. I know I'm not supposed to be happy about someone else's misfortune, but seriously, Darlene asked for it.

5
Celeste Boudreaux

Me and Jimmy have been dating for near about four years now. We could've started right after the ten-year reunion, but he's a little slow when it comes to romance. I had to tell him we was meant for each other before he saw it for himself.

Now I'm trying to figure out a way to get him to propose. The women's magazines say there's nothing wrong with the woman asking her guy to marry her, but somehow it won't seem as real if he don't get down on one knee to pop the question. I did manage to get him to the county health department for a blood test last week, just in case we might wanna have a quickie wedding while our friends are in town for the reunion. But the second we got to the door, he said no way was he gonna tie the knot any time soon. He just went to get me off his back, and now he couldn't go through with it. The way he shivered made me wonder which he was more afraid of: getting married or having someone draw his blood.

I finish putting on my mascara the way Priscilla taught me to do it. I start to turn away from the mirror when I notice a few stray hairs beneath my perfectly plucked eyebrows. Shoot. Keeping up with the facial hair is a time-consuming ordeal.

I wince as I pluck each little hair. One of these days I think I might spring for another one of them wax jobs and get the pain over with all at once.

Every day, Priscilla's beauty advice rings through my head. I've never liked her all that much, but she does know how to make a woman look good.

"Now that your face and hair are your best features," Priscilla said, "you should call attention to them with a flattering neckline and jewelry."

So I open my jewelry armoire—the kind you can get at the mall for half-price during the after-holiday sales—and select what the magazines call a "statement necklace." I'm wearing a universally flattering turquoise top, so I pick a chunky, coral-colored choker and some big wide hoop earrings. According to fashion experts, a girl don't have to wear matching jewelry. In fact, matchy-matchy went out in the 1950s.

In spite of all the fashion studying I've been doing over the past five years, I'm still a tad uncomfortable calling so much attention to myself. Standing in front of the mirror, I feel like a fraud. Hiding inside this pretty girl is a dorky wallflower. But I remember something else Priscilla said. "Lift your head a couple of inches, straighten your back, and smile. Everyone else will think you have confidence, and eventually you will too."

I wonder how long it'll take for me to feel it. You'd think five years of looking like this would give me all the assurance I need, but I'm not sure I'll ever get past my insecurities.

Maybe staying in Piney Point held me back, but I reckon it's too late to fix that. I know my place, and it's right here. Besides, what I do is important, and most of the time I don't mind my job. I like having folks depend on me and respect me for what I know.

My job as a private-duty nurse changes, depending on the condition of my patient. The last man I sat with needed companionship and a little help with feeding. I was his day nurse. His night sitter was a man who helped him bathe and take care of more intimate details of grooming. Now I'm working with Liz, a younger woman who fell headfirst out of a three-story building in Hattiesburg. In my book, she's fortunate to be alive, but she constantly complains about this and that, and sometimes she even says she wishes she was dead. If it weren't for that, I would've asked more questions, like how the incident happened that put her in the wheelchair in the first place. There's some conflicting talk. Some folks say she jumped when her boyfriend told her he was leaving her for someone else. Other people claim he pushed her before leaving and is covering his tracks. She's such an angry person she won't talk about it—not even in court with lawyers breathing down her neck. Whatever the case, she's paralyzed from her neck down, and she needs round-the-clock help.

Her mama sold their farm out near Columbia and moved to Piney Point after the incident so they could be near the hospital in Hattiesburg. Her mama reminds me of my own, and that's not a good thing. Liz went from being independent in her own apartment to being treated like a child and stuck in the smallest bedroom of her mama's house.

I arrive at my job five minutes early. "You're late," Liz's mama says as she flings the door open.

"I—"

She cuts me off. "Just go on back to Liz's room. I have to leave now. They had a big party at the country club last night, and it'll take all mornin' to get the place back in shape." Liz's mama works on the cleaning crew at one of the country clubs in Hattiesburg. She don't make a lot of money, but that don't matter to me since the insurance company pays my salary.

When I get to Liz's room, I pause and knock. Even in her condition, I think it's important to let her keep a certain amount of dignity. I don't like her much, but she's one of God's children, and I try real hard to be respectful of her personal space.

"Come in," Liz hollers.

As I open the door, she eyes me up and down before settling her gaze on my necklace. I'm uncomfortable under such intense scrutiny, but I remember Priscilla's words, and I lift my chin.

"Did you know you clash?" she asks.

I instantly reach up and grab hold of my necklace. "It's a fashion statement piece."

She cackles. "Whoever told you that?"

"It's in all the magazines," I reply. Why I'm letting this mean girl affect me so much, I don't know, but what little confidence I had when I left my place has vanished.

"It doesn't matter anyway, since you won't see anyone important here." She glances over her shoulder. "Get me my drink. I'm thirsty."

Throughout the remainder of the day I wait on her hand and foot, and she doesn't even bother to thank me. As the time to leave draws close, I start watching the clock. She notices.

"Got a date?" she asks.

I nod. "Jimmy and I are going out to dinner."

"I hope you plan to go home and change clothes first."

Of course I will, after what she's said. But I don't know why I even think about taking advice from someone who either tried to do herself in over a guy or was pushed. I'm not sure which is worse since they're both so bad I can't even comprehend.

The second her mama returns, I bolt out of the house, hop into my car, and head home. Jimmy don't like to waste time picking me up. He says he'd rather meet me places. I've questioned that, and occasionally he gives in, but most of the time I drive to wherever he wants to go. Oh, and he likes to go

Dutch . . . claims he's a women's libber. Funny that he is because I'm not, but oh well.

When I get home, I scroll through the caller ID and see that Laura has called. She has my cell number, but I told her not to bother me when I'm with a patient, since they're paying me by the hour.

Instead of listening to my voice mail messages, I call Laura back. I've found it's easier to go ahead and do that, since most likely the voice mail will tell me to call. I'm all for skipping unnecessary steps.

"What do you want, Laura?" I ask.

"Did you see the invitation?"

"No, why?"

"Don't you ever open your mail?" Her voice sounds strange, but I've come to expect anything from Laura. I used to think she was weird. However, after witnessing what she has to put up with, I understand . . . and I'm glad Pete Moss only had eyes for her—even when I tried to get his attention back in high school and a few times after that, until I realized I was making a fool of myself.

"I open all my mail, and I didn't get an invitation."

She mumbles some words of frustration. "Come by later, and I'll hand you one."

"Why bother? I know when and where we're having the parties."

"I want you to see the invitation."

"Why?"

Laura's sigh echoes through the phone lines. "You sound like a three-year-old. Just come by this evenin', and you can see for yourself."

"I have a date with Jimmy," I tell her.

"Yeah, I know. Just stop by on your way to the diner and get your invitation. I gotta run. The girls are hollerin' at each other, and I best go intervene before one of 'em kills the other."

After we hang up, I go change clothes, all the while fussing at myself for acting on one of Liz's mean comments. But if I don't, I know I'll be self-conscious all through dinner, and it won't be fun at all.

Before my makeover, I knew who I was, and I was okay with it. At least, I thought I was. Being a wallflower is a way of life that a girl accepts if she don't know nothing else. After Priscilla got ahold of me, and I took one glance in the mirror, something inside me snapped.

I'd walked into the Cut 'n Curl an ugly duckling without hope, and I came out looking like a pretty woman who might stand a chance of getting what she wanted. At first, the feeling was liberating, but as time passes, I grow more and more insecure.

All sorts of self-doubting thoughts enter my head every morning before I leave the house. Does this skirt make my butt look huge? Is my top too low cut? Did I miss plucking a stray hair on my eyebrows, chin, or neck? Did I go too heavy on the blush?

Liz's comment makes me realize that no matter how much I try or strive for outer beauty, I'm still the same ugly duckling on the inside. People know that about me, so the only person I might be fooling is myself, and even that's not working anymore.

Clad in a gauzy white top that don't clash with my coral-colored choker and a dark brown skirt, I head out the door to meet Jimmy. But first, I swing by the Mosses' house to see why it's so important that I see the invitation.

She greets me at the door before I have a chance to knock. Grinning, she thrusts an envelope at me. "Open it."

"I don't want to be late." Even as I say those words, I rip into the invitation and pull it out. There's my name in fancy letters, right beneath Laura's. "Why'd you go and put my phone number on here for everyone to see?"

Her mouth flops open. "Are you kidding me? You griped about all the work you had to do last time without the recognition. I can't do anything right with you, can I?"

The feeling is mutual. And that pretty much sums up Laura's and my relationship.

I tell Jimmy all about it. He just shakes his head and says, "I thought you and Laura made up. I thought y'all was friends."

"We are."

"You have a strange way of showin' it."

6
Priscilla

This time I don't have nearly as much to do to get ready for the class reunion. Now that my office manager has proven her ability to run the business, even if she can't keep an assistant, all I have to think about is getting myself ready on a personal level and figuring out what's going on with my parents. Mother has never been one to disclose anything she considers none of my business, but in my mind, it *is* my business. I mean, these are my parents—my family, my fortress, my protection. Even when we disagree, I know they're always there. Five years ago, I thought things had changed, but during my few short visits between then and now, I realized that was temporary. For several years, the chasm seems to have grown.

Then there's Maurice. Last time, I harbored some hope that Maurice and I would get together, but after that happened I realized it wasn't a good thing. He was an opportunistic cad when we were teenagers, and he hasn't changed a single bit. I cringe when I think about how Tim must have felt when I let him know that my feelings for my high school flame had been reignited. Why Tim would want to go back and put himself through the torment again is beyond me. I did apologize—profusely—but still . . .

I think he understands that although I love him to pieces, my feelings for him aren't romantic. He was a humongous help at the ten-year reunion, running errands and doing the leg-work no one else wanted to do. On top of all that, he's sweet, and everyone from my high school class likes him. Whenever I go back to my Piney Point salon these days, people ask how he's doing. They obviously assume we're a couple.

Mother has actually offered to let him stay with them, but I tell her everyone will be much more comfortable if he stays in a hotel. I know I'm being presumptuous by not extending the offer to him, but I also realize the talk that'll spread like wild-fire if people know how much my parents like him. At least Mother does. I'm not so sure about Daddy, who's been keeping to himself a lot since I left town. Even Mother says she doesn't have any idea what's on his mind lately. When I start to offer advice, she reminds me I have very little experience with men because I've been working so hard at building my beauty shop business.

All I've ever really wanted from my parents, besides their love, of course, is for them to be proud of me. When I won the title of "Most Likely to Succeed" back in high school, I ran straight home and bragged to Mother and Daddy. They said they weren't surprised in the least. In fact, they expected noth-ing less from me.

Then when I started college at Ole Miss, they let me know I could come back and finish my studies at the University of Southern Mississippi after I had a year away from home. Mother has always held to the belief that part of the college experience is having to do without the comforts and safety net of home. At first, I accepted that, even though I was burned out on traditional studies. But as the first semester progressed, I became increasingly agitated by doing something that went against what I've wanted to do since my middle school years when I started playing with fashion and hair, standing in front of the mirror and seeing what a cute hairstyle and fashionable clothes could do. Then that dream morphed into the desire to build a beauty business that would help thousands of women look their very best.

I'll never forget that look on Mother's face when I showed up on her doorstep announcing I'd dropped out of college and enrolled in the Pretty and Proud School of Cosmetology. Mother pulled me inside and looked around like she was worried one of the neighbors might have heard me. Then she pulled the typical parent trump card, railing about how they'd given up everything to make sure I had a proper education. I have no idea what they gave up because they pretty much had everything they said they wanted.

Daddy didn't say a word. He simply turned around and walked out of the room, leaving me there alone with Mother ranting on and on about how she'd had such high hopes for me. At the time, I thought their disappointment was all directed toward me, but after the last reunion, I know better.

I walk into the Cut 'n Curl office and see a new person sitting at the reception desk. She's on the phone, but she grins and motions for me to have a seat. She obviously doesn't realize who I am, and I don't want to embarrass her, so I try to mouth *I'm Priscilla Slater* as I continue walking past her and toward what used to be my office and is now where Mandy hangs out behind a closed door.

"Excuse me," the receptionist says into the phone. "I have to deal with something here. Hold on." She cups her hand over the mouthpiece and looks me in the eyes. "I'm sorry, ma'am, but the office manager is busy right now."

I force a smile as I lean toward her. "I'm Priscilla Slater, and Mandy is expecting me."

It takes a few seconds for my name to register. Suddenly, her eyes widen, and all the color drains from her face. She loosens her grip on the phone, says, "I'll call you back," and drops it into the cradle, all the while not taking her eyes off me. "I am so sorry. I had no idea."

"Hey, don't worry about it," I say. "Honest mistake. I'll just knock and let her know I'm here."

She nods and watches with her eyes still wide as I walk past her. I knock on the door softly at first, then after Mandy doesn't respond, I knock harder.

"I told you not to bother me," she hollers. Then I hear the squeaking sound as she pushes her wheeled chair away from the desk. A few seconds later, the door opens, and she sees me. "Oh. I am so sorry, Priscilla. Come on in."

I step into her office, leaving the door open. "So have—"

"Close the door," she says.

I make a face. "But why?"

She shrugs. "I just like it that way. It's easier to concentrate."

This doesn't sound like the Mandy I first hired. Back then, she needed constant social interaction, which was why I let her hire her first assistant, Becca. Together, they painted my eggshell walls hot pink and added cheap prints from the dollar store. I've noticed that each time I return, some of the garish décor has been toned down, and now it practically looks businesslike.

I shut the door and sit down across from Mandy. "How's your new assistant working out?"

She shrugs. "I like Clarissa, but she can't seem to stay off the phone."

"Have you talked to her about it?"

"I shouldn't have to."

The girl looks awfully young. Even though the door is shut, the walls are thin, so I lower my voice to make sure it doesn't carry to the reception area. "Sometimes you need to be direct with people to get what you want." I remember when I first hired Mandy and how immature she was. And now look at her.

"I'm not so sure that always works. I was direct with Becca, and she got her feelings hurt and walked out."

"Direct in a good way," I say. "You don't want to be confrontational. If you want to continue managing people, you'll have to learn that skill." I'm giving her an example right now, and I hope she reads between the lines.

Mandy tilts her head and gives a slight nod. "Yeah, I do remember you being that way with me. I'm just not sure how to handle Clarissa."

"I'll tell you what. I'll see what I can do before I leave today. Make sure you pay attention, though, because I'm counting on you to handle everything while I go through my next phase of expansion."

"Everything?" she asks, her eyes lighting up.

I level her with my gaze. "Everything that happens in this office. Nothing else."

She chuckles. "You're not lettin' me get away with anything are you?"

"I just want things to run smoothly around here, and you do a good job as long as you don't overstep."

"Okay, I'll keep everything here . . . in this office . . . " She lifts one eyebrow and grins. " . . . under control."

The phone rings, and we both stare at it, until the light starts blinking and Mandy's phone beeps. She smiles at me before picking up the phone. "Okay, I'll take it." She pauses with her finger over the blinking button and says, "It's the accountant. I've been working on last quarter's report for him."

"Okay, go ahead and take the call. I'll go out there and get to know Clarissa a little better. When you're done, come out and join us."

She nods and punches the button. "Hey, so what can I help you with?"

I marvel at how far Mandy has come and how she's grown into the job. Since I've only heard about Clarissa, I'm not sure how to appeal to her, so I step into her area and smile. She nervously starts straightening her desk that is cluttered with an equal mix of business and personal items, which I'm fine with as long as she does her job.

"So how do you like working here so far?" I ask.

She shoves a few things into the top drawer, slams it shut, and looks up at me with an awkward half-grin. "So far I like it, but there's really not all that much to do."

"Would you like more work?"

"Um . . . I guess that would be okay, but not too much . . . I mean, it's not like I'm getting paid a fortune or anything . . . well, that's not what I mean either . . . " The look of horror on her face betrays her nerves.

"That's okay, Clarissa, I understand. You haven't been here long, so Mandy doesn't know what all you can do yet. One of the most important aspects of this job is to provide a professional but friendly front for anyone who walks in or calls."

"Yes, ma'am." She folds her hands on top of her desk and stiffens her back.

"But you don't have to be too stuffy or anything. We're in the beauty business, which is very personal and touchy-feely. We like getting to know people, and we want them to be comfortable around us."

She nods. "I understand."

I see her eyes dart to something behind me, so I glance over my shoulder and spot Mandy standing in the doorway of her office, listening. Now is the ideal time to show how to be direct but in a nonconfrontational way.

"For example," I add, "when you get a business call, you can ask about the other person's family or something you know about them before you conduct business. By the same token, when you get a personal call, that's fine, too. You can be short but sweet, letting them know you're at work."

Mandy takes a few steps forward and puts in her two cents. "And when you have personal visitor, I'm sure they'll understand that you're working, so they can't hang out here all afternoon."

Clarissa's mouth opens for a moment, and I feel the tension. Before I have a chance to smooth things over, Clarissa jumps up from her seat and runs toward the restroom.

"Did I say the wrong thing?" Mandy asks.

"You didn't say anything wrong, but I do think your timing needs work. I'm afraid she feels like we ganged up on her."

"What would you have done if you were me?"

"I'm not sure, but it's too late to worry about that now. Why don't you have a heart-to-heart with her after I leave?"

"I hope she doesn't walk out on me like the last girl . . . er, like the last several girls did," Mandy says.

"If you really like Clarissa and want her to stay, let that be the first thing you tell her." I pause to think. "Let's come up with an employee handbook so this won't happen again, okay?"

She chews on her lip then nods. "What a great idea. Want me to start working on that right away?"

"Yes, but don't show it to anyone before I take a look at it. I might want to add some stuff."

"I'll get right on it."

I nod toward the restroom. "I think I best leave now so you can talk to her privately." I bend over, pull out a slip of scrap paper, and jot a note to Clarissa letting her know I'm happy to have her at the Cut 'n Curl. "Make sure she sees this."

"I'll call and let you know what happens," Mandy says. "I'm real sorry I botched things up so bad."

I flick my hand. "You're fine. I'm just happy to have you here so I can be free to do what I have to do."

"Oh, that reminds me," Mandy says as she shifts from one foot to the other. "I've been thinking about this whole expansion thing. Is there any chance we'll need a bigger office?"

"I haven't really thought about it. Why?"

She shrugs. "Just wonderin'. My mama's cousin has some property near downtown, and I said . . . I mean, he asked if you might be interested."

"Probably not anytime soon. Maybe in a few years, if I get the gig on the TV Network Shopping Channel."

Mandy rubs her arms and giggles. "I get goose bumps just thinkin' about that happenin'."

"They have my latest proposal."

"I can't believe they turned down your Smooth as Silk product line," she says. "Before I started using it, my hair was coarse and dry."

"You sound like a TV commercial. Maybe I should have sent you to sell them on the idea." I grin at her. "So far, you've been the biggest cheerleader for that line. The product selection committee said it wasn't unique enough."

"Well, let's just hope they see the value of your hair volumizing system." She pats the top of her head. "It's simply the best thing since sliced butter."

"Sliced bread," I say. "I pray they'll like it as much as you do."

"If they don't, I got a good mind to go up to their offices and give them the what-for."

"With you on my side, Mandy, I don't see how I can miss. We'll just keep tryin' until we hit on the perfect product that makes them sit up and take notice."

"Once we do, hoo-boy, watch out. Here comes the queen of beauty products, ready to set the world on fire."

I can't help grinning at Mandy's belief in my company. What she lacks in people skills she more than makes up for in enthusiasm.

When I hear the sound of the faucet running in the restroom, I walk toward the door. "I'm outta here. Let me know if you need anything."

Before Mandy has a chance to say a word, I leave the office so she and Clarissa can have some quality time to hash through a few things. I get into my car and say a silent prayer for both of them to find their way through the sticky thicket of balancing business, personal life, and their feelings.

Once I'm home, I ponder which number to call—Laura's or Celeste's. The concept of having co-coordinators makes sense, but it puts all the graduates of our class in the position of having to choose one of them, and knowing those two, they're keeping track.

I go back and forth. On the one hand, Laura had the entire responsibility on her shoulders last time, so it makes sense to go to her. But on the other hand, Celeste has taken on more challenges, and she needs to prove herself capable. The thing is, I don't want to hurt either of their feelings, so I decide to call both of them.

Since Laura's name and number are first, she's the one I start with. Pete answers the phone.

"I'd like to speak to Laura please. This is Priscilla Slater."

"I know who you are. I'm standin' right here lookin' at the caller ID."

"Hey, Pete. I'm just RSVPing to let y'all know I'll be at the reunion."

"Laura ain't here."

"Would you mind letting her know?"

"What do you think I am? Her secretary?"

"Um . . . no, that's not what I think." I ponder what to do next and realize this is an excellent excuse to call Celeste.

"Why don't you call back in about an hour?" he says. "She should be home by then." I hear one of the kids hollering in the background. "I'm babysittin' the young'uns, so I gotta go." He hangs up without so much as a good-bye.

I'm stunned by the fact that Pete said he was babysitting their children. It's not like they're just Laura's. I'll call Celeste now.

She answers before the first ring stops. "Hey, Priscilla, are you coming to Piney Point early like you did last time?"

"Yes," I say slowly. "In fact, that's why I'm calling. I wanted to let you know I'll be there."

"Good. I want to book an appointment for the day of the reunion before you get all filled up."

"Why don't you call Sheila and let her know?" I say.

"I tried that, but she said she needs to talk to you first."

"Okay, I'll call her after we get off the phone."

"You do that, and while you're at it, tell her I want the nine-o'clock appointment."

My, my, my, Celeste sure has gotten bossy. But I let it slide and get off the phone. Then I call the Piney Point salon to let her know I'm coming early and to pencil in Celeste's name at nine.

"She's been buggin' the daylights out of us. I'm glad you finally talked to her. I wasn't so sure you'd want the hassles like you had last time."

"Sorry. I hope I don't disrupt things too much while I'm there."

"It does get a little crazy around here when folks find out you're in town, but I'm always happy to have you here. We miss you somethin' crazy, Priscilla."

"Oh, one more thing before we hang up. I'm thinking about going short with my hair and getting rid of the highlights, so put me down for a cut and color."

Sheila laughs. "You're too young to be goin' through a midlife crisis, so what's up with messing with your gorgeous hair?"

I run my fingers through the hair I've kept highlighted and a little longer than shoulder length. "I think it's time for change."

"We'll take a look at it when you get here. I've always thought you'd be a cute redhead."

7
Laura

Pete comes walkin' into the house and dumps a stack of mail onto the counter. He picks up one envelope and waves it in the air. "Looks like we got some sort of invitation from Uncle Snub." He laughs. "Like he thinks we'd ever go to anything of his after what he did to us."

Shortly after Pete and I got married, his rich uncle forgot to mail us an invitation to Cousin Buffy's wedding, hence Pete dubbing him Uncle Snub. His name is actually Peter, Pete's namesake, but my husband doesn't want to admit that, since Uncle Snub actually fits him better.

I nod toward the envelope. "Open it."

"What's the point? We're not goin' anyway, regardless of what it is." Without another word, he drops the envelope into the garbage can.

I rush over to rescue it from the coffee grinds and empty wrappers. As I lift it, I can't help feeling the fine linen paper and noticing the hand-lettered calligraphy. "It looks important. Maybe he's extending the olive branch."

"I don't see no olives on that thang." Pete shakes his head. "Miss Pudge, I'm afraid you're just settin' yourself up for disappointment. I know you wanna get in good with the rich folk, but you married me, so that's not likely to happen."

"This *rich folk* just happens to be your daddy's only brother," I remind him.

"Maybe so, but he don't never come around much, except to flaunt his money."

I've carefully lifted the flap of the envelope so as not to tear the fine paper, and now I'm pulling out the contents. It's obviously an invitation, and my heart pounds with excitement. "There's gonna be another Moss wedding," I say. "Chandler's gettin' married on July Fourth."

"My uncle must be runnin' out of friends, or we'd find out after the fact. Throw that back in the trash and stop actin' like you wanna go."

But I do want to go. I love weddings, especially when I know they'll be elegant, and there's no doubt in my mind Uncle Snub—Peter—will make sure his son will have the finest wedding money can buy, even if the girl's folks can't afford it.

"Who's the unlucky girl?"

"Someone named Ainsley Chadwell." I look up at Pete. "I've never heard of her."

"Me neither. I'm sure the girl comes from high fallutin' money."

That's all the more reason I want to witness Chandler Moss tying the knot. Ever since I was a little girl, I've dreamed of princess weddings, with a dashing groom whisking his beautiful bride off in a gilded carriage. Sometimes I'm the bride, but most of the time it's some perfectly beautiful creature who doesn't have frizzy hair or a single freckle on her heart-shaped face. And she certainly doesn't have bulging, cellulite-dimpled thighs.

"Better get rid of that goofy look before the kids come downstairs," Pete says, "or they'll think their mama done got the Old-Timers disease."

I swat at Pete with the envelope. "Stop makin' fun of the way I look. I hate when you do that."

Pete opens his mouth to comment, but I give him the look that's supposed to shut him up. It doesn't always work, but this time it does. After he got alcohol poisoning at the last class reunion, we went through counseling to figure out what our deeper problems were. The psychologist said we needed to learn unspoken communication that every husband and wife are supposed to have, but we obviously didn't get the instruction book when we got married.

"If you really wanna go that bad, go right ahead," Pete says as he strolls toward the door. "But don't expect me to put myself through that kinda misery."

"You make it sound like torture."

He stops and turns to face me. "If it quacks like a duck . . . "

After he leaves me alone to figure out what to cook for supper, I can't help thinking about all the things I've missed out on just because he's not comfortable in certain situations—namely all those that involve his family or my family or weddings or funerals or any other occasion that requires wearing a suit. Both his mama and daddy have siblings who have pulled out of their humble beginnings and made something of themselves. According to Pete, nothing divides a family more than money or lack of it, and I think he's probably right. Pete's mama and daddy are sweet and loving, but they can't seem to get past thinking anyone who drives a Cadillac or one of "them fancy furren" cars is a card-carryin', snobby millionaire. They even look at my mama as someone who's made something of herself, just because after she left Daddy, she married a man who owns a used car lot.

The phone rings and I absentmindedly answer it only to discover that Pete's on the upstairs extension. I hear him laughing and talking to Jimmy, his partner in all things centered on booze. I cup my hand over the mouthpiece and listen.

"Good move takin' the preparty to the house," Jimmy says. "That way you won't have to worry about drivin' home." He laughs. "A man can guzzle a lot of beer in three hours. How'd you get Laura to agree to that?"

"I told her she could hire someone to clean the house. That woman'll do anything to get out of work."

They both crack up. My ears get hot, my eyes moisten, and my lips quiver with the urge to let 'em have a piece of my mind about tricking me, but I decide to keep my yap shut to find out what else they've got up their sleeves.

I stay real quiet as I listen to memories of drinking and potty jokes—nothing that interests me—until I spot the tops of kids heads passing the kitchen window. I hang up the phone as fast and quiet as I can.

"Mama, I'm starvin'," Bubba says as the screen door slaps shut. "Got anything good?"

I point to a basket filled with all the cheapest snack foods—all carbs—on the kitchen island. "Help yourself, but only one each. I want y'all to eat your supper."

"What're we havin'?" he asks as he inspects the contents of the basket and selects the one with the highest sugar content. As he rips it open with his teeth, little Jack indiscriminately grabs something from the basket.

"Meat and vegetables," I reply.

"With cheese?" Jack asks.

"Of course, doo-doo head. Mama always feeds us cheese 'cause we don't drink milk."

As much as I hate to admit it, Bubba's right. I put cheese on almost everything because it's the only way I can get calcium in them. In fact, I use so much cheese I have a whole shelf dedicated to jars of Cheez Whiz in the pantry. Every six weeks or so, the Piggly Wiggly has it on sale, buy-one-get-one-free, and that's when I stock up.

I send the kids out of the kitchen after they finish their snack. The girls are up in their rooms, pretending they don't have a family. Boys and girls sure are different. I discovered that when I caught Renee playing with Bubba's matchbox cars. Instead of going *vroom-vroom* and crashing them into furniture like Bubba would have done, she had them all lined up according to size and color. "Ain't they purty, Mama?" she asked.

Memories of their younger days dance in my head, and I can almost imagine being back in the "good ol' days." But other thoughts snap me back to reality. I was always up to my elbows in young'uns and rarely able to go anywhere without them 'cause the only way I could hire a sitter was to cut into my grocery money, and as it was, my food budget was bare-bones. Pete still can't understand why I'm not able to feed a family of six on less than a hundred dollars a week. If we just had girls, maybe, and that's only if I kept up with coupon clipping, but boys are bottomless pits. They can be shoveling food in their mouths and still complain about starving to death.

Renee's actually a good eater, but it shows. She still has a roll of baby fat around her midsection, and Bonnie Sue takes every opportunity to remind her. That little Bonnie Sue is a handful ever since making the cheerleading squad at the Piney Point Middle School. Renee is more like her mama was at that age: a little bit heavy and socially awkward, even though she tries real hard to fit in. The big difference between us is she hasn't figured out how to worm her way in by offering something other people want.

Yeah, I admit it. I wanted folks to like me, so I catered to the popular kids and made them think they needed me.

That's how I managed to snag Pete. He was part of the cool crowd, although that faded a bit when people got sick and tired of some of his drunken shenanigans. None of the other girls would date him because he had a knack for embarrassing them in front of their friends. But since all my so-called friends were in a crowd I didn't quite fit into, I didn't much care. Pete could embarrass me all day long, and I kept coming back for more.

I used to wonder if Pete really loved me, but I learned in counseling that he just has a different way of showing his love. But it still hurts my feelings when he pokes fun at me and gets the kids in on it. How am I supposed to get their respect when they're laughing about my fanny jiggling or my inability to get anything done right the first time?

But then when someone outside the family says something not so nice about me, Pete is willing to fight for my honor. In fact, he misunderstood something Jimmy said once, and he just about decked him, until Priscilla's friend Tim stepped between Pete's fist and Jimmy's face. Later on, Pete felt real bad about what he'd done, but would he man up and apologize? No sirree. He says men understand stuff like that, and apologizing only makes things awkward. I'm not so sure Tim agrees with him, but I've noticed Jimmy has more respect for Pete after that incident.

For the third day in a row, I dump some canned vegetables into a casserole dish, add meat, and cover it in cheese. I've gotten in a slump, so I make a note to go over to Mama's and thumb through her cooking magazines for some new, quick-and-easy recipes. Mama is known as the queen of quick-and-easy, and she brags about it every chance she gets. Her husband, Randy "Save-a-Lot" Elmore, turns the phrase around and makes it sound obscene. When other folks call her that, all they really mean is Mama knows how to cut corners to get jobs done fast.

I slide the casserole into the oven and putter about the kitchen some more as my mind races through the list of all the things I have to do for the reunion. Even though I added Celeste's name to the invitation, I still feel responsible for everything getting done.

"You do too much for everyone," Pete complains constantly.

"That's because people don't seem to know how to do for themselves," I argue.

He always shakes his head and snorts. "How you expect 'em to learn if you don't give 'em half a chance?"

Bless Pete's heart, he simply doesn't understand, and I doubt he ever will. There are different types of people in this world, and I just happen to be from the group that straightens up other people's messes. I've learned that the easiest way to do that is to prevent stuff from happening in the first place. Only problem is, now that we have three young'uns who have entered the dreaded hormonal years, stuff happens so fast I feel like I'm juggling knives and lit torches. And I've been cut or burned a few times over the past ten years.

I call everyone down to the kitchen right before I take the casserole out of the oven. "Mm," Pete says as he walks up to his spot at the head of the table. "Smells delicious."

"It's the same thing we always have." I can't help it if I sound grumpy, but I'm getting tired of eating the same old cheese-covered food. I want something different. Something with a little spice and not so much goo. Something cooked by someone else who brings it to me and places it on a white tablecloth. With candles and a centerpiece. A table with a view. And a bill that Pete picks up afterward and pays without making a rude comment.

To my surprise, Pete tells everyone to bow their heads. Normally, I'm the one issuing that order. He clears his throat.

"Dear Lord, heavenly Father, Jesus, I want to thank you for this food my wife has cooked up for the family. Make sure she knows how much we all appreciate her, and let her find a way to get this reunion done without losin' her mind like she did last time."

I lift one eyelid and take a peek at my husband, who is staring and grinning right back at me. When I shake my head and close my eye, he continues.

"I pray that you'll keep findin' ways to make us appreciate each other and bless this food we're about to eat. Amen."

"Daddy, that was a real good prayer," Jack says.

"I thought it was stupid," Bonnie Sue says. "You're the one who lost your mind last time you and Mama had a reunion."

"What are you talkin' about, Bonnie Sue?" Pete says.

She slams her fork down on the table, bobs her head and smirks. "Everyone at school was talkin' about how drunk you got."

Pete's face turns flaming red. "I . . . "

He turns to me with a helpless look. I know he wants me to say something, to save his image with the kids, but I can't think of anything. "Bonnie Sue, Honey, your daddy is a good provider, and he comes home every night, so you should count your blessings."

"That's right." Jack grins at Pete before looking at Bonnie Sue. "All my friends' parents are gettin' divorced, but Mama and Daddy ain't." His face crinkles as he turns to me. "You and Daddy ain't gettin' divorced, are you?"

"Aren't. No, of course not." I turn to Pete and force a smile. "Are we, Pete?"

"Huh-uh." He makes a goofy face. "Unless you know somethin' I don't know."

I wish Pete wouldn't joke around at a time like this, but he's always had a hard time when talk turns to more serious issues.

Then I look around at the kids and see that they respond to his lighter talk. "Looks like y'all are stuck with the family stayin' together," I say, trying to stay in the same tone, but I get the feeling I'm falling flat on my face.

Bonnie Sue shrugs. "Divorce isn't so bad. Mackenzie's daddy buys her all kinds of things when she goes to visit him. She even has a smartphone."

Pete leans back in his chair and juts his chin. "My kids is smart enough on their own. Y'all don't need a smartphone."

I scan the kids' faces and see their exchanged glances, letting me know they've been discussing something among themselves. Even though I have no doubt they're conspiring against me and Pete, I'm still happy to know they're doing it together. I always wished me and my brother could have been closer, but after Mama and Daddy's divorce, he started smoking dope and stayed stoned pretty much all the time. Once he was grown, he became a drifter, taking odd jobs just long enough to make money he needed for more dope and something to eat. As far as I know, he's never had to live on the street because he has enough sense to meet people who don't mind letting him sleep on the couch. That's a good thing 'cause Randy kicked him out of his and Mama's doublewide, and Daddy wasn't about to let a druggie stay with him and my stepmom, who only recently retired from being head of ROTC at Southern Miss.

We eat the rest of our supper in relative silence, with the exception of Pete's or one of the boys' disgusting sounds. The girls groan and say, "ew," and, "gross," while I pretend not to hear. I've discovered that when I make a big deal of revolting habits, it just eggs them on. Pete claims that's what normal boys do, but I wouldn't know since I haven't been around much of anything that's considered normal by most people's standards.

After supper, everyone disappears so quickly I don't have a chance to assign kitchen duty. But that's okay by me because I like having the kitchen to myself. It gives me a chance to think in silence, without someone else interrupting.

I put the rest of the casserole in the fridge and turn around to see Celeste standing by the door, arms folded, staring at me with a smirk. Years ago, that would've made me jump, but I'm used to the unexpected.

"How'd you get in here, and how long you been standin' there?" I ask.

"One of the boys let me in and long enough to hear you mumblin' to yourself," she says.

"What do you want?"

"Nothin'. I'm just here with Jimmy. He said he and Pete had something to discuss, so I came along with him."

I hadn't planned to do any reunion work, but for lack of something better to say, I ask, "Have you gotten any RSVP calls yet?"

"Yeah, but only about a dozen or so."

I frown. I've only gotten three. Why are folks calling Celeste and not me? No matter how much I don't want it to, the very idea of our classmates choosing to call her over me hurts my feelings real bad.

"Some of them said they tried you first, but Pete took the calls, and they were afraid you might not get the message," Celeste adds.

That makes me feel a little better, so I smile. "I'll have to talk to Pete about that. Have a seat. Want some iced tea?"

She sits down while I walk over to the fridge and pull out the pitcher I'd just put away. I still have my back to her when she asks, "Do you think Priscilla knows about Didi and Maurice?"

8
Priscilla

I try to hold myself back from going to the Cut 'n Curl administrative offices or Mandy will think I'm checking up on her. And to be totally honest, that's exactly what I'd be doing. It's hard to let go of the control that got me where I am, but I realize that to move to the next level of my career, I have to trust others.

Clarissa seems like a nice person, but it's hard to imagine her and Mandy getting along for more than a few months. In spite of her early days of having to be told what to do practically every moment of the workday, Mandy is demanding and difficult to please. I could see it on Clarissa's face. Maybe I should stop by just for a minute . . . nothing more than to have a presence and show that I'm happy to have her.

Tim calls my cell phone. "You might want to go to Piney Point early again," he says. "Sheila won't tell you this 'cause she don't want to get you all worked up, but their phone's been ringin' off the hook with folks who want you to do the same thing for them you done for Celeste."

As he rambles on and on about what a difference I made in Celeste's life, I consider his suggestion. Since I've been working from home—that is, when I'm in Jackson and not on the road looking for more salons to add to my ever-growing collection—I don't think it'll be any different working from my parents' house. Mother and Dad finally relented and had high-speed Internet installed, and they're gone most days, so I can conduct whatever business I have to do from there.

"Thanks for the tip, Tim."

"I'm sure Uncle Hugh won't mind if you need me longer than a week. He's always happy to help you."

I laugh. "No, I wouldn't want to do that to you, but thanks."

"Really, I don't mind."

Tim sure is persistent, which I'm sure is one of the reasons he's so successful in sales. The other reason is that he's cute and harmlessly flirty—two factors that come in handy for a guy in a female-dominated business.

I really don't want Tim hanging around Piney Point the whole time I'm there. "Why don't you plan to arrive the week-end before? That'll give you an extra few days, and you won't have to use up all your vacation time."

I stifle a laugh as he sighs really loud. "Okay, I'll do that then. But I might just happen to be in the area a little early, since I'll have to follow up on the extra orders on hair color that week at the Cut 'n Curl."

Amazing how quickly the gray comes in once it starts. Most of us were still in our twenties at the last reunion, but over the past five years, I've noticed more silver and white hairs popping up on my own head, so Tim is probably right. We'll be doing more color than usual that week.

"Oh, before I forget, Angela Stanton at Making Waves wants to talk to you."

I think back and try to remember Angela Stanton. "That name doesn't ring a bell."

Tim chuckles. "She's in Birmingham, and she's interested in helping you add to your long list of acquisitions. I can imagine how annoyin' it must be havin' folks constantly after you for—"

"Is her salon profitable?" I ask, interrupting him. I've always liked Birmingham, and if it's in a good location with a steady clientele, this might be perfect.

"I've never seen her bottom line, but if having all her chairs full is any indication, then I would say it is."

"Great! Give her my office number and have her talk to Mandy."

After Tim and I hang up, I call Mandy and tell her to expect a call from Angela Stanton from Making Waves. I then call Laura Moss to let her know Tim will be available to help. In the background, I hear her children shrieking.

"Is this a bad time?" I ask.

"Yes, it's a terrible time. I have to nag the young'uns to make them get ready for school. But you don't have kids, so I don't expect you to understand."

I was just trying to be polite. Besides, I have no doubt that any time is bad in the Moss household. "Sorry. Wanna call me back later?"

"No, I don't have free long distance, so you call me," she says. "Give me about an hour." *Click.* She hangs up on me.

I reflect on the ten-year reunion and how difficult everything was for Laura, with her children demanding so much of her time, while her husband stayed drunk pretty much the whole time I was in Piney Point. Sympathy for Laura edges out some of the annoyance.

Once I get back to my townhouse, I make myself a cup of coffee and carry it into my small office. I've created a happy place to do business by enclosing a section of my porch and decorating it in soft, buttery yellows and greens. It overlooks a tiny flower and herb garden filled with plants that don't require much maintenance. Although I rarely cook for myself, I like having fresh herbs.

I've switched from my old desktop to a laptop computer so I can take everything with me. One of the vendors on the TV Network Shopping Channel has a line of luggage for businesswomen, so I invested in a carryon combination briefcase-overnight bag that is perfect for my laptop, toiletries, and a change of clothes. My life is neat and orderly, and my career is heading in the right direction—all because I've spent time setting goals, planning, and working hard. When I'm in Jackson, I attend a small church close to home. I have very few friends outside of work, and I rarely date, so the only thing that's lacking for me is a social life. Before I turned thirty, I figured I had plenty of time for that.

Now I'm starting to consider my biological clock. If I want children, I need to ramp up the dating. I also like the idea of having a close friend—a confidante who understands me. Too bad I haven't met that person yet.

I send a couple of follow-up e-mails to commercial real-estate brokers, letting them know when I'll be in their areas to view new properties. I've been in a major growth mode for the past five years, adding to my list of Prissy's Cut 'n Curls on the eastern side of the US. I started out in Mississippi, expanded throughout the Southeast, and now I want to have a presence all the way up to New York City.

Once I hit send on the last e-mail, I glance at the clock. It's still too early to call Laura back, so I decide to call my parents' house, hoping to leave a message. Mother still snubs the fashion and beauty industry and anything else she deems superficial.

Both of my parents generally have early morning classes, so maybe they're not home. After the third ring, hope rises that

I'll get away with leaving a quick voice-mail message. Then I hear the familiar sound of Mother's voice.

"Hi, Mother. I didn't expect you to be home."

"Then why did you call?"

Instead of answering, I get right to the point. "Apparently, I'll need to come to Piney Point at least two weeks early."

"I already said you can stay here for . . . two weeks."

"Okay," I say. "Just making sure."

"Will you have a date for the reunion?"

"Tim is attending with me."

I hear the whistling sound of her breathing between her teeth—something she does when she's annoyed. "I'm talking about a real date, Priscilla. If you keep stepping out with Tim, men will think you're attached, and you'll never meet someone special."

I'm not likely to meet someone special at my fifteen-year class reunion, but I don't dare state the obvious. Instead I try to reassure her that I don't go everywhere with Tim.

"We'll talk later," Mother says. "I have some advisory appointments at the college."

After we hang up, I take a chance and punch in Laura's number. She's quick to answer and breathless.

Since she seems to be in a hurry, I get right to the point and tell her Tim will be available to help at the reunion. To my surprise, she doesn't seem happy about it.

"I thought you'd have a real date this time, but I guess it's okay if no one else is interested."

My hackles rise, so I take a deep breath. "Laura, Tim is a very sweet man who has offered to do whatever you want. If you don't need him, let me know so I can tell him not to bother taking his hard-earned vacation to be at your beck and call for *anything* you need."

"Oh, I didn't say we can't use him. I'm just sayin' that by the time most people reach your age, they've been romantically . . . involved at least once."

I get what she's saying, and she's right, but coming from Laura, it's annoying. "I'll be taking appointments, starting two weeks before the final party," I say. "If you have time, I'd like to do your hair, gratis." I half expect her to argue, but she doesn't.

"Good. I'm glad I don't have to ask. I'd like the works . . . that is, if it's part of your offer."

How can I turn her down after all the work she does for our graduating class? "Of course I'll give you the works. How about coming in first thing the morning of the final event?"

"Perfect 'cause I'll need to hurry home and make sure the house is picked up, since we're hosting the preparty there. You haven't forgotten, have you?"

"Are you sure you wanna do that?" I ask. "It seems like it would add to your stress."

She lets out a diabolical chuckle. "Honey, you've known me long enough to know I'm not one to run away from stress, 'cause every time I do it catches me and makes my life even more miserable."

Sympathy takes a tiny tug at my heart. Laura has always been the underdog, in every aspect of her life. I also know that she puts herself in the position of getting trampled—and I mean trounced—yet she continues to do it.

"I'll help you as much as I can between appointments," I offer.

"Don't you worry about that. Celeste is my co-coordinator, and I plan on makin' her earn her title."

"Just know I'm there if you need me." I start to tell her good-bye when she takes a breath, letting me know she's not finished with the conversation.

"Have you heard about Didi Holcomb yet?"

Didi has held a grudge against me, ever since I beat her out of the class valedictorian title by a fraction of a percentage point. She gloated when I presented her with the award for "Most Successful" at our last reunion. Laura thought it was fitting for me to give it to her since I was voted "Most Likely to Succeed" back in school. I suppose she sees Didi's becoming an ear, nose, and throat specialist as being more successful than owning a chain of thriving hair salons. Oh well.

"What about Didi?"

"You obviously don't know." Laura pauses to clear her throat. "She and Maurice have . . . well, they got together shortly after the last reunion."

"Got together, as in—?"

"As in engaged."

Now I'm stunned.

"They're getting married?"

"Priscilla, honey, that's what getting engaged generally leads to," Laura replied. "Although they are taking their sweet time about it. At first we thought it was because she had to move her practice back to this area, but she did that two years ago. They've had plenty of time to tie the knot, but . . . well . . ."

"So they've been engaged all this time, and they're still not married?"

"Yeah, that's what I said."

Even though I got over Maurice the instant I realized who and what he was, this still comes as a blow. "Thanks for the warning."

Laura chuckles. "I'm not sure if it's him or her with cold feet, but you know what they say about a long engagement."

Actually, I have no idea what *they* say, but I'm ready for this conversation to end. Speculating about anything related to Maurice means I have to think about him, and I've managed to forget about him for more than four years.

DEBBY MAYNE

"Hey, Laura, I gotta run. Why don't you make a list of anything I can do to help with the reunion?"

"Okay, and I'll look through some magazines for hairstyle ideas. I think I'm ready for something new. I've sort of gotten into a rut."

She can say that again. Laura Moss has worn the same blunt-cut chin-length style since middle school.

After I'm off the phone, I don't even try to work. The image of Didi Holcomb with Maurice Haverty plays in my mind. Didi is cute in a bookish sort of way, and that's never been the type of woman who caught Maurice's eye. He's more of an intelligent version of Trudy Baynard's ex-husband Michael, whose ideal female standard leans more toward Barbie doll than real women with brains.

My cell phone rings, jolting me from my thoughts. It's Mandy asking if she can bring in more temps for a massive mailing she has planned after I close on a small chain of salons in the Carolinas.

"That would be fine if we had a place to put them," I say.

"Oh, that's another thing. My uncle's best friend has some warehouse space we can rent temporarily . . . for a big discount, of course."

When Mandy sets her mind to something, I've learned it's best not to argue, unless I have a good reason. "How much?" I ask, knowing I'll probably give her the go-ahead.

"Thirty dollars a day plus electric, and that's a steal, considering how much space he has."

"That does sound good. How long do you think it'll take to finish all the lick, stick, and stuffing?" I ask, referring to our nickname for putting together direct mail pieces.

"All depends on how many temps we hire. I figure if we bring in four people, we can get it done quick enough. Eight people might go twice as fast, but the temp agency fees will wind up much higher than the daily rental on the warehouse."

"Good thinking," I say. "Wait until the closing to set it up, though. You never know what might happen at the last minute."

"Yeah, I do know. I'll tell my uncle what you said so he can have his friend pencil us in. I won't sign anything yet."

Mandy has turned out to have a better business mind than I ever would've thought. But I still have to keep an eye on her to make sure she remembers who owns the Cut 'n Curl.

9
Celeste

Sometimes I'd like to rearrangé Laura Moss's face, she makes me so mad. She put my name on the invitations without telling me, and now she's acting like I should feel honored to have all this extra work flung at me.

Then I remember who I'm dealing with. Laura comes from a family that defines dysfunctional. Her mama left her and her worthless, dope-smoking brother with their ex-military daddy to run off with some pit-crew member from Daytona. When that didn't work out, she tried to pry Laura's daddy loose from that lady ROTC drill sergeant he didn't waste no time getting involved with. I felt sorry for Laura when her mama settled for Randy Elmore, the owner of Save-a-Lot Used Cars, and somehow managed to get custody of Laura and her sorry, no-good brother, who wound up running away within the first month.

The whole town got rather excited when Mrs. Elmore went off the deep end and wound up at Whitfield, the state-run mental institution near Jackson. What I heard was Randy had her committed 'cause she'd go weeks without doin' the laundry and fixin' his supper. Instead, she sat around reading trashy magazines and nipping at the cooking sherry. Word on the street was there was all kinds of garbage all over the house, and it smelled to high heaven. I'm sure Randy made it sound worse than it was since what she was doing wasn't enough on its own to have her committed. The one most of us pitied was Laura, who tried to pretend everything was just hunky-dory at home. That's something you can't hide in a town as small as Piney Point.

I once had the biggest crush on Pete Moss, but when I saw how he defended Laura during her family's rockiest times, I knew I didn't stand no chance at all. I still liked him, but I backed way off . . . not that I was ever all up in his face or anything. The most I ever did was stare at him during study hall, and when he looked right at me, I sometimes managed to smile, but I mostly just looked away 'cause my face got so hot I thought it might burst into flames. The eye-opener for me was when someone mentioned Laura's mama being committed to the looney bin and how it might be in the genes, and Pete Moss went after that boy with both fists swinging. Good thing for him one of the teachers in the cafeteria could vouch for Pete when he said he wasn't the one who started it.

Laura's mama came home for a little while but relapsed and got sent back. When she finally made it home again, Laura was committed to keeping her there, and she took charge. Of everything. After a full day at school, she went home and cleaned the house and did laundry. She cooked meals, although I have to admit I heard they were atrocious. But at least she did it. And then the one time she talked back to her mama, she was sent to live with her daddy. There she wasn't allowed to touch a thing. Her daddy and stepmother ran their house like a military institution. They never liked Pete, but Laura didn't much care—not after all they'd been through together.

As time went on, most people forgot about Laura's mama, including Laura, I think. Otherwise, why would she let a certified crazy woman watch her young'uns? Not that it happens all that often, since Mr. and Mrs. "Save-a-Lot" like to gallivant around, flying here and there or taking cruises, every chance they get. Randy obviously cared enough to stick around, but I still have an issue with the way he showed it in the beginning.

Even though I know better than to think Pete Moss would ever pay a bit of attention to me, my childhood crush has lingered way longer than it should have—even with all his drinking and carrying on. The crush has faded maybe, but I still feel it a tad every now and then.

Jimmy is the next best thing to Pete, although he's not all that bright, and he don't clean up quite as well. The one thing I like better about Jimmy, though, is he knows when to put down the booze. Pete don't.

I've been getting one call after another, people asking questions about the reunion. Some folks call me first, and others call me after getting the run-around from Pete when Laura ain't home. She thinks he don't know much about what's going on, but I seen that look in his eye when he's pulling someone's leg.

Jimmy's supposed to stop over for dessert tonight after supper. He called earlier, obviously hoping I'd ask him to come for supper, but I promised my patient's daughter I'd stick around so she could run a few errands after work. My new patient is Myra Chapman, a sweet but feeble old widow woman who thinks her husband is off at war. According to Miss Myra, Colonel Chapman is coming home soon. Her daughter asked me not to say anything about Colonel Chapman being dead for near about twenty years.

"Celeste, c'mere, girl!"

I hear Miss Myra hollering, and I'm on the other side of the house—a monstrosity of a mansion with seven bedrooms, a living room, den, and a library. The house is old, though, and it needs quite a bit of work. When Miss Myra got sick, the doctor recommended putting her in a nursing home, but her daughter refused, saying there's no way she'd have her mama put in one of them places after all she'd done for the family.

I make my way down the hall to Miss Myra's bedroom, where she's on her side, trying to reach something on her nightstand. I rush to her side and steady her.

"You need to be careful, or you'll fall," I tell her.

"I need my chewing gum."

"Your daughter took away your chewing gum, remember?"

Miss Myra mumbles a few obscenities as she rolls back over on her back and looks up at me with her faded blue eyes framed by barely visible white eyelashes. "Why does life have to end this way?"

I stand there and stare down at the woman. "Your life hasn't ended yet."

As she turns her head from side to side, I feel a tightening in my chest. Miss Myra grew up in this big old house, moved out when she got married, and after her parents passed away, she and her family moved back in. All but one of her children abandoned her when she stopped giving them the money they constantly had their hands out for, and now she's very sad all the time. In some small and selfish way, that makes me feel better about my own pitiful existence, living in a tiny apartment. My mama helps me out once in a while, but I'd never do to her what Miss Myra's young'uns have done to her.

Leaning over and taking her firmly by the arm, I slowly pull her to a sitting position. "Let's get you sitting up for a while, Miss Myra. We don't want you getting bedsores."

"Bedsores? I've only been here since last night," she says.

"That's why you don't have 'em yet."

The wrinkles in her forehead grow deeper as she ponders my comment. Next thing I know she's cackling.

"You're a piece of work, Celeste. Anyone ever tell you that?"

"Just you." As I help her out of the bed and into the chair beside it, I think about how most people never pay enough attention to me—or at least they never did until my makeover five years ago—to tell me anything they notice. Now people look at me with amazement and comment on how they never thought I could look so good. I'm not sure how to take it, but Jimmy says I should just say thank-you.

"The colonel should be home any day now," she says as I set her tray of oatmeal and prune juice on the table. She grins up at me with that spark I see in her eye whenever she talks about her late husband. "We need to get the house ready for the big-gest party Piney Point ever saw."

"I'll talk to your daughter about that."

Miss Myra frowns. "She doesn't like the idea of making such a to-do over the colonel's homecoming. Says it'll make him uncomfortable." Her shoulders rise and fall as she lets out a long-suffering sigh. "I reckon she's probably right. He's always been such a quiet man. Strong and silent."

I lift her bowl of oatmeal and hold it closer so she can at least attempt to feed herself. When she looks directly at me, I see tears forming.

"What's wrong, Miss Myra?"

She dabs her eyes with the hanky she's been holding. "He's not coming home, is he?"

I feel a clenching sensation in my heart. This is the moment I prayed would never have to happen.

"I-I'm sure you'll see him again . . . at least one of these days." On the other side of the Pearly Gates.

She opens her mouth without reaching for the spoon, so I take it as my cue to feed her. After she swallows her first bite of oatmeal, she pushes my hand away. "I'll see him in heaven. Lord, I pray that happens sooner than later."

"It'll happen in His own time," I say. "In the meantime, we need to make sure you stay healthy. I'm sure the Lord has some reason to keep you here."

Miss Myra ponders my comment and finally nods, obviously having a lucid moment. "You're right, Celeste. Anyone ever tell you you're a smart woman?"

I don't think anyone has ever told me that. "Just you, Miss Myra. Just you."

She remains in an alert state throughout the entire day. By the time her daughter gets home, I've fed Miss Myra her supper and tucked her in for the night.

"How'd Mama do?"

I tell her about our conversation about the colonel, how much her mama ate, and how she cooperated for her sponge bath. Instead of looking pleased, she frowns.

"Do you think it's a sign?" she asks.

Now I'm confused. "A sign?"

"Yeah. I've heard people rally right before they die."

I gasp. I hadn't even thought of that. "I certainly hope not."

Miss Myra's daughter has always been a negative Nelly, so I don't put much stock in her comments. However, after I leave the mansion, I have a bad feeling in the pit of my stomach.

Jimmy and I have just settled onto the sofa with our plates filled with chocolate cream pie when the phone rings. I stare at it, and he points.

"You gonna answer that or just let it ring?"

Without saying a word, I get up, go into the kitchen, and answer the phone. "She's gone, Celeste. Mama's gone."

I mumble a few words as numbness creeps over me. When I return to the living room, Jimmy looks at me with concern. "What happened?"

"I'm unemployed. Again."

10

Priscilla

All the way to Charlotte, I reflect on how my business has grown. And it keeps on growing.

I step off the plane in Charlotte and go straight to baggage claim. Then I hop into a cab to go to my hotel. Tomorrow I'll own another chain of salons to bring my total number up to fifteen. It'll be nice to head into the reunion with that behind me.

The closing goes off without more than a few minor complications. I have to write a check for the discrepancy in closing paperwork, but it's not a deal-breaker. The former owner balks at signing the noncompete clause, even though this is the first I've heard about it. His agent pulls him aside, talks some sense into him, and he finally relents. One of the salons is in a flood zone, so I have to call my insurance agent to add more coverage on the building. By the end of the business day, all the papers are signed, and I have a bunch of new employees.

I spend the next couple of days going to the salons within driving distance. There are two more—one in Apex and another in Cary, both suburbs of Raleigh—but I decide to wait until another time to visit them. I've been in contact with the managers of those salons, and they seem perfectly content with the transfer of ownership. In fact, one of the managers swore me to secrecy before letting me know she was glad to be out of the hands of the former owner, who was a tyrant. "I hear you're progressive and fun to work for," she added.

I smile as I think about the excellent relationship I have with all my salon managers. We're like family. I care about them and their families, and they know it. When they tell me about a new technique or process, I encourage them to take whatever classes they need, and the Cut 'n Curl office sends them a check to cover their expenses. Apparently, that's not the norm, but no one has ever accused me of being normal.

Since my flight doesn't leave for Jackson until tomorrow, I head back to my hotel room to prepare for my meeting with the TV Network Shopping Channel. The execs have granted me a one-hour meeting, and during that time, I have to demonstrate the product, show the value to customers, convince them I'm using high-quality materials, and show my on-air personality. Since I've never been on TV before, I'm nervous about it, but they've said they have coaches.

The only people who know the details of what I'm doing are Mandy and Tim. Other folks are aware I'm hoping to take my products to TVNS, but they don't know I have a solid appointment. Just thinking about it gives me shivers.

I've made my notes and am getting ready to practice the first part of my presentation in front of the dresser mirror when my cell phone rings. It's Tim.

"How'd it go at the closing?" he asks.

"It's a done deal."

"I'm proud of you, Priscilla."

"Thanks. We had a few little glitches, but nothing we couldn't take care of."

"So what's next on your bucket list?"

"TVNS." I pause to let the tingles pass. "In fact, I was just workin' on the proposal when you called."

"You'll knock 'em dead, Priscilla. You always do."

I chuckle. "Well, let's hope they don't fall over dead before they offer me a spot. Did you know that they have annual sales of nearly a billion dollars?"

"Uh, yeah, I believe you might have mentioned that a time or two."

"Or a dozen," I say with a giggle. "I can't believe the time is almost here for me to kick my career up to the next level."

"Priscilla, honey, you done kicked your career up way higher'n anyone else I know in the beauty salon business."

"You know what I ultimately want, though."

"Yes, Priscilla, I know what you think you want."

"What's that supposed to mean?"

He audibly exhales. "I probably shouldn't be tellin' you this, but I've never been one to keep my mouth shut, and that's not gonna start now, so here goes. You think your goal in life is to be on some fancy TV show hawkin' your hair products when you only want the same thing everyone in the whole entire world wants . . . " His voice trails off.

"And what does everyone in the world want, Tim?" I can't help the fact that my voice sounds mocking, even to my ears.

"Do you really wanna know? I mean are you ready for this?"

"Yes, of course I am. What do you think I really want?"

"Okay, you asked for it. All you really want is for people to accept and respect you. 'Specially them folks you went to school with. I got news for you, though. They respect you a whole lot more than you realize."

"That's not—"

"I'm not finished. Back when you was still in school? All them folks knew you'd be successful. And when you didn't finish college, you assumed everyone else thought the same thing your mama and daddy did. But that's not the case at all."

"I think my classmates see the error of their decision now, though. Remember, I had to give Didi her award plaque for actually bein' the most successful?"

"Yeah, but that don't mean nothin'. Didn't look to me like many people voted. I think it was just Laura Moss's way of puttin' you in your place. She's not exactly the happiest person in Piney Point."

He has a point. "Maybe you're right, Tim, but I really want to be on TVNS."

"I know you do." He drops his voice to where I can barely hear him. "Just remember that there'll always be something you want that you don't already have. It's okay to go after it, as long as you know that's not all there is to life. I hope you haven't become so numb to real relationships that you wouldn't know a good one if it bit—" He cuts himself off. "You know what I mean."

"Yes, I think I do." I smile. I've known Tim for about eight years now, and this is the most philosophizing I've ever heard from him. "You've been thinking about this quite a bit, haven't you?"

"Yeah, Priscilla, I have."

Why do I think there's more behind what he's already said? Perhaps it's because I have a hunch I know what he's referring to, so I don't mention it. Tim still wants a romantic relationship with me, although every now and then, I can see some of his interest fading a tad.

We hang up, and I go back to rehearsing in front of the mirror. Only now, I'm not nearly as into it. Tim's words echo in my head.

I know that my professional goals aren't all there is, but I also realize I haven't worked on any other part of my life.

If someone were to ask me to describe myself, I could pretty much sum it all up by saying I'm a hair salon chain owner.

I live in a townhouse in Jackson, but lately I've been spending more time on the road than at home. During the day, I visit salons I own or might consider buying, and at night, I've been working hard on my hair system that I hope TVNS will let me sell on air. That'll pretty much make me a household name, since Mandy has convinced me my name should be on the product. I have to admit she's right.

⁂

My flight back to Jackson is short. I pull my luggage to my car in long-term parking and hoist it into the trunk. I drive home, still thinking about what Tim said. That man is a good friend, but sometimes his words get under my skin, and I can't seem to shake them. What if Tim is right and I've become too numb to understand a personal relationship?

Years ago, Dad told me that love is different for everyone. He used examples of the difference between his and Mother's love for me and my love for them. "Our love for you is more of the protective variety, while you love us because that's all you know." Then he explained his love for Mother. "Once upon a time, we got all excited about every little thing we discovered about each other, but over time that's changed. We've become comfortable, and our expectations are low." Even if he tried, he couldn't hide the sadness in his eyes, and it broke my heart.

I always used to assume I'd eventually find the right guy, get married, and have at least one kid, all the while working on my business plans. After all, that's what adults do, right? I'm not sure at what point my vision for myself changed. All I know is that the image of being a wife and mother seems as foreign as life on Mars, and I realize my vision wasn't really my own. It was what Mother planted in my head. We made amends five years ago, but at some point I think we started sliding backward.

When I arrive at my townhouse, I have to step over boxes on the front porch. Looks like UPS and FedEx had a party while I was gone.

It takes me less than five minutes to drop my luggage on the floor in my room and go back downstairs to push the boxes inside. I plop myself down on the floor with my box cutter in hand and start the arduous task of getting into them. I only know what's inside one of them—some of the competitors' products from the TVNS channel I ordered before I left town. I never expected to see them arrive so quickly.

Since that box is clearly labeled with the network logo, I push that one aside for last. Each box holds something completely different. One is a tin of designer cookies from Tim. I smile as I open it and pull one from the top. It's delicious with its buttery, melt-in-your-mouth texture and chunks of chocolate, but I doubt it's worth whatever he paid for it.

The next box has Mother and Dad's return address, written in her extremely neat cursive. Inside there's a note. *Dear Priscilla, I cleaned out your grandmother's personal items before we took her to the assisted living residence, and these are the things she said she wants you to have. Love, Mother.*

As I lift hand-crocheted doilies, tarnished costume jewelry, and a moth-eaten wool coat, my eyes sting with tears. Granny was always so independent and remained on the farm until she wasn't able to carry on with her normal life anymore. She once told me that as long as she could pick her own butterbeans, she was perfectly self-sufficient. I sure hope they have butterbeans in that place where she now lives.

A couple more of the boxes are from mother with even more stuff from Granny's farm. I'm happy to have all this memorabilia, but I wonder why Mother mailed it to me instead of waiting until I came to town for the class reunion. It would have saved her a boatload of money.

As I pull things from the boxes, I place them into piles—one to display, one to store, and another to decide what to do later. My first inclination is to donate them to Goodwill, but knowing Mother, she'll ask about the things next time I see her, and I've never been one to lie.

The last box is from Hugh Puckett, Tim's uncle, with his New York City return address clearly printed on top. I have no idea what he'd be sending to my home address, and now that I think about it, I don't remember ever giving it to him. I need to have a chat with Tim about not giving out my personal information to anyone. I realize this is his uncle, but all my dealings with Jerry have been professional, so there's no reason for him to send stuff here.

A formal looking card rests on top of the bubble-wrapped item, so I open it first. *Priscilla, congratulations on adding to your growing stable of salons. May you have a future filled with success and beauty. This is a small gift that you can take with you during all your travels to visit your salons. Your supplier and friend, Jerry Puckett.*

I lean back and read it again and again. Isn't that the sweetest note?

Since the box is tall, I stand up and gently pull out whatever is inside. It's a little bit heavy, but I manage it by bracing the box with my feet while tugging with both hands. It's squishy.

I finally get the item out and place it on the coffee table. With enthusiasm and force, I rip the bubble wrap from the item to expose a large leather tote. An obviously *expensive* large leather tote. It's buttery yellow leather, my favorite color, with my initials embroidered on the side in a deep hunter green. I run my hands over the soft, pebbled walls of the bag and luxuriate in the feel. This is something I never would have bought for myself, but I absolutely love it.

Throughout my childhood, Mother insisted on providing the most economical wardrobe we could find for me because, in her words, "It's silly to spend much money on clothes you'll only wear for a little while. Either you'll outgrow them, or they'll go out of style." The few times I dared to beg for something with a label I could proudly display, she sternly put her foot down. "No one will ever know the difference unless you tell them."

But they did. Everyone knew most of my clothes and handbags came from the big-box discount store on the edge of town or one of the charity thrift shops in Hattiesburg, even though both of my parents had good jobs and could afford more. I babysat a few times so I could buy my own clothes, but small children intimidated me, so that didn't last long. I was never proud of my clothes and accessories, but because I wasn't paying for them, I learned to put some of my cheap wardrobe pieces together in a more fashionable way. I did the most with what I had, including cutting my own hair and adding a little color to my face with dollar-store makeup. Mother insisted I study my brains out, which she said I would be grateful for later. I have to admit it was sort of nice to be called up on stage and presented the "Most Likely to Succeed" plaque.

I caught myself stroking my new tote as though it were a kitten. Even though I've been buying much nicer handbags since being out on my own, I knew this one was special. So special, I doubted any of the stores in Hattiesburg—or Jackson, for that matter—carried anything like it.

Okay, this is ridiculous. I place the tote on the coffee table, stand up, and break down all the boxes for recycling. The temptation to do an Internet search on the brand name on the label hovers in my head, and I resist as long as I can. That lasts all of thirty minutes. I finally plop down in front of my laptop, flip the top to wake it up, and type the name of the designer in the search engine box.

Oh my. It's an even nicer tote than I thought. As in four-digit nice.

I gulp and slowly turn around to face my new tote. Now that I know how much that thing is worth, I'm going to be paranoid about carrying it. It also makes me uncomfortable to get something so lavish from a vendor.

But that's silly, I tell myself. It doesn't matter how much it costs, it's still just a handbag. I remind myself that Jerry's not just a run-of-the-mill vendor. His products just happen to be the best in the industry, and one of the lines he couldn't make successful is one I'll probably use for my own private label.

I cross the room, pick it up, and pull it closer. Yes, I'm hugging my bag. A bag like this one deserves a little extra love.

11
Laura

As much as I don't want to, I actually pity Celeste. Her patient passed away, and now the medical agency she works for has informed her that there are no new people needing to be sat with. Her only other option is to go back to being a nursing assistant in a home.

"I hate doing that." She shudders. "Too much lifting and too many people hovering."

"It doesn't have to be permanent," I remind her.

She lifts her top lip and bares her teeth in a way that reminds me of one of them dogs Mama and Randy used to keep in their yard to protect their double-wide. I thought it was cruel to the dog, until he bared his teeth at me—just like Celeste is doing now.

"All righty," I say. "Maybe that's not such a good idea."

Her shoulders slump. "I don't see any other option. I have to make a livin'. It's not like I have a man *supporting me*."

I plant my fist on my hip and give her a double head bob—the kind my young'uns do to annoy me. "Just what are you trying to say, Celeste?"

"I'm saying you don't have to worry about workin' all day every day, just to pay the bills."

That does it. I can't let her get away with thinkin' I don't work. "What in the world do you think I do all day? I got a house to clean, young'uns to feed, and a husband who doesn't do a thing but come home wantin' his supper."

She drops her scary look and smiles. "I really got your goat, didn't I?" .

"You sure did, and I suggest you don't do it again. I'm sick and tired of people assumin' things about me, just because I choose to be a stay-at-home mama. It's honorable, and it's good for the young'uns. They'll grow up knowin' I was willing to make sacrifices for them. They'll—"

Celeste holds her hands up as she takes a step away from me. "Whoa there. I didn't mean to get you all riled up like this. We got work to do, so let's get off this tangent and do it."

I hand her a stack of busy work—mostly name matching, place card making, and vendor phone numbers for following up to make sure they're gonna have stuff ready on time—hoping she won't make any more personal comments. She takes a look at what I shove at her and squints as though she's thinking of something then slowly looks up at me. I have a hard time holding eye contact with her glaring at me like that.

"Seriously?" she says.

I blow a breath upward, and my bangs fly up. "What, Celeste?"

"Any monkey can do this. In fact, you can probably get your kids to do it."

Rage surges. "Are you callin' my young'uns monkeys?"

"Stop it right now, Laura. I wasn't doin' any such a thing. All I'm sayin' is that I want to do some of the important stuff."

"Like what?" I ask.

She rolls her eyes as she flaps her arms. "How should I know? You won't let me see anything but this . . . this . . . "

"Okay," I say as I reach into my canvas bag and feel around for the pack of envelopes. "These are the reminders we need to send out a week before the reunion."

"Reminders? Are you kidding me? Why are we wastin' our time remindin' people of somethin' they already said they was plannin' to attend?"

She obviously doesn't remember that a bunch of people who said they were coming to the last reunion were no-shows. "I wanna make sure they don't forget. We wasted our budget on food no one ate last time 'cause folks forgot they said they'd be here."

"Maybe something came up at the last minute."

"Maybe," I agree. "But that's just downright tacky if they don't at least let us know things have changed."

She looks back and forth between the envelopes and me. "I don't know about this."

"Just do it, Celeste. You said you wanted more important work, and I'm givin' it to you."

One more dirty look my way, and she picks up the envelopes. "I best be gettin' home 'cause I gotta get up bright and early to go down to the nursin' home for a job interview."

As I walk Celeste to the door, I wonder why she has to make everything so difficult. If she'd just do what I tell her without arguing, we would've been done by now.

After she leaves, I lean against the door, close my eyes, and allow the pent-up energy to flow from my body. Seems folks always like to talk about what they wanna do, but when push comes to shove, they balk when they think they'll have to work. Case in point, Celeste keeps hounding me to give her more work, but she thinks every job I give her is unnecessary. And she's always correcting me on how I deal with folks.

I walk back into the kitchen and see that Celeste has left the cards on the table. I'm not sure, but I think she's what folks call passive aggressive to the point of being downright tacky.

Granted, I don't always know proper etiquette since Mama wasn't the best role model. I'm not putting her down. I'm just being real. Back when other girls' mamas were helping them choose a china pattern or teaching them the fine art of making the perfect centerpiece, my mama was busy canoodling with some pit-crew guy in Daytona. Even after returning to Piney Point, it was obvious Mama was more concerned with her own love life than my future happiness and standing in the community.

Some folks might say I married up when Pete and I said *I do*, and they're probably right. Back in high school, he hung around with the popular kids, and everyone wanted him at their parties 'cause he was the only person with the nerve to end the night with a tabletop song, or if the occasion called for it, a mooning. The big problem holding him back from snagging a more appropriate mate for life was his drinking. And that's where I came in. Pete knew back then that I loved him no matter what. He still knows that. He might be a drunk, but he's no dummy. Having me in his life keeps him fed and worry-free 'cause I do all the worrying for the both of us.

I'm the one who totes the kids to and from school, team practice, and the mall. When they were little, I was the one they came to for snacks, Band-Aids, and a listening ear. Now that listening ear is starting to go deaf, but I pretend to hear what they're saying, while my mind races over my to-do list for the rest of the day.

Lord knows if it weren't for me, my young'uns wouldn't get a bit of Christian learning. Pete hates going to church, but he does it for me—mostly 'cause he knows if he doesn't get up and get dressed on Sunday mornings, he won't get his honey-baked ham or fried chicken dinner later that afternoon. Sunday dinner is the one meal I splurge on nearly every single week. I even pull out all the stops with Mama's potato salad, one of the few recipes she has that doesn't make my family gag. Mama's not the best cook in the world, but one thing she always says is, "Women need to know how to make good potato salad, how much sugar to put in the sweet tea, and how to sit over a public toilet seat without touching it." The last item on her list is a whole 'nother topic that doesn't need exploring at the moment.

"Laura!"

The sound of Pete's voice reminds me where I am and the fact that my family has sacrificed enough, and now it's time to give them the attention they demand. Every. Single. Night. I have to drop my jaw to keep from clenching my teeth.

"Coming!" I holler right back.

"Where's my white T-shirt?"

I blink as I try to remember where I last saw it. "Have you checked the hamper?"

I hear the sound of creaking floorboards as he stomps across the bedroom and enters the bathroom. "Yeah, it's in here. Never mind."

The thought of him pulling that smelly old T-shirt from the dirty clothes hamper and wearing it to bed makes me gag. "I'll be right up there to find you something else, Pete."

I've made it up three steps when he appears at the top of the stairs, wearing his old white T-shirt. "But I like this one."

"I bought you another three-pack. Wear one of those."

He shakes his head. "They ain't worn in yet."

"How do you expect them to get worn in if you don't wear them?"

He doesn't grace me with an answer, so I make a mental note to do whatever I can to distress his new T-shirts. I can't have him sleeping in something that'll wake me up from the stink every time he does his whale-flopping in bed.

"At least take that thing off and let me spray some fabric freshener on it," I say as I follow him into the bedroom.

He scrunches up his nose and shakes his head. "Phewee, no thanks. I hate that stuff. Makes me smell like a girl."

I would threaten to sleep on the couch if I thought he'd either give in and change shirts or at least argue with me. But he won't, so I don't.

Until I fall asleep, his T-shirt's *manly* smell wafts over me every time he rolls over. I'm definitely doing laundry tomorrow, and I'm going to make sure he can't tell the difference between his worn-in shirt and his newer ones.

The remainder of the week goes by fast, between laundry, carpooling, packing lunches, throwing meals together, and breaking up fights between my young'uns. The boys aren't so bad this week. The girls are a mess.

Renee wakes me up hollering for me. "Hurry up, Mama, I'm dyin'." Then she lets out a shriek like I've never heard in my life.

I jump out of bed, my heart racing, and rush to Renee's room, not knowing whether I'll see her on the floor with broken bones or someone standing over her with a knife. When I get there, I see her writhing around, moaning. I sit down on the edge of her bed.

"I hurt so bad, Mama, make it go away."

"Where does it hurt?" I feel her forehead and gasp at the clammy skin.

She screams and thrashes, kicking off the covers, and that's when I see the dark stains on her sheets in the dim light coming from the full moon outside her window. "Honey, I think you got your period."

"Make it go away. I hate it."

"It'll go away in a few days, but in the meantime let's get you cleaned up."

I help her into the bathroom where I have supplies stashed for this very moment. I just wish it hadn't happened in the wee hours. Once she's taken care of, I change her sheets and help her back into bed. By now it's less than an hour from when I need to be up, so I don't bother going back to my own bed. Instead, I go downstairs to have some quiet time. An hour later, I hear the first alarm clock blaring that crazy music the kids like. First young'un downstairs is Bonnie Sue, and she doesn't even bother with a good-morning greeting. Renee is right on her heels.

"Mama, tell Renee to stop talkin' to me in the hallway at school. She's embarrassin' me."

Renee plants her face inches from her sister's. "I just wanted to know if you were comin' straight home after sixth period."

"You shoulda asked me before we left the house."

"But I didn't. What's your problem?"

Bonnie Sue turns and looks to me for support. "Mama, tell her, okay?"

"How you feelin', Renee?" I ask.

She shrugs. "Not good. Can I stay home from school?"

"No." Guilt washes over me. "But if you get sick at school, I'll come get you."

Bonnie Sue rolls her eyes. "You're such a baby *and* a dweeb."

"Snob," Renee says in her annoying teenage voice.

"Am not. I just don't like associating with dweebs."

"Who's the dweeb? You priss all over that school, thinkin' anyone cares you're wearin' that fancy little designer skirt."

Now she has my attention. "What designer skirt?" I ask.

Bonnie Sue rolls her eyes and starts to walk away, but I grab her arm before she gets far. I pull her close and look her in the eye, waiting for her to explain.

"Stop it," she says as she tries to yank away from me, but I still don't let go. "You're hurting me."

"If you think you're hurtin' now, just wait 'til you see what I do if you don't tell me about your designer skirt."

She looks at me as though trying to decide if I'll make good on my threat—which I rarely do—so I put on my crazy-mama-don't-take-no-prisoners face. "Let go, and I'll tell you."

I loosen my grip, but only a teeny bit. I don't want her taking off. "You better tell me, Bonnie Sue."

"Yeah," Renee says. "Go ahead and tell her how you got that skirt, and while you're at it, you might wanna tell her about all that eye makeup you been puttin' on after you get to school."

"Eye makeup?" I squint and study my younger daughter's face. We have a rule in the Moss house. Makeup is allowed in phases. Eleven years old, a tad of pink lipstick. Twelve, a little face powder to dust off that shine. They can start with one coat of mascara when they get to high school.

"You are such a toad!" Bonnie Sue shouts at her sister as she bolts toward the stairs.

"Come back here right this minute, Bonnie Sue, or you're grounded." I glance over at Renee, who is sporting a self-satisfied smirk. I wag my finger at her. "And don't you think for one minute you're off the hook, period or no period. I'll deal with you later." I take off after Bonnie Sue, who has reached the top step and is heading toward her room. "No slammin' doors," I remind her. "We need to talk. Now."

When she turns and gives me that jaw-jutting, determined look she's used since her first two-year-old temper tantrum, my heart lurches. She's still that same little girl, but now she's as big as me and noticing boys. And apparently not only noticing them but trying to lure them into a web she doesn't even know she's spun.

She narrows her eyes and pouts. "What?"

"It's time we had ourselves a mother-daughter talk."

Bonnie Sue bobs her head, making me want to knock it right off her shoulders, but I'm not that kind of mama, so of course I just play it out in my mind. She throws herself across her twin bed and doesn't even bother turning to look at me. Instead of insisting she look me in the eye, I perch myself on the corner of her bed, inspect my fingernails, and think about how to put my feelings and thoughts into words without sounding as crazy as I feel.

"Bonnie Sue, you're growin' up so fast my head is spinnin'," I begin, wishing the perfect words would just plop into my head. "It's just that . . . well, I don't want you to try to act older than you are."

"Mama, everyone's wearin' mascara."

"Everyone?" I know exactly what she means. But I can't help giving her the age-old comeback. "First of all, I'm sure not everyone is wearin' it, but even if they were, does that mean you have to do it too? I never thought of you as a follower." That is true, too. "Your daddy and I knew you were a leader from the moment you popped outta me, with that loud, commanding voice and your ability to get the attention you wanted."

"I'm not bein' a follower. I just want to look cute." She dares a quick glance in my direction but quickly looks away.

I touch her back and feel the pent-up tension. It breaks my heart for her to be so stressed out at her age, but there's just some things a mama's gotta say. "So tell me about the skirt."

As far as I know, she doesn't own a designer skirt. Holding my breath, I pray she came by it honestly, even though for the life of me, I can't imagine how that would happen.

She shrugs and starts playing with the satin corner of the blanket at the foot of her bed. "It's just a skirt."

My mama radar sounds off loud and clear. "I'd like to see it."

Silence fills the room, making me even more uncomfortable than the night Pete mooned the entire cheerleading squad, while I drove the car, embarrassed beyond belief. I hear a light sniffle.

"Bonnie Sue?" I touch her arm, and she jerks away from me. I get up and walk toward her closet.

"No, don't."

I stop in my tracks and slowly turn around to face her. "What is going on, Bonnie Sue? What are you not tellin' me?"

She bursts into tears . . . and I mean the crocodile tears with the heaving sobs and total inability to talk. This is obviously worse than anything I could have imagined, and I still can't figure out what it is. Unless . . .

"You didn't . . . um, do a five-finger discount, did you?"

Her sobbing stops as she scrunches her flaming-red, tear-streaked face and gives me a look like she just saw me for the first time. "What are you talkin' about, Mama?"

"Just tell me about the skirt, Bonnie Sue. Where is it, where did you get it, and why are you so upset about it?"

Bonnie Sue growls as she hops up from the bed, lifts the corner of her mattress, and whips out a very tiny piece of material. We both stare at it for what seems like forever before she throws it at me. "Okay, so here it is. Now what're you gonna do to me?"

I pick up the dark pink garment and turn it over in my hands. When I look up at her, she has that old defiant look back on her face. "This isn't even enough material to cover your behind. How'd you get out of the house without me seein' it?"

She rolls her eyes. "I wore my dorky jeans to school and put the skirt on when I got there."

"But why?" I'm obviously missing something. "Why do you think you have to hide your clothes?"

"Because you want me to be like Renee, and I'm *so* not like her."

The other question still haunts me, and she's obviously found ways to skirt the issue. If I weren't so mad, I'd probably laugh.

"Okay, now that I know what it is, tell me where it came from."

She folds her arms, forms an exaggerated frown, and stares down at the floor. "I don't—"

"You do and you will."

I watch my daughter process her answer and have a flashback to my own childhood. My mother and I didn't get along all that well, but this conversation actually reminds me more of a situation with my ROTC stepmother.

Her body starts shaking, and the tears begin to stream. She opens her mouth a couple of times before she finally blurts, "Okay, I kiped it. Are you happy?"

"You what?" I think I know what she's saying, but I need to be one hundred percent sure before I react.

"It was at La Boutique in Hattiesburg. The saleslady was actin' all suspicious, followin' us around like she thought we were thieves or something. When I tried it on in the dressin' room, she walked right in on me 'n my friends and told us to get outta her store. She don't allow teenagers to come in there without their parents."

I open my mouth to ask a question, but she plows right on through. I don't have a chance to say a word.

"I tried to tell her I needed to take off the skirt, but she never gave me the chance."

"Didn't she see it on you?" I ask.

Bonnie Sue looks down and mumbles. "No, I kept my coat on."

I feel my shoulders sag and my body go limp. Until now, the biggest thing I had to worry about was a drunk husband and spirited young'uns. Now I have to deal with the fact that I've raised a thief.

12
Priscilla

Three more days before I go to Piney Point. I could wait another two days, but I want to settle in and spend some time with my parents. Off and on for the past five years, they've acted strange. Every once in a while I like to drop in on them for a day or two. Last time, they seemed fine, but the time before, they were getting ready to head off in their separate ways—Mother to the coast with some friends and Dad to an academic seminar at Ole Miss in Oxford.

"I thought you liked to go to Ole Miss," I said to Mother after Dad drove away.

She shrugged. "I do, but your father will be with his friends, and I'd rather spend time with the Classy Lassies than sit in some hotel room."

Really. Ever since Mother got into this barely-old-enough-Red-Hat group, she's acted like a college sorority girl. I think Dad's annoyed by the whole thing, but he's not about to tell Mother what he really thinks. He never has. Dad has always been one of those live-and-let-live types. He has strong opinions, and they eventually come out, but he's never direct. Mother, on the other hand, doesn't hesitate to say what's on her mind.

"I just wanted to make sure y'all were okay," I said. I brushed her cheek with a kiss before hopping back into my yellow sports car to head back to Jackson.

Now that I'm getting ready to stay with them for a couple of weeks, I've started thinking about their relationship. Dad once said every marriage has phases, but this one is lasting a mighty long time. I can't help worrying. It's like they're married, but they're not.

I'm probably worrying needlessly, I think as I go through the clothes in my closet. I'll need a different outfit for each special event while I'm in town, but I can do laundry and wash my work clothes. Since I now have a salon rule of dark bottoms and light tops, I pull out every single pair of navy and black pants I own and toss them onto the bed. I choose a variety of white and off-white tops to mix and match with the pants and some scarves to add a touch of color.

I go back into my large walk-in closet to pick out shoes when the cell phone in my pocket rings. It's Celeste. Odd. She's not one I hear from often.

The instant I say hello, she starts right in. "I'm worried sick about Laura, and I don't know what to do."

"What happened?" I've been worried about Laura too, ever since the last reunion. After Pete wound up in the hospital with alcohol poisoning, I thought he might straighten up, but last I heard, he was back to hitting the bottle just as much as ever.

"She refuses to get out of bed. Pete can't even talk her into getting up."

"Do you know why?"

"No," Celeste says softly. "But I've heard rumors she had some serious trouble with one of her daughters."

"Have you tried talking to her?"

"Yeah, I tried, but she refuses to see me. We still have so much to do I'm at my wits' end. And you know how Laura is—such a Miss Do-it-all. I don't even know what she's started or finished. I don't know how all this reunion stuff is gonna get done."

I tuck the phone into the crook of my shoulder and start packing as Celeste fusses and fumes about how everything is now on her shoulders, but Laura won't even give her what she needs. "What do you want me to do?" I ask as soon as I can get a word in.

"When can you come to Piney Point?"

"Um . . . " There goes my plan. "How about tomorrow?"

"You can't come tonight?"

Without argument, I go back into my closet and pull out my overnight bag. "Sure, I can go tonight, but I'll have to come back to Jackson tomorrow. I hadn't planned—"

She cuts me off. "Good. I'm surprised you're able or even willin' to do this on such short notice, you bein' so busy and all. But Pete, he said you wouldn't let us down. I still have some doubt—"

"Celeste, if you want me to go tonight, I have to get off the phone, toss some extra clothes into a bag, and make a few calls before I leave."

As soon as we hang up, I call Tim, but he doesn't answer. Since I know he's more likely to check his call log than listen to messages, I don't leave one. Next, I call Mother.

"You're what?" I hear the annoyance in her voice.

"Never mind. I'll just find a hotel room in Hattiesburg." I could drive back to Jackson tonight, but there's no telling how long it'll take to get through to Laura, and I hate being on the road so late.

"You'll do nothing of the sort, Priscilla, but I don't under-stand why you couldn't have given me more notice. I'll call your father and have him pick something up on his way home."

"Don't do that." I try to explain what's going on, but she doesn't seem to think it's an issue I need to worry about.

"Why did Celeste call you? She's a grown woman and per-fectly capable of doing whatever she needs to do. Isn't she one of the co-coordinators?"

"Mother, I really need to get on the stick. I'll see you in a few hours."

"I don't think Teresa changed the sheets on your bed, and she's already gone home for the day."

"Don't worry about it."

Mother worries about every last little detail when it comes to anything having to do with me. Too bad she doesn't put that kind of energy into her marriage. I catch myself and remem-ber how I've recently noticed that Dad hasn't exactly been the "husband of the year."

I call Mandy's cell phone to let her know where I'll be. "I thought you weren't leaving for a few days," she says.

"I'll be in the office sometime tomorrow, but I'm not sure what time."

"Oh, okay. So why did you call me?"

I don't have a good answer, so I tell her I'll see her soon and get off the phone. I forgo calling Tim again, since I figure he'll probably know where I'll be before I get there. He's good at that.

Three hours later, after I deposit my overnight case at Mother and Dad's, I'm standing on the Moss doorstep. Pete comes to the door looking ragged as ever.

"I don't know what to do," he says as he opens the door and steps back for me to go inside. "She refuses to do anything around here, and these young'uns are just about to drive me up the wall. They act like they're starvin' to death, but I bought 'em Happy Meals."

"How old are your children?" I ask. If I recall correctly, Happy Meals are designed for the toddler crowd.

Pete shrugs. "I dunno, ten or so? Laura always keeps up with that."

"Let me try to talk to her." I nod toward the stairs. "Is she in the master bedroom?"

"Yeah." He gets out of my way as I head upstairs.

As I pass three bedrooms, all with open doors, I see unmade beds and a tiny bit of clutter, but nothing like what I expected. I knock on the only closed door in the hallway. No answer.

"Laura," I say softly. "It's me, Priscilla. May I come in?"

"Miss Priscilla?" I turn around to see who's behind me, and I see someone who looks to be a teenager. I'm not sure who she is, but I think she may be one of Laura and Pete's daughters. It's been a while since I've seen any of their children, so the vision is rather surprising.

"I'm here to see your mother," I say.

The girl slowly shakes her head as tears stream down her face. "It's all my fault. I told her something that upset her so much she won't talk to anyone or eat or nothin'."

Guilt is a powerful thing. "What did you tell her?"

Her chin quivers, but she doesn't answer my question. We just stand there staring at each other for a while, before I finally break the eye contact and knock on Laura's bedroom door again.

"Laura," I say a little louder. "If you don't answer, I'm coming in."

"Go away." Her voice is muffled. "I don't wanna talk to you."

I hear the sound of feet scurrying away behind me. Making the decision to impose on someone who has just told me to leave, I turn the knob and push the door open. "Laura, everyone is worried about you—Pete, Celeste, your children."

She bolts upright in bed, startling me, rubs her eyes, and starts laughing. Not a ha-ha-funny sort of laugh. It's more of an I'm-ready-for-the-white-coats-to-take-me-away cackle.

I have no idea what to do now, so I just stand there looking at the silhouette of a wild woman in a semidark room that reeks from the smell of dirty sheets and pent-up anger. Her laughter eventually winds down, and she flops back on the pillow.

"Everyone can rot as far as I'm concerned. They don't really care about me. All they want is clean clothes and food on the table. Oh, and now I find out one of my girls is a shoplifter, just so she can make her friends think she's better than she is. Nothin' I do around here matters anymore."

Well, at least I've gotten to the heart of the problem. Laura Moss, control freak extraordinaire, has lost control of her family. I'm sure by now she probably realizes she lost control of everything else when she married Pete Moss.

"Um . . . " I try to think of some brilliant comment that will get her out of bed, or in the very least make her sit back up and argue with me. Instead, I wimp out. "She probably didn't mean to do that. Maybe if you—"

That does the trick. Laura not only sits up, she hops out of bed and opens the door, jabbing her finger toward the hallway. "Get out of my bedroom, Priscilla. You have no business interfering in my life."

Okay. I follow her order and leave, only to be met by five pairs of eyes trained on me as I make my way down the hall. I open my mouth to explain, but Pete shakes his head.

"I coulda told you what would happen, but I didn't expect you to give up so fast." He rakes is fingers through hair that looks like it hasn't been shampooed in weeks. "I thought you might be able to use some of your smarts to make her come to her senses."

No one is that smart. Besides, I think she's clinically depressed.

"Have you considered . . . getting her some help?"

Pete nervously glances at his children before settling his gaze on me. I now realize I shouldn't have said that in front of the children, but it's too late now. *Lord, please give me the right words to say. I don't want to make a bad situation worse.*

"I called her mama," Pete says, "and she said she'll check in on Laura tomorrow on her way to get her nails done."

"Celeste asked me to come to see if I could help, but it doesn't appear that Laura is interested in anything I have to offer."

Pete motions for me to follow him back downstairs. Three of the children go back into their rooms, while the girl who admitted guilt comes with us.

Before Pete says a word, the girl looks at me with the most pitiful expression. "I didn't really even want that skirt. A bunch of my friends was tryin' stuff on and I didn't want to just stand around looking dorky and I pulled it off the rack to try it on and the lady, she got all Cruella on me and . . . " She looks over at her daddy and bursts into tears.

I realize Pete clearly doesn't know what to do when he shuffles his feet and moves away from his daughter. This family needs way more help than I'll ever be able to give.

But I still feel the urge to do something, at least to smooth things over for the moment. "Did you try to talk to that woman?"

The girl folds her arms, closing me off. "Why would she talk to a thievin' preteen?"

"Bonnie Sue." Pete tilts his head toward her and gives her his version of a loving look. "You're not a thievin' preteen." I'm glad he finally said her name because I'd forgotten it.

"Would you like for me to talk to her, Bonnie Sue?" The instant those words escape my lips, I regret saying them. But now that I've started, I can't very well wimp out on her. "Not that it'll make any difference, but I can at least vouch for the fact that you're so upset."

"I don't know," she says as she turns back to Pete. "Daddy?"

"I don't reckon it'll hurt nothin'. It's not like there's anything in this for Miss Priscilla."

"When we go, I think we should bring that skirt back to show you mean what you say."

A flash of rebellion crosses her face before she nods. "I can do that, but Mama will have to wash it first."

"That's not necessary. Just put it in a bag, and we can take it back tomorrow. When do you get home from school?"

The next day I leave the Piney Point salon and drive over to the Mosses' house to pick up Bonnie Sue. Laura answers the door.

"You're not goin' anywhere with my daughter," she says.

I'm so happy to see her out of bed, bathed, and dressed that I smile. "I told her I'd take her to La Boutique so she can explain—"

"That's not necessary," Laura says. "I've decided it's best to let it go, and maybe it'll all blow over."

"Things like this don't blow over on their own."

Laura snickers. "Maybe in your neat, tidy little world they don't, but I have a messy life, and I've decided to turn over a new leaf. No more tryin' to take control of everything. Most problems will go away if you just let them be."

"I'd really like to help." I hate being so persistent, but Bonnie Sue is such a young, impressionable girl, it would be a shame to go back on my word. "What if you ever want to shop at La Boutique?"

She snickers. "In case you haven't noticed, that's not exactly my kind of store."

True, but I don't believe in limiting options. "What about Bonnie Sue? What if she wants to shop there?"

"Mind your own business, Priscilla."

She's right. I take a step back. "Okay, so I guess you don't need me."

"I didn't say that. Celeste said we need to give you somethin' to do, since you came all the way over here."

"You don't have to." I take a step back, wishing I could run but not wanting to evoke Laura's ire.

"Give me just a second. I have a tub of envelopes that need stuffin' and addressin'." She chuckles. "I figure you'll need somethin' to do since you're stayin' at your mama and daddy's house for two and a half weeks."

"Actually, I'm going back to Jackson now, but I'll be back here the day after tomorrow. Can it wait?"

Laura's jaw tightens. "I shoulda known better than to think you actually wanted to do anything constructive. I reckon I just have to do it all myself if I want it done on time. That's the way it always is." She exhales and rolls her eyes. "Celeste likes to moan and groan so much about all the work she has to do, I hate giving her more."

Is she trying to guilt me into doing this job? It's obviously working. I extend my hands. "Okay, I'll take them. When do you need the work done?"

13
Celeste

Looks like my plan backfired. I coulda got Laura back on her feet, but it's been obvious since day one that there's too much work for two people. When I called Priscilla, I assumed she'd show up, get Laura moving again, and maybe take some of the busy work off our hands. Now all I hear from Laura is "Priscilla this" and "Priscilla that." You'd think they were best buddies or something.

I hear Priscilla didn't even warm the bed at her mama and daddy's house. She came to Piney Point, did what I asked her to do, spent the night in town, and got up bright and early to go back to her fancy job in Jackson, taking some of the work with her. I reckon she has an assistant who can do all the busy work, so she's not gonna be too put out.

She has a way of getting all the attention when she's around. But I have to say she did an excellent job of getting me started on my makeover. Even Pete took an extra glance when he thought I wasn't looking.

After the newness of the new haircut and makeup wore off, I took matters into my own hands and had my nose shortened and straightened. And now I'm looking into Botox. That wrinkle between my eyes is starting to make me look cross-eyed. Jimmy says he likes me the way I am, but I've been around long enough to know how men are. They think they want something 'til a prettier, shinier thing floats by, and then they'll take off, stomping all over your heart as they exit.

I might not have ever had a boyfriend before, but I seen it happen to plenty of other girls. Take Trudy, for example. That girl used to be gorgeous back in the day. And looky what Michael done to her. Yeah, I gotta keep this up, or I'll find myself single again. And that ain't no fun when everyone else is all paired off.

Granted Jimmy wouldn't have been my first choice a few years ago, but now I know who I am, and even with my face all done up, I'm not a big enough catch for someone like Michael or Maurice . . . or even Pete. What blows my mind is how Laura, frumpy as she is, managed to catch him and keep him. That girl wasn't ugly, but I never would have called her pretty either. She used to be a little bit chubby, but now she's all spread out and squishy looking. I suspect having them four young'uns might have something to do with Pete putting up with her. That would be a lot of child support.

I'm sorta the opposite of Laura, what with being so scrawny. I used to get teased about it, but now when I look at the models in the magazines, I'm happy I don't have to worry about going on some starvation diet.

Every once in a while, Jimmy feeds me thick-crust pizza and doughnuts, trying to fatten me up, but it don't work. I eat 'em, but I don't know where they go. I think I know why he wants more meat on me. His mama don't like skinny women . . . says they can't be trusted.

I rummage through my jewelry box for my hoop earrings, getting ready for my date with Jimmy. He's the night watchman at the resin factory in Hattiesburg, so we can't go out much in the evening. I try to take advantage of all my time with him to look my best and make sure other folks around town see us together.

One of the fashion magazines I started subscribing to had an article about how to look youthful and effortlessly stylish, and hoop earrings were one of the ways to do that. So I went out and bought myself a pair, and ya know, I think they're right. There's just something about a big ol' honkin' hoop earring that softens some of the sharp angles on my bony face. See, I'm a little older now, but it's never late to start learning all about looking good. I add one of my chunky necklaces to complete the look.

Jimmy arrives right when I walk out the bedroom door. He takes one look at me and shakes his head. "Boy howdy, Celeste, you sure do look fine. But we're just goin' to the movies. Why'd you go puttin' on all that . . . " He wiggles his fingers around his neck. "You know."

"We might just be goin' to the movies, Jimmy, but I like to look nice," I say in my best southern belle voice that I been working on for a while. "Never know who we might run into."

He gives me a look of confusion but nods. "I reckon that makes sense."

On the way to the movies, I do most of the talking. When I realize he ain't said much, I shut my mouth, fold my arms, and give him one of them looks.

"What?" he says.

"Have you heard a word I said?"

"Yes, of course I have. You said—"

"Never mind what I said. What's got you all in a snit?"

"I saw Maurice this afternoon at the mall, and he was askin' about Priscilla." Jimmy frowned. "Ya know, after everything I heard about what happened between them, I'd think he'd want to forget about Priscilla."

"Why are you so worried about Maurice? It's not like y'all ever been friends before."

"I know, but I have a bad feelin' he might start somethin' at the reunion, and I know how much work you and Laura put into it. I wouldn't want—"

My heart flutters. "You're worried about me?"

"Yes, of course I am, Celeste. You're my girlfriend, and I want you to be happy."

He couldn't have said anything more romantic if he'd tried. "That's sweet, Jimmy." I pull a tissue from my purse and dab at my eyes. "Just remember that we can't control Maurice and his philanderin' ways. And Didi's not likely to act out in front of folks. She's too worried about what other people think."

"Yeah." He nods. "That's true. I guess I'm worryin' for nothin'."

I pat him on the arm as he pulls away from the light. "You're a good man, Jimmy. And don't let no one ever tell you otherwise."

"Why?" He cuts a look over at me. "Has someone said somethin'?"

"No." I laugh. Whoever said women were obsessive about themselves never met Jimmy. "Let's try to enjoy the night."

14
Priscilla

When I arrive at my parents' house to stay for the next two weeks, I can tell something is different, although whatever it is isn't obvious. There's just something I can't put my finger on.

Mother comes out from the kitchen and greets me with one of her professional smiles. "I wondered what time you'd arrive." She glances up at the clock on the mantel. "Your father should be home in an hour or so."

The way she says that is odd. There's an unsettling tone to her voice, and she quickly looks away.

"I'll just put my things away then," I say. "I have to make another trip to my car."

"Go on ahead. I'm putting the finishing touches on supper."

As I bring in my bags and put everything away, I think about Mother and how she's never been all that domestic, yet she always resisted getting household help, until recently. And her cooking? That's always been a joke around the house. Mother is good at cooking just a few things that she'd rotate every few days. If we wanted something different and Dad hadn't already picked up something on his way home from work, he and I either had to cook it ourselves or get takeout. We had all the good places on speed dial.

I join Mother in the kitchen after all my things are unpacked. "What can I do to help?" I ask.

Her mouth is in a straight line as it always is when she has to concentrate. "Why don't you fill the glasses with ice?" She looks up at the clock again and nearly drops the platter. "Your father should be home any minute."

Something is definitely going on, and it doesn't appear good. "Mother, is my being here putting too much strain on you?"

"No," she snaps. "I mean, things are always a little different whenever you're around, but we love you, and you're always welcome to stay whenever you want."

She has said that so many times over the past few years, I know it's rehearsed. Another thing I know is that I won't be able to get an answer just by grilling Mother with questions. I'll either have to continue trying to read between the lines or catch her and Dad slipping up and saying something they don't intend for me to hear.

Taking the path of least resistance, I do everything Mother asks of me. I have just put the flatware on the table, when I see Dad standing at the door.

I scurry across the kitchen for a hug from my favorite man, and that's when I notice the overnight bag on the floor behind him. He sees me looking at it but doesn't say a word. If the tone in the house were different, I might ask if he's going somewhere, but I don't.

"I better go wash up," he says as he takes a step back. "If y'all are hungry, go on ahead and start without me."

"Don't take forever, George," Mother says in her professor voice. "I left the college early to prepare a nice dinner for the family."

Whoa. I haven't heard Mother talk like that since I dropped the bomb on her and Dad about leaving Ole Miss and starting beauty school. Mother doesn't yell, but I think I'd rather hear that than the icy tone.

Mother finds things for her and me to do while we wait for Dad to wash up. He finally joins us in the kitchen, rubbing his hands together, fake smiling.

"Smells delicious, Suzanne."

She glances at me before turning her attention to him. "I prepared one of the dishes Dr. Bromley recommended."

Dr. Bromley is one of the biology professors at the Piney Point Community College. She has to be at least eighty, but she's still going strong. After her husband passed away about ten years ago, she bought a small cottage a half mile from PPCC so she could walk to work. I'm sure all that exercise is what keeps her so healthy and young acting.

"Must be good then." Dad glances nervously around the table, until his eyes settle on his regular seat.

I look up at Mother, who is standing there, waiting, almost as though she's not sure what to do next. I let out a nervous giggle, which grabs their attention.

"What's so funny?" she asks.

"Nothing." I pull out my chair. "I'm hungry. Let's eat."

On the surface, everything appears normal. But the undertone of everything about the meal—from the blessing to the last bite of dessert—is charged with tension.

I'm relieved when we're finished. "Why don't y'all go on into the living room and watch some TV while I clean up?"

"No," Mother says. "You haven't seen your father in a while, so y'all go chat. It won't take long to get everything in order here."

Dad has already left the kitchen, which annoys me. It's not like Mother stays home all day. They both have demanding jobs, so I would think he'd want to help out. Under normal conditions, I would have said as much to Mother, but this doesn't appear to be the right time to add to the tension.

"Are you sure?" I say. "I can help—"

"No. Scoot. You're in the way."

Feeling like an intruder in the house I grew up in, I do as Mother tells me to. Dad is sitting in the rocker-recliner, staring at the blank TV.

"Have y'all rearranged the furniture?" The chair is on the opposite side of the room, and the sofa has been moved and now rests diagonally in the corner. There are a few more floral arrangements, and some of the pictures on the wall have been repositioned.

"Your mother has." He feels around on the table beside the chair before pulling his hand into his lap.

"Where's the remote?" I ask.

Dad gives me a look I can't decipher. "I have no idea."

For Dad not to know where the remote is, there has to be something dreadfully wrong. And it's not something I can ignore any longer.

"What's going on around here?" I wave my arms around, gesturing first to the furniture then to him. "I feel like I've been abducted by aliens and dropped off on another planet."

"Ask your mother. This whole thing was her idea."

"What whole thing? You're not making a bit of sense."

The sound of Mother clearing her throat grabs my attention. I look toward the doorway.

"I was hoping we wouldn't have to tell you this, but I think it's time."

"Suzanne," Dad says. "If this isn't the best time—"

Mother holds up her hands to shush him. "No, I think we might as well get it over with, George." Her shoulders rise and fall as she takes in a deep breath and exhales. "Priscilla, your father and I have been drifting apart over the years, and we've decided to separate."

In a matter of seconds, my entire world has turned upside down. "You can't." My voice comes out in a squeak as my throat constricts. All my life, I've felt secure, knowing my parents were always there. Together.

Dad stands and shoves his hands into his pockets. "We can and we have."

"But when? Why?"

Mother and Dad look at each other, and Dad nods for Mother to tell me. "Your father moved out three years ago."

I mentally flash back to the times I've stopped by over the past three years, and I can remember some things that should've been red flags. Dad was never there, unless I called in advance to let them know I was coming.

"We want different things," she adds.

"But what about me?" That sounds selfish, even to me, but the words fall out of my mouth before I have a chance to think.

Dad chuckles. "You're a grown woman, Priscilla. It's not like there's a custody issue or anything."

Yes, I'm a grown woman, but that doesn't make this any easier. How can I know that they won't push me out of their lives, after they do that to each other? Even worse, what if one of them meets someone new? I shudder.

"Is there . . . another woman?" I ask Dad.

He glances over toward Mother before smiling at me. "No, I wouldn't do that . . . at least not until the divorce is final."

"Divorce?" Even after hearing they've separated, the word *divorce* sounds even worse. "Can't y'all at least try to make it work? See someone?"

"We've done all that," Mother says. "The problem is—" She stops abruptly. "Okay, we've said everything you need to know. Don't go trying to make us feel guilty because it won't work."

I hate divorce. I've never liked it, but now that it's affecting me, the very thought of it makes me sick to my stomach.

"Now that we have everything out in the open, Suzanne, there's no need to continue with this charade." Dad takes a few steps toward their room . . . or her room. "I'll get my things and leave."

"But—" I have no idea what to say next.

Mother remains standing in the same spot, but her head is bent, and she's looking at the floor. I close the distance between us and put my arm around her. She stiffens at first, but then she relaxes as she puts her arm around me in one of the rare hugs I've gotten as an adult.

"I love you, Mother . . . and I love Dad too. I wish y'all had told me."

"We discussed it and decided it would be better if we waited. Your father said he didn't want to interfere with your business, since you seem to be doing so well. I know how you feel about your beauty shops, so I went along with him."

This sounds like a veiled way of blaming Dad, but I let it drop. No point now in even bringing that up.

"My family will always come before business," I say. "But I appreciate y'all thinking about me." Even I hear a hint of sarcasm in my words. "What now?"

Mother shrugs and pulls away from me—a position I'm most familiar with. "Your father will go to his apartment, I'll retire to my room to read, and you'll do whatever you normally do at this hour of the night."

She leaves me standing there staring after her. I want to chase her down the hall to her room, but I know that won't do any good. My body goes from the numbness of shock to anger toward both of my parents. How can they do this? I don't understand why, whatever the problem is, they can't work it out.

I can't stand there all night, so I make my way to my old room that was once my cheerful sanctuary. Now it's oppressive and gloomy. What did I ever see in that lemon-yellow bedspread? I yank it off the bed and toss it to the chest that used to be my mother's. She called it her *hope chest*. I let out a maniacal snort as I reach for the envelopes Laura has asked me to address. At least I have something to do. And then I pray. *Lord, please don't let my parents split up. If there's anything I can do to help, show me.*

⤝⤞

The next morning I drive over to the Mosses' house to deliver the cards. Laura answers the door.

"You're not gonna mail 'em?" she asks.

"You didn't say you wanted me to mail them. You just said you wanted them addressed."

She growls. "It's common sense, Priscilla. If all these reminder cards have to be addressed, most people would assume they need to be mailed."

I have to bite my tongue to keep from saying what's really on my mind. "Okay, I'll go to the post office now."

"Mama!"

"Go back to your room, Bonnie Sue, and don't come out until I tell you to." Laura turns to me. "I swear, I don't know what I'm gonna do with that girl."

"Why isn't she in school?"

Laura's frown deepens. "You obviously don't have young'uns, or you'd know that school's out for summer."

"I have to go to the bathroom!" Bonnie Sue hollers.

"Okay, you can go to the bathroom, but you better get right back in your room." She spins around and faces me again. "I been thinkin' about your offer."

"My offer?"

"Yeah. You offered to go to La Boutique and try to fix things."

"Um . . . what about it?"

"While you're out mailin' those cards, why don't you swing by La Boutique and see if you can't straighten things out?"

"Are you sure?"

Laura gives me one of her are-you-kidding looks. "Of course I'm sure. You've known me long enough to know I only say what I mean."

"Okay, I'll do it." I know I need to have my head examined, but I'm thinking that if Bonnie Sue's story is accurate, we can smooth everything over. If she's lying, having to face the store clerk might put the fear into her, and she won't ever do it again. And maybe Laura will realize she's not the only capable person around. "But I'll only do it if Bonnie Sue goes with me."

"That could be dangerous. I don't know about lettin' my daughter go off with someone she doesn't know."

"Don't you think it would be more effective for her to go with me?" I challenge. "Besides, you just said you didn't know what you were going to do with her. Maybe this will shed some light on what the best course of action may be."

"Aren't you all la-di-da?" She glances over her shoulder, still holding the door from the inside with me standing on the porch. When she turns back to face me, she has a completely different expression. "I reckon it won't do any harm. It's not like I haven't known you all my life." She sighs. "Besides, how much worse can it get than it already is?" Before I have a chance to say another word, Laura turns around and yells. "Bonnie Sue, get down here right now. You're goin' somewhere with Miss Priscilla."

I barely have time to catch my breath before Bonnie Sue arrives. "I have the skirt in my purse."

Once we have our seatbelts fastened, Bonnie Sue rummages through her purse and pulls out the tiny skirt. It's all wadded up, and I see a smudge of a stain on the side.

"How many times did you wear that?" I ask.

"Just once." She shakes it out, and I'm stunned to see how tiny it is when she holds it up.

We drive straight to the post office first, and since it's already getting hot out, I tell Bonnie Sue to go inside with me. She starts to argue, but she stops herself and agrees. The line is rather long, but it's moving quickly. I recognize a few faces, but I don't know anyone well enough to strike up a conversation. Bonnie Sue, on the other hand, seems to know most of the people in there, and several of them say something to her.

As soon as we get back out to the car, she cowers lower in her seat. "I've never been so embarrassed in my life. Don't ever make me do that again."

"Embarrassed?" I look at her as she peeks out the side window. "Why were you embarrassed?"

"Are you kidding me? Who goes to the post office and stands in line with their mother's friend?"

"I—" I don't know what to say. It never dawned on me that anyone of any age would be embarrassed to be seen with me.

"I'll try not to put you through that again." I smile to myself as I think about how much worse she'll feel after visiting La Boutique.

After turning off the car, I turn to Bonnie Sue and see that she's hyperventilating. "What am I supposed to say?"

"Just tell the woman what happened." I reach for her hand. "But before we go in, why don't we say a prayer?"

Bonnie Sue goes from being a tough acting preteen to a little girl in a matter of seconds. Her palm is damp, and her hand is shaking.

I say a short prayer for guidance and mercy. After I say *Amen*, she follows suit. "Ready to go?" I ask.

She hesitates but nods. "Okay."

The bell on the door jingles as we walk in, and a blonde woman about my age comes out from the back room. As soon as we lock gazes, I recognize Carolyn from my beauty school class. She tried so hard to do a good job, bless her heart, but she never could get the hang of cuts, color, perms, or anything to do with hair. The first time she messed up, I helped her out. The second time, I covered for her. After that, there was nothing I could do, but before she quit, she told me how much she appreciated all my help.

"Priscilla? Priscilla Slater? You sure have turned into quite the celebrity! What brings you here to La Boutique?" She glances over at Bonnie Sue who is trembling slightly to my right. When she looks back at me, I see the confusion on her face.

"I need to speak to the manager, if you don't mind."

Carolyn beams. "You're talkin' to her."

"This is my friend's daughter, and it appears there's been some kind of misunderstanding." So much for letting Bonnie Sue handle things on her own.

I explain what I know, and Carolyn asks Bonnie Sue a few questions. I'm proud of the girl when she answers all the questions with "Yes, Ma'am." Laura has taught her children manners.

Fifteen minutes later, Bonnie Sue and I are back in the car, not only with an apology from Carolyn for the misunderstanding, but with a twenty-five-percent-off discount card for the next purchase. Bonnie Sue handed Carolyn the skirt and apologized profusely as I'd instructed her to do. I'm happy because I feel that this has taught Bonnie Sue a valuable lesson. "So what did you learn from that?"

She looks at me with way more admiration than anyone deserves. "You really are famous, aren't you?"

I can't help it if Carolyn has been following my career, all the way down to the fact that I'm about to pitch to TVNS. That seems to have impressed Bonnie Sue the most.

"I don't know about famous."

"But you are. That lady called you a celebrity." She settles back in her seat, grinning. "I'm hangin' out with a famous person. Just wait'll I tell my friends. They'll be so jealous."

15
Trudy

Rumors have been flying ever since the class reunion invitations went out. Mama doesn't hesitate to call me when she gets home from her weekly appointment at the Cut 'n Curl to catch me up on everyone's business. I suspect most of what I'm hearing is factual—at least in someone's mind—and what's not totally factual has at least a grain of truth.

Today is Thursday, Mama's regular day to get her hair done before the weekend, so I expect my phone to ring any minute now. She's all excited about me coming home for the reunion, but she's made me promise not to starve myself half to death like I did last time.

"Instead of not eatin', why don't you work out like Amy's been doin' to get ready for her weddin'?" she asked last time we chatted.

"I hate sweating." The truth is, I've spent all my money on clothes and makeup, and I can't afford a gym membership. Sure, I could go for long power walks like my neighbors Alan and his wife do every afternoon after work, but it's awful hot lately. We have a gym at my apartment complex, but there are always a bunch of young, Barbie-doll women who'll make me look huge in comparison. And we all know how women use floor-to-ceiling mirrors to compare.

"Surely there's somethin' you can do besides limit yourself to rabbit food."

"Don't worry, Mama. I'll do what I can, but I won't stop eatin'. In fact, I'm on a health kick these days." I turn the topic to my weekly grocery list, hoping she'll lay off the talk about working out. I've done a bit of that in the past, but it's not something I stay with long enough to do me any good. I hate pain.

This time when Mama calls, I'm all worked up and ready for an argument, until she drops the bomb. "Michael's latest girlfriend is pregnant." Then I go numb.

As I fall back onto the chair behind me, I open my mouth to speak, but no words will come out. *My ex is about to be a daddy?* All I can do is let out a tiny grunt.

"Apparently," Mama continues, "she gave him an ultimatum. Either marry her, or her daddy will ruin him for life."

"Who's her daddy?" I manage to squeak.

"Senator Showers."

Now I'm in total shock. Senator Showers has two children— one boy who is just now finishing up law school at Ole Miss and a daughter who graduated from high school a year and a half ago. I suppose I shouldn't be all that surprised. Michael has always favored girls over women.

"Are you still there, Trudy?" Mama asks.

"Yes, Mama, I'm here." My voice is barely above a whisper. "Is . . . is he bringin' her to the reunion?"

"I would assume so, unless her father takes him out to the woodshed first, and he can't walk." Mama laughs at her own joke, which I don't think is so funny. "Who knows? They might even show up as a married couple. Are you okay with that?"

What choice do I have? "Of course I am. It's been over between me and Michael for years."

"Sweetie, don't feel like you have to lie to your mama. I remember all the stories about what happened at your ten-year reunion."

"Those were just stories. You should know better than to believe everything you hear at the beauty shop."

"I been around a lot longer than you, Trudy, and I know there's somethin' behind every morsel of gossip."

So she's always said. "Mama, I really need to go now. I have a bunch of stuff to do before I go to bed tonight, and tomorrow is gonna be a long day."

"Don't work yourself to death, Trudy. You know what they say about all work and no play. Besides, I think you need to find yourself a good man and think about having your own family soon."

"Bye, Mama."

All sorts of thoughts flit through my mind as I pile clothes into the washer. I'm barely thirty-three, yet I've gained enough weight to put me two sizes larger than I was when I was still married to Michael. We got enough money in wedding gifts to put a down payment on a house shortly after we got married, and the real estate agent was so enamored of working with Michael that he cut his commission to practically nothing. Even the seller cut us a deal, enabling us to buy a much bigger house than we needed. Michael liked living there for status. I saw it as a place that was big enough to raise children, but every time I brought that up, Michael reminded me that pregnancy would stretch out my gorgeous body, and it might never come back.

In a way, the joke's on him now, but I don't feel like laughing. He's got his jailbait girlfriend, and she's the one who'll wind up with the stretched-out body. I glance at my backside in the mirror behind me and sigh. No telling how bad I'd look if I'd given birth.

All my friends with kids don't seem to mind the fact that their wiggle has turned to jiggle when they walk. It makes me wonder why I'm still into the whole perfect-body notion that most everyone else has already gotten past.

I'm tempted to forgo the healthy dinner and nibble on lettuce leaves like I used to. But images of a pregnant belly remind me that even if I do care—not saying I do—what Michael thinks, at least I won't be compared to a skinny little stick-figure girl with big boobs. That is, if Mama's right and Jenna Showers really is pregnant with Michael's baby, and he's forced to marry her. Love for Michael is a fleeting thing, which leads me to wonder how long his relationship will last with Jenna Showers, even if she is pregnant. The biggest advantage that girl has is her daddy, who can make or break anyone's career in the state of Mississippi.

The more I think about Michael and Jenna, the more I realize how perfect she is for him. And that just proves that I'm completely over him because before, the very thought of another woman being with him sent me into the darkest emotional hole anyone could imagine.

As my clothes go through the laundry cycles, I tidy up my apartment and start thinking about what to wear to the reunion. Even with my employee discount, I'm not sure my budget can handle a new outfit—at least not one I'd want to be seen in. It's bad enough that I'm still driving the same old car I was ashamed to take to the reunion five years ago. The difference now is I don't care as much about the car. It is what it is, and it has nothing to do with me as a person. But still . . .

My mind wanders to other options. Now that Alan's married, trying to find a way to borrow his car is out of the question. Renting one won't work because of the car rental stickers all over the bumper.

Then the solution dawns on me. I can tell everyone my car is in the shop, and I'm driving the mechanic's car. That'll involve having to fib, but it's not like it'll hurt anyone. I'll have to put more thought into that, but at least I have a plan if nothing else comes to me.

16
Priscilla

What do you think you're doing, Priscilla?" Mother asks as she stands in my bedroom doorway, a semiscowl on her face.

"I'm trying to get the room neatened up a bit before I go to the salon."

"That's what Teresa's for." She comes into the room and thumbs through the closet, inspecting my clothes. "How much did you pay for all these . . . clothes? They look expensive."

They are, but I don't tell her that. Mother is a society snob, but she's always been a reverse snob about fashion. She seems to think anything that doesn't come from a thrift store, clearance rack, or discount store should be outlawed. All she's ever cared about is education, and quite frankly, her nagging about it has only made me want to go in the opposite direction.

"Some of them are, Mother, but you don't have to worry about it. I'm doing just fine."

She pulls out my most expensive blouse, inspects it with a curled lip, and puts it back. "I bet you bought most of them new, too."

"And you're right."

"Have you even been to a resale shop since you moved out of the house?"

"Of course I have." I smile, trying to lighten things up a bit and make her happy. "You've taught me well, and even though I make a good living, I still like to save a buck if possible."

The lines on her face make her look much older than her almost-sixty years. "Doesn't look to me like you've saved many . . . bucks."

She's obviously not going to let go of this issue, so I walk across the room, place my hands on her shoulders, and look her squarely in the eye. "Please don't do this. I'm in a business that's all about outward appearance, and I just happen to feel very good about it."

"I don't know how you turned out this way." Is that a tear I see forming in her eye? "I wanted so badly for you to embrace real values and not something so . . . " She waves her hand toward the closet. "So ostentatious."

"So are we going to church tomorrow?" I ask.

"Yes, of course. Why wouldn't we? You know I never miss church."

"How about Dad?"

She closes her eyes and swallows hard. I can tell this is really tough for her. "Your father hasn't warmed a church pew in . . . I don't even know how long it's been."

"We all went together last time I was here," I remind her.

"But that was only for show because you were here."

I back away from Mother as I think about the odd comments from people on that Sunday. Several of the men told Dad they were happy he'd decided to return. When I asked him about it later, he changed the subject, and Mother jumped right in to keep me from bringing it up again.

"That explains a lot," I say. "Why did you keep the separation a secret from me? It's not like I'd never find out."

"We wanted to make sure that's what we wanted. No point in upsetting you."

"But I am upset. And it has more to do with not telling me than anything else."

Mother folds her arms, juts her chin, and stares me down. "Okay, Miss Priss, tell me what you would have done if we'd told you."

"I . . . I would have tried to help you two work through things. We could have sat down and found a solution to your problem."

"We've been working on solutions for years."

"I don't think y'all tried hard enough."

"Bingo. That's exactly why we didn't tell you. We're done trying to find solutions. We're ready to move on." She breaks eye contact and heads out the door. "Don't bother doing all the housework, or Teresa won't have anything to do."

Before Mother gets completely out of earshot, I let her know I might not be home for supper. "Laura is still struggling to finish all the jobs she's committed to."

"Maybe it's not her fault," Mother says, which surprises me. She's never been a Laura Moss fan.

"I'm sure you're right. She has her hands full with Pete, the four kids, and trying to get this reunion whipped into shape."

"Since you have so many plans while you're in town, I'll keep mine with the Classy Lassies."

"I would hope so."

When she first joined the Classy Lassies, Dad didn't understand her wanting to do so much with the Red Hat group, after doting on him all their married life. But he somehow got over it . . . at least I thought he did. Maybe that's part of their problem—that she went from centering her whole life on Dad and me to wanting to have a bunch of girlfriends to hang out with. Since Mother doesn't do anything halfway, I suspect she most likely overdid her Classy Lassie socializing.

After I get my room straightened, leaving only a few things for Teresa to do, I head out to my Piney Point salon. Sheila is at the front desk, talking on the phone and jotting something in the appointment book. She glances up at me, winks, and points to the floor area. I look up and see Chester smiling back at me.

"How in the world have you been, Priscilla? We have been so excited about having you back here. There's some cake in the break room."

I pat my hips. "Cake is the last thing I need, but thanks for the warm welcome. How're the facials coming along?"

He shakes his head and makes a clicking sound with his tongue. "I never thought Piney Point could support an aesthetician, but, girl, it sure can. After what you did for Celeste, it's like all the women in town are comin' out of the woodwork, wantin' the same miracle done on them."

"And I'm sure you're doing a wonderful job with them," I say.

"Celeste and Laura both insist on you doing their faces, but I've taken all the rest of the appointments for facials." He lifts his comb and pumps the chair with his foot simultaneously, raising his client high enough to work on her hair. As he detangles her hair, he continues chatting about how busy the next couple of weeks will be.

I'm unable to get a word in edgewise, until Sheila shows up and rescues me. "C'mon back here, Priscilla. I gotta show you somethin' I think you'll like."

Chester grins. "If you're talkin' about the new microwave-convection oven . . . Oops!" He covers his grinning mouth. "Sorry. I didn't mean to ruin the surprise."

"Well, you've gone and done it again, Chester, but I'm sure she'll still wanna see it." Sheila grabs hold of my arm and practically drags me to the back room. As soon as we're there, she closes the door behind me. "That man is driving me insane. He never knows when to stop talkin'."

I laugh. "So y'all are enjoying the oven I sent?"

"Of course we are, but that's not why I wanted to talk to you. In case you haven't noticed, Piney Point is growin' like a weed. We need to bring in more hairdressers, or we'll have to start turnin' folks away."

"You know I trust your judgment on that," I remind her. "You've never had to ask permission to hire a new hairdresser before."

"I know, but that leads to somethin' else." She extends her arms out to her sides. "Where we gonna put another hairdresser? As it is, we've got the chairs all crammed together on the floor. That's another thing Chester talks about—gettin' outta his space." She snorts. "To tell ya the truth, I don't know who wants it more, him or me. I'd love to be in another room most days."

Last time I was at the salon, which wasn't all that long ago, I did notice the close quarters. "Maybe we can knock down the wall to the private area and put a couple of chairs there."

"Where will Chester do the facials? You know most women don't want everyone seein' them with all that goop."

"Good point. Let me see what I can do while I'm in town." I add one more thing to do on my mental to-do list that is already too long.

A look of concern clouds Sheila's otherwise cheery expression as she touches my arm. "Are you okay, Priscilla? You seem unhappy about something."

I don't want to discuss my parents' marital issues, so I force a smile. "No, nothing's wrong. I just have quite a bit to do."

"I'm sure you do," she says. "But there's something different about you."

"There is?"

"Yeah, you've lost a bit of that spark, that energy that buzzes every time you're within twenty feet of this place."

I laugh. "Maybe that's a good thing? I don't want to electrocute anyone."

"How's Tim?"

So she thinks I'm having man trouble. "Tim is doing great. He's coming with me to the reunion again."

"Is there something you haven't told us?"

"No, Tim and I are still just very good friends. I don't have time for anything else."

Sheila shakes her head and tsks. "That's a downright shame. Haven't you ever heard that love makes the world go 'round?" She twirls her finger in a circle around her ear.

"Yeah, and it makes you crazy too. That takes way more energy than I have."

"Any luck yet with TVNS?"

"I had an appointment for last week, but the executives called to reschedule." My hope is fading, but I try not to let Sheila see that.

"I'm sure it'll happen when it's supposed to," she says in her motherly voice. "In the meantime, you have lots of appointments." Her lips tilt into one of her lopsided grins. "You made Celeste look so good last time, everyone wants your magic fingers on their hair."

"Good." Relieved to have an opening to leave this discussion that has grown way too personal for my comfort, I lead the way out of the break room and toward the floor. "Let me take a peek at the appointment book before I go see someone at the real estate office."

I see that there's nothing on today's page, but starting Monday, all the times are filling in. Sheila points out the fact that my days right before the reunion are filled, and people are still calling.

"We got more men wantin' work this time. Not just the standard haircut."

Chester speaks up behind me. "Looks like metrosexuals are movin' into the 'burbs. I'm glad men are interested in cleanin' up a bit." He shudders. "The unibrow just kills me."

Sheila glances at me, winks, and nods. "Yeah, that unibrow thing is deadly."

One thing I've noticed over the years since I've owned more than one salon is that each place has its own personality. This one in Piney Point is filled with good-natured ribbing, playfulness, and laughter. The salon in Jackson has always been more businesslike, and I wonder if that's because my office is upstairs and the newer hairdressers are concerned that I wouldn't approve of horsing around. The Hattiesburg salon is generally filled with girls from the University of Southern Mississippi who can afford getting their hair done at an upscale salon. Or more accurately, their parents can afford it. We also have more waxing and facials in Hattiesburg. I've learned to study what I call the heartbeat of each salon before I buy it so I know what I'm getting into. It's always been much more than a good haircut and color. It's more about how we're making our clients feel when they leave.

I like how Sheila once put it. "If they're not standin' a little taller when they leave, we missed somethin'." That about sums up my philosophy.

It's Saturday, and I'm concerned about the commercial real estate office not being open. Jackie Miller, the owner who inherited the business from her father—and he inherited it from his father—is a few years older than me and the only woman I know who has as much ambition as I've always had. I like the fact that she gets me.

As I round the corner, I see that the lights are on in the front of the real estate office. They used to have their own redbrick building, over by the old train station, but her father moved closer in so he could be in the heart of Piney Point. Jackie told me he liked being closer in to feel the heartbeat of the town.

Jackie looks up from the reception desk as I walk in. I'm surprised to see her there, since last time I was here she was in a big office in the back corner.

"Hey there, Priscilla. I heard you were in town. Want some coffee?"

I glance around before turning back to face her. "No thanks. I know you're probably busy, so I won't take up all your time."

She laughs and gestures around the quiet office. "Things have been a little slow lately. In fact, when Georgette retired, we decided not to replace her."

Georgette had been the receptionist in the Miller Real Estate office for as long as I could remember. I loved walking in and seeing her glowing face framed by that gorgeous red hair. That woman could multitask better than anyone I've ever known, and I used to tease Jackie that she better watch out, or I'd steal her for the Cut 'n Curl.

"Does she need a job?"

Laughing, Jackie shakes her head. "No, I think she was relieved. She's worked hard all her life, and now it's time to go have some fun. Whatcha need?"

"The Cut 'n Curl is about to burst at the seams, and there's not much room for internal expansion, so we need more space. Any ideas for a new location?"

She twists her mouth and chews on her lip as her thinking furrow forms. "Right off the top of my head, I can think of several options. When do you wanna start lookin'?"

"I'm here for the reunion, and the closer we get to the big party, the less time I have."

"How 'bout right now?" she asks.

Another thing I like about Jackie is her sense of urgency. "Sure, sounds good."

"Let me go grab my stuff, and we can go lookin'."

Within minutes, we're walking the streets of downtown Piney Point. The first place we enter has been vacant for more than a year, and the stench overwhelms us.

"Phew-ee," she says as she waves the air in front of her nose. "I reckon this is what an old deli smells like when it's been closed up without air-conditionin'."

We walk around the space, and I try to imagine where everything will be. It has possibilities, but it's not exactly what I have in mind.

"Put this on the long list," I say. "Where to next?"

"C'mon, I have a few more within walkin' distance, and then we can go for a drive."

Every place we look at has potential. I'm able to envision my salon in each one, but nothing really strikes me as the perfect place for the Cut 'n Curl.

After we walk through the last place on her walkin'-distance list, she grins at me. "You're not lovin' any of these, are you?"

"No, but I don't hate them either."

"Tell you what. I have a place in mind that you'll either love or hate—no in between. It's been sittin' vacant since . . . I don't know, maybe the last world war?"

I laugh. "What place is that?"

"Instead of telling you, I want to take you there. Granted, you'll have to use your imagination, but knowing you like I do, I don't think that'll be a problem."

We drive about a mile before she pulls into the parking lot of an abandoned building that was once the ice factory. And she's right. I don't think it's been occupied in my lifetime—unless you consider the four-legged rodent population.

"Ready to go take a look-see?" she asks, an amused grin playing on her lips.

I swallow hard. "I think so. Is it safe to go inside?"

She tilts her head back and howls with laughter. "It's been checked out, and from what I know, the building won't cave in over us." She digs in her bag and pulls out a pair of flats. "I'm glad you're not wearin' high heels."

"It looks terrible." The bricks are discolored where someone tried to remove the graffiti. The few windows that aren't broken are cloudy. The parking lot and grounds around the building are in such a bad state of disrepair I imagine a movie studio setting a horror film there. The only thing that looks decent is the tin roof.

"If you think this is bad, wait'll you see the inside."

She isn't kidding. The second we walk in, something runs across the floor in front of us. The stench nearly knocks me over. Jackie motions for me to follow her.

As we walk through the building, the flaws are obvious, but she's right. I can see the potential. "How much of the building is available?" I ask.

Again, she laughs. "You're kiddin', right?"

"All of it?"

She nods. "Yep, and it can all be yours for a rock-bottom price that the owners should be happy to get, considerin' how long they've been tryin' to dump it."

Jackie tells me the price, which is very low, but I've been in business long enough to know it'll take way more than that to renovate it. My first reaction fades as I see the potential in the combination of architectural details—that is, if we can safely save them—and the size.

"You're right. I do love the . . . potential, but . . . " I look around and shake my head. "Let me think about this, okay?"

"Of course. This is a decision that I'm sure you'll need to ponder for a while. If you have any questions, or if you'd like to look at it again, just call or stop by. You know where I'll be."

17
Tim

I just happen to know where Priscilla is, and it's taking every bit of holdin' myself back not to go to Piney Point. Mandy likes to keep me informed, even though I think she's had a crush on me off and on since I've known her. She flirts like nobody's business, until she starts datin' someone, and she goes all professional-girl on me.

I can't believe I'm feelin' this way about Priscilla since hope for anything between us faded years ago. Her ten-year reunion was a real eye-opener, when she made it clear how she felt about that loser Maurice. I know I'm obsessing over what he did to her, but I can't help wondering what she sees in him . . . or at least what she *saw* in him before he showed his true colors. I could've told her he was tryin' to use her, even though I didn't know how. But no, she had to find out for herself that all he wanted was her money.

After we got back home to Jackson, she told me all about what happened. My heart did a few extra bumpity-bumps, hopin' that meant she'd freed feelings from that guy and was ready to take a better look at me. I even took her to a romantic dinner, hopin' to score some points. She let me know all she saw in me was friendship.

So I did what any man would do in that situation: I went out and found me a girlfriend. She was a pretty girl, too—all nice and soft and blonde—and she liked me way more than I deserved, considerin' the circumstances. I might coulda fooled myself into thinking I was in love with her, but I didn't do that. It wouldn't have been fair to her or to me. I want that feeling like I get when I'm with Priscilla—like I don't give a rat's behind what else is going on in the world 'cause all that matters is being with the one I love.

After me and that girl broke up, I started hanging out at the Cut 'n Curl offices again. It's not like Priscilla didn't egg me on either. In fact, she came right out and told me she missed seeing me. So I thought maybe all she needed was a little time apart, and now she'd be ready for a relationship. I was mistaken, though, so I went right out and did it again. That girl wasn't as nice when I told her I wasn't feeling it. She cut one of the tires on my company car. If no one else had seen her do it, I might have let her off, but she was stupid enough to get caught by a cop riding around in an unmarked car. I was sorry she had to go to jail, but I wasn't about to bail her out after all the threats she made.

Good thing I work for my uncle, or I might have found myself without a job, 'cause first thing she did when she got outta jail was call my boss and tell him she knew for a fact I'd been stealing from petty cash. Before I knew what she was like, I spent big bucks on dates with her. I mean, a guy's gotta impress a girl these days or she won't give him the time of day. I seen enough of them reality shows to know that. When she asked if I was rich, I joked around and said I had a hefty petty-cash fund. I didn't think she'd take me seriously.

So when Zenith called Uncle Hugh and blabbed about me stealing from petty cash, he outright laughed in her face. Then he called and asked me what kinda girls I was seeing. I told him what happened, and he said never, ever do that again, or I might be standing on the unemployment line. I doubt he'd follow through with that kind of threat since we're related and all, but I don't wanna tick him off again. Of course I don't say that 'cause he's gotta think he's making a point to keep me outta trouble.

"Find yourself a nice girl, and you won't have to worry about impressing her," he told me.

I did find a nice, girl—Priscilla—but she don't love me back. That's another thing I won't tell him. "I'm workin' on it," I say.

If Sheila had her way, me and Priscilla would be married and have a kid or two by now—at least that's what she says. Chester, on the other hand, don't seem to like me much, if his sourpuss face every time I step into the Piney Point Cut 'n Curl salon is any indication. Last time I was there, I tried striking up a conversation with him, and he just snarled and walked off. Sheila told me not to pay him any mind . . . he's just in a snit.

Priscilla says to wait until the weekend before the reunion before going to Piney Point. I look at the calendar and see that I still have to wait four more days, since I count Friday as the start of the weekend. Last time, I had no idea what I was getting myself into, but this time I know full well that I'll be running myself all over town, picking up messes Laura starts. It's hard to imagine her ever being called the organized one. That girl don't finish much that she starts.

Me and Jimmy get along pretty well, until Pete's in the picture. When that man drinks, hoo-boy, he has him some serious anger issues. I was worried he might get mean around Laura and the kids, but according to everyone I've talked to, he never lays a hand on his family. He's more likely to wrap his truck around a pole, and I know that's true 'cause I seen that firsthand.

I go over a mental list of things to do to get ready for my trip to Piney Point. I have all the clothes I need, and I just got a haircut last week. Then I remember the vocabulary book Priscilla gave me. After that last dinner we had together, I put it away, figuring I didn't need it no more, but maybe I can show her what she's been missing. Besides, even if I don't stand a chance with her, I don't want to make myself look stupid just 'cause I don't talk smart.

18
Priscilla

On Monday morning, I get up and prepare for my day at the Piney Point salon. As I dress, I ponder the vulnerability I've recently seen on Mother, who has been my fortress ever since I can remember. When I got home on Saturday, I was surprised to see her sitting in the living room, staring at a blank TV screen, her jaw slack. I asked about the Classy Lassies, and she just silently shook her head, stood, and walked to her room, leaving me wondering if something terrible had happened. I had to cajole her into going to church with me yesterday—something that I've never had to do. She's withering right before my eyes. The signs may have been there, creeping up as my parents' relationship deteriorated, but until now all I noticed was how they seemed cool to each other.

I walk into the kitchen and prepare the coffee. Mother has either left without a cup, or she's not up yet, which is strange. Once I hear the coffee brewing, I go to her room and lightly tap on the door. I hear rustling on the other side of the door.

"Mother," I say softly. "I started the coffee. Would you like me to make you some breakfast?"

"No thanks, dear. I'll be right out. Just give me a few minutes." Her light tone sounds forced.

About fifteen minutes later, Mother and I sit across the table from each other, mugs of coffee and bowls of oatmeal in front of us. "You really didn't have to do this," she says. "I'm perfectly capable of fixing my own breakfast."

I smile at her. "You've always done so much for me, I figured it was time to pamper you a little."

"That's sweet." She stares at her oatmeal. "I'm really not all that hungry."

"Just eat a few bites. You need it to start your day, remember?"

She nods as she lifts her half-filled spoon to her mouth. This role-reversal thing is rather frightening, and I wonder how long she's been like this. Mother has always been slender, but now she's getting downright skinny.

I'm so concerned about her I count the number of bites she takes—seven very small ones, not enough to get through the morning. She stands, carries her bowl to the sink, rinses it, and sticks it in the dishwasher, looking robotic and remaining silent.

"Why don't you bring a banana or granola bar with you?" I ask. "I'm sure you'll get hungry later on." Did I just say that? I'm becoming my mother.

She smiles and nods. "Of course."

Her compliance is unsettling. I've always been able to count on Mother being argumentative, regardless of the topic. I can't wrap my mind around how to deal with her like this.

"What do you have on your agenda today?" she asks in a monotone.

"I have a few haircuts, and then I'm going to take Chester and Sheila over to a new location I'm considering for the salon."

She lifts an eyebrow, the first sign of interest I've seen in her this morning. "New location? What's wrong with the one you're in now?"

"We've outgrown it."

Mother's jaw tightens, an expression I'm more familiar with and oddly feel more comfortable with. "Have you outgrown it, or do you just have the urge to change?"

"Mother, please." I try to hide the joy of seeing Mother's usual state of disapproval return. "It's all about business, and without growth, some businesses wither and die."

"Your father said the same thing when I told him you were adding to your holdings. He said in your field, change has to happen, or you become dated and stodgy."

I suspect he was talking about more than just my business. At the risk of having to face her ire, I nod. "He's right."

"Maybe so, but I don't see why you can't update the space you're in now."

"Mother." I tilt my head forward and look at her from beneath my recently shaped brows. "Please don't do this."

She waves her hands around. "All right, I'll stay out of your business. What does an English professor know about *beauty shops*, anyway?" Her emphasis on beauty shops reminds me of her attitude toward what I've chosen to do for a living. Tim has called my parents intellectual snobs. I defended them, and he apologized, claiming it just "slipped out," but deep down, I agree with him. If it's not bookish or influential on the universe, they don't see the value—especially my mother. Dad has never been nearly as emphatic about this view, which leads me to believe he either disagrees, or he hasn't put as much thought into it and goes along with mother to keep from having to discuss it later.

I give her a hug and tell her I love her before I leave the house because you never know what might happen, and it wouldn't be good to have negative comments be our last. She gives me an air kiss and says she loves me too.

Sheila and Chester are standing behind an empty chair when I arrive. "Hey, I've got a surprise for y'all."

Chester looks down at my hands and leans around before straightening and looking me in the eye. "I don't see anything. What is it?"

"When's your next appointment?" I look back and forth between them.

"My first one's not for another hour and a half," Sheila says.

"And my first appointment of the day called and canceled." He glances at the clock. "So I have at least that long."

"Okay, c'mon. We're going for a ride."

On the way to my car, I call Jackie and ask her if she can meet us at the old ice factory. "I'm on my way," she says.

Chester has to sit in the front seat because I drive a sports car, and he's over six feet tall. Sheila folds herself into the back-seat and leans forward to make sure she doesn't miss anything.

"This is excitin'." She giggles. "I love surprises. Does it involve food?"

"No, it's much better than food."

Chester snorts. "All depends on who you're talkin' to. Sheila likes her doughnuts." She playfully smacks him on the shoulder.

We pull into the parking lot that is even worse than I remember. I get out and wait for Chester and Sheila before fanning my arms out. "Well, what do y'all think?"

"About what?" Chester frowns and looks around, his gaze settling on the dilapidated building.

"If everything goes the way I hope it does, you're looking at the new Piney Point location of Prissy's Cut 'n Curl."

"You have got to be kidding me," Sheila says. "Have you lost your mind?"

I laugh. "Yes, but I think that's what keeps me going—trying to find it."

"I've heard this place is haunted." Chester shudders. "I think I can feel the ghosts swooping around me now, letting me know they don't like this a bit better than I do."

"C'mon, y'all. Look at it this way. We can gut the place and make it like we want it."

"It's huge." Sheila takes a tentative step toward the building and stops when Jackie pulls into the parking lot. "But won't the renovations cost a fortune?"

"Probably. I'm going to call an inspector to find out if there are any structural problems before I make an offer."

"I don't know, Priscilla," Chester says. "This isn't what I had in mind."

Sheila playfully punches him in the arm. "What did you have in mind?"

"Something newer." He narrows his yes and juts his chin. "Something not quite so scary."

I have to admit, when Sheila mentioned that we needed to expand, I envisioned something similar to what we already had, only larger. And my first reaction to this place was the same as Chester's.

"Ready for the grand tour?" Jackie approaches with a face-splitting smile. "I hope our little buddies stay away this time."

Chester's eyebrows shoot up. "Little buddies?"

"Never mind the little buddies." I cut a quick glance over to Jackie, and she winks. "Try to keep an open mind, okay?"

Sheila looks horrified. "Are there bugs in there?"

Jackie and I exchange a glance and smile about Sheila's question. I say a silent prayer that all we see are bugs.

Chester walks up and stops to wait for the rest of us. "Scared?" Sheila asks.

"No, of course not. I was just waitin' for y'all. You know, ladies first and all."

"Sure," Sheila pats him on the arm. "Don't worry, Chester. I'll protect you."

Jackie unlocks the door and steps inside. We all follow close behind, no one veering far from the rest. With a wave of her arms, Jackie encourages us to explore. "Check it out and talk about it. I've contacted the owner, and he's willing to work a sweet deal for the right buyer."

"Oh, I'm sure he is," Chester says as he nearly bumps into me when I stop. "This place is one hot mess—even worse than Celeste's hair before Priscilla got hold of it before the last reunion."

"Chester!" I can't allow my hairdressers to talk about our clients like that, although he'd verbalized exactly what was on my mind.

He shrugs. "Just sayin'." Something catches his attention, and he points. "Hey look over yonder. That is way cool."

"Is that an elevator?" Sheila asks.

"Yup." Looks like Chester's fear has subsided as he steps away to inspect the antique elevator. When he gets directly in front of it, he looks up. "Where's this thing go?"

"There used to be offices up there," Jackie explains. "Back when it was an ice factory, they did most of the work in an open area, but half the building had a second floor."

"We can do that here," Chester says, clearly letting his enthusiasm for the elevator take over.

Jackie laughs. "I doubt that thing works. Even after the last owners stripped away the second floor, they kept the elevator for decoration."

"It looks awful to me." Sheila touches one of the beams in the center of the room. "But I can see the potential of the space."

"Yeah, we can put the mud baths over there . . . " Chester waves toward the back corner and sweeps his hand, pointing a few yards away. "And over there we can have showers and massage rooms—"

"We're a hair salon, Chester," Sheila reminds him. "Just because you're doing a few facials every now and then don't mean we have to get all carried away."

Jackie turns to me. "What do you think?"

"I'd like to have an inspection as well as a survey of the lot and building so I can show it to the designer I used to build my Jackson salon and offices."

"Right." She jots down some notes. "We'll also need to contact the historical society and find out what your restrictions are."

Chester rolls his eyes. "Oh honey, this place is such an eyesore I would think the historical society would be happy about anything we do to it."

"Not necessarily," Jackie says. "They've been known to keep projects from moving forward. However, I think that if they know Priscilla is involved, and it'll be for an existing successful business, they're more likely to approve changes as long as they aren't terribly intrusive."

"One thing I know we'll need is a massive plumbing overhaul." I look at Sheila. "And I'm sort of on the same page as Chester. With all this space, we can make this into a day spa."

Now that I say this, Sheila's eyes light up, and she smiles. "Really? Are you serious? We'll have one of them day spas where people go to get pampered, and they're willin' to pay a fortune for a good haircut?"

I can't help laughing. "As long as I own it, we'll always charge a fair price, but we have to take our expenses into account."

Jackie drops her notebook into her bag. "Would you like me to get the ball rolling on this?"

I turn to Chester and then Sheila, who are both nodding like a couple of bobbleheads. I laugh. "Sure, sounds good. But for now, we need to get back. I have a few calls to make, and these two have appointments."

All the way back to the salon, Chester and Sheila jabber over each other, talking about what kinds of things we can do in the new salon and day spa. I'm startled when Sheila gasps.

"We can't keep callin' it Prissy's Cut 'n Curl—not if we have all that other stuff. I mean, no offense or anything, but the Cut 'n Curl name sounds a little . . . well, country, if you know what I mean."

"We've always been that." Chester sounds defensive. "Back when Dolly owned us, we were Dolly's Cut 'n Curl. I'd hate to change the name to somethin' all uppity, just because we offer more services."

I let them discuss the name of my business as though I'm not even in the car. When it all comes down to the final decision, it's mine and no one else's. But I listen just in case they have ideas I might want to incorporate.

As they argue, I listen, and occasionally, I can't help chuckling. They both make very good points, but in such a comical way. Sheila wants to call it Prissy's Day Spa, but Chester wants to keep the Cut 'n Curl name.

I park my car in back of the salon, and we pile out to go inside. Chester holds the door for Sheila and me, but he stops me before I enter. "Why have you been so quiet? Tell us what you think we should call it."

It's sweet that he's using we, so I don't call him out on it. Instead, I just smile and say, "I dunno. I'll have to think about it. Why don't you talk to the other hairdressers and come up with a list? Just remember, though, that we're a long way off from finalizing this deal. We've just started looking, and as you said yourself, the place is a hot mess."

Chester doesn't just get the hairdressers involved, he has customers voicing their opinions. And one of Chester's clients expresses her concern that I'm sure others have thought about but haven't mentioned. "Don't go gettin' all fancy on us with the prices 'cause you know what they say about fancy, right?" She tilts her head up and bats her eyelashes. "Fancy is as fancy does."

I have no idea how that saying applies, but I nod as I put the finishing touches on her daughter's haircut. "Don't worry. We'll do our best to keep our prices in line. The last thing we want to do is lose our loyal clients."

The woman's shoulders relax. "Good 'cause I never had nobody do my hair like Chester here. He knows how I like it, and he don't try to talk me into changin' it."

After she and her daughter leave, Chester blows out a deep breath. "I got no idea what that woman was talkin' about. I been tryin' to get her to change her hair for the past five years, but she insists on wearin' it in that same dowdy style."

"There are ways you can get her to change without upsetting her." I spend the next fifteen minutes sharing some techniques for gradual changes that allow clients to get used to something new.

He nods in agreement. "See? That's why you're the business tycoon, and I'm the lowly stylist."

"I wouldn't say that, Chester. If you weren't an excellent stylist, you wouldn't be working here." I pause to let that sink in. When I see him smile, I add, "All you need are a few psychology techniques, and your customers will allow you to do whatever you think will look good on them."

"So true," he says. "I'll work on that. By the time we move to the ice factory, people will come to me begging me to do whatever I want, and they'll leave happier than ever."

Sheila stops, shears in midair over Mrs. Hatcher's head. "Dream on, big boy, dream on."

Mrs. Hatcher cackles. "All depends on what you want to do. If you tell me you can make me look twenty years younger, I'd say go for it."

"I don't know how you can possibly look twenty years younger, Mrs. Hatcher," Chester says. "What are you now? Twenty-nine?"

"I better keep an eye on you, Chester, or you'll wind up stealin' all my customers away."

Mrs. Hatcher makes eye contact with Sheila in the mirror, smiling with her whole face. "You know I'd never leave you, Sheila. I started coming to you when you were fresh out of beauty school. How long's that been? fifteen, twenty years?"

Sheila frowns. "I don't think it's been anywhere near that long."

I just happen to know it's been much longer than that, but I don't say anything. After I finish cleaning my station, I head to the back and get my tote. I walk past Chester, and he does a double take.

"Where'd you get that bag? It's gorgeous! I think that's the one I saw in last month's *Elle*."

"It was a gift, and thank you. I like it too." Rather than wait for more comments or questions, I leave the salon. Even though I've bucked my upbringing and wear designer labels, I'm still uncomfortable calling attention to them.

As soon as I walk into the house, Mother confronts me. "So you're buying the old ice factory? What are you thinking, Priscilla? Have you lost your mind?"

19
Celeste

On my way to the Cut 'n Curl on Wednesday, I pass the old ice factory and laugh. Priscilla has always been one of those weirdo, studious types, but in the past she had more common sense than most. Now she's done gone and put an offer on a building no one in their right mind would even step foot in, let alone go for a beauty treatment.

Reality hits as I ponder the idea of finding another beauty shop, and I feel my perfectly tweezed eyebrows drawing together. Weird as Priscilla is, she knows her stuff when it comes to beauty.

I park my car and walk into the salon and see Priscilla standing at the front desk looking all full of herself. If I didn't depend on her to make me pretty I'd want to rip her face off. Back in high school I didn't like much of anyone, especially the girls who thought they were either too pretty or too smart to hang out with me. Not that I went to all that much trouble to make friends, 'cause I didn't. Why would anyone wanna be friends with a loser? I shudder and try to shake off that old feeling that keeps rising inside me.

"Hi there, Celeste," she says, grinning like she means it. "Ready for your facial?"

"Ready as I'll ever be." I try to act all normal, like this is something I've been doing all my life. In reality, I'm still trying to get used to looking good, and being in the place where it all started makes me all squirmy inside. It's like they're on to my secret, and they know I'm a fake. Which I am. I mean, think about it. I walk in being the town ugly duckling and walk out looking like this. No fooling anyone here.

We sit down across from each other at the little table in the private room at the back for what she calls the *consultation*. I don't wanna talk about it. I just want to git 'er done.

She looks me over and jots down some notes. "Looks like you've kept everything up, Celeste. Good job." She puts down her pen and leans back in her chair. "There's only one thing you need to be careful of, and it's pretty common."

"What's that?" I just know she's about to tell me in the nicest way she knows how that I'm back to being ugly.

"Before I say anything, I want you to know you look fabulous. It's just that . . . well, you're overplucking your eyebrows." She smiles. "A lot of women do that. They figure if a little plucking makes them look polished then more plucking is even better."

"I like 'em this way." Why is she still grinning at me like that? I know she's not stupid, but she sure looks like the town fool, sitting there with that smile on her face, even though she knows I'm not gonna change my mind.

"Tell you what, Celeste. Let me show you what I mean." She picks up a makeup pencil. "I'll fill in one of your brows just a teeny bit, and we'll look at the difference between the two of them. That way you don't have to make a commitment. If you don't like it, all you've done is confirmed it."

Leave it to Priscilla to find a way to get what she wants. I try to bob my head, but I haven't quite mastered the technique yet. I'll have to watch more reality TV. "That's fine."

She leans toward me and brushes the pencil across my eyebrow a bunch of times, in tiny strokes. When she's done, she's back to smiling. "There we go. Take a look and see for yourself."

I pick up the handheld mirror and look at myself every which-a-way—my whole face all at once, the left side covered, and then the right side covered. Well color me shocked. The girl's right again.

By the time I'm ready to leave, I'm missing the top layer of the skin on my face, I have a new-and-improved mascara that makes my eyelashes all flirty and blinky, my lips are moistened with color that won't rub off even when me and Jimmy smooch, and I have eyebrows that frame all this beautifulness. And I've booked my next appointment for a hair consultation and cut. I don't know how Priscilla does it. I'm happy for how I look, but I still don't like her much.

Mama has already paid, so all I have to do is leave a tip, which Priscilla says isn't necessary, but I do. After all, a girl's got to have pride if she has nothing else.

On my way out the door, I pass Chester's area, and he winks. "Lookin' good, girl."

I sling my bag over my shoulder and keep walking. It bugs me when I don't know why someone's complimenting me—if he's trying to keep me coming back or if he really means it. Either way, it makes me uncomfortable. I mean, all my life I've been homely, so of course I don't take to all this attention like a natural-born pretty girl.

Sheila is standing at the front desk writing in her appointment book. She looks up at me and blinks. "You keep lookin' better and better all the time, Celeste. I'm glad you've found your natural beauty."

My lips twitch, and I grin back at her. I don't mean to; it just happens. Something about Sheila makes her seem real.

I switched schedules with one of the second-shift nursing assistants at the nursing home, so I have to go get ready for work. As much as I hated going back to a regular job after my last private-duty patient died, I've discovered it's sorta fun to have coworkers. They crack jokes, and even when I don't think they're funny, I laugh because it makes me feel like I'm part of something—a feeling I've always wanted but never had until I got done over. And most of these folks didn't know me back in the days when I was downright uglier'n a mud fence. All they see is the beautiful new me.

20
Priscilla

We'll need to have the electricity turned back on," Jackie informs me during our discussion about having an inspection of the old ice factory. "I'll see if the sellers will foot the bill, but be prepared if they won't."

"Tell you what," I say. "Don't even bother asking them. I'll pay."

"It still has to be in their name."

"That's fine. Just tell them to let me know when the bill comes in, and I'll cover the cost."

"You're too easy, Priscilla." I hear the smile in her voice, which makes me happy. Real estate in Mississippi has been hit hard, and Piney Point has practically tanked. There's no doubt in my mind that Jackie's scrambling to make half the money she used to make when the economy was better.

"What else do I need to do?"

"Just sit tight until we get the inspection done. Do you want to have your design guy come in this week, or do you wanna wait for the inspection?"

It doesn't take long to make that decision. My *design guy* just happens to be one of the best remodelers in the state, and he's super busy. "I'll wait. No point in wasting his time if the inspection doesn't check out."

"Good thinkin'. The place has been sittin' vacant so long there's no tellin' what might be wrong with it."

"Let's just hope there's nothing that can't be fixed."

"I been in this business long enough to know that near 'bout everything can be fixed if you're willin' to cough up the money."

I laugh. "That's how it is with almost everything, including my business."

"Yeah, you got that right. I've seen Celeste since you worked your magic on her."

Not one to ever trash talk my clients, regardless of how I feel about them, I change the subject. "With the reunion coming up next week, I might be out of pocket between now and then, so don't feel like you have to rush anything."

"Tell you what. I'll get the electricity turned on and order the inspection. Unless there's a problem, I won't need you for anything until it's time to make a decision."

"Perfect. Thanks, Jackie."

"No problem."

Each day that leads up to the reunion is busier than the one before. I know I'll be slammed next week, so I'm trying to give Mother the attention she seems to need.

"If I wind up moving the Cut 'n Curl to the ice factory, there'll be plenty of room for administrative offices," I tell her during dinner on Thursday. "That way I can be closer if you need me."

"No, that's silly. Besides, I don't think that'll happen because once you get your people in there they'll tell you how ridiculous you're being, thinking you can go in there and make that old ramshackle of a building into something you'd want your name on."

As I look at Mother, I wonder if she's talking about her own pride and having her friends wonder about her daughter being in that old building. Although she openly shuns anything to do with external beauty, she's still an intellectual snob.

"I know you don't like that place, Mother, but think of it this way. It's a historical building, and we're going to recycle as much as we can."

She frowns and hesitates a moment before nodding. "Yes, there is that. But you have to admit the place is quite an eyesore."

"Right now it is, but try to envision it." I lift a hand and slowly wave it through the air. "The rustic building against the backdrop of a manicured lawn and a nicely paved driveway with fresh lines painted for parking. The canopied entrance welcomes visitors who walk into a full-service salon where they'll get pampered and primped. They'll tell all their friends about it, and before long, we'll be known as the people who take the old and ugly, and make it new and pretty."

Being an English professor, mother loves symbolism. I see her eyes start to sparkle as she finally gets it. "As much as I hate to admit this, you might actually have something, Priscilla."

To drive my point home even more, I add, "Remember when you told me that wearing clothes from a thrift store was actually doing a service by keeping it from the landfill? Think of what I'm doing in the same way."

"You're really stretching this a bit too far, Priscilla. Stop while you're ahead."

I laugh and get up to clean the kitchen. "Why don't you go finish up your summer schedule planning, while I do the dishes?"

Since Teresa is due to come in the morning, I wipe down the appliances. Mother doesn't want anyone, including our cleaning lady, to think she's dirty or messy. In fact, I think since she's had Teresa coming to the house, she does more housework than she did before.

———⌇———

I awaken the next morning to the sound of loud voices in the house. Before I have a chance to sit up in bed, Mother's at my door, a look of horror on her face.

"What's wrong?" I rub my eyes and try to wrap my mind around being up at—I glance at the clock—six thirty.

"The ice factory."

Teresa is right behind her, hollering, "The whole place is on fire! You should see it. They had to call in the Hattiesburg Fire Department to come help put it out."

"Fire?" I hop right out of bed and grab my robe. "The house—?"

Mother shakes her head, but I see the look of concern on her face. "No, honey, the ice factory."

I follow Mother into the living room, where she turns on the television to see if any of the local stations are covering the news. And they are, all from different angles. We flip from one channel to the next to see if there's anything that can be saved, and it appears that won't be the case.

"Well, looks like your salon plans have just gone up in smoke."

Disappointment floods every inch of my body. "I better go call Jackie."

Mother stops me and looks me in the eye. "I know you're disappointed, sweetie, but things have a way of working out. I'm sure you'll find something even nicer."

I smile. "I hope so."

She moves to the side so I can go to my room and call Jackie in private. Jackie answers before the end of the first ring. "I was just about to call you. This is terrible. I had the electricity turned on right after I told the sellers you were willing to pay. They were eager to get movin' on the deal."

"Now what?"

"I'm not sure. Let me think about it. In the meantime, I can scout out a few more places, but they'll likely be out a ways. We've already looked at everything downtown."

"Don't worry about it now, Jackie. I'm not in a hurry."

"I—" She stops herself before continuing. "I would really like to help you find the perfect place, Priscilla . . . that is, if you still want to move."

"Don't worry about that, Jackie. If . . . I mean *when* we move, you'll be the one who handles it."

"Thank you, Priscilla. In the meantime, I need to call the sellers and let them know you've changed your mind."

"I'm sure they'll know that."

"Not necessarily. Some buyers would still go through with a deal, but with changes in the contract, of course."

"They would?"

"Yeah, but generally that happens if the buyer plans to raze the structures and start over."

"So would I be able to get it for a little less money?" I ask.

"Not necessarily . . . at least not if they have time to think about how much time the buyer will save starting from scratch rather than having to retrofit the building to suit their needs."

Hmm. A speck of an idea flits through my mind, and I don't want to waste time, or I might miss out on a fantastic but time-sensitive opportunity. "Why don't you hold off on talking to the sellers for just a bit? I need to discuss something with my staff."

"But the building . . . I mean, there's nothing left . . . "

"I know. Just trust me on this, okay?"

"Oo-kaaaay," she says slowly. "Want me to call you later?"

"Sounds good."

After I get ready for work, I head for the door. Mother tilts her head and gives me a curious look. "What's going on, Priscilla? You look different." She narrows her eyes. "You look happy."

"I have an idea that just might wind up being the best one I've ever had."

"Uh-oh. I know what it means when you get one of your sil—" She pauses to smile. "One of your ideas." For once, Mother resists the urge to call what I'm doing a silly frilly business, and I appreciate it.

All the way to the salon, I hum the tune to "She Works Hard for the Money." It's still playing in my head as I walk into the shop. The whole place is buzzing with the news of the ice factory as the early-shift hairdressers talk about what I'll do next. The commotion doesn't even stop when I walk in.

Sheila's wiping down her station, and Chester's placing his combs in the disinfectant solution. Neither of them looks up, even though they both pause momentarily, letting me know they're aware of my presence.

"Hey, I have an idea I want to share with both of you," I say as I stand between them.

Sheila leans on the counter and looks me in the eye. "You sold us on your last idea, only to have it burn down this mornin' . . . in case you haven't heard."

"I heard." I motion for her and Chester to follow me as I walk back toward the private room we've been using for facials.

Chester closes the door behind him and glares at me. "I didn't like that place, until you got us all excited about addin' all the extras. Don't get us worked up again." He lifts his hands and drops them, slapping his sides, his lips turned downward at the corners, defying his words. "I think it's a sign that we should just stay put."

I frown right back at him. "So you're saying you think that this incident at the only place we've seriously considered should affect the salon's future?"

He folds his arms, flattens out his lips, and nods. I turn to Sheila and see her standing there staring at me, wearing an expression I can't read.

"Okay, here's what I'm thinking, but remember it's just the beginning of my thoughts." I lower my voice so they'll have to lean closer to hear what I'm saying. "We need to find out what the fire inspector's report says first, of course, but if the building isn't salvageable, I might go ahead and purchase the property to build a brand-new facility. There isn't any commercial land left that close to town, and it's really a good location."

"A brand-new salon, just like the one you have over in Jackson?" Sheila asks, a light of interest flashing in her eyes.

"Something like that, only better. How about a brand-new building that is a replica of the old ice factory but with everything brand-new? We can even call it Prissy's Cut 'n Curl and Ice Factory Day Spa." I give them a moment to wrap their minds around the idea. "And I'm thinking the two of you—with input from the rest of the staff—can help me work up the plans to make it exactly how we want it."

Chester's eyes widen, a childlike grin replaces his frown, and he lifts his hands straight up. "Priscilla, you are a genius, girl! I love that idea."

Sheila snickers and gives him a sideways glance. "Chester, you are one fickle dude."

He rolls his eyes at her and smiles at me. "I wouldn't call me fickle. Open-minded is more like it."

Sheila glances at the wall clock and darts toward the door. "I'm expectin' my first appointment any minute. We can talk about this later."

"Me too." Chester runs out the door right behind her.

As soon as I'm alone, I wonder if I've done the right thing by telling them my initial thoughts because anything can go wrong. My motive was to give them some hope, but if something happens again, they may lose faith in my ideas, and it'll take even longer to build them back up. I have to laugh at my own worries. It took me every bit of fifteen seconds to reignite their spark, so even if I have to spend a whole minute convincing them my next idea is good I can deal with it.

21

Laura

No, Bubba, you cannot go out with your friends tonight."

"But, Mama . . . " He takes time out to sniffle. "It's Saturday." My fourteen-year-old stands there looking like he might burst into tears just because I said he wasn't allowed to hang out with that bunch of hoodlums he thinks are his friends.

"What part of *grounded* don't you understand, Bubba?"

"That's just stupid. We didn't do nothin' wrong . . . just TP someone's yard."

"The mayor's yard," I remind him. "Talk about stupid."

"I didn't know." If he thinks those crocodile tears will break me, that boy has another think coming.

"What's the problem?" Pete asks as he pulls out a chair and plops down into it. "Got any coffee?"

I pour Pete's coffee, dump a bunch of nondairy creamer and sugar into it, give it a twirl with the spoon, and hand it to him. "Bubba thinks we should let him hang out with those . . . " I cut a glance over to my son who has now turned to his daddy for mercy. "Those awful boys." *Please, Pete,* I silently beg with my eyes. *Back me up on this, just this once.*

Pete takes a sip of his coffee, chuckles, and shakes his head, still smiling. "I don't see what the problem is, Laura. That was just a boyish prank that didn't hurt nobody."

Times like this I want to strangle my husband. I feel like I'm raising four underage young'uns and an overgrown, over-age toddler.

"Pete . . . " I stop and see that he's not even listening to me. Instead, he's staring at our son.

"Bubba," Pete says. "Your mama don't want you hangin' out with them boys."

"But they're my friends."

Pete nods. "I know they are, and I understand why you're just dyin' to hang out with 'em tonight. That's why I thought I'd offer somethin' that should make both you and your mama happy."

Now I'm curious. My husband might be an overgrown young'un, but he does have an interesting way with our offspring.

"If I can get your mama to agree to this, we'll let you hang out with your friends, but only on one condition." He continues staring at Bubba, whose face has lit up. "I can come along, just to make sure y'all stay outta trouble."

Bubba looks horrified. "No, Daddy. That wouldn't be cool."

Pete continues grinning as he sips his coffee. "That's the deal, Bubba. Take it or leave it."

Bubba scowls down at his toaster pastry but doesn't say a word. I can tell he's thinking over his daddy's offer. After a tense couple of minutes, Bubba shakes his head. "Nah, I'll just stay home tonight." He picks up the pastry and gobbles it up in three bites as I stand there in silence, watching my now-brilliant husband looking all smug and pleased with himself.

After Bubba leaves, Pete winks at me. "Ya gotta know what makes a boy tick, sweetie. I gave him a choice, and he's the one who decided he'd be better off stayin' home."

I scramble up some eggs for Pete and toss in some extra cheese for helping me with Bubba. He eats them before they have a chance to get cold—the one thing I can count on from every single solitary member of my family—and gets up when he's done, leaving his plate on the table—another thing I can count on if I don't remind them to carry it to the sink. But that's okay now because I'm still happy about him backing me up with our boy.

"Whatcha gonna do today?" Pete asks.

I shrug. "I thought I'd finish up some of the work for the reunion."

"Finish up?" He pauses by the door. "You mean you're almost all done?"

"You know better'n that. I've got my list for each day, and today I have to—"

"Look, Laura, I can't stand around listenin' to your list. I promised the guys I'd go help mount the engine on Trey's Camaro."

Whenever Pete helps the guys with anything, I know there's drinking involved, and I'm not likely to see him again 'til suppertime. At least I don't have to deal with feeding lunch to a half dozen half-drunk, starving men this time. A flash of pity for Trey's wife flashes through me, but it doesn't stay long when I think about her cleavage-baring tops and shorts that make her legs look longer than they really are.

"Have fun," I say, knowing it's pointless to even try to talk him into helping me get through my list.

I've barely finished doing the breakfast dishes when the doorbell rings. All the young'uns are home, so one of them should get the door. But then the doorbell rings again.

I wipe my hands on the dishtowel and answer the door, mumbling about how if it wasn't for me, nothing would get done around here. Celeste, Jimmy, and Tim stand on the other side of the door.

"Hey y'all," I say, not giving a hoot that Celeste and Jimmy look annoyed as all get out. "Wanna come in? I just dumped the last of the mornin' coffee, but I can fix some more."

"That would be good." Celeste takes a step inside, and the men follow. "We're all done with what you gave us to do. You need to give up some control, Laura. I woulda thought after last time—"

Tim holds up a hand. "Laura, please let us help you. I'm in town for a whole week, so I can run all the errands you need and be your right-hand man . . . that is, if you let me."

In my book, the best thing Priscilla Slater has going for her is Tim Puckett. Too bad she doesn't see husband potential in him.

"Okay." I open my folder and scan the list of things to do this week. I reckon it won't hurt to delegate a little more from my list.

We spend the next hour discussing and arguing about who should do what. Every now and then Tim plays referee, giving me a break from having to deal with Celeste's know-it-all attitude that started when she got all prettied up at the Cut 'n Curl five years ago.

"Mama!" The sound of little Jack's shrieking voice at the top of the stairs goes all through me. "Tell Renee to get out of my room."

"Mama," Renee hollers. "I'm not in Jack's room. He's in mine!"

"Don't make me come up there," I holler right back as I tromp to the bottom of the stairs. "Jack, get out of Renee's room."

"She stole my computer."

"Here's your stupid computer . . . " I watch in horror as Renee storms toward the top of the stairs, pulling back the arm that holds Jack's secondhand laptop he saved his allowance for.

"Don't you dare throw that," I yell. "Because if you do, you're gonna pay for it."

Renee rolls her eyes, growls, and puts it on the floor. "Here's your stupid computer. Don't even think about goin' back in my room, or I'll—" She clamps her mouth shut and looks down at me.

"You'll what?" Jack taunts.

"Jack, pick up your computer and go to your room right this minute." I point my finger at Renee. "And don't take anything else without askin' first."

When I rejoin the reunion committee, I notice looks of pity on all their faces. Celeste even tries to be nice. "Looks like you got your hands full, Laura. Why don't I make the place cards?"

"I was gonna hand-letter 'em." I can't give up without at least a hint of an argument.

"I can do that . . . " She looks at the men before turning back to me. "Not as good as you, of course, but I don't think no one will much care."

"Okay, here ya go." I shove the box of place cards in her direction, trying not to let 'em see me hyperventilating. It's hard for me to give up so much control, but I know I have to do it, or everything will get all wacky on me again.

After they leave, I go back to the kitchen and pour myself another cup of coffee. Then I sit down at the table and try to organize my thoughts, but too many things remind me of the last reunion, and I feel paralyzed.

When Pete was in the hospital with alcohol poisoning five years ago, we both had to spend time with the counselor, who gave both of us some things to work on. I thought my part was silly, but I was willing to do whatever it took to help Pete get better. He's not drinking quite as much as he used to, but he still hasn't given it up. The counselor said even a sip is too much for Pete, considering he's an alcoholic and all, but as long as he doesn't drive after drinking or hurt any of us, I can live with a little bit of drinking. After all, like Pete reminds me all the time, he was a drinker before we got married, and I knew that going in. It took a while for him to get his license back, so I had to carry him everywhere he went. Every once in a while, if I was up to my elbows in something, he'd take the car a short distance, being careful to stay off the main roads so as not to let any of Piney Point's finest see him.

He has his license back, but they're still watching him like a hawk, and he knows it. That's why I expect him to call me this afternoon to come get him from Trey's. One thing is a given: there will be drinking when he and his friends get together.

22
Priscilla

I arrive at the salon first thing Monday morning and find Jackie waiting for me in the reception area. She stands and smiles when I walk in.

"Hey." I motion for her to sit back down, and I join her. "Any news yet?"

"This is one of those good-news-not-so-good-news things."

"What's up?"

"The preliminary report on the fire is that it started when the electricity was turned on. Apparently, some of the . . ." She shudders. "The rodents had chewed through the wiring."

"Good thing no one was in the building at the time." I pause long enough to see that she's squirming. "So what's the bad . . . er, not-so-good news?"

"The historical society wants more of an investigation, since it would have cost a small fortune to retrofit the building to almost any business that bought it."

I feel a headache coming on. "So what are they saying, that I started the fire?"

"No, they're not saying that at all. They just want to make sure the report is accurate."

"So what do you recommend we do now?"

She whips some papers from her briefcase and presents them to me. "Submit a fresh contract and let's try to get them to agree to the same price as soon as possible . . . at least before someone else offers more to purchase the land now that it's vacant."

"Let me think about it, okay?"

Jackie tilts her head, smiles, and slowly nods. "Okay, but not too long."

"How about until tomorrow morning?"

"I'll be here first thing in the morning. If you decide earlier than that, you know how to get in touch with me."

I have two morning appointments that should keep me busy and my mind on something besides the new location, but that doesn't happen once Sheila and Chester start talking about it. Even my clients chime in.

"If you know you need to expand, and that's the only place available, why wait?" my second client says.

Chester nods so hard Sheila teases him and says if he keeps it up his head might fall off. "We know that's where we need to be. I even dreamed about it last night, and you know what happens when I dream about stuff."

"Yeah," Sheila says, cutting her gaze over to me. "It means you're gonna drive us crazy with every last detail."

Chester places his knuckles on his hip, bobs his head and pouts his lips. "It means, my friend, that we're supposed to be there. That place is perfect for the Cut 'n Curl, and you know it."

I take another snip of my client's hair as she starts her spiel about why I need to sign the contract. "I've always wanted to get pampered at a day spa, and when I heard your plans, I talked to my bridge group, and they were talkin' about havin' a spa day every month."

This conversation the three of us had a few days ago wasn't a cross-your-heart-and-hope-to-die secret discussion, but I would have preferred they didn't discuss it with clients. Oh well, too late for that now that my client's bridge group knows.

By noon, I know what I need to do. I call Jackie, and she doesn't hesitate to drop everything to bring the contract for me to sign.

"You'll be so happy you did this," she says as she drops the paperwork into her briefcase on her way out the door.

I sure hope she's right. My head is still spinning at the speed of my decision. I've always been one to act fairly quickly, but never without considerable thought and prayer, which reminds me. I bow my head and pray that the Lord will guide me through whatever He has in mind for me, in spite of my lack of attention to Him.

"Honey, I've been prayin' for you all along," Sheila says when I open my eyes. "I know you think you're alone in all this, but trust me when I tell you we'll stick by you no matter what."

My eyes mist as I nod. "Thank you, Sheila. It's nice to know you're right there with me."

"It isn't easy bein' you." She gives me a hug. "Folks might think just because you're a successful businesswoman you don't have any doubts, but I know better."

"Am I that obvious?"

"No, not really. If I didn't understand human nature you'd have me fooled, but no one is always one hundred percent self-assured."

"Thank you, Sheila." We lock gazes, and I feel the love flowing between us. She's one of my favorite people in the entire world. She's not old enough to be like a mother to me, so I guess I can say she's like an older sister I never had.

Once my afternoon appointments start, the rest of the day goes by quickly. I walk through the door of my parents' house—or more appropriately these days, Mother's house—only to be confronted by the woman who has never approved of my business. "So you're actually going through with it, I hear."

I close my eyes for a moment to catch my breath and to prevent an outburst I'll later regret. "If you're talking about purchasing the ice factory property, yes, I do have a contract on it."

"That's exactly what I'm talking about. Why are you doing this? I can understand some of your other decisions. You've always been the rebellious daughter, but this is beyond any of your other pranks."

Now I can't let it go. "Prank? You think this is a prank? Mother, I've done quite well, and it's because I know what I'm doing." Some of my earlier doubt creeps up on me, but I quash it.

"You do realize that if you're in over your head, and I think you are this time, your father and I aren't in a position to bail you out."

That does it. I can't let her continue talking to me like this. "Mother, I love you, and that'll never change, but one thing I need to remind you is that I've never asked you to bail me out of anything." I speak with a firmer voice than I've ever used with my parents, and for a moment, fear flows through me.

She blinks, but my comment doesn't prevent her from continuing. "This is a huge mistake, Priscilla."

"Maybe so, but it'll be my mistake."

"I think this is a very bad business decision." Mother obviously doesn't know when to stop. "Even your father agrees with me on this."

Laughter escapes my throat. "How can you and Dad talk about my business when you can't even fix your own marriage?"

A flash of anger darts from her eyes. "Our marriage is none of your business, Priscilla."

"Oh, but I disagree. You and Dad are my family. Y'all are all the family I know, thanks to the fact that both of you have tried so hard to keep me from getting to know most of my relatives. Y'all even limited the amount of time I could spend with my own grandmother."

Mother's chin quivers as she sinks into the chair behind her. "I only wanted what was best for you. Your father and I always wanted you to have a good education so you wouldn't wind up in a bad way."

I close the distance between us and kneel down by her side. "You and Dad did a good job of showing me that it's possible to follow my dreams as long as I work hard. That's what y'all did, and that's what I've done."

"But . . . " Mother looks at me with tears in her eyes.

I can't let her say something she'll regret, so I squeeze her hand and speak before she has a chance to finish her thought. "But we have different dreams. You and Dad shared the dream of getting advanced degrees and teaching college, and y'all both accomplished that. My dream is to have a successful business that will continue to grow as long as I'm able to make it happen. I love what I do, just like you and Dad love what y'all do."

Mother swallows hard and blinks. "We used to, but I'm not so sure anymore." She pats my hand as her expression softens. "You've had a long day, sweetie. Why don't we have some supper and watch a little TV?"

I can't remember the last time I watched TV, and I don't really want to now, but I don't want to let the opportunity to spend more time with Mother slip by. She's obviously down, and if it's something that'll make her happy, I'll do it.

I nod. "Let's go fix supper."

"I thought we'd just have canned soup and grilled cheese sandwiches."

Not my favorite, but if that's what she wants, that's what we'll have—without an argument from me. "You heat up the soup, and I'll grill the sandwiches."

Less than an hour later, we're finished cleaning the kitchen after supper. "Let's put on our pajamas," she says. "That way we can completely relax and enjoy the rest of the night."

Once we're all comfy, we settle in the living room—Mother and me in the matching rocker-recliners she and Dad bought after I moved out. "Want a snack?" she asks.

"I better not. Eating late will only make me puffy in the morning."

Mother nods. "Yeah, good point. I've developed some bad habits that I need to stop." She pats her tiny belly. "Like late-night snacking. I've put on a few pounds."

We catch the tail end of Mother's favorite game show. "Have you ever thought about trying out for 'Jeopardy'?" I ask. "I bet you'd be good."

Mother shrugs. "If they ever come to Mississippi looking for contestants, I might consider it."

"Instead of waiting for them to come to you, why don't you find out where they'll be and go to them?" The realization of one of our biggest differences dawns on me. Although she managed to pull herself out of the poverty she grew up in, she still isn't as aggressive as she could be.

"I might just do that."

Mother picks up the remote and starts to channel surf. She's about to flip past TVNS, when I lift my hand. "Stop right there," I say.

She gives me a curious look. "What are you talking about?"

"TVNS. That's what I'm aiming for."

"TVNS? Don't tell me you're still on that kick, Priscilla"

I'm not sure about my timing, but I figure the opportunity is there for me to let her know where I stand with the shopping network. As I talk, I see a smile flickering on her lips. And then she giggles. I can't remember ever hearing my mother giggle like that.

"What's so funny?"

"I can just picture you on TVNS holding up one of your shampoos, telling all the lonely housewives who watch how pretty they can be if they use your product. Sort of reminds me of some of the early commercials back in the day."

She has a point. I open up a bit more and tell her that some of my products have gotten to the final stages in the network's decision in the past, but they've ultimately gotten shot down because I don't have enough to offer.

"So what are you gonna show them next?"

I tell her about the complete big hair system. "Of course, it'll have to go through their stringent QA process, but I have confidence in what I do."

She reaches up and wiggles her fingers over the crown of her head. "You're talkin' about the stuff that makes your hair look fluffy on top?"

I nod. "Yes."

She tilts her head back, laughs, and shakes her head. "I don't know if that's something women outside the South would be interested in."

"We'll see," I say. I'm tired of defending myself.

"You can call it Priscilla's Fluffy Hair Goop."

"I'll have to think about it."

Mother points the remote toward the TV. "Mind if I change the channel?"

"No, go ahead."

As she settles on a reality show that I never would have expected her to watch, I think about all the products I can sell on TVNS, including volumizing shampoo and conditioner, hair gel, and modified rattail comb. I need to make a final decision on the name of my line and go from there.

During commercials, Mother looks over at me but doesn't say a word. I used to have a pretty good idea what she was thinking, but now she has a different expression. Could it possibly be respect? That might be a stretch, but it sure doesn't look like vehement disapproval.

23
Tim

I kept trying to tell myself I was over Priscilla, but when I see her working her magic on her client's hair, I get that old belly-flop feeling that lets me know I'm not. She has a way of making you think you're the only person on earth when she does your hair. I know 'cause she's done my hair a bunch of times.

Last night I spent about an hour trying to come up with a word from *A Hundred Days to a Smarter Vocabulary,* that book she gave me years ago, the one that teaches you how to learn a new word every day. At first, I followed it according to the instructions, starting from the front and working my way to the back. The problem was that some of them words aren't natural. Take the word *abhor* for instance. I tried to use it, but it made me feel downright uppity knowing I could have just said *hate* instead. So I stopped. The only time I even look at the book anymore is right before I see Priscilla. And that hasn't been all that much recently. Last night I studied three new words that looked like I might be able to work into a regular conversation, since I knew I'd be seeing her today. Much as I hate to admit it after all these years of getting shot down, I still wanna make Priscilla proud of me. Uncle Hugh has teased me about it a time or two, letting me know I should be past wanting some woman's approval. But she's different from most women, and I just can't help that she makes me feel like a teenage boy again.

The list Laura Moss handed me is lame, but I promised I'd do everything on it . . . and I already have. Now it's time to work on more stuff that she thinks she'll be able to do herself but most likely won't get around to. One thing I learned about Laura five years ago is that she bites off way more than she can chew, and then she makes things worse by trying to take a bite out of everyone around her. I ain't letting that happen this time. I aim to be what Priscilla calls *proactive*. I grin at the thought of how much smarter I am, just for knowing that girl.

Priscilla glances up and catches sight of me. I grin and try to act cool with a wave, but in reality, I'm not cool at all. In fact, I'm sweating bullets. Not only is it nearly a hundred degrees outside, simply looking at Priscilla still sets my blood to moving faster.

She motions for me to come over to her station, so I do, trying real hard to go slow and not act like I'm all anxious about seeing her. "What's up, Priscilla?"

"As soon as I'm finished here, I thought we could go over our to-do lists."

I wave mine. "I'm all finished. Got somethin' you want me to take care of?"

"I did everything on mine too. We really need to get Laura to relinquish more of the work, or we'll wind up with a huge mess on our hands and find ourselves scrambling at the last minute." She makes a funny face. "Again."

Relinquish. I make a mental note to look that up later. I think I know what she's saying, but I don't want to take a chance and make an idiot of myself.

Then I figure now's the time to try some of the new words I learned. "I perused her list last time I saw her, so I know some of the stuff that's on there. I think she'll be all jubilant if everything runs smooth this time."

Priscilla grins. "You still have that vocabulary book I gave you?"

Trying to act cool again, I shrug. "I'm sure I have it somewhere."

She smiles as she hands her client a mirror and spins the chair around. "Take a look at the back and let me know if you like it."

"You look real pretty, Ms. Pointer."

The elderly woman smiles up at me. "Why thank you, Tim. You're such a sweet boy."

Priscilla gives me a curious look but don't say nothing. Ms. Pointer nods and says she loves her hair, and they walk to the front desk to square the bill. After Priscilla returns, she laughs as she sweeps the floor beneath her chair. "You amaze me, Tim. Sometimes I think you fit in here more than I do."

"It feels like home to me." As soon as I say that, I regret it. Priscilla has made it very clear that she's never fit in at Piney Point, which is why she only comes home when she has to.

"C'mon, let's go to the back so we can talk in private."

I follow her to the back room. She closes the door and turns around to face me. "Coffee?"

"No thanks. I had my daily cup before I left the hotel. So what did you need to get all private about?"

She glances down at the floor and slowly raises her gaze to mine, a worried look on her face. "We need to figure out a way to keep Pete from drinking too much, especially at the reunion party."

"Yeah, I agree. But that's hard to do with Pete. He's real sneaky."

"True, but I think we can outsmart him."

"Whatcha got in mind?"

Debby Mayne

She mentions different ideas, including one to replace all the alcohol with colored, flavored water. I can tell Priscilla ain't been a drinker. Anyone who tosses back the whiskey like Pete does will know the difference right off the bat. In fact, he could probably name the brand after sniffing it real good.

"I'm not so sure that'll work," I tell her, "but I'll try to come up with somethin'. In the meantime, I need to stop by and see Laura. I got her bonfire permit, even though I don't think we'll be needin' it after hearing the weather report for the weekend."

"That might not be a bad thing." Priscilla chuckles. "Without the bonfire, we won't have a place for the keg."

I lift one eyebrow and shake my head. "I'm sure Pete will find a place . . . like maybe his garage, which would be worse."

"True, I hadn't thought about that. What can we do?"

Be still my heart—Priscilla is asking me for advice. "I'll come up with something." And I fully intend to. No way will I let this woman down. "I'll head on over to the Mosses' house now. Anything I can do for you?"

She ponders that for a while and shakes her head. "No, not today. Are you going to the committee meeting tonight?"

"Of course. No way would I miss it."

"You're amazing, Tim." Priscilla leans over and gives me a hug. I wanna pull her into my arms and never let go, but I'm afraid that would scare her away. Instead, I try to pretend it don't matter, while my insides is quaking with pure joy.

She backs away from me, taking a piece of my heart—something I can't help, no matter how much I tell myself no woman's worth wanting as bad as I've wanted her since we first met. "Tell Laura I'll see her tonight."

I lift my hand in a pretend salute. "Will do."

All the way over to Laura's my mind races through different scenarios. Me and Priscilla would be so good together, if she'd only relax and let herself feel it. Even though I tell myself that,

198

I know deep down that if it's not there, well, it can't be forced, no matter how much the other person wants it.

Laura answers the door looking like a wild animal got ahold of her. "Come on in, Tim. I have to deal with my young'uns, but it shouldn't take long. I'll be right with you."

"Want me to wait in the kitchen?" I know the way, since that's where our meetings were last time.

"Sure, go ahead. And tell Bubba I need him upstairs."

When I walk into the kitchen, I see Bubba playing tabletop football with his Fruit Loops. There's a mess of 'em on the floor where he missed his goal.

"Whatcha doin', Bubba?"

He don't even look at me when he talks. "What's it look like I'm doin'?"

"Your mama wants you upstairs."

Bubba just sits there flicking his cereal across the table. I wanna smack him, but he's not mine, and I think it's illegal to do that. The boy obviously needs some serious parenting.

"Did you hear me, Bubba?"

"Yeah, I heard you." He stands and starts heading in the direction of the stairs, walking slow as a turtle with a broke leg.

Since I know Laura will hit the roof if she sees the mess on the floor, I look around for a broom to sweep it up. I don't see one, so I bend over and start picking up the colorful cereal.

"Whatcha doin' down there?"

I glance up and see Laura standing over me. "Cleanin' up the mess on the floor."

"It's not your mess to clean up." She's talking to me like she talks to her kids, and that annoys me to no end.

Rather than show my irritation, I keep picking up the Fruit Loops. She gives up and heads over to the coffee pot. "Cream and sugar?"

"Sugar, no cream." After I pick up the last of the cereal, I straighten up and extend my cupped hand. "Whatcha want me to do with this?"

She points to the garbage can. "Did you have a chance to get the bonfire permit yet?"

After she puts the coffee on the table, we sit down and discuss all we've done so far and what we have left to do. I express my concern about the weather, and I see the lines on her face grow deeper. The committee meeting is tonight, but with so little time left to get stuff done, we can't wait. "We need an alternate plan."

Laura shrugs. "I'm fresh out of ideas."

"Then let me worry about it, okay? There's no sense in you adding it to your list that's already way too long for one person to handle."

Her lips start to twitch before she breaks into a smile. "Tim, you are one of the sweetest people I've ever known in my entire life. I wish Pete could be more like you. Shoot, I think most women wish their husbands were as kind, considerate, and . . . well, you know."

"Thank you." I feel my face heating up. "Why don't I see if I can figure out a backup plan for bonfire night, in case it rains? It's gettin' mighty cloudy out, so I checked the weather report, and it just might." I stand and push the chair back beneath the table.

She does the same thing. "I don't know, Tim. I'm pretty sure if it rains, everyone will find another place to party."

"Like your garage?" I lift an eyebrow and wait.

"Um . . . yeah, I think it's probably a good idea to come up with an alternate plan. Why don't you do that?"

"Any ideas?"

She scrunches up her face. "Not that I can think of right off the bat, unless . . . Maybe you can talk to Mr. Danny at the hardware store. He books the VFW for certain functions. They might be able to work out a deal with us."

"Is there room in the budget if they charge?"

"No, but Mr. Danny has a daughter who would've graduated with my class if she hadn't . . . well, gotten herself in a family way . . . back when it used to matter if a girl was married." She rolls her eyes. "If the hall is vacant that night, he might be willin' to let us use it if we promise to clean up afterward."

"And that's if it rains, and we have to move the party indoors," I remind her. Chances are good that'll happen, according to the weather report on the Internet.

Laura rips a sheet of paper from her notebook and jots down some information. "You know where Olson's Hardware is downtown?"

I nod. "Next to Olson's Cafe, right?"

"Yep. Mr. Danny should be there since he manages the place. Tell him I told you to ask for him."

I fold up the paper and stick it in my pocket. "Let me go run and take care of this. I'll let you know what he says when we have our meetin' tonight."

She walks me to the door and stops. "Tim?"

I turn around and face her. "Ya need somethin' else?"

She swings her arms and makes a face. "Thank you. I'm sorry I've been so difficult."

I wink and point at her. "I don't even know what you're talkin' about."

She closes her eyes, smiles, and blows out a breath. "Thank you."

The sound of her kids squabbling grabs her attention. Not missing a beat, she leans back and hollers, "Don't make me come up there." Then she slams the door in my face.

24
Priscilla

My time in Piney Point is flying by. I have an uneasy feeling on many levels. Tim is very comfortable taking over some of the reunion preparation, which may seem good on the surface, but I have to admit it sort of bothers me. I mean, this is *my* class reunion, yet he's more connected than I've ever been. No one knows how hard I tried to fit in. I've accepted the fact that it never happened; however, with Tim getting so involved, I feel as though I'm having to relive the days of my teenage insecurity. I have to ask him what's going on, for crying out loud. Shouldn't it be the other way around?

And then there's the issue of the property. I wasn't completely blindsided by the fact that we've outgrown our space in the old salon. Every once in a while I've looked online to see what else is available. When I came back to work, the claustrophobic atmosphere made it clear that I couldn't continue to avoid the problem, and I needed to do something ASAP. Sheila and Chester have been with me since the beginning of my career. They've been nothing but supportive, with encouraging comments and stepping up when needed. There's no doubt in my mind that they'll do a nice job of overseeing the transition from the old to the new space. Granted, they rarely see eye-to-eye on anything, but that'll keep the two of them in check.

Then there's the issue of my parents' marriage. The fact that they haven't actually divorced yet leads me to believe there still might be some hope. If there's anything I can do to help them find their way back together, I will, although Mother has told me to mind my own business and turns back to whatever TV show she's watching at the moment. But I hold to the notion that it *is* my business. They're the only family I have.

Celeste is my first appointment of the day. I brace myself for her snarkiness that she doesn't even try to hide, even when I'm holding tweezers or shears.

I walk into the salon, greet everyone who's there early, and head on back to the private room to set up for Celeste's appointment. She says she wants the works, since her mama's paying. I lay out all the cleansers, creams, and makeup I plan to use as I wait for her.

"Hey. I'm in sort of a hurry today," Celeste says as she breezes into the room. I turn around and see that she's already in the chair, ready to get started. "Let's get this thing going. You have an hour to do whatever it takes to keep me beautiful."

I have to bite my tongue and dig deep to get into professional mode. "I was hoping I could show you some of the latest eye-shadow techniques that'll bring out those gorgeous eyes of yours." I turn my head and wait for her reaction. "It might take more than an hour, though, so if you're in a hurry, I'll just freshen you up a bit."

"Latest techniques?" She chews on her bottom lip as she ponders what to do.

Score. "It's what all the models are doing these days." I look at her and wait.

"Let me make a call." She nods toward the door. "May I have some privacy please?"

Looks like I got to her. "Yes, of course." I stand up and leave the room.

Two minutes later, I hear her calling my name. "Priscilla, I'm done." When I walk back into the room, she wiggles around a bit in the chair. "Looks like I have more time after all."

"Good. Now let's get started."

Throughout her facial and makeup application, I try to keep the conversation on what we're doing. Every now and then she makes comments about Laura, Pete, and even Tim, but I don't want to go there with Celeste while I'm working on her face, so I steer the conversation back to how beautiful she's becoming. Besides, gossip has never served any purpose other than to make the people doing the talking feel better than the ones they're discussing, and that's only momentary. I'm not saying I've never been guilty of gossiping, but when I do, I regret it later. More times than I can count, whatever I've said has come back and bitten me on the backside later.

I've just shown her how to apply the plum and gray eye shadow to give her the current smoky-eye look, when she glances up at me. "So I hear you found out your parents are splittin' up. I guess they were just waiting to make sure you could stand on your own two feet."

I resist the urge to turn her smoky eye into a black-and-blue one. As I scoot my chair away from her, I grit my teeth. "My parents' marriage is not open for discussion."

"Ooh, touchy subject, huh?" She snorts. "You better get used to it, though. Piney Point is a small town, and people will talk. Most everyone already knows your daddy moved out."

That does it. I stand, brush my hands together, and wave my hand toward the door. "We're done."

"But we haven't done the mascara yet." The sound of her whimper annoys me even more than I already am.

"Nothing's changed with mascara. You know how to do that already."

Her nostrils flare as she stares at me, but I refuse to back down. She's treading in an area I'm not ready to discuss with anyone, let alone Celeste who grates on my last nerve. When she sees I'm firm, she stands and struts toward the door before turning back to face me. "You are way too sensitive, Priscilla. But I reckon I shouldn't expect nothin' else from a girl who was always a prima donna."

Prima donna? Me? Never. I open my mouth, but I'm so stunned by her comment I can't even speak.

"See you Friday mornin' for my haircut. I'd really like me some bangs, I think. I hear it makes ya look younger."

I remain standing there staring at the door as she leaves. Why do I let Celeste affect me like this? Or more like it, why do I even care what she thinks?

Throughout the day, as my classmates come in for their new hairdos for the reunion, my mind keeps taking me back to Celeste's comments. After I finish my last appointment of the day, Sheila comes up from behind and puts her arms around me, gives me a squeeze, and lets go.

"I don't know what's been buggin' you all day, but I can tell you're worried about somethin'. If it has anything to do with movin', don't worry about us here. We'll be just fine."

"No, I'm fine." I turn around to face her.

"I mean it, Priscilla. I don't wanna stress you out or nothin'."

"Sheila, I want you to be completely honest with me about something, okay?"

Concern deepens the lines between her eyebrows. "Of course, I wouldn't ever lie to you. You know that."

"Do you think I'm a prima donna?"

Sheila rolls her eyes and shakes her head. "Are you kiddin' me? You're anything *but* a prima donna. I've never known

anyone more concerned about other people than you. Why?
Did someone tell you . . . ?" She narrows her eyes. "Is that
what's been buggin' you all day?"

I slowly nod. "It's strange how much it bothers me."

"Just tell me one thing. Was it Celeste who told you this?"

"Yes."

"Listen to me, Priscilla. Celeste has never had even a smidge
of tact. That girl runs off at the mouth more'n anyone I know,
and she's only gotten worse since her makeover. Matter of fact,
I'm the only hairdresser who'll work with her when you're not
here. She's the reason Germaine walked out and never came
back. No matter what anyone does, Celeste isn't happy. What
galls me is she brags about how you're her regular hairdresser
when you're in town, and she has to settle for the rest of us
when you're not."

"Oh." Celeste is even worse than I thought. "No one should
have to put up with that, including . . . especially you."

"Trust me, I'm a big girl, and I can stand up for myself. Last
time she mouthed off, I pointed to the door and told her not
to let it hit her in the backside. She didn't give me no more lip
after that."

I laugh. "Good. I'm glad you set her straight."

"Now all I have to do is set you straight. You are so not a
prima donna. Most people see you as a kind woman who puts
up with way too much from people."

"Oh, I'm sure there are others who don't like me much."

"If you're talkin' about some of your sorry classmates, it's
just because they're jealous. Don't worry about them."

Sheila is loyal to a fault, and it only makes me love her more.
"Thanks. I need to run home now and make sure Mother is
okay."

"My small group has been prayin' for your mama and daddy.
I know how hard their separation must be on all three of you."

This is the first she's mentioned anything about my parents' split. "Thanks for the prayers. I wish I could figure out a way to make them come to their senses."

"I know. I think the same thing about a lot of folks I know. Me and my husband don't always see eye-to-eye, but we figure that's how it'll be with anyone you're married to. When I hear about people splittin' up over not bein' soul mates, I wonder what they been smokin'." She clicks her tongue once. "Soul mates. I'd like to know who came up with that idea."

"I believe everyone has a soul mate," Chester says from behind me. "Havin' that one person in your life who totally *gets* you would be a wonderful thing."

Sheila sticks her fist on her hip, bobs her head, and makes a face at Chester. "So tell me, Mr. Relationship Expert, how long you been married?"

He snaps a towel at Sheila. "You know I never married, but that's because I can't find my soul mate. When I do, though . . . " He looks off into the distance with a dreamy expression.

"It'll be a cold day in July," Sheila finishes before turning back to me. "Stop lettin' people like Celeste play with your mind. I'd be willin' to bet every woman in your graduatin' class would give her eye tooth to be you."

"She's right," Chester agrees. "So what brought all this on?"

"Nothin'." Sheila winks at me. "It's just girl talk. Nothin' you'd be interested in . . . or would it?"

He snaps the towel again and walks away. "Obviously not."

Sheila and I look at each other, and I can see she's trying as hard as I am not to laugh—at least until Chester is out of hearing distance. Then we both let loose.

"I don't know what I'd do without him," Sheila says. "Whenever things get too serious, he has a way of lightening things up."

I call Mother on my way to Laura's house for the committee meeting. She doesn't answer, so I leave a message reminding her I'll be home late.

As I turn onto the street in the Mosses' suburban neighborhood, I see a row of cars parked along the curb in front of Laura and Pete's house. Looks like I'm the last to arrive, but that can't be helped.

I park a half block away and half-walk, half-run up the sidewalk. Before I get to the door, Bonnie Sue flings it open. "Hey, Miss Priscilla. They're waitin' on ya." She grins with hero worship, which makes me very uncomfortable.

"Thanks, Bonnie Sue."

I walk past her, and I'm almost to the kitchen, when I hear her coming up behind me. When I turn around, she stops. "Miss Priscilla, I have a favor."

"Sure, what is it?" I'm already a few minutes late, so I figure another minute won't matter.

"Can you teach me how to wear makeup right? I mean, Mama told me I'm too young, but all the girls wear it at school, and Mama said if I can learn the right way to wear it—"

"Sure, I'll be glad to." I glance at my watch. "When?"

"Tonight?"

I let out a sigh. "Okay, if the meeting doesn't go on too long, and it's all right with your mother, I'll be happy to spend a few minutes on some simple makeup tips. How old are you?"

She straightens her shoulders. "I'll be eleven on my next birthday, and I'm in middle school."

Her thick eyeliner, clumped mascara, and heavy blush makes her look like a little girl who got into her mother's makeup bag. "There are ways to enhance your looks with makeup and still look your age."

"Priscilla, is that you?" Laura calls, her voice getting closer. When she sees me talking to her daughter, she stops and scowls at Bonnie Sue. "I told you not to pounce on her the minute she gets here. Sorry, Priscilla, but my little girl is tryin' to grow up too fast."

I let out a nervous laugh. "I understand. I hope you don't mind if I give her a few tips after the meeting."

"If *you* don't mind, that would be great. Come on back to the kitchen. Looks like we might get rained out, but Tim has saved the day." She shakes her head. "He's turning into our class's knight in shining armor."

When I walk into the kitchen, I see Celeste, Jimmy, Michael Baynard, some young girl sharing his chair, Didi Holcomb, and Tim sitting around the table. "Hey, everyone. Sorry I'm late." Since Didi's here, I wonder where Maurice is.

Celeste points to Tim. "Looks like we're havin' the bonfire at the VFW, only it won't be a bonfire."

"What'll we do for entertainment?" Michael asks. "It's too late to hire a band."

"We're havin' a band on Saturday." Laura gestures around the table. "Any ideas?"

Jimmy raises his hand. "I like karaoke."

Didi rolls her eyes, but she doesn't offer a better suggestion. Everyone just looks at each other, until I comment.

"Karaoke can be fun," I say. "Where can we get a decent karaoke machine and music?"

Pete comes walking into the kitchen with his empty beer can. "One of the guys at work has a good one. I'll ask him."

"Good. Now there's one more thing we have to cover," Tim says. "Regardless of where we have this party, we have to hire an off-duty sheriff's deputy. Apparently, that's a new city policy, after what happened at the last reunion."

Laura shakes her head and slumps down in her chair. "We don't have any more money left in the budget, and it's too late to ask for everyone to pay."

"How much does the deputy cost?" I ask. "If it's not too much, I'll cover it."

"Get a load of the rich girl." Didi's voice drops at the end.

Laura waves her hand to dismiss her. "Hush up, Didi. You're just jeal—"

"Oh, all right," Didi says, waving her left hand around. "I'll pay half. If Priscilla and I split the cost, it won't be too much of a burden on anyone."

I know that no matter what I do, I get under Didi's skin. She obviously wants to make sure I feel some of the competition, or she wouldn't be flashing her multikarat rock every time she speaks.

25
Trudy

Mama reminds me to call the Cut 'n Curl to get my hair done by Priscilla, so I call to try to set an appointment. I don't recognize the voice of the girl who answers the phone . . . someone named Nicole.

"I'm sorry, but she's booked until next week, after the class reunion," Nicole says. "She'll be here for a few days next week. Can you see her on Monday?"

"No, I really need to see her tomorrow or Saturday." Before, I couldn't have cared less about having Priscilla do my hair, but now that I know she's booked, I want her real bad. "Can't you work me in on Saturday? Please?"

"Um . . . " She covers the mouthpiece for a few seconds. "What did you say your name was?"

"Trudy. Trudy Baynard."

"Okay, just a sec. I'll see if she can squeeze you in." Once again, she covers the mouthpiece. I don't know why she doesn't punch the button to put me on hold. I've been to the salon, and I've sat in the reception area long enough to know they have a fancy system. After less than a minute, she comes back, her voice all cheerful sounding and smiley. "Ms. Baynard, Priscilla says she can see you at two o'clock, as long as all you need is a cut and style."

Yes! At least someone in Piney Point thinks I still got it! "That's all I need." After I get off the phone, I feel as though I've scored something real big. I used to take Priscilla for granted back when she first started working for Dolly, when the place was called Dolly's Cut 'n Curl. Who would ever have thought she'd wind up being a big-shot hairdresser? Even Joel, my hairdresser in Atlanta, knows about Priscilla.

After the last reunion, I went in to see him, and he asked me who redid my hair. I told him, and he went from acting all haughty and full of himself to being impressed. "Priscilla, as in Priscilla Slater?"

I nod. "Yes, how do you know her last name?"

"Trudy, sweetheart, any hairdresser who keeps up with the latest in the industry knows the name Priscilla Slater. That woman is simply the latest and greatest."

I puff out my chest and smile. "We went to school together."

From that moment on, Joel has treated me like a superstar. All I have to do is answer questions about Priscilla and act like we were close friends back in the day. That's not exactly a lie either. I mean, we didn't hang out all that often or anything, and she wasn't, like, in my wedding or even one of the guests for that matter, but I did say *hey* to her when we passed in the school hallways. And she did my hair when I used to go to the Cut 'n Curl, before I moved away from Piney Point when I was still married.

I lean back on the bed in my old room that Mama has kept decorated exactly how I had it in high school. There's a picture of me accepting the Miss Piney Point crown, all my teeth sparkling white, tears making my eyes shiny, my hair fluffed out and perfect, as the mayor looks at me with pride. The words he said to me that night—"Represent Piney Point well, Trudy"—

still play through my head. I'm pretty sure I did a good job of representing Piney Point, even though I didn't win Miss Mississippi. In fact, I wasn't even one of the top five finalists.

When Mama comes to the door, she knocks, even though the door is open a few inches, and she's looking right at me. "Everything all right, Trudy?"

"Why wouldn't it be?" I don't move from my half-lying-down, propped-up-on my-elbows position.

"Did you ever get hold of Priscilla?"

"I called her salon and booked an appointment for Saturday."

"Oh." Mama pushes the door open a few more inches. "I'm goin' shopping in Hattiesburg. Wanna join me?"

"Sure." I rise from the bed and slip into my Cole Haans. "Where ya goin'?"

"I thought I'd stop off at the home decorating store and see if there's anything that Amy might like."

I wish I'd asked before I agreed to go. I'm sick and tired of everything being all about Amy. Ever since she announced her engagement, it's *Amy this, Amy that.*

"Why doesn't she register and make it easier on everyone?"

Mama shrugs. "I've tried to talk her into it, but she says it feels uncomfortable—like she's asking for presents."

"That's part of the fun of it," I say. "Maybe I can talk some sense into her while I'm here."

"Oh, I forgot to mention she's not gonna be back until next week. As soon as school let out, she went down to the coast with some of her schoolteacher friends. They're having a bachelorette weekend."

If it had been anyone but Amy, I would've imagined a bunch of wild women cutting loose in Biloxi. But since this is Amy we're talking about—sweet, never-miss-church-always-perfect Amy—I suspect all they'll do is lay out in the sun, chow down at the all-you-can-eat buffets, and walk on the beach. Oh, and they'll find some nice little church to attend on Sunday morning.

I don't ever openly complain about Amy, though. She's the one who stayed home to help Mama and Daddy after me and our oldest sister, Patty, got married. Not that they needed all that much help. It's just that Mama and Daddy always wanted to travel and go on cruises, but they didn't want to leave the house empty. Now that they got that out of their systems, I reckon Amy feels free to do her thing.

As we drive around Hattiesburg looking for places to spend money, Mama tells me about Tyler and his family. "They're not moneyed, but they're good people."

Being *good people* is important to Mama, but I've never understood exactly what she means by that. I used to assume it meant they were law-abiding folks who had high-paying jobs, but even some of those don't make the cut, according to Mama.

"Tyler is a minimalist," Mama says when I pick up a pretty throw pillow that's very pretty and lacy all over. "He doesn't like too many frills."

"Oh." What a shame, I think as I put the pillow back on the shelf. "How about a spice rack?"

"Hmm. I don't know. They've leased a small house that he's already moved into." She pulls out her cell phone and mouths that she's going to call Amy. I listen as she asks about the kitchen and bathrooms. After she gets off the phone, she shakes her head. "They don't have much countertop space, so no on the spice rack."

Two hours later we head home with nothing but a set of bath towels and kitchen linens. "That was a waste," I say.

"Not really. The bath towels are very nice, and I'm sure she'll appreciate the dish towel and pot holders you picked out."

I've always had to work hard to not show my annoyance with both Amy and Patty. Being the middle child put me in the position of never doing anything first or last, so I had to really stand out to be special . . . or even noticed for that matter.

As soon as we turn onto my parents' street, I see an unfamiliar car in the driveway. "Looks like you have company, Mama."

She leans forward and squints to get a better look. Then she points. "I believe you're the one who has company. Looky who's on the front porch."

What is Michael doing at Mama and Daddy's? I turn to Mama. "Did you set this up?"

"No, I promise I didn't. In fact, knowin' what I know about that two-timin', sorry, good-for-nothin' buzzard, I'd never invite him to our house."

That's my mama. At least I believe her now.

As soon as she pulls into the driveway beside Michael's car, I get out and stomp over to see what he wants. "Hey, what are you doin' here?" I don't want to waste time.

He looks up, and that's when I see how swollen his blood-shot eyes are. His skin looks sallow, like he's been pullin' several all-nighters in a row. "Trudy, I need your help."

"What happened?" I can't help it. When he looks at me with that sad face, the urge to take care of him takes over. However, I resist putting my arms around him.

"I'm in trouble, and I want you to help me get out of it."

"You're in trouble?" *Lord, forgive me for not bein' sad.*

He nods. "Yeah, that's what I said. See, Jenna—that's my girlfriend . . . or *was* my girlfriend—is tryin' to trap me . . . " The puppy-dog eyes get droopier. "She says she's pregnant, and now she wants me to marry her. I'm just not ready to do that again, Trudy. The first time nearly got me—" He stands up and comes toward me with his arms out.

"Whoa." I hold up my hands to stop him. "So after you dump me for some young bimbo, and then you dump her for another one and another one, you go and get yourself in trouble?" I can't believe I ever loved this sorry excuse for a man. "And you expect me to help you?"

"Yeah, I got it all figured out," he says, dropping the pitiful look. "Me and you can get back together . . . at least for the reunion and maybe a little while afterward. When Jenna sees there's no hope for me and her, she'll go away."

"Are you kidding me?"

He looks confused. "Why would you think that?"

"No way would I bow down to your level. Go find someone else to help you with your scheme, Michael."

"It won't work with anyone else. See, since me and you were once husband and wife—"

I jab my finger toward his car and take an aggressive step toward the man I once thought I loved but now can't even stand the sight of. "Get out of my yard, Michael. I don't ever wanna see your face around here again."

On the way to his car, he glances over his shoulder. "At least think about it, Trudy. It'll be a win-win situation. You can help me get off the hook, and I can be your date so you won't have to go to the reunion alone. I know how you hate goin' places by yourself."

"Go. Now."

I fold my arms and watch him back out of the driveway. Once he's gone, I brush my hands together. The way I feel now, I know I'm completely over him.

Mother is waiting on the other side of the door. "Trudy, honey, I'm so proud of you. You've finally become the woman I always hoped you'd be."

Feeling happy all over, I head to my room. It sure does feel mighty good to have told Michael to hit the road. This reunion should actually be fun now.

26
Priscilla

I wake up early on Friday morning to the sound of voices coming from somewhere in the house. That's odd. Now that Dad's moved out and Teresa is off today, the only person Mother has to talk to is me, unless she has company. The clock reads 6:30 a.m., so that's not likely.

Since I'm not sure who's out there, I slip into a pair of jeans and a T-shirt. I step into a pair of flip-flops and mosey on out to see who Mother is talking to. Even before I get to the living room, I recognize Dad's voice.

He sees me and opens his arms wide. "C'mere, Priscilla. Give your old dad a hug."

"Old? I hardly think of you as old." All the while I'm talking, I'm moving toward him. He pulls me in for a humongous bear hug. "What are you doing here?"

"Your mother called me last night. We've been talking."

"Since when?" Then it dawns on me that Dad's wearing the shorts he always puts on when he first gets out of bed in the morning. "Were you here all night?"

"Pretty much, yeah," he says. "Your mother is concerned about you."

"Tell her the whole story, George."

I look up at Mother who is standing in the doorway holding a couple of coffee mugs. "Good morning, Mother."

"Want some coffee, Priscilla? I would have gotten you some if I'd known you were up."

"I'll get it, but first, tell me what's going on. Are the two of you . . . ?" I glanced back and forth between them. "I mean, does this mean . . . " How awkward!

Dad watches Mother as she sets down the mugs and settles into her chair. "This has nothing to do with"—she glances at Dad, who nods—"*us*. I called your father over last night because I'm concerned about you."

"Why are you concerned about me?"

"I think you're losing touch with reality. All you think about is business, and although you've done quite well, considering . . . you know. This nonsense about buying the ice factory property and going on TVNS just seems rather strange, even for you."

"I still don't understand why you called Dad."

He leans forward, turns his focus to me, and steeples his fingers. "Priscilla, there are some things you need to know about your family history. My grandfather had some problems when he got older, and your mother thinks you might have inherited some of them."

"Problems? Like what?"

"He became rather . . . confused as he got older. He was always tinkering in the barn, trying to invent something that would change the world. Granny never minded because it kept him out of her hair, but one day he came in and said he'd found a way to stay alive forever, but they'd have to pack up and move to a cave in Tennessee." He pauses. "I understand he grew rather agitated when she told him he was talkin' like a crazy person."

I'd heard about my great-grandfather, the inventor, but this is the first I've heard about the cave thing. "What happened?"

"Of course, Granny wasn't about to pick up and leave the house she'd lived in ever since she'd been married, so she called her brothers to come help her out."

Dad obviously doesn't want to tell me all the details about what happened to his grandfather, or he would have. "So you think I'm starting to do crazy stuff?" I turn to Mother. "Are you saying I'm crazy?"

"No, sweetie, that's not what I'm saying, but I want to make sure you keep your feet solidly planted rather than get all caught up in believing you're something you're not . . . " She casts a look at Dad before turning back to me. " . . . or thinking you can do the impossible."

I'm dumbfounded. This has caught me so off-guard I don't have a defense.

Dad continues. "My uncle wound up in Whitfield after he tried to jump off the roof holding onto an umbrella and a bunch of helium balloons."

Now he's implying I'm certifiable. "Um, Mother, Dad, I'm not doing any of those crazy things. I've never wanted to move to a cave, and you're not likely to find me on the roof. I'm just trying to grow my business."

"But TVNS?" Mother shakes her head. "That's the strangest thing I've ever heard of. After you told me about it, I watched it to see what it's all about. I don't understand why you'd even want to be on that channel. Have you seen what those people do?"

"Yes, of course I have, Mother. Millions of people tune in to watch demonstrations of products and buy things." I turn to Dad. "Have you ever seen it?"

He glances at Mother and turns back to me. "Yes, your mother showed me the channel last night. I have to admit I was rather intrigued, but your mother reminded me that I've always liked strange and unusual things."

"But it's not so unusual. Do y'all realize there are other retail networks that do the same thing? They wouldn't be there if they weren't successful . . . making money."

"Is that all you care about?" Mother asks. "Making money? Don't you even care about how this will make the family look?"

Frustration wells inside me. They've turned my career dream into a crazy scheme simply to make money and taint the family reputation.

Mother continues. "You know we were very unhappy when you dropped out of school to pursue this path that doesn't utilize your intelligence, but we thought you were just rebelling and would eventually see the light." She glances at Dad who remains impassive. "After you kept opening new salons, we realized your pride got in the way, but at least you were able to make a living."

I let out a whispered grunt. "Y'all don't get it, do you?"

"We got that you needed to exert your independence." Mother holds out her hands. "But now you've crossed the line, and we can't allow you to continue on this path of self-destruction."

"Your mother feels that my moving out might have put you over the edge, so we've . . . " He looks at Mother. "Why don't you tell her?"

"We've decided that your father should move back home to give you the stability you obviously need right now."

"I—" The instant I open my mouth, I remember what I've been praying for and the fact that I asked the Lord to show me how to help. *This wasn't what I had in mind, Lord.*

"We're not saying we'll stay together forever, but for the time being . . . " Mother smiles at Dad, and he smiles back his encouragement. "This is the best thing we can do to help you."

This discussion has gone too far, so I stand up. "I'm going back to my room."

"Everything we do is because we love you," Mother calls out.

I close the door behind me and lean against it. *Very funny, Lord. Your sense of humor astounds me. I pray for a way to help bring Mother and Dad back together—to have them agree on some-thing. The only thing they see eye-to-eye on is that I'm crazy.* I chuckle. I totally didn't see this one coming.

It's too late to go back to bed, so I get ready for the day. A glance out the window lets me know the weather report was right, and it looks like we'll be having tonight's event at the VFW. I sure hope Pete follows through with the karaoke machine, or we'll have a bunch of people in a big room with nothing to do but drink.

When I get to work, Sheila looks stressed. "We've had two cancelations already, and with this weather, we expect more to come. Folks from your class want to reschedule tomorrow, but we don't have enough openings."

"I can work a little later tomorrow." I open my tote and pull out a solution that's guaranteed to stop frizz. "Here's a product that just came out of development. Maybe we can try it on those who don't cancel."

Sheila takes the bottle, turns it over, reads the back, and smiles. "Looks like this might be the answer to all our prayers today." She tries to give me back the bottle, but I shake my head and laugh.

"What's so funny?"

"You don't wanna know. Keep that bottle. I have several more." I start toward the back room to put my things away, and I can hear Sheila trotting along behind me.

"You seem different today, Priscilla. Did something hap-pen? Are you okay?"

I'm tempted to tell her nothing is different, but I really need to talk, and she's the person I trust most in the world . . . at least at the moment. "To be honest, I'm not sure. Some strange stuff is happenin' at the Slater house."

She looks up at the clock on the wall. "I have a little time if you'd like to talk now."

As I tell her what's happening with my parents, she nods and gives me an occasional smile. "So now my parents are back together, but only to gang up on me and protect me from myself . . . from accomplishing what I've wanted to do since I first saw TVNS."

"I have to admit, Priscilla, you're in the most unusual pickle I've ever seen. I'll have to think on this one."

"In the meantime, we better get out there, or the other hairdressers will come looking for us."

Chester stands at his station, watching us as we walk out of the back room. "What's the big secret? Y'all leavin' me out again?"

"No, of course not," Sheila says. "Did you know that Priscilla has a new product that's guaranteed to fight the frizz?"

"Honey, I don't think nothin' will work on a day like today. At least everyone has to deal with the same conditions." He finishes getting his station ready as I start working on mine.

Midway through the morning, Chester approaches my station. "Got anymore of that magic frizz serum? It seems to be workin'."

"I put some out on the table in the break room. Help yourself. Just remember that a little bit goes a long way."

He grins and gives me a thumbs-up. "I'll go easy on it. We don't want to overdo it again, do we?"

I laugh and shake my head as he walks toward the back. Last time I told him to use just a little bit of conditioner, he didn't realize just how little, and it took him a half dozen washings to get it out of his client's hair. After she left, he groaned. "That stuff was like shellac."

I'm pleased with how this new anti-frizz product is working out. Two of our clients have called in after they got home and said even the rain didn't ruin their blowout.

After my last morning appointment leaves, I sit down in the break room with my peanut butter sandwich. Sheila comes to the door, holding the phone out. "Mandy. She says it's urgent."

I push my sandwich back and take the phone. "Hey, Mandy, whatcha need?"

"TVNS called and said they need to see you as soon as possible."

"TVNS?" My heart pounds at the mere mention of the station call letters. "Are they seriously considering my product line?"

"They've narrowed it down to the final three items, and they can only choose one for next season."

"But . . . " I remember them saying they'll need more information before final approval. "When do they need to see me?"

"Tomorrow if possible, but I told them you'd be out of town all week, so they said the Thursday after the reunion at the very latest."

Okay, calm down, I tell myself. No way can I even consider going tomorrow. "Can you call them back and let them know I'll be there that Thursday?"

"I would, except they want to speak directly to you." She waits for me to get a pen and something to write on before giving me the call-back information. "Sounds like you've finally got a real shot at this."

"I sure hope so, Mandy. Thanks."

After we hang up, I sit back in my chair and stare at the woman's name and number. I'm supposed to stay with Mother through part of next week, and now I'll have to give her a good reason for leaving. I can only imagine what she and Dad will say when I tell them I need to cut my visit short to take an appointment with an executive at TVNS. *Lord, you may be laughing, but I still don't see the humor.*

27
Tim

I been trying all week to give Priscilla the space she needs, hoping she'll come to me and say she misses me somethin' awful and she realizes now that she can't live without me. But that's not happening. Instead, I'm running myself ragged trying to please another woman whose husband looks at me like I done lost my marbles. Yeah, I'm talking about Laura Moss, gestapo of her high school graduating class.

Here it is Friday already, the day before the big event, and I've only seen Priscilla a handful of times. And some of those times have been when I stopped off at the Cut 'n Curl and she was too busy to do more than wave. I'm beginning to wonder how smart it was to come to Piney Point. All it does is aggravate me to no end.

I used to try to impress her by showing her I was smart enough to learn big words, but I'm not blind. I can see her amusement when I say stuff wrong. It don't come natural to me like it does her. When I say stuff like *adversity* and *capacious*, chances are, I'm getting it wrong. I might have studied the meaning of them, but using them is a whole 'nother story.

Priscilla was born into a family that uses big words every day. My family used to laugh at folks like hers. Called them uppity snobs tryin' to put on airs. Of course I'd never tell Priscilla that 'cause I was taught to never be rude, no matter what. And when I talk to her, I think about what I'm saying before I let it leave my mouth. Most times I think I do just fine, but like I said, it don't feel natural. When I get tired and talk like I think, I see her little smile. At least she don't correct me like I suspect Laura does Pete. If I didn't know about his drinking back in high school, I would've thought Laura drove him to it.

I'm fixing to go on down to the VFW hall where Pete said he'd meet me after he gets off work, which should be . . . about fifteen minutes. I just hope he ain't had nothing to drink yet, or I'll be setting it up all by myself. Pete's not a bad guy when he's sober, but all it takes is a couple of drinks, and hoo-boy, he sure does fly off the handle at the drop of a hat. And then he falls asleep, no matter where he is—might even be behind the wheel of his truck.

At least this time we have a sheriff's deputy, thanks to Priscilla and that Didi girl footing the bill. Pete won't be able to pull one of his typical shenanigans. Not that getting drunk and wrapping your truck around a tree isn't serious, 'cause it is. But Pete seems to think it's normal, and he still hasn't learned his lesson.

I pull my company Buick into the parking lot of the VFW hall, and who do you think I see? Pete's standing beside his truck, swigging from a can. I groan until I realize it's a sody pop. Good for him.

It's been drizzling off and on all day. The weatherman can't seem to make up his mind when it's gonna stop, so it's a good thing we had an alternate plan. As soon as I park and get out, Pete ambles toward me.

"Hey there, Tim. I got the karaoke equipment in the truck. Wanna give me a hand with it?"

He loads me up with stuff, leaving a small shoebox filled with CDs for him to carry in. I don't say nothin' since he's a ticking bomb, and I'm not in the mood for a black eye, no matter how manly it makes me look.

"Just set that stuff over there." Pete points to a long foldout table by a small stage. "We'll get some of the guys to help later."

"It's just a karaoke machine. We can do it now since we're right here."

He turns the can upside down over his mouth, finishes it off, crumples it in one hand, and tips his head forward. "Then by all means, go right ahead. I'm not stoppin' ya."

As I set up the karaoke machine, which involves pulling it out of the box and attaching the extra speakers and microphone, he talks on his cell phone. "Where can I plug this in?"

Pete punches a button on his cell phone before slipping it into his pocket. "What do I look like? an electrician?" I just happen to know Pete ain't stupid, so this is his way of asserting himself.

I walk around the perimeter of the hall until I see an electrical outlet. Off to the side is a box filled with an assortment of extension cords. I rummage through the box 'til I find one that looks like it'll reach the karaoke machine.

The whole time I'm working, Pete stands around looking like he's itching to be somewhere else. That makes me want to crawl, just to get his goat. But I don't. I have more things on my list, and I've never been one to let things slide.

Once the karaoke machine is all set up, I test it to make sure it works. And boy, does it ever. I snort when Pete jumps near 'bout outta his drawers at the sound of my voice booming through the hall. "Why'd ya go and do that?"

I grin right back at him. "Just testin' the equipment. Sounds like it works just fine."

"Let's get outta here before the women come to decorate."

"Why?" I ask. "Afraid your wife might put you to work?"

His nostrils grow big, and I have the weirdest feeling in my belly that he's about to charge like a bull, but he don't. "Naw, it's not the work that bugs me. I just don't wanna have to deal with that girly streamer stuff my wife likes so much."

I laugh. A mental picture of Pete taping sparkly streamers to the ceiling is hilarious. "She did put up a lot of stuff like that at the last reunion, didn't she? But that was for the big party. I don't reckon she'll do that tonight, since this is supposed to be a bonfire."

"You obviously don't know my wife very well. You done?"

I take a long look around at the naked walls and cheap-tile floor. "Yeah, I reckon I am."

"Good." He struts to the door. "C'mon, let's go."

I'm happy to see Pete turn in the direction of his house. Maybe he won't stop off anywhere for a drink before the party. Even though Laura can be a bear to deal with, I feel sorry for her having to handle four rebellious kids and a husband who most likely will never grow up.

After checking off the next few items on my list, a sense of accomplishment comes over me. Years ago, right after I started working for my uncle, I called on Priscilla when she was still working on the floor as a hairdresser. That woman has always been able to do more in a day than most people do in a week, so I asked what her secret was. She told me she kept lists—a master list for the month, a weekly list, and a daily list with every single thing she needed to do that day. It took me a while to remember and get the hang of the list thing, but once I did, I discovered how much more I could do. And when I go to bed at night, I feel real good about myself for doing so much every-day and crossing through each thing. Used to, I'd stare up at the ceiling worrying about stuff and wondering where all the time went. Uncle Hugh noticed how much more I was selling, and he gave me a raise. Now I don't go nowhere without a list, and I keep doing better and better in business. That's what I call job security.

I get everything done and head on back to my hotel room. More hotels have opened since the last reunion, and I picked me out a real nice one with a workout room and a breakfast bar with all kinds of fancy muffins and pastries laid out every mornin'.

Priscilla hasn't called me yet, and I ponder what to do. We need to talk to make arrangements for tonight, so I go ahead and punch in her number, and she answers right away.

"Hey, Tim. I just pulled my phone out of my bag, and I was about to call you. Looks like we're not having the bonfire tonight. Good thing we had an alternate plan."

"I know. Did you talk to Pete or Laura?"

I hear her take a breath, almost like she's expecting something bad to happen. "No, why?"

"Me and . . . I mean, Pete and I set up the VFW hall for karaoke."

She laughs. "As long as I've known you, I don't think I remember ever hearing you sing."

"And you're still not likely to."

"Come on, Tim. It's karaoke. No one expects you to sound like a rock star."

"Oh, trust me when I tell you that's not what I'm worried about. Folks will think someone's been hurt if I start tryin' to sing. Mama always said I couldn't carry a tune in a bucket."

I love the sound of her laughter. "So what's the final count on the reunion?"

This is when I have to break the news. "Not as many as Laura expected. She kept sayin' there was gonna be at least sixty folks, but now it looks like we'll have closer to forty, includin' the guests. Maybe not even that many."

"That's too bad, but I suspect more people come to the ten-year and twenty-year reunions than the ones in the middle."

"That's what Laura said." I glance at my watch. "Hey, I better finish so I can shower and shave. Can you be ready in an hour or so?"

"Of course. Would you like me to drive?"

"Nah, I'll come get you, and I'll drive."

After we get off the phone, I hurry with my shower, shaving, and hair combing. Then I'm on my way over to pick up the girl I used to hope I'd be married to by now. Although I know that's not likely to ever happen, I still pretend she's mine. Uncle Hugh used to encourage me to keep after her, but lately even he's been telling me it's time to move on.

I knock on the door of her parents' house, and her daddy answers, surprising me since I thought he'd moved out. "Hey there, Mr. Slater. I came to get Priscilla."

He steps back and motions me inside before hollering. "Priscilla, your fella's here."

I barely blink my eyes when she appears from around the corner, looking more dazzling than a bunch of diamonds in the snow. Her hair frames her smooth, creamy face, and she looks slammin' hot in a pair of jeans with colorful stones running down the outsides of both legs. I look at her feet and see that she's rockin' a pair of sandals with her hot-pink polished toes peeking out. This is all stuff I wouldn't have noticed before I got into the beauty business. All I woulda seen is how good she looked. Now I know how all the parts work.

"Hi there, Tim. You're right on time." She reaches up and gives her daddy a big hug as I stand there with my chin hanging practically to the floor.

28
Priscilla

Tim has been awfully quiet since he picked me up from my parents' house. Maybe Dad said something to him about my . . . craziness.

"So I wonder if everyone who's going to the reunion tomorrow night will be there tonight," I say, trying to break the silence and make conversation. "Do you know if anyone called people to tell them we've moved indoors?"

Tim shrugs but keeps his eyes on the road. "Laura and Celeste were supposed to do that, but with them, ya never know."

"I'm sure they did if they said they would." I look around as we pass all the familiar places I grew up around. Even when I was a child, I knew I'd eventually leave Piney Point, but it would always be home.

"So did you have a good day?" he asks. "I hear you were busy at the salon."

"Yes, I worked until closing. People were still calling to get appointments for tomorrow." This conversation is starting to feel awkward and stilted, but I don't know what to do about it.

"I know how you hate to say no to people who need you," he says.

"You're one to talk. But I did say no to the last few. My final appointment is at four, and that's just for a cut and blow dry."

"Can't blame folks for wantin' to look good at the reunion. But with just a few people comin' to the reunion, I wouldn't think you'd be all that busy."

"It's not just reunion people. Other women have been holding out on getting their hair done when they heard I was going to be in town." I decide this is as good a time as any to tell him the news since word's already out. "I heard from TVNS. They want to see me next week. Looks like there's a chance I'll be sellin' my hair care package on air very soon."

Tim pulls up to a light and turns toward me, his face beaming with pure joy. This man is so good to me. I don't know anyone else who is as sincerely happy about my success as he is. "That's great news, Priscilla."

"Oh, that's not all. Remember that guy who sold me his salons in North Carolina?"

"Yeah, the one who wanted to concentrate all his time in New York City, right?"

I nod. "He's going through a divorce, and his wife insists on splitting everything right down the middle. She's put her half of the New York salons on the market, and I'm thinking about buying them."

This time his face registers surprise. "You've always wanted some places in New York." He sighs. "Must be nice to have all your dreams come true."

"It's very nice, but there's one thing I don't know how to handle."

"I can't imagine anything you can't handle, Priscilla. You're an amazing woman."

"Maybe so to you, but tell my parents that. They think I've gone off the deep end." I flinch. "I think they're even talking about having me committed to Whitfield."

He laughs. "Now I know you're kiddin'."

I'm not so sure. "At any rate, they've been talking again over"—I do air quotes with my fingers—"their concern about me."

"Whatever it takes to make them get on the same team," Tim says. "So tell me all about your plans to visit TVNS." He crinkles his forehead. "Hey, they're in New York, right? You can kill two birds while you're there."

"That's what I was thinking. I'm trying hard not to get my hopes up about either venture. The salons might not be as nice as I've imagined, and from what I understand, the TVNS spot isn't a done deal until they run a video test on me and the contract is signed." I pause. "Besides, I'm one of three they're looking at."

"You'll do it, Priscilla. I've never doubted for one second your ability to get everything on your bucket list." He pulls into the VFW hall parking lot but doesn't make a move to get out of the car, so I lean back and fold my arms.

"So do you have a bucket list?" I ask after a few seconds of silence.

"I did, but I'm not sure what I did with it." He winks and before I have a chance to say anything else, he opens the door and hops out of the car.

On our way into the hall, I hear a loud, screeching voice with tinny background music over the speaker. I nudge Tim and laugh. "Sounds like the party started without us."

Laura greets us at the door. "Y'all finally made it. What took you so long?"

"Um . . . " Tim looks at me.

"I had to work. We came as soon as we could. Do you need me to do anything?"

Laura gestures around the room. "I think Celeste and I about have everything done, but we sure could've used you to help hang the streamers."

I look up at the ceiling and see about a dozen strands of scrawny looking silver and blue streamers waving in the breeze coming from the air-conditioning vent. "You and Celeste did this all by yourselves?" It's about the tackiest looking decoration I've ever seen, but I'm not about to hint that it isn't beautiful, or there's no telling what Laura might do. I've seen her in her pre-snit mood, and I know she's heading there now.

"Pete wanted to put the keg by the stage, but I made him move it to the back." She points over to the corner where half a dozen guys are standing, plastic cups in hand. "I told him he better stop before he gets wasted this time. I'm not puttin' up with any of his . . . his you-know-what."

Tim laughs. "Maybe I can help you out here. Let's see if we can get Pete singin' karaoke. I figure as long as he's usin' his mouth to sing, he won't be chuggin' beer."

Laura shrugs. "I doubt it'll do much good, but you can give it a try."

"Why don't you go talk to Pete while I—"

Laura grabs me by the arm and tightens her grip. "Don't look now, but guess who just walked in."

With that kind of reaction, I have to turn around. It's Didi Holcomb—*Doctor* Didi Holcomb—and Maurice Haverty. I feel the blood drain from my face.

Celeste walks up and leans into me. "Don't they look happy? I never would have imagined Maurice Haverty and Didi Holcomb together, but they're such a cute couple, aren't they?"

"Yes, very cute," I say.

"Did you see that rock on her hand?" Celeste holds up her hand and wiggles her fingers in front of her face. "I wondered how Maurice came up with the money to buy that thing, what with his business strugglin' so lately. I asked Mama, and she said the ring is Didi's family heirloom."

"The ring was Didi's?" The instant I say that, I wish I'd kept my mouth shut. Last thing I need is anyone thinking I have even a smidge of interest in what happens between Didi and Maurice.

"Yep. And Maurice insisted on havin' it appraised. You know how Mama is friends with Ruby over at Olson's Jewelers. Ruby told Mama that ring is so valuable it can't be duplicated."

I bet Maurice is happy about that, but I don't say it. Instead, I nod and pretend to be only slightly interested. "I hope they're very happy together."

Celeste lifts one of her carefully manicured eyebrows. "Do you? I mean, doesn't it suck at least a little that he dumped you after that last reunion."

I pull back. "Dumped me?"

"Yeah." A look of pity flashes across Celeste's face. "Maurice told Didi, and she told some people at the doctor's office all about how you thought he was comin' on to you, when he was just tryin' to be friendly."

"Is that what he said?" My pride is coming on strong, and I want to stand on a table and holler out what really happened. But I take a deep breath and force myself to act calm.

"I don't think he was sayin' it in a mean way or nothin'. It's just that Didi don't want to upset you. You know how she is—always tryin' to keep the peace and make sure everyone is happy and feelin' good."

Yes, I do know how Didi is—as jealous as she is intelligent. But again, I keep my thoughts to myself.

"At any rate, Maurice is head-over-heels in love with the girl, and who can blame him?" Celeste sighs. "She's a successful doctor in Hattiesburg, and she bought a house in the nicest area."

"That's wonderful, Celeste." I've heard about all I can stand for now. "I need to run and make sure Tim is okay. He's helping out way more than he should, considering how this isn't even his class."

Jimmy walks up. "Either of you want a soda or beer?"

"I'll get my own, thanks." I leave Celeste and Jimmy.

Before I'm out of earshot, I hear Jimmy. "Did I say somethin' wrong?"

"Nah, she's just jealous about Maurice and Didi." In spite of better judgment, I slow down to hear the rest of what Celeste has to say. "That had to be rough, seein' the two of 'em walkin' in here tonight lookin' all dreamy-eyed at each other."

Now I want to run, but I don't, or people would really think I have an issue with Maurice and Didi. Deep down, I can't help wondering if he really feels something for her besides lust for her money. Didi has always wanted whatever I had, and now that she's with Maurice, she probably feels like the tables have turned. Everyone in the school knew about my crush on him and how hurt I was that he didn't have feelings for me. I'm sure Didi assumes she's scored a victory in this competition.

The sound of Pete's voice as he sings "Puff the Magic Dragon" echoes throughout the hall. He really gets into the performance, strutting around the small stage, leaning toward the crowd, and wiggling his eyebrows when he sings about frolicking in the autumn mist.

Tim walks up beside me. "He's actually not a terrible singer."

"I'm sure he's even better when he's not drinking." I smile and lean closer to Tim. "Thank you for helping out all week. I don't know what we would've done without you."

He smiles. "My pleasure. I have to admit I feel a lot closer to some of your classmates than I do my own."

Then it dawns on me that we haven't talked about any of his reunions. "Did you go to your class reunion?"

"Yes, and it was very boring compared to yours. Then again, I graduated with several hundred people, so the mood was a lot stiffer."

Stiff? Sort of like how Tim is acting now. "Are you okay, Tim?"

"Yes, I'm fine." He clears his throat. "Wanna do some karaoke? I can put you on the list."

I laugh. "No thanks. I'd rather enjoy everyone else."

"Good 'cause I'm up next." Pete is wrapping up his song, so Tim hands me his drink. "Mind holdin' this for me? I don't wanna spill it."

"I thought you weren't going to do karaoke."

Tim shrugs. "I reckon I changed my mind."

I take the drink as Tim runs up onto the stage and grabs the mic. Thunderous applause jolts me into the realization that Tim has become one of the most popular people here.

"Thank you," he says, curling his lip Elvis style. "Thank you very much." The music begins, and within a few seconds, Tim gyrates as he sings "Hound Dog."

A handful of people now line the stage, all of them clapping along. Every once in a while, someone hollers or screams, and this fuels Tim's kitschy performance. I have to admit it's one of the funniest, most entertaining things I've ever experienced in Piney Point. What he lacks in musical ability, he makes up for in performance.

"Your boyfriend seems very sweet," Didi says as she sidles up next to me.

I turn in her direction and see that she's alone. "Where's your . . . boyfriend?"

She grins. "Maurice and I decided that since we see so much of each other, it's a good idea to mix and mingle while we're here. After all, how often do we have so many of our old friends in one place?"

Old friends? I don't remember Didi having any *real* friends, but I don't tell her that. "So how do you like working in Hattiesburg?"

She shrugs. "I preferred working in New Orleans, but Maurice and I found it too difficult to sustain a long-distance relationship. His business has been in the family for so long I couldn't very well expect him to pick up and leave."

"No, of course not." I bite my lip to keep from saying any more.

"How are your little beauty shops coming along? I hear you've expanded a bit."

"Yes, in fact, all of them are doing quite well." I'm so tempted to tell her I'm about to be on TVNS, but I know it's my pride stepping in the way of common sense, so I cough and take a step back.

"You okay?" she asks. "There's something going around. I've seen quite a few patients lately with inflamed throats and ear infections."

I hold up my hands. "No, I'm fine. Every once in a while I get a tickle in my throat." *Like when I want to tell someone what a fool she's being but can't.*

She leans over, smiles, and waves her fingers. "Maurice can't keep his eyes off me. He is so cute."

"I—"

Before I have a chance to congratulate her, she places her hand on my arm. "Oh, Priscilla, I am so sorry. That was horribly insensitive of me to say that to you, after he . . . well, since he had to let you down. I promise I had nothing to do with that, even though we did get together a few weeks later."

"You did? A few weeks?"

She nods. "Yes, he went all the way down to New Orleans and walked right into my office, just to tell me he couldn't stop looking at me at the last reunion." With a tinkling laugh, she adds, "I guess I don't have to tell you no one has ever said that to me before."

"I'm happy for you, Didi." I smile back at her, trying hard to get past the look of condescension on her face. "I really am."

"Good." Her tone lets me know she doesn't believe me. "I better go check on Maurice. He has a tendency to wander when I'm not around."

She doesn't know the half of it. I'm just glad I found out what a snake he was before it was too late. If I thought it would do any good, I'd let Didi know what I'm pretty sure Maurice is up to, but she'd just think I was talking out of jealousy.

"Hey, Priscilla," I hear from behind.

I turn around and see Trudy Baynard looking at me, a shy smile on her face. That seems odd, considering how full of herself she once was.

"Hi, Trudy. Did you just get here?"

She nods, looks around, and finally turns back to face me. "Have you seen Hank?"

"Hank? As in Hank Starkey?"

"I don't know any other Hanks." Her vulnerability flickers in her eyes, but she quickly glances down at the floor.

29
Trudy

Now I remember why I've never been all that close to Priscilla Slater. When she looks at me, I feel like she's seeing right through me and can tell I'm faking my confidence most of the time. Even back in high school, she made me uncomfortable.

Priscilla squints like she's trying to remember something. "I'm not one hundred percent sure, but I think Hank sent an RSVP that he was coming."

"If you see him, let him know I'm here, okay?"

She nods as I back away. "Of course."

As soon as I can do it without seeming rude, I turn my back to her and shudder. I'm having the hardest time not reverting back to my old high school ways. And as I walk past a group of former wannabes, I have to psych myself into thinking they aren't looking at me, wondering why I let myself get so fat. But I refuse to do what I did last time and starve myself half to death. Last I remembered about the reunion was the room spinning before I passed out, and I woke up in the emergency room with some goofy doctor telling me to hold still so I wouldn't yank the IV out of my arm.

The room is humongous, and there aren't nearly as many people as there were at the ten-year-reunion bonfire. I reckon some of the people decided to just attend the final event, since the bonfire really wasn't worth repeating.

"Hey, Trudy." Celeste's scratchy voice hasn't changed much since high school. "Help yourself to something to drink." She points to a long table filled with homemade treats and coolers filled with cans of soda. "It's right over there."

"Thanks."

"In case you're wonderin', Michael isn't here yet, but he should be here shortly. At least he said he was comin'."

I've been divorced from Michael since long before the last reunion. You'd think people would have gotten the message by now that we're no longer accountable to each other.

Movement over by the entrance catches my eye. As soon as I see that it's Hank, my heart starts hammering ninety-to-nothin'. Who would've ever thought Hank Starkey could do that to me? Obviously, Marlene saw something in him five years ago that I missed. But, boy, do I see it now. There's something about him that oozes confidence . . . and success.

Back in the day, I thought I loved Michael because he was so good looking and because he'd make a good provider. Oh, and all the girls wanted him, which only made him all the more attractive to me. Now I realize what I really loved—or thought I loved—about Michael was his confidence and commanding presence. Seeing him on my parents' front porch looking all pitiful was a real eye-opener. Hank, on the other hand . . . I look up at him strutting across the hall like he owns the place, his head held high, and I know what attracts me to a man. And from the looks of things, I'm not the only one. A couple of girls whose names I can't remember have made their way to him, but if his body language is any indication, he's not interested in them. I want to approach him, but I've never liked to show hero worship, even if I felt it.

"Laura told me to bring you this."

I turn around and see Celeste carrying a little plate with a sandwich and some fruit. "I'm not hungry."

Celeste leans toward me and whispers, "Just take the plate, okay? I don't care what you do with it. Laura said she don't want you passin' out again."

"I—" Oh, what's the point in arguing? Celeste thrusts the plate toward me again, so I just take it to keep her from hounding me.

"Good girl." She glances up, widens her eyes, and shakes her head. "Boy howdy, he sure has changed."

"Who?" I turn around and see Hank heading toward us. "Oh, you mean Hank."

"Yeah. Everyone else is pretty much the same as they was back in high school, but he's got somethin' special now."

I look back up at Hank who makes instant eye contact with me. That's when I see the old Hank from the halls of Piney Point High School, looking at me with wonder and adoration, and I like it. Michael has never looked at me like that.

As he gets closer, he grins and lifts his hand in a self-conscious wave. "Hey, Trudy. You look nice tonight."

Celeste's eyebrows shoot up, but she doesn't say a word. She backs away and disappears, leaving Hank and me standing there, just the two of us.

"Thank you, Hank." I give him a once-over and can't help noticing that he's wearing designer clothes. "So do you."

"Are you with . . . I mean, do you have a . . . um, are you with someone?"

I shake my head. "No, I came here alone. Why?" I find myself feeling all self-conscious, and I don't know what to say.

Hank looks around for a moment before zooming in on me. The intensity of his gaze takes my breath away. "Would you like a drink to go with your food?" He nods toward the plate Celeste brought me.

"I would love a drink."

He hesitates for a moment before lightly placing his hand in the middle of my back. "C'mon, let's go see what they've got."

Heads turn as we walk across the room. I can just imagine what people are thinking. And for the first time I can ever remember, I don't much care.

The perfect gentleman, Hank waves his hand over all the soda cans before pointing to the punchbowl. "Just tell me what you want, and I'll get it for you."

I choose a can of ginger ale, which he opens and pours into a cup filled with ice before handing it to me. Michael would never have done that. If anything, I would have taken care of him.

"I think I'll have the same." Hank reaches over and grabs himself a can of ginger ale. "I'm glad you're doing well. I was worried about you when you passed out at the last reunion."

"I know." I take a sip of my drink and smile at him. "Marlene told me."

He pursed his lips. "What else did Marlene tell you?"

"She said y'all broke up."

Concern washes over his face as his gaze intensifies. "Did she tell you why?"

I slowly nod, set my drink and plate down on the table, and take his free hand in mine. "I want you to know that I think you are one of the sweetest, smartest people I've ever known."

"You do?"

"Yes." I glance down at the floor and sigh before looking back up at him as a shot of confidence bolts through me. "I've been such an idiot not to notice before, but I was too wrapped up in my own little fairy-tale world to know what was real. I like you, Hank Starkey. You're a real man."

"You have no idea how happy you have just made me." He tilts his head toward my plate. "Now I want you to eat that sandwich so you don't get sick. Let's go over there so we can talk."

Over the next hour, Hank and I catch up on what we've been doing for the past fifteen years, while the voices of various classmates fill the room with ear-splitting noise. Pete Moss seems to have more than his share of time at the microphone, and Priscilla's boyfriend keeps egging him on, shoving him up onto the stage. When I see Tim take the cup of beer out of Pete's hand to replace it with the microphone, I realize what's going on.

"I'm proud of you, Trudy," Hank says. "I know how disappointed you must have been when your marriage to Michael didn't work out, but you got right back up on your feet and made a life for yourself." His smile widens, and I can tell it's real because his eyes crinkle. "You've become quite the businesswoman, I hear."

He makes me feel really good about my decisions. "How about you?" I say. "How did you get in the position of ownin' so many companies? I thought you were just . . . I mean I thought you were a CPA."

With a self-conscious shrug, he replies, "I just happened to be in the right place at the right time, and I figured I might as well go for it."

"Sounds like everything you touch turns to gold."

Hank chuckles. "Not exactly. I've had a few failures. But I once heard that you only have to be right fifty-one percent of the time to be considered a success."

"That's more than most people." I look around and catch a few people staring at us, looking confused, but it doesn't bother me. "I'd venture to say most of these people are happy with everything as it is, and they're not willin' to take the chances you've taken."

"Maybe so, but we all find happiness in different things."

"Are you happy?" I ask.

He smiles, takes my hands, and squeezes them. "I am now."

30
Priscilla

I've rarely been surprised by anything people do, but I can't help staring at the sight of Trudy sitting in the corner, holding hands with Hank Starkey. That is the least likely pairing I ever could have imagined.

"Looks like love is in the air for some of us," Tim says as he joins me. "I'm glad she finally got past that whole Michael thing."

"Yeah, me too, but I'd hate to see Hank's heart get broken."

Tim snorts. "No one likes a broken heart, but look at it this way. He's enjoyin' the heck outta sittin' there with her right now. I expect this is the best thing that's ever happened to him."

"And I suspect you're right." The look on Hank's face is one of total adoration and pure bliss. "It looks like Trudy is enjoying the attention too."

"Maybe she's been out in the world long enough to realize things aren't exactly as they seemed back in high school."

I blink as I wonder if Tim's comment is about the topic at hand, or if he's subtly trying to tell me something. "Point taken."

He turns his attention back to the stage, where Pete looks like he's about to fall over from exhaustion. "I'm not sure how much longer I can keep him up there singin'. He's startin' to lose his voice."

As if on cue, Pete's husky voice cracks. He pulls the microphone away from his mouth and stares at it. "Sorry, folks, but I'm done for the night. I gotta keep up the health for the big event tomorrow."

Tim gives me an apologetic look. "I better go escort him off the stage and do what I can to keep him from the keg. I wish y'all didn't have to have alcohol at these things. Makes it hard for people like Pete." Our gazes lock for a few seconds before he takes off toward Pete.

I wish the same thing, but someone always orders the beer, and Laura's never able to stop it. Laura is running around the VFW hall, making herself appear busier than she needs to be. But that's just how Laura is: full of nervous energy and a temper that no one wants to ignite.

It doesn't take long for Pete to join his buddies by the keg. Tim stands there with the guys for a few minutes before joining me.

"I tried, but the pull of the beer is stronger than anything I can say." He gives me an apologetic look. "I'm sorry."

That's when I realize how much pressure Tim has felt to be responsible for so much at my reunions. "It's not your fault, Tim."

"I know, but I did promise Laura I'd do what I could to keep him from drinkin' all night."

"And you did exactly that. He sang for a good two hours. I'm sure that'll help."

"Let's hope so."

"At least he didn't drive here, so we shouldn't have to worry about an accident on the way home."

I look at the exit and see the deputy. Patrick Moody is a good ten years younger than us, but he has such a commanding presence, I don't think anyone would want to cross him. He's aware of Pete's problem.

Jimmy approaches. "Have you seen Celeste? I swear, that girl pulls the best disappearing acts. Every time we go somewhere I spend half the time lookin' for her."

Tim winks at me. "I know the feelin', Jimmy. Have you tried lookin' in the ladies' room? That's a very popular place for women."

"Priscilla, will you go see if she's in there?"

"Sure. Be right back."

I'm happy to do what Jimmy asks, since I've run out of things to talk about with Tim. We're both doing our best not to broach the topic of our relationship.

As soon as I push open the main door to the restroom, I hear whimpering in a stall. "Celeste?" I say.

"Go away, Priscilla. I don't wanna talk to you."

"What's wrong?"

"I told you to leave me alone."

"I'm not leaving until you tell me what's going on."

The stall door opens, and out walks Celeste, her eyes red and swollen, mascara dripping down her cheeks, creating a path of paleness where her blush once was. She makes a beeline for the sink.

"What happened?" I grab a paper towel, wet it, and hand it to her. "Did someone say something?"

She sniffles and hiccups. "It's terrible, Priscilla. Just terrible."

"I don't know what someone said, but remember that people are always saying things they don't really mean."

"Oh, he meant it, all right."

"Who, Jimmy?"

Celeste shakes her head as she turns around and leans back on the sink, creating a wet spot on the back of her silk dress that I can see in the mirror behind her. "No, Pete."

"Pete upset you?"

"Yeah, while he was up there singin', he kept on lookin' at me. It's no big secret that I took advantage of that time when he and Laura broke up, and for a while, I thought of ways to keep him next time it happened . . . "

"Don't tell me you still want to be with Pete," I say in total bewilderment.

"No, of course I don't, but he hurt my feelings."

Now I'm really confused. "He hurt your feelings because he kept looking at you while he was singing?"

"It's what he was singing when he was lookin' at me that hurts."

"Sorry, Celeste, but I wasn't listening to every song. Just tell me what he was singing that upset you so much."

" 'How to Get an Ugly Girl to Marry You.' " She sniffles again. "Before he started singin' that song, he dedicated it to me and Jimmy."

I want to smack Pete Moss. In the three minutes it took him to sing that song, he undid all the work we've done to ramp up her self-image.

"He's right, ya know. There's nothin' I can do to make the ugly girl inside me go away." She glances at herself in the mirror. "See? I can't even cry pretty."

"No one is pretty when she cries."

"Some people are. Look at Demi Moore in *Ghost*. She made fellas swoon when she cried."

"That's a movie, Celeste. She also had a team of makeup artists making sure her blush didn't run, and I'm sure she practiced getting the tears to fall just right."

She shakes her head, her chin still quivering as tears continue streaming down her cheeks. "Face it, Priscilla, I'm still an ugly duckling, no matter how much work we do on my face and hair."

"You are not—"

I'm interrupted by a loud banging sound on the restroom door. "Celeste, Priscilla, are y'all still in there? Is everything okay?"

I touch Celeste's arm, and to my surprise, she doesn't pull away. "Jimmy's really worried about you," I whisper. "Why don't you freshen up a bit, and I'll go talk to him."

She nods. As I walk out of the restroom, I'm not sure what Celeste will do, but I do know she's still in a bad state.

Jimmy pounces on me the second I walk out of the restroom. "Is she okay? Do I need to go in there and see about her myself?"

"No, she'll be fine. Just give her a few minutes to . . . " I turn to see what Jimmy's looking at behind me and see Celeste walking out, her face still streaked with tears and her clothes damp from leaning against the sink.

"She don't look fine to me." Jimmy doesn't waste a second before rushing to Celeste's side. Together they walk toward the exit and leave the party.

Now I need to let Laura know two of the committee members are unavailable. She'll be furious, particularly if she finds out her husband had something to do with it. I decide it's best just to say Celeste isn't feeling well and had to go home.

Laura's reaction is about what I expected. "Not feelin' well? You think I'm feelin' all that great? And she took Jimmy with her? It's not fair that I'm stuck with all the work—"

"Calm down, Laura." I place my hand on her shoulder. "You still have Tim and me. What do you need us to do?"

Laura glances around the room. "Maybe you can go talk to Didi. She said she's not sure she and Maurice should go to the party tomorrow night, since you're clearly not over him."

"What?" I can't help the fact that my voice has suddenly turned squeaky. "Where did she get that crazy idea?"

Laura shrugs. "Maybe something you said or did last time you talked to her?"

"I didn't say . . . " I try to think of exactly what was said, but I can't remember. "I'll go talk to her, but I'm not sure what kind of reassurance I need to give her that I'm completely over Maurice."

"Based on how you're actin' now, I'm not so sure I believe you, but all righty then, go ahead and tell her whatever you think will get her to change her mind. After all this money we spent on food, I don't want it to go to wa—"

"Okay, I'll go talk to her now." I have to get away from Laura before I say something I'll later regret. She has a way of angering me, even when she needs something from me.

Didi is standing over by the edge of the stage, looking like the wallflower she always has been, only this time with a huge rock on her hand to keep her company. As I approach, she looks me in the eye and smiles.

"Hey, Priscilla. Too bad it's raining out. A bonfire sure would've been nice."

"I know." I stop a couple feet from her, glance over my shoulder to make sure we don't have an audience, and turn back toward her. "What's this I hear about you not going to the big party tomorrow night?"

She shrugs. "I don't want to make things any more difficult for you than they already are."

"So tell me why you think it might be difficult for me." I fold my arms and glare at her.

"I don't want you to have to see Maurice and me together and so . . . happy. It must be excruciating."

"No." I can't help laughing. "In fact, it gives me a warm feeling all over to see you and him together. It lets me know that all's right with the world."

She gives me a dubious look. "Are you kidding me? I've seen how you look at us."

"I don't know how you interpret my look, but you're obviously missing something. Granted, it's no secret I did have a huge crush on Maurice back in high school, but I've matured quite a bit since then, and my feelings have changed. I have different goals now. You understand that, don't you, Didi? After all, I vaguely remember you once saying that getting married wasn't in your future because you wanted to have a larger impact on the world than settling down with a man would allow."

"Um . . . " She crinkles her forehead, obviously searching for something to say.

I shrug, satisfied that I've rendered her speechless. "So looks like things have flip-flopped. You're the one who wants to settle down, and I'm the one making a splash."

As soon as I say those words, a combination of satisfaction and regret washes over me. I've never been snarky, but I have to admit it sure feels good to put someone like Didi in her place.

She glances down at the floor before raising her gaze back to mine. I hold my breath waiting for a reaction, then she slowly nods. And I don't feel any better now than I did when I first approached her.

31

Laura

Last night wasn't bad, but I wouldn't call it a success either. Pete managed to get through the party at the VFW without passing out, which for him is a big accomplishment when there's a keg. But people started leaving early, so by the time we had to shut things down, all the folks we had left were me, Pete, Priscilla, and Tim. Hank and Trudy offered to stick around if we needed help cleaning up, but I could tell they wanted to get outta there. I would never have believed those two would get together if I hadn't seen it with my own two eyes.

Bubba was still up when we got home, but he wasn't happy about having to sit at home to look after his brother and sisters. "I'm not doin' it again," he says as he stomps into the kitchen for breakfast. "Bonnie Sue and Renee went at it again. They're both just stupid girls, and I wanna smack 'em."

"Don't you dare," I say. "If you have trouble you can't deal with, you know you're supposed to call your granny."

"I ain't callin' Granny. She's meaner'n either of them."

Good point. "Would you rather we get a babysitter for tonight?"

Bubba frowns. "Who for?"

"You and the rest of my babies who can't stand the thought of their mama and daddy having a couple of nights out every five years."

He makes a disgusting noise that sounds like a cross between a snort and cough. "It's not fair."

I put down the bowl I've been holding, walk right up to my oldest child, bend over, and shake my finger in his face. "Look here, Bubba, you and the rest of the young'uns got it easy around here. I cook all your meals, wash your clothes, tote you around everywhere you need to go. Life hasn't exactly been easy for me. Just this once try not to be so selfish and do somethin' for me."

He starts out looking me in the eye, but as I talk, his gaze slowly falls to the floor. When I'm done, I remain standing over him, glaring down at his face that's starting to sprout a few whiskers. My heart twists as I realize my boy is turning into a man right before my eyes. I wish Pete was willing to take a bigger part in teaching him to be the kinda man he should be, but I'm afraid Pete doesn't have a clue himself.

"Got that?" I ask after a long moment of silence.

Instead of answering me directly, Bubba looks back up. "Whatcha cookin' for breakfast?"

I smile. No argument means he's in agreement . . . at least, that's what I'm counting on. "Eggs and bacon and biscuits."

"Got any of that jelly with chunks in it?"

I point to the cupboard. "I just bought a brand-new jar of strawberry preserves. Why don't you get it out while I finish cookin'?"

Once I started cooking the bacon, the smell draws the rest of the family into the kitchen. Bonnie Sue is already dressed.

"Where do you think you're goin'?" I ask.

Bubba snickers. "What makes you think she's goin' anywhere?"

"She's wearin' her good jeans."

Bonnie Sue sips her orange juice. "Mama, can you take me and some of the cheerleaders to the mall?"

"I got a ton of stuff to do for the reunion party tonight. Can't you get one of the other girls' parents to take y'all?"

"Tracy's mama is on a retreat, Bailey's daddy has to work on Saturdays, and Darla's stepmother is gettin' her nails done."

"I'll take 'em," Bubba says.

"That's stupid." Bonnie Sue rolls her eyes. "You don't even have your license yet."

"But I can still drive, and I'll be real careful."

I glare at Pete. "Have you been teachin' Bubba to drive?"

He shrugs. "The boy's gotta learn sooner or later. I figured it wouldn't be a bad idea to give him some practice."

Sometimes my husband doesn't have the sense God gave a billy goat. "He's not supposed to be drivin' 'til he gets his learner's permit."

"That's just a technicality." Pete grins up at me. "I learnt to drive when I was eleven."

"That's 'cause you learned on your granddaddy's farm. It's different these days."

"Stop it, both of you. I hate when y'all fight."

I look over at Renee. "We're not fighting. We're just discussin'."

"Sounds like fightin' to me." She plays with the bacon on her plate.

"Want some more eggs?" I ask little Jack. He's been mighty quiet since he sat down at the table.

"Yeah."

I lift my eyebrows and give him one of my firm looks. "Yes, please?"

"Cut the boy some slack," Pete says, undermining my authority, which grates me to no end. "He's bein' good."

"I want my young'uns to have manners."

Renee stands up so quickly she knocks her chair over. "I'm sick of y'all fightin' about everything all the time. I can't take it anymore." Before I have a chance to say a word, she storms out of the kitchen and stomps up the stairs.

"Now look what you gone and done," Pete says. "Are you happy now?"

"What I did?" I jab my thumb to my chest. "All I want is to have happy, polite young'uns who respect others. If I left parentin' up to you, they'd act like a bunch of animals."

"This is stupid." Bonnie Sue gets up and leaves.

"Mama, can I please have some more eggs?" Jack asks. "I'm real hungry."

"Uh . . . oh, sure." On my way to the stove, I cut as dirty of a look as I can manage over to Pete who sits there looking like the cat who just finished eating the mouse.

"What time you and Daddy leavin' for your party?" Bubba asks as I scoop some eggs out of the skillet onto Jack's plate.

"We're startin' the party here, remember?" Pete says. "And we expect you young'uns to behave yourselves in front of all your mama's friends."

Jack laughs. "How about your friends, Daddy? Do we have to behave with them?"

"Nah, my friends are a buncha good-for-nothin . . . " His voice trails off as he sees the daggers I'm shooting. "Y'all best stay up in your rooms 'til we go to the school."

The boys look back and forth between Pete and me in silence. Pete finishes his breakfast, belches, and shoves back from the table. "I reckon I best get the backyard cleaned up a bit so folks don't think we're slobs. You boys wanna help?"

Both Bubba and Jack hop up to help Pete. If I had asked, they would've grumbled. I don't get how Pete can be the way he is and still get such an instant response when he asks for something. It isn't fair.

I'm nearly done cleaning the kitchen when the phone rings. It's Celeste.

"I just wanted to let you know I'll be a little late to the reunion tonight."

"But you're on the committee. You have to be here early to help set up for the preparty."

"I can't." I hear someone talking in the background before she adds. "Neither can Jimmy."

"I'm sorry, Celeste, but we really need both you and Jimmy. You can't bail out on us now."

Before I can say another word, Celeste hangs up on me. I try to call her back, but she doesn't answer.

A glance at the clock lets me know I barely have time to do all the work that's gotta get done before folks start showing up for the preparty. I walk over to the backdoor, open it, and holler, "Pete, c'mere. I need to talk to you a minute."

"What?" Pete looks up from the bush he's trimming. "I'm busy."

"I know, but I need to talk to you."

"Then you come out here and say whatever you gotta say. I wanna get this done, and if I keep hoppin' every time you say hop, it'll take me all day."

I suck in a breath, count to ten, and puff out my cheeks as I blow it out. Pete can really get on my last nerve.

When I walk up beside him, he turns off the hedge trimmer. "Whatcha want?"

"Celeste just called and said she and Jimmy are gonna be late for the party."

Pete grimaces. "Who's gonna drink with me?"

"Maybe this is a good time to quit."

He tilts his head back and lets out a belly laugh. "Good one, Laura. So why are they gonna be late?"

"She wouldn't say. Pete, I have a bad feelin' about this. Something's goin' on with them."

"Probably just a little spat. Couples have 'em all the time."

I think about that and make a decision. "I'm gonna go over to Celeste's apartment and see what's goin' on."

"You can't," he says as he lifts the hedge trimmer into position. "You have to stay here and get the house ready for the preparty."

"I'm comin' back soon." I close the door to stop the argument that is quickly going nowhere, grab my purse off the hook by the door, and run out to my car so I can leave before Pete comes inside.

When I pull into the parking lot at Celeste's apartment, I see that her car is in its usual spot. Good. She's home. I need to get to the heart of what's going on with her. After she got all weird last night, I've been worried, but I don't know why 'cause she's not the nicest person in Piney Point. I reckon it's sort of like that worn-out shoe thing. You know it's not good for your feet, but you've had it so long you don't wanna get rid of it.

I lift my hand and knock on the door. No answer, so I knock again, only this time a little louder. I wind up banging hard on the door and yelling, "Celeste, I know you're in there, so you better open up."

The door to the apartment next to Celeste's opens, and a man sticks his head out. "She ain't home."

"Where is she?"

"How would I know? She left with that feller she's been seein' real early this mornin', and I ain't seen 'em since."

"Thanks." I go back to my car, take another look around the parking lot, and head back home. As annoyed as I get with Celeste, it's not like her to abandon her responsibilities on the class reunion committee. Until now, I hadn't realized how much I've come to depend on her.

32
Priscilla

When I arrive at Laura and Pete's house late, I discover that none of the guests have arrived yet, which is a good thing since they're not ready. As I help them finish setting up, I can't help noticing the tension between them. "Are you stressed about this party?" I ask.

She levels me with one of her looks that has always made me cringe. "What do you think?"

"What can I do to make it better?"

She lets out a wicked-sounding laugh. "Are you kiddin' me? Make this thing better? The only way that'll happen is if no one shows up."

I put down the folding chair and turn her to face me. "Why did you do this to yourself, Laura? You didn't need to have the preparty here. In fact, what's the point of even having a pre-party? From what I can tell, it's just an excuse for people to get drunk before they attend the reunion."

Laura points to Pete. "It was all his idea, and I figured it would be better here than at some other place where I couldn't control things."

It's always been about control with Laura. "Since everything is already in motion, let me take over so you don't have so much on your shoulders. Where's Celeste? Shouldn't she be here to help?" I pick up a folding chair and start to open it.

She shakes her head. "You're not gonna believe this."

"What?"

"She and Jimmy took off and won't be back until after the party starts."

I let the chair slide to the floor. "What? She's supposed to be here helping out." I flash back to the night before. "I hope she's okay."

"Oh, I'm sure she's just fine. They just found somethin' better to do, that's all." Sarcasm drips from her words.

"But why today?" I think back to last night and how distraught Celeste was. "Never mind. I'm sure she has her reasons."

"What would be a good reason to leave us with all this work she's supposed to be helpin' out with?"

As we make a row of folding chairs, I explain how upset Celeste was. Since I'm not sure what Laura will do if she finds out her husband was responsible for what happened, I leave that part out.

"So let me get this straight." Laura stands up and looks at me with confusion. "Celeste felt ugly, and she's using that as an excuse to bail out on us?"

I nod. "Yup. That about sums it up. She'll probably show up at the party in the school cafeteria looking better than ever. I think she feels she has to prove something."

"It's about the stupidest thing I ever heard, but I have to admit it sorta makes sense, with it bein' Celeste and all."

I decide to check on Celeste after I leave here. "Do you have any idea where she might be?"

Laura shakes her head. "I went to her apartment to drag her over here, but her neighbor said she left with Jimmy early this mornin'."

One thing I can count on at my class reunions is to expect the unexpected. When Tim shows up, Laura and I tell him about Celeste and Jimmy, and he doesn't act surprised.

"Jimmy was really worried about her last night. I'm sure he's doin' what any man would do for the woman he loves." He moves the sofa to the spot where Laura wants it. "Any other heavy liftin' you want me to do?"

Laura points to the dining room table. "We need to put the leaves in the table. They're in the hall closet."

Tim gets right to work pulling out the table leaves and putting them into place. Every now and then, like now, I feel a tiny spark of attraction for him, but I respect him too much to act on it. Laura occasionally gives me a look, and I have to turn away.

Pete comes walking in from the backyard, tracking mud on the carpet. Laura opens her mouth to say something, but she winds up clamping her lips together. Pete leans over to kiss Laura on the cheek, but she dips low and scoots away from him.

Laura rests for a moment with her hand on her hip as she looks around the room. "We're missin' somethin' here."

"Everything looks fine to me." Tim brushes his hands together. "I reckon I need to get back to the hotel and get ready for the party. I'll get here a little bit early in case you have some last-minute stuff."

As soon as I can leave in good conscience, I take off to get ready. I'm almost to my parents' house when my phone rings. It's Mandy calling from the office phone.

"Sorry to bother you, but the executives at TVNS want you to call them. It's urgent."

"It's Saturday, Mandy. What are you doing at the office?"

"We've been swamped with some of the direct mailing, and I needed to come in and catch up."

"But I thought . . . Can it wait until Monday?"

"No, they're having a meetin' right now, and they said if you wanna be in their spring lineup, you need to call them today."

I'm home now, so I park the car and jot down the number for TVNS and thank Mandy for being so diligent. She has me repeat the information to make sure I have it right.

"Oh, and don't tell your mama I called."

"Why?"

There's a brief silence on the phone. "I just think it would be best if you didn't."

"Okay." I close my eyes and say a prayer for my nerves to be steady enough to hold a somewhat intelligent conversation.

Robert Waddell, the head of product development answers and informs me that we're on speakerphone with the heads of all the departments at TVNS. They take turns asking me one question after another, until I finally manage to answer everything under the sun about my "big hair system."

"That'll be it for now," Robert says. "We'll see you next week."

"Does that mean you still want me to fly up there?"

I hear mumbling on the other end of the line. "Of course. We'll need to see how you are on camera."

After hanging up, I rub my sweaty palms on the sides of my jeans. If I'd known when I started trying to get on TVNS what I know now, I'm not so sure I would've gone through with the plan. I remind myself that I'm almost there—merely days away from achieving my ultimate career dream.

Mother is waiting for me in the living room. "Where have you been?" Before I have a chance to answer, she continues. "Don't you have to leave for the reunion soon?"

"I'll be fine." Mother seems to forget that I've been on my own for a while now, and I don't need her hovering or nagging me about being on time.

Mother follows me back to my room. "What were you doing out in the driveway?"

"Mandy called, and I had to write some stuff down." Oops. I forgot Mandy said not to tell Mother she called.

"I told her not to call you because you're very busy with your little reunion parties."

"Did you actually come out and tell her that?"

"Yes, sweetie, I did. I know you think you have to get on that silly TV network, but how can you take anything like that seriously?"

"Wait a minute. You've decided that you know more than I do what I should have?"

"Don't get all testy on me, Priscilla. I'm your mother, and I think I know what's best—"

"No. You don't know anything about me. All you know is what you want me to have, and that's why I don't like talking to you about anything." I walk into my room and have to hold myself back from slamming the door. Mother has a way of reducing me to feeling like a rebellious teenager.

She knocks on the door. "Priscilla, please try to listen to reason." I hear her take a deep breath. "Maybe you can tell me your plans so I can understand better."

The teenage girl deep inside me wants to tell her to go away, but my grown-up self can't. I open the door and stare down at my mother who seems to have shrunk in the past few minutes. "Your reason is obviously different from my reason," I say softly. "I'll discuss my plans with you, but not if you continue to insult me or try to belittle what I consider important."

"But Priscilla, you have to—"

"No, I don't have to do anything. I've never asked you for money or anything other than acceptance. I even paid you back the money from the college fund that I used to get through beauty school. What is it you don't understand about my personal goals?"

Mother's face contorts in pain. "How many times do I have to tell you that your father and I had such big dreams for our only child. We thought you'd get a college degree, maybe meet someone nice in school, and settle down to have a family." She holds her hands out to her sides. "It doesn't look to me like you're even considering settling down. I may never be a grandmother." She sniffles. "And you're our only hope."

I try to offer a reassuring smile as I place my hand on her shoulder. "You never know what might happen in the future. I haven't met my Mr. Right yet, but it could happen any day at any time."

"But what about Tim? He seems awful nice, and you have to admit, he's willing to put up with a lot."

"I'm not going to marry a man just because he's willing to put up with me."

"I would love some grandchildren, and you're getting to the age—"

I hold up my hand to stop her. "If this is all about having you some grandkids, you could have increased your odds by having more than one child. I don't like all the pressure being on me."

"You think I'm pressuring you?"

I nod. "Yes, Mother, I've always felt the pressure to be everything to you and Dad. I had to make good grades and keep up a certain image. When I made a career decision y'all didn't expect, I let you down. And now you're putting pressure on me to give you grandchildren."

"We love you, and we've done the best we can."

"I know, and I appreciate that. You've given me *your* best. Now why don't you let me show you *my* best?"

She holds my gaze for several seconds before backing away. "I better let you get ready for your party tonight. After all, that's why you're here, isn't it?"

Once she's gone, I ponder her last comment. Is the reunion the real reason I'm here? I don't have to go to a party to see the people I grew up with. What is it about the actual event that has people scrambling around for a few hours of pretending to be something they're not? Even I put on a tiny bit of an act, making people think that nothing bothers me, that I'm in control of my life and can do anything I set my mind to. No one has any idea how hard I've worked or how many failures I've had. In fact, I've been trying to get products on TVNS since the last reunion five years ago, and until now, I haven't even gotten to second base.

As I ponder some more, I shower and put on the dress I'd bought for the occasion. As always, I'm ready early. Tim isn't due for another fifteen minutes. There's nothing else to do in my room, but if I go out to the living room, I risk facing more guilt-laced comments from Mother.

33

Celeste

I feel like pinching myself. Jimmy is driving us back to Piney Point so we can go to the fifteen-year reunion . . . as a married couple. Some folks would say that's an odd way to spend our wedding night, but I don't wanna miss everything I been working on for the past six months.

Oh yeah, that's right. Jimmy and I got married this morning. We tried to find someone in Mississippi to marry us, but there's that little issue of not having a blood test, since we decided to do this late last night. Alabama has basically no requirements—no blood test, no waiting period, no nothing. Just find someone who's allowed to marry folks, and you're good to go.

"You okay?" Jimmy asks as he turns off the interstate toward Piney Point.

I sigh and smile at my new husband. "I'm doin' just fine. Are you happy you married me?"

The corner of his bottom lip twitches letting me know he's still having a case of the nerves, but he nods. "Very happy. I never seen myself as a married man, so I'll have some adjustin' to do." He cuts a glance over at me. "It don't quite seem real yet."

I giggle. "I know, but it will when we move all your stuff into my apartment."

"What's wrong with my apartment?"

"C'mon, Jimmy, you know exactly what's wrong with it." I shake my head. "It's a dump. You don't expect me to live in a dump, do you?"

"I like it. Why you callin' my place a dump?"

I'm not ready to have my first marital fight, so I decide to change the subject. "Everyone will be surprised we got married."

"Probably. Where'd you put our marriage license?"

"In there." I point to the glove compartment.

"I hope you didn't bend it. We gotta get it framed, and it won't look nice if it's bent."

"Framed?" I open the glove compartment and see that it's not only bent but also ripped where it got caught in the latch. Uh-oh. I glance back at Jimmy and see that he notices. "Sorry."

"It's all right. I just hope that's not a bad omen."

I wave off that comment. "I don't believe in omens, and neither should you. The Lord doesn't care if our marriage license is torn. All he cares about is puttin' Him in our marriage."

"How's He gonna feel about us not gettin' hitched in the church?"

"God's everywhere, so I don't think it matters."

Jimmy grows quiet as he continues to drive and, I hope, think about what I just said. I allow myself to ponder how this whole wedding thing happened. Okay, so maybe it wasn't a real wedding—more like a civil ceremony with me, Jimmy, the justice of the peace, and the JP's next-door neighbor to sign the witness line. After I came out of the bathroom at the VFW, Jimmy felt so bad about me getting all upset over Pete's song he was willing to do anything to make me happy. That conversation will forever be burned into my mind.

"That's just plain mean," Jimmy said. "I wouldn't marry no ugly girl."

"Are you sayin' there's no hope for us gettin' married?" I asked.

"I ain't sayin' that. I would never call you ugly, Celeste."

"So what are you sayin'?"

I'll never forget as long as I live how Jimmy got down on one knee—which was a might difficult in the VFW gravel parking lot—and proposed. As soon as I told him I'd marry him, I asked when, and he said as soon as possible before he chickened out. Knowing Jimmy the way I do, it didn't take much convincing to get the show on the road. I was a tad worried he'd back out and not pick me up at sunrise like we'd planned, but he was at my door before that.

"You're early," I said.

"I didn't get no sleep. You ready to go get married?"

And the rest is history. I hold my hand out and look at the simple gold band we picked up at the discount store. Jimmy said he wasn't ready to wear a ring, and I didn't push. I figure I can do the wifely thing and trick him into wearing one later.

"Where should I go first?" He's at the point where he has to turn left or right, all depending on whose place we go to first.

"Since you don't have as much to do, why don't we go to yours first?"

He scrunches his forehead. "Nah, I reckon we can go to yours first. You can take your shower and bring all your girly stuff to my place to get ready while I shower and shave."

This man obviously needs quite a bit of training, but I have the rest of my life to do it. "Okay, that's fine . . . honey." It feels strange to call him this term of endearment, but that's what husbands and wives do.

"What'd you call me?"

"Honey?" I give him a look as a wave of shyness washes over me.

"Don't call me that, Celeste."

"What's wrong with callin' you honey? We're married now. Husband and wife. That's how we show we . . . um, we . . . " I want to say *love each other*, but the words won't come out.

"You best think of somethin' else, Celeste, 'cause I don't like bein' called *honey*." He grows silent before adding, "And I don't wanna hear no *sweetie pie* or *sugarplum* neither."

I can tell I got my work cut out for me—way more than I ever would've imagined. "Whatever you say, sugar britches." I let out a nervous giggle.

The creases in his forehead grow deeper. "Celeste, I'm warnin' you."

Jimmy is obviously not in the mood for fun, so I say, "Okay, whatever," fold my arms, and stare straight ahead. I'm sure the biggest problem between us right now is a huge case of the nerves.

I shower as quickly as possible, and because I never go out anymore without at least some makeup on, I do the bare minimum before stepping out of the bathroom. Jimmy is pacing in my living room.

His face is still crinkly when he looks at me. "Does it always take you that long to take a shower?"

"I'm a woman, Jimmy."

"I know that." He still looks pained. "C'mon, we best be gettin' outta here so I can get ready . . . unless you don't wanna go to the reunion. We don't have to, ya know."

"Oh yes we do. We're on the committee."

Jimmy looks at me but don't say nothin'. I can see that something's buggin' him. And then it dawns on me.

"You're not ashamed you married me, are you?"

His eyes widen. "Now why would I a-married you if I was ashamed? That's ridiculous."

I start to feel okay, but he still hasn't answered my question. "Just answer me."

"No, Celeste, of course I'm not ashamed." He comes toward me and puts his arms around me, the first sign of affection he's shown since we tied the knot. Although his movements are stiff and awkward, I appreciate how he wants to put me at ease. "I was gonna ask you to marry me later, but since you was in such a bad way I figured it wouldn't be a bad idea to go ahead and do it."

"You were . . . I mean you really did plan to propose later?" Relief floods me, and that's when I begin to feel a tad more confident.

We didn't start out with that heart-thumping, crazy-in-love feeling you get when you're infatuated with someone. We moved a whole lot slower, and it just happened. Don't get me wrong. I do sometimes feel that flutter when he's around—like now—but it goes a whole lot deeper than that. I've gotten to know Jimmy, and I know he's not one to take off when things don't go his way. He might be a touch stubborn and crotchety sometimes, but I can live with that.

"Let's go." He tugs me toward the door, but I stop. "What?"

"I have to get my stuff. You don't expect me to go to the reunion lookin' like this, do you?"

"What's wrong with the way you look?" His lopsided grin makes me a little dizzy. "I like it."

An hour and a half later, we're on our way to Laura and Pete's house. "I bet everyone will be surprised," I tell him.

"Nah, I don't think so. I done told Pete I was thinkin' about askin' you to marry me."

"You did?"

He nods. "Pete said he thought it was a good idea. He's been worried that I'm not eatin' right, and he said if you could cook near as good as Laura, I'll be healthy in no time."

I know how Laura cooks, and I would never call it good or healthy. But I don't say that since there's no point. Instead, I nod. "I do like to prepare healthy meals."

"Not too healthy. I don't wanna shock my body. Might make me sick."

We pull up in front of the Mosses' house. Before Jimmy has a chance to get out, I take his hand. "Let me say a prayer before we go in."

Jimmy groans, but he don't argue. I keep it short so he don't get too antsy.

34
Priscilla

It's almost time to start cleaning up when Celeste and Jimmy arrive. Laura and I approach them at the same time, coming at them from two different directions.

"Where you two been?" Laura demands.

They exchange a goofy look, and I step back. Something is different between those two.

"Alabama," Celeste says.

"What in the world were you doin' in Alabama when you were supposed to be here helpin' us set up?"

Celeste looks at Jimmy, who now has beads of sweat forming on his forehead. He rubs the back of his neck and looks down. "Gettin' married."

Laura pulls back, her eyes looking like they're ready to pop right out of her head. "What?"

Celeste holds up her left hand and points to her ring finger. "Me and Jimmy got married today."

The low murmur in the room instantly stops. Laura's chin falls slack.

I reach for Celeste to give her a hug. She stiffens, but I pull her close anyway and whisper, "Congratulations," before letting go.

Pete appears, hands Jimmy a cup of beer, and slaps him on the back. "Couldn't wait, huh?" He laughs and lifts his own cup. "Here's to the happy couple."

Jimmy starts to take a swig, but Celeste gives him a look, and he sets down his beer. "I . . . I'm drivin', so I better not drink."

"Nonsense." Pete picks up Jimmy's beer and hands it to him. "You got you a wife now. She can drive."

As Celeste and Jimmy continue giving each other looks, I glance over at Laura who has retreated from the group and sits on the arm of the sofa, still looking stunned. I join her.

"You okay?" I ask.

Laura nods. "I just can't believe they did that. I mean, I figured they'd probably eventually get married, but I thought I might get to be matron of honor, since Celeste and I . . . well, we've sort of become best friends." She sniffles and looks me in the eye. "I never had a best friend before . . . well, not countin' Pete."

"She can still be your best friend."

With tears in her eyes, Laura flicks an invisible piece of lent from her clothes. "But I won't be in her weddin'." She swallows hard. "I never been in someone else's weddin' before."

Celeste separates herself from the group still standing around her and Jimmy, and joins us. "Laura, I could hear everything you was sayin'. I had no idea bein' in my weddin' was so important to you." Her chin quivers, and tears spring to her eyes. "I didn't even know Jimmy was already plannin' on askin' me to marry him until today, when he told me after we done tied the knot."

"Well, I knew," Laura says.

As I watch these two awkwardly show their affection for each other, an idea springs to mind. "Hey, why don't y'all still have a wedding?"

They both look up at me, and Celeste nods. "Ya know, that's a good idea. We can have a little weddin' at the church and have a reception and serve cake and punch and everything." She cuts her gaze over to Laura. "And you can put on your prettiest dress and be my matron of honor. I'll even get my cousin to take pictures."

A grin plays on Laura's lips. "When do you wanna do this?"

Celeste taps her finger on her chin. "We'll have to do some plannin', but since we're already married, it shouldn't be too hard."

As the two of them chatter about Celeste's upcoming wedding, I back away from them. Tim joins me by the kitchen.

"Can you believe it?" he asks.

"I wouldn't have guessed it, but now that it's happened, I can see it."

Tim grins. "This actually seems more romantic than a traditional weddin'."

"Deep down, you're pretty romantic, aren't you?"

He nods. "Yeah, I reckon I am."

"You're an unusual man, Tim."

"Not as unusual as you might think. Most men appreciate a good romance, but they don't like to admit it."

More than ever, I wish there was a stronger chemistry between Tim and me. He'll make someone a fabulous boyfriend and husband someday. Then it dawns on me. As long as I have such an active part in his life, he's not as likely to move on.

"We need to talk soon," I say.

"Me and you?" He lifts his eyebrows. "We talk all the time."

"No, I mean *really* talk. About us. About what we want in life."

"So what are you sayin', Priscilla? Are Jimmy and Celeste givin' you some ideas?"

Uh-oh. I think Tim's reading me wrong. "Not ideas about getting married, but what they did is bringing some things to light."

The sound of scuffling above us captures all our attention. "Mama! Tell Jack to stop hittin' me!"

Laura's nostrils flare as she storms away from Celeste, past the other guests, and stomps up the stairs, growling and mumbling what she wishes she could do to her children but won't because she'd be arrested. We all look around at one another in awkward silence, until Laura returns. "I told them young'uns they better behave, or I'm not givin' 'em a dime."

"You're givin' 'em money?" Celeste asks.

Pete snickers. "Yeah, she told 'em we could either hire a babysitter to watch 'em tonight, or we can pay them to behave while we party." He leans toward Tim and whispers, "Don't tell anyone, but I got the old lady across the street watchin' the house and makin' sure no one comes and goes while we're not here. I don't trust my young'uns as far as I can throw 'em."

I glance at Tim, and he raises his eyebrows. "Oh." He takes a sip of his soft drink. "I think we need to help clean up and get goin' to the school. Me and Pete got the streamers hung, but I'm worried the tape didn't hold. We might need to reinforce the decorations."

I know this is Tim's way of getting out of an uncomfortable discussion, so I nod. We need to continue our talk later, in private. "Then let's do it."

As Celeste and Laura sit on the sofa planning the wedding, Pete, Jimmy, Tim, and I pick up some of the trash. It doesn't take long because most of the guests have left. I'm glad Laura's not acting as frantic as she has been.

Tim and I make our exit without being noticed, since everyone is now clustered on the sofa, loveseat, and chair in Laura and Pete's living room. All the way to the school, Tim talks about what he and Pete did to the cafeteria. I know he's focusing on that to keep from talking about weddings and marriage.

We walk into the dark cafeteria that still smells like school lunches, even though school's been out for more than a week. I find comfort in the fact that certain things remain constant.

Tim feels around for the light switches and flips them. "Looks good." He points to one streamer that has fallen. "I'll stick that back up, and we're good to go."

The cafeteria is not nearly as heavily decorated as the gym was five years ago, but I know that's because Laura handed the task over to her husband. I have to admit I'm surprised she did that. The decorations at the last class reunion were over the top, and they took forever to remove.

"The band should be here soon," Tim says. "Pete says they're able to play all styles of music."

I laugh. "Zeke Jacoby is a character." All the members of Zeke and the Geeks were in the Piney Point High School marching band, and if there had been a prize for worst music, they would have won, hands down. But Zeke, who was a year ahead of me in school, has always been a sweetheart, someone who went through middle and high school in a state of cluelessness that endeared him to everyone, regardless of social status. He never realized he wasn't handsome, so others managed to overlook it too. He wound up marrying one of the Olson girls and now manages the IT department of the family business.

The sound of a truck pulling up out front gets our attention. Tim walks over to the door before turning to let me know Sonya the caterer has arrived. I'm surprised Laura was willing to hire a caterer, but as things change, I see that she's coming to realize quite a bit. It's part of the growing process that I've seen in myself as I develop my business.

"Just put it all on that table in the back," Tim says.

"You got a tablecloth?" Sonya asks.

Tim stands there scratching his head. "Um . . . I don't know nothin' about a tablecloth."

Sonya looks at me and winks. "I have a spare one in the truck. Y'all can borrow it. Just make sure no one walks off with it."

Tim and I help Sonya carry everything into the cafeteria, but once we have everything out of the truck, Sonya asks us to leave her alone. "This is one of those jobs that one person can do better than three."

"We still have half an hour." Tim looks around. "Zeke should be here any minute. I hope he's not late."

"Don't worry about so much. Even if Zeke shows up late, everything will turn out just fine."

Sonya has everything on the table within fifteen minutes. "I left the wrap on the platters. All you have to do is remove it right before the party starts. I'll be back before the party's over to get all my stuff outta here."

Tim walks her out to her truck, while I look over the food Sonya has carefully prepared and laid out. She's done an excellent job with presentation, and I see that she's also placed her business cards around the table. I take a couple—one for me and one for Celeste, in case she decides to have her wedding catered.

When Tim walks in, he tries to pretend he's not worried, but I can tell he is. "Zeke's not here yet, and the party is supposed to start soon." He rubs his neck as he paces in front of the refreshment table. "Where's Laura and Pete? I can't believe the person in charge of this whole thing ain't even here yet." He stops and gives me a sheepish look. "Oops. I mean she *isn't* even here yet."

I smile. "Stop worrying so much, Tim. Everything will be just fine." In spite of my reassurance, I've been thinking some of the same worrisome thoughts as Tim. Laura fussed and worried over every last detail of the ten-year reunion, but this one almost seems like an afterthought.

The flash of headlights as the cars pull into the school parking lot gives me a moment of panic. When I see that it's Laura and Pete and Celeste and Jimmy, I let out a sigh of relief.

The first thing out of Laura's mouth when she enters the cafeteria is, "Where's Zeke? Isn't he supposed to be here already?"

Tim shrugs. "He's not here yet."

Back in frantic form, Laura shouts over her shoulder. "Pete, call Zeke and tell him to get over here right this minute."

"Calm down, Laura. He'll be here."

As if on cue, another truck pulls up in front of the cafeteria. One of the band members hops out and comes inside. "Sorry we're late, folks. They messed up our pizza order, so we had to wait for them to cook us another one. We ate as fast as we could."

Laura runs outside to give Zeke a piece of her mind, while the rest of the band members start carrying stuff inside. Add guests arriving to the mix, and chaos abounds.

Tim approaches me with a crooked grin. "Ahh, the sounds of having fun. Can't get any better than this." He shakes his head. "Maybe y'all should consider having the next reunion at the country club. At least there they'll have someone to coordinate it."

"What? And take away all Laura's fun? She'd never forgive us for that."

"Hey, you two." Celeste motions us over. "I need someone to check people in and give them their name tags."

I step forward. "I'll take care of that."

"And I'll go see if I can rescue Zeke from Laura's wrath." Tim waves as he takes off toward the stage, where Laura is still gesturing wildly as she hollers at the man who is supposed to supply the music but looks like he might change his mind. I have faith that if anyone can save the moment, it's Tim.

The moment I sit down behind the registration table, I see Didi and Maurice walking toward me. He's a couple of paces ahead of her, and she has to take little skipping steps to catch up.

I rummage through the name tags to find theirs and hand them over as soon as Maurice gets to the table. "Here ya go. I already put a checkmark by your names." I have to dig deep for the self-restraint required not to glare at Maurice. He's such a worm.

"Maurice, can you wait just a minute? My feet are killing me." Didi limps up to the table.

"I told you to wear flats and carry your heels in your bag." The sound of impatience in his voice reminds me of the times when I used to chase after him for interviews back when he was a football player and I was on the school newspaper staff.

"You did not." Didi stops, plants her fist on her hip, and bobs her head—looking more like a teenage girl on a reality show than an ear, nose, and throat doctor. "In fact, you're the one who said I should wear heels because they make my legs look—"

"Women." Maurice snorts as he gives me a look that makes me want to smack him. "Seems there's nothing I can do to make 'em happy."

"Maybe you should try being nice," I say. "I've seen you act before. I'm sure you can pull it off."

Didi narrows her eyes and comes toward me with determination. "What did you just say to my fiancé?"

Maurice leans away, arms folded, an annoying grin on his lips. "Ooh, I love a good catfight."

"Sorry, Maurice," I say, "but there won't be any catfights tonight. Didi and I are both reasonable, professional women who would never stoop that low." I look her in the eye and see the low simmer brewing. "Right, Didi?"

35
Laura

The reunion party got off to a rocky start, with Zeke and his buddies being late, but everything seems just fine now, thanks to Priscilla's fella, Tim. He's a real gem. If she was as smart as everyone seems to think she is, she would have married him already. But no, she's too focused on her career and all those sky-high goals. One of these days she'll wake up and realize how she's been chasing after the wrong thing.

I look around the room and see Celeste flashing her ring finger, thinking folks will be impressed that she finally tied the knot. Problem is, there's no bling on that finger—just a tiny gold band that I can barely see from where I stand.

Jimmy is still walking around in a daze. What can I expect? It's his wedding day, and they're sharing it with their high school graduatin' class. How pitiful is that!

Over by the registration table, Priscilla sits there pretending not to be bothered by the fact that Didi has gotten her hooks into Maurice who is, in my book, too pretty for any girl in Piney Point. I don't think there's a mirror in the whole town he hasn't made friends with. The problem is, the mirror doesn't show what's behind the pretty face. I've never much liked Maurice, and even though Pete used to hang out with all those guys from the football team, he hasn't either. He used to call Maurice a player.

Pete's still a little ticked that I insisted on us coming to the reunion party together, in the same vehicle. He says he likes knowing he can leave whenever he wants, but I figure if I'm stuck here, he can deal with a few hours of being someplace he doesn't wanna be.

Everything seems to be running smoothly, so I head on over to the refreshment table to get something to drink. I pick up a can of soda and turn around in time to see Deputy Patrick Moody walking toward me, that same look of determination I used to see on his face when I babysat him. He's cute in a military sorta way.

I smile real big to welcome him, but he doesn't smile back. Someone should've taught that boy some manners.

"Mrs. Moss, where's your husband?"

Something about the way he says that sends a shiver through me. "Why? What's goin' on, Patrick?"

"We need to find your husband."

I start to argue, but he tightens his jaw and pushes back his shoulders, letting me know he's in charge. Okay, so I have to find Pete in order to find out what has *Deputy Moody* in such a snit.

"Is that him over there?" Patrick points over toward the rear exit.

I look up in time to see my husband tossing back something in a paper bag. How on earth did he find alcohol here? I know I didn't bring any, and Jimmy's been with Celeste.

"Looks like it," I say between gritted teeth.

Patrick takes off toward Pete, and I'm right on his heels. I want to get someone to warn Pete to put away his booze, but there's no time. I brace myself for a scuffle.

"Pete, I'd like to have a word with you and Mrs. Moss." Oh, so Patrick is on a first name basis with my husband but not me? I'm not sure whether to take that as a compliment or an insult.

Rather than try to hide his paper bag, Pete holds it up in a salute before putting it down. "Can you give me a few minutes?"

"No, sir, I can't. There's been an accident."

My heart stops. "The young'uns."

Pete's face goes all sickly pale. He tosses his bag into the trash can and turns to face Patrick. "What happened?"

"Your neighbor Mrs. Crenshaw called 911 after she couldn't get in touch with you. Said your children went out for a joy ride in the truck." He looks down at his feet. "I went lookin' for 'em and when they spotted the blue light, we had a little chase. Until they got to the curve in the highway goin' to Hattiesburg, and the oldest boy lost control of the vehicle. Good thing they were wearing seatbelts." He pauses. "I have to admit I haven't seen many teenage joy riders wearin' seatbelts."

My stomach roils, and I fall into Pete. Fortunately, he's still able to hold me up.

"The kids are all fine, but your truck . . . " He holds out his hands. "You'll need to call your insurance company . . . and maybe a lawyer"

I look at Pete, whose face has gone slack. "You sure the kids is all right?"

Patrick nods. "Pretty shaken but fine. The oldest suffered a few scrapes on his arm, and one of the girls has bruises, but it doesn't look like anything's broken. They're at the sheriff's office right now."

"Just wait'll I get ahold of 'em," Pete says. "They coulda been killed."

"Yes, sir."

"C'mon, Pete, we need to go get 'em outta jail." I tug on my husband's arm.

For the first time since he arrived, Patrick cracks a smile. "They're not in jail, Mrs. Moss, but they'll probably wish they were after your husband sees his truck."

"Let's go," Pete says. "C'mon, Laura."

I touch Patrick on the arm. "Are you sure my young'uns are okay?"

"Positive. We wouldn't still be standin' here if they weren't."

"Give me a second to let someone know where we're going."

And I know just *who* to tell. Priscilla. When push comes to shove, she's the most responsible person in the entire room.

"I'll take care of everything," she says. "Call me later and let me know how everything went."

I take off after Patrick and Pete. "We'll be right behind you," I say.

Patrick turns around and looks me in the eye. "You are driving, right, Mrs. Moss?"

"Yes, of course."

"Just makin' sure."

All the way to the sheriff's Piney Point office, Pete grumbles about how the young'uns can't be trusted. "I can't believe Bubba would take all the kids on a joy ride when we're gone."

In my mind, I blame Pete for teaching Bubba how to drive so early, but I don't say that now. It's already bad enough knowing his truck's been all smashed up.

As soon as we walk into the reception area, Bubba leans over and puts his face in his hands. Jack sits on the edge of the chair, his face pale, eyes wide. Both girls hover in the corner, sitting all close and snuggly as though they're depending on each other for life. Funny how they hate each other except when they're in trouble together. There is something about bad stuff happening to draw you closer.

Pete marches right up to Bubba and stands there staring down. Bubba doesn't look up. Instead, he keeps his head lowered, but I see his leg shaking and his hands dripping with sweat.

"Bubba." Pete's voice is low and firm. "Look at me, son."

Bubba's leg stops moving as he slowly lifts his head. "I'm sorry, Daddy, I didn't mean to do it."

"Didn't mean to do what?"

"I don't know." Bubba's whiny voice reminds me of when he was four and upset when I caught him eating ice cream out of the carton in the middle of the kitchen floor.

"Are you sayin' you didn't mean to steal my truck or you didn't mean to get caught?"

Bubba bursts into a crying jag. I'm tempted to go over to him, put my arms around him, and tell him everything will be okay. But I don't because everything *won't* be okay. I've always had a tough time making my young'uns behave, but until recently, I trusted them to do the right thing. Between Bonnie Sue stealing that skirt from the shop and now Bubba taking off with his daddy's truck without permission, I realize we have much more serious issues than the little squabbles and temper tantrums we've dealt with since they were born.

Pete looks down at me, his eyes filled with emotion like I've never seen. "Why don't you go see about the girls, and I'll have a talk with the boys?"

I nod. Pete has never offered to deal with anything related to the young'uns, except when it's playtime. Maybe this is the Lord's way of waking my husband up to his parental responsibilities.

Renee turns her entire body away when I approach them, but Bonnie Sue looks me squarely in the eye. "You shouldn't have left Bubba in charge. He's nothin' but a troublemaker."

My little smart-aleck daughter has hit a nerve. "What do you think you're talkin' about, Bonnie Sue? Seems I remember you thinkin' you can help yourself to a five-finger discount."

She shrugs. "That's all in the past. Priscilla Slater took care of that for me. She's a celebrity around here, and she can do anything."

I grit my teeth and count to ten. "Priscilla Slater is more than just a celebrity," I say in a low growl. "She has worked hard for everything she has, including all those fancy salons. You owe her big-time."

Bonnie Sue's eyes go into half-mast position as she bobs her head. "She told me I don't have to do nothin'." This town is full of bobbleheads.

"Priscilla's not your mama. I am. I'm gonna have a talk with her and tell her you're workin' off all she did for you."

"Work?" Bonnie Sue says that word like it's disgusting.

"That's right. Work. I just happen to know they could use someone to help clean up between customers, and I think you're just the one to do it."

"But Mama—" She looks me in the eye and shakes her head as she lowers it.

"That'll teach ya to press your luck with me and your daddy. Now you'll think twice before gettin' in the car with someone who shouldn't be drivin'. And next time I hear about you stealin' . . . " I shudder. "You don't wanna know what I'll do." I turn to Renee, who has been discretely watching out of the corner of her eye. "And you, young lady . . . "

Renee holds her hands up. "I didn't do nothin'."

"Except get in the car with your brother who don't think about the consequences."

"He told us to come on."

"Oh, so all someone has to say is 'come on,' and you'll do whatever they want you to do?"

She slinks back in the seat. "No."

"You're all grounded for a month." I step back so I can look both of my daughters in the eye. "You can go to school and church, and that's it. No more goin' out with friends, no nothin' for a month."

"But Mama," Bonnie Sue whines. "I'm a cheerleader."

"It's summer." I lift an eyebrow and hold her gaze, until she finally backs down and looks away. "We'll see how you behave this summer before I decide if you can try out for cheerleading again."

"I have band camp," Renee reminds me.

This one's hard for me. I've been lookin' forward to band camp for months 'cause it's an organized event sponsored by the school, and that's one less bored kid to deal with during the summer. But I have to stay strong.

"No band camp this summer, missy." My stomach hurts as I say the words, but I know it's for her own good.

"But I ha—" She scowls. "It don't start 'til July."

"We'll see about it then," I say.

Renee joins her sister in sulking and acting all put out. I glance over my shoulder and see Pete kneeling down by the boys, their heads lowered. Could they be . . . praying? Nah, Pete only prays when I tell him to. I take a step back so I can hear what he's saying. Well, I'll be. They are praying. *Lord, you sure do have an interestin' way of gettin' folks' attention.*

We have to fill out some paperwork before they let us go. Finally, an hour later, we're on our way home.

"Don't y'all have to go back to the reunion?" Jack asks. Seems he's the only one of the four who's still talking to Pete and me.

"Nope. We're not leavin' you young'uns home alone again for a very long time." Pete glances over at me. "Y'all have to prove we can trust you again. Right now I don't trust any of you any farther than I can throw you."

Little Jack laughs but quickly quiets down when his siblings give him dirty looks. The rest of the trip home is quiet.

As soon as we walk in the door, Bubba heads for the living room and grabs the remote. Pete points to it. "Put that thing down, son, and go to your room."

"But, Daddy."

"Nope. All four of you, go to your rooms. Your mama and I have some things to discuss."

The firmness in his voice is so rare the kids don't know what to say. I'm stunned as I watch them head off to their rooms without another argument.

Once they're gone, Pete pulls me into his arms. "When was the last time I told you I love you, Miss Pudge?"

Back in the day when he first called me *Miss Pudge* after I put on a few pounds, I was highly offended. But tonight, as he embraces me so tenderly, I actually find comfort in the familiar. I rest my head on his chest, and he gently strokes my back, letting me know we're in this together.

"If it'll make you happy, I'll even take you to my cousin's weddin'." He leans away and grins at me. "I know how much you wanna go. And I think it might be good to connect with some of the family we haven't seen in a while."

Is it possible he's actually turned over a new leaf? I don't remember him ever being this agreeable to seeing Uncle Snub before.

I sigh as I close my eyes and imagine the fairy-tale wedding we're about to attend. I wonder if my pink lacy dress still fits.

36
Priscilla

Your phone has been ringin' like crazy," Celeste says as she lifts my handbag from beneath the table and thrusts it at me. "It must be important."

Jimmy holds up his phone and shows me the back of it. "You oughta get one of these here belt clips so you don't miss your calls."

"I'll think about it." I take my bag and go into the ladies' room, where the noise from Zeke and the Geeks doesn't sound nearly as bad as it does in front of the speakers. When I look at the phone, I see it's from the Moss residence.

I dread the very thought of calling Laura back. Shortly after she and Pete took off, word had reached us about her children going for a joy ride and getting into an accident. According to the source who just happened to overhear Patrick Moody talking to Laura and Pete, no one was seriously injured.

Instead of calling them back, I check my voice mail. Surprise. Laura isn't the one who called. It was Bonnie Sue.

"Priscilla . . . I mean Ms. Slater, you really have to talk to my mama. She got real mad at me and my sister and brothers just 'cause we went for a little ride in Daddy's truck. We planned on comin' back before they got home, but Bubba was too busy

288

fiddlin' with the radio to see the tree. I'm innocent. Honest. Me and little Jack was sittin' in the backseat mindin' our own business . . . " *Click.*

I punch the number to listen to the next voice mail. "Sorry. I thought I heard Mama at the door. Mama and Daddy's so mad they're not even yellin' like they always do. We're not allowed to go anywhere for a whole month. Not even Renee, and she's supposed to go to band camp. If she don't go, they won't let her be in the marchin' band next year. You're the only one . . . " *Click.*

I sigh as I press the number for another message. "That time it really was Mama, but she went back downstairs. Please talk to Mama. You're our only hope, on account of you're famous and all. Maybe she'll listen to you. Even Daddy's mad, and he never gets mad."

This is ridiculous. I don't even bother listening to the rest of the message since it's all about getting Bonnie Sue off the hook. I've always known having children was a tremendous responsibility, but the Moss kids have shown me how frustrating the parenting job can be. I'm not sure I have, or ever will have, the patience for it.

I spot Tim out of the corner of my eye and think about how supportive he's been. He turns and catches me watching him, and he waves.

This reunion has a completely different feel to it. There are fewer people, and everyone has mellowed out a bit. Of course, I mean everyone but Didi. I always considered her very book-smart, but she's never had much common sense, which, until now didn't matter. I wonder if she and Maurice actually will get married or if she'll remain in a state of limbo while he sucks her bank account dry.

Looking around, I think about all the people in the cafeteria, who are either engrossed in discussions with old friends, running around trying to network, or slow dancing to something that only vaguely resembles music. The only surprise I see is Trudy draped over Hank, swaying to the sound, occasionally lifting her head for a kiss. Michael isn't here yet, and I wonder if he comes, what he'll think about his ex-wife cozying up to the class nerd.

"Kinda makes you wanna go back to the high school days, don't it?" I turn around and see Tim.

"Right." I roll my eyes. "More like makes me want to run away and never come back."

"Aw, c'mon, Priscilla. It's not so bad. Everyone's doin' their own thing, havin' a good time, chillin' to the music."

"Music?" I laugh, and he smiles as he offers his hand.

"Care to dance, pretty girl?"

"Sure." I take his hand and follow him out to the makeshift dance floor, where there are only two other couples.

Tim is a good dancer, but even he has trouble finding the beat. Finally, he just steps back and forth, and I follow.

"So are you still gonna go to New York City?" Tim whispers.
"Yes."

"Uncle Hugh wants me to come up for a visit." Tim straightens his arms, holding me at a distance so he can look me in the eye. "Maybe we can work somethin' out to see each other while we're there."

I smile and refrain from mentioning that we see each other as much as we want to in Mississippi. No point in risking hurting his feelings right now.

Celeste comes up and taps me on the shoulder. "Me and Jimmy wanna wrap this thing up on time, this bein' our weddin' night and all."

"Okay."

I look at Tim who winks at me before turning to Celeste. "Y'all can go on and leave now if you want. Me and Priscilla can take care of everything."

Celeste ponders that and shakes her head. "Nah, I don't think Laura would want me to do that. She's countin' on me to make sure things run smoothly, and the caterer is supposed to come take all her stuff outta here before we leave."

Tim starts to argue, but I squeeze his arm. He gives me a puzzled look, and I shake my head. He finally sighs and says, "Okay, we'll help make sure everyone's out on time."

Celeste smiles and wanders on back to her new husband who still appears stunned. I look up into Tim's eyes. "I sure hope everything works out for them."

"I'm sure it will, once Jimmy gets used to the fact that he's a married man." Tim chuckles. "I just think it's funny he couldn't think of no other way to cheer her up last night."

Maybe that's for the best. Other couples, including Trudy and Michael, and my parents, planned their lives together for years, and now look at them.

37
Trudy

Hank has his arms around me so tight I can hardly breathe. I'm still not sure what Marlene saw in him, but I aim to find out if it takes me forever. As of right now, though, I can't get past the point that I'm hugging on the guy my husband used to make fun of back in high school for being so nerdy.

Don't get me wrong. I was never mean to him, but when it was just me and Michael, we would laugh at the comments that came out of Hank's mouth, his joy from the robotics team winning the regional championship, and of course the calculator he never went anywhere without. Now I'm trying my hardest to find some common ground.

"What did you and Marlene used to talk about?" I ask when the song ends.

He looks at me with those soulful eyes I never noticed until a few days ago. "Why do you keep asking questions about Marlene?"

I shrug. "I just wanna make sure you're over her before anything happens . . . well, before you and I start . . . "

"Don't you worry about that." Hank grins at me. "I'm completely over her. She's a sweet girl, but truthfully, she was always second to you in my heart."

That's really sweet, but it still doesn't change the way I'm feeling. Or more like it, *not* feeling.

"Marlene is so pretty . . . " I look at Hank and force a smile. "And she got all the way to second runner-up in the Miss Mississippi pageant. I didn't even make the top five."

He brushes the bangs back from my forehead, and I shake my head to put them back into place. I spent good money on this wispy look, and I don't want him messing it up.

"Seriously, Trudy, you worry too much about things like that. If I were one of the judges, you would have *been* Miss Mississippi."

I have no doubt he's telling me how he really feels, and I want to take it as a compliment, but it's hard knowing his history. "Thank you."

He reaches toward my bangs again, and I back away. "Please don't mess with my hair. I hate people touching it."

A look of dejection flashes on his face. "There are so many things I still don't know about you. In all the years I've been watching you and thinking I'd never stand a chance of getting this close to you because of Michael, I didn't realize you didn't like people touching your hair."

I bite my lip to fight the tears that threaten to fall. It's not that I don't like people touching my hair. I used to love it when Michael would run his fingers through my hair and pull it away from my face so he could see me better. It's Hank that I don't want messing with my hair.

"But now that we're getting to know each other better, we can take our time to learn what we like and don't like."

"Don't forget, Hank, I live in Atlanta, and since I work in retail, I can't get away very often."

"That's okay. I just closed a deal on another company that has offices in all the major cities, including Atlanta."

I should be flattered that Hank, who has turned his geeki-ness into a thriving business empire, is interested in me. But every now and then, I glance over at the spot where Michael and I used to eat lunch together—at least when he wasn't sit-ting with his football player friends. Maybe if I see Hank in a less familiar setting, I'll feel different. Yeah, that's gotta be the problem. Alan is just as geeky as Hank, yet I was able to get past that and consider a relationship—at least after seeing Marlene bein' so interested in Hank. I've even heard from some of the teenage girls I help at the store that *geek* is the new *cool*.

"Can we leave now?" I look up at Hank, who still has a dreamy look in his eyes. I wish he didn't adore me so much. I know, that's what I say I want from a guy, but deep down, I think I must enjoy a challenge, which Michael definitely was. I wish I could stop comparing everyone to Michael, but being around all my old classmates reminds me of how things used to be.

"Sure." He grins. "Would you like to go over to my place in Hattiesburg?"

I shake my head. "No, I'm very tired."

He doesn't bother to hide his disappointment. "Okay, that's fine."

All the way to my parents' house, he talks about when we might be able to get together again. I wish he would give me a little bit of quiet time. Michael and I used to have long stretches of silence that I thought were annoying at the time, but look-ing back, I realize I came to find comfort in them.

When we make our last turn toward my parents' house, I spot Michael's car at the curb. The house is dark, but the front porch light is on, and Michael is sitting on the steps, his head down, shoulders slumped—almost like last time.

"Is that . . . ?" Hank's jaw tightens. "What's he doing here?"

"He didn't show up at the party." I can't stop looking at Michael, but that old familiar flutter in the tummy doesn't happen. "I have no idea what he's doing here."

"I'll tell him to get lost." He pulls into the driveway and puts the car in park.

I place my hand on Hank's arm. "No, don't. Something is wrong, and I don't wanna be mean."

"But he's—" Hank looks at me and shakes his head. "You're still in love with him, aren't you?"

By now I know for sure I'm not in love with him. "No, I'm not in love with him anymore, but he and I have a history."

Hank slams his palm on the steering wheel. "That's what bugs me. If he doesn't stay out of your life, there's no chance for us."

"Don't say that, Hank. Michael has nothing to do with . . . us." I'm not sure I'll ever feel anything romantic toward Hank, but at the moment, I want to find out what's going on with Michael and let him know he's responsible for whatever he's going through.

I look back over at Michael and see that he's watching us. There's no doubt in my mind that he's not worried about anything happening between me and Hank. Michael has always had a superiority complex. All he has to do is snap his fingers, and he gets what he wants. Maybe that used to be the case, but not anymore.

"Why don't you pick me up in the morning for church?" I smile at Hank.

He glances over at Michael then back at me. "Are you sure about that? What if the ex wants to take you to church?"

"The ex doesn't always get what he wants."

"Okay. What time?"

"Church starts at eleven, so how about ten-thirty?" I sigh. It's time to go face Michael. "Well, are you gonna walk me to my door?"

Momentarily flustered, Hank scrambles to get his seat-belt unhooked, opens his door, and gets out, while I wait for him to come around to get me. No matter how independent I've become, I still enjoy some of the old-fashioned southern etiquette in a dating situation.

He casually places his arm over my shoulder, but I can tell he's nervous about encountering Michael. When we get within a few feet of the steps, I turn around to face Hank and say in a voice loud enough for Michael to hear, "I had a wonderful time tonight, Hank. Don't be late pickin' me up in the mornin'."

I can tell he's not sure whether or not to kiss me, so I stand on my tiptoes, give him a quick little lip smack, and back away from him. The stunned look on his face is so comical, it makes me want to laugh, but I don't.

"G'night, Hank."

Hank slowly walks toward his car, gets in, and backs out of the driveway. When I turn around to face Michael, I see him staring at me in disbelief.

"What was that all about?" He doesn't even bother to stand up.

I put my fist on my hip and stare down at him. "I'm the one who should be askin' you that question. Why are you sittin' on my porch again?"

"Trudy . . . " He finally stands up and reaches for me. When I don't move toward him, he jerks his head back and pats the spot beside him. "C'mere."

I fold my arms. "No. I'm not taking orders from you any-more, Michael."

"But you and I . . . we're meant to be together. I've made some big mistakes, Trudy, and I want you to know I'm ready to take you back."

"Yes, you've made some humongous mistakes, but I'm not going back to you." I tilt my head forward and glare at him. "Ever."

"Oh, Trudy honey, that's the most ridiculous thing I've ever heard. You know we'll wind up together."

"*Honey*? Uh-uh. You lost the right to call me honey when you said I wasn't good enough for you." Disgust toward Michael starts to flow through me, and that gives me the courage to say what's on my mind. "How about your pregnant girlfriend?" I have no intention of going back to Michael, regardless of the girlfriend, but I'm curious what his plans are. "Are you just gonna cast her aside like you do everyone who cares about you?"

He pouts, but I can tell it's fake because he has his body in the old stance he's always used to show his power over everyone. "You've never turned me down before, Trudy. What has that . . . " He makes a face. "What has that sorry excuse of a boyfriend of yours said about me?"

I give him one of those smiles he used to tease me about giving people who don't really matter—the kind that shows all my teeth but doesn't crinkle anything on my face. "You may not believe this, Michael, but my . . . boyfriend doesn't say *anything* about you. We have much more important things to discuss."

"Important things? Like what?" He leans closer and tries to hold my gaze like he did when we were too young to know what love was.

"That's really none of your business."

"So do you think you and what's-his-name have a future together?"

I shrug. "Maybe, but that's really not your concern, now is it?"

Michael's shoulders slump. "I'm not sure how to deal with this situation I'm in."

"So now you're calling your pregnant girlfriend a *situation*?"

He nods. "She trapped me."

I can't help laughing at the ridiculousness of his comment. "You weren't exactly innocent."

"But I was. I never told her I wanted to settle down. She asked me to move in with her, but I told her I wasn't ready for a commitment."

"Looks like your actions speak louder than your intentions." They always have, but at least I was smart enough to hold out. "In case you didn't know this before, if you don't want a commitment from a girl, there are certain things you shouldn't do."

"I didn't ask you for a lecture, Trudy. All I wanted was your help, but now I see what kind of friend you truly are."

"I'm not your friend, Michael. I'm your ex-wife, and I have no intention of getting you out of any mess you got yourself into, just to stroke your ego."

"You need to get past your grudge."

"I do?" I laugh right in his face, and *forgive me, Lord, but it feels mighty good*. "I have yet to see why."

"It's not very becoming."

The front porch light blinks at us—the sign that my parents know I'm on the front porch, and they want me to come in. "You need to leave now."

Michael doesn't budge from his spot on the step. He just stares at me as though that will change my mind.

I point to his car. "Leave. I have nothing else to say to you."

"I'll call you tomorrow so we can talk about it when you have more time and you're not so cranky."

"No, don't. I'm going to church with Hank, then later on, I'm heading back to Atlanta."

He frowns. "You've really changed, Trudy."

"Yes, Michael, I have changed." *Thank you for that, Lord.* "I've grown up, and it's time for you to do the same." I open the door and see Daddy standing there. I take a step inside, lean over, give him a hug, then look back at Michael. "Good night." Then I close the door behind me.

"What was that all about?" Mama asks in her sleepy voice as she walks up from behind Daddy. "Was that Michael I heard you talking to?"

"Yes, he was sitting on the porch waiting for me to come home from the reunion."

Mama's eyes squint with concern. "Is there a chance—?"

"No, Mama, there's no chance on earth for Michael and me to ever get back together, if that's what you were asking."

"So you had a nice time with Hank?"

I nod. There's no point in going over all the details about my conflicting feelings, but I want to reassure her that my evening went well. "I had a wonderful time with Hank . . . so much so, he's picking me up for church in the morning." I hug her and give her a kiss on the cheek. "Go back to bed now. Love you."

As I lie in bed a half hour later, I reflect on the night with Hank. I remember seeing him at the ten-year reunion and thinking about how sweet he was with Marlene. That was when I made my decision to give Alan a chance once I got back to Atlanta, but he surprised me with his announcement that he'd gotten back with his old girlfriend. I was disappointed, but the experience taught me a valuable lesson: sometimes things aren't as they seem, and just because someone is geeky doesn't mean he's not worth loving. Hank is very similar to Alan, only I knew him back in high school, when Michael and I were the hottest couple in town. It's difficult to get past the image, but I really need to work hard at seeing beyond the facade. So what if he's a *Star Wars*–loving, graphing calculator–toting, infrared pen–loving, sports-hating, championship-debating nerd? He's got enough redeeming traits to capture and break the heart of the second runner-up in the Miss Mississippi pageant. And I can be pretty certain he won't ignore me when the Super Bowl is on, even if the New Orleans Saints are playing.

38
Priscilla

I shouldn't be surprised by anything that happens in Piney Point, but I have to admit a few things have caught me off-guard. First, being faced with Laura and Pete's daughter's shoplifting unsettled me, but Carolyn's reaction at the shop threw me for a loop. She should never have made such a big deal of my career success. As it stands now, Bonnie Sue will think that if she's successful or well known, she can get away with theft. I've never stolen a thing in my life.

It's Monday morning, and I already have a full schedule for the week. I'll need to make sure everything is in order here at the Piney Point salon, drive over to Jackson to check on Mandy, then fly up to New York for my appointment with the TVNS execs. Every time I think about it, I get a tummy flutter.

But before I leave town, I need to have a chat with Bonnie Sue—that is, if Laura lets me. After her kids got into trouble on the night of the big party, she's acting even more cantankerous than before, and she's always been the type to let you know when she feels put-upon.

Mother comes to my bedroom door to let me know that my second surprise is on the phone. It's my Realtor.

"Hey, I got good news."

"They accepted my offer?"

"Well . . . " Her voice gets a little scratchy as the pitch goes up. "Not exactly but close."

I grab a pen and paper to jot down the notes. "Okay, I'm ready."

She gives me a list of the seller's conditions and lets me know their asking price has shot up. "That's what I was afraid of," she says, "but I thought if we gave them an offer quickly enough, they wouldn't realize the place is worth more as a vacant lot."

"That's okay," I say. "Their asking price is still in my range."

"So you wanna take their counter?"

"No, of course not. I want to get the best deal I can." I give her a counter to their counter. When I hang up, Mother knocks on my bedroom door. She's obviously been listening from the hallway.

"I couldn't help overhearing." She takes me by the hand and leads me to the edge of the bed, where I sit and she stands. "Please, Priscilla, I beg you to think this through before you become even more committed than you already are. Buying that property is a huge investment, and if you change your mind . . . " She shakes her head. "It'll be an even bigger mess." She might be talking about my offer on the old ice factory, but I see the parallel of her relationship with Dad.

"Mother, my commitment is already established. I have several dozen people working for me already. They depend on my business to support their families. I consider that much more important than the building."

She ponders that, even though she continues to frown. I wonder if she catches the depth of what I'm saying. "Your father wants to discuss this with you before you make any final decisions."

I let out a deep sigh. "Okay, but I have to leave on Wednesday to go to New York."

"That's okay. He's in the kitchen waiting for you now."

I should have known that. "Let's go have a chat with Dad."

"You go on ahead, dear. I have to straighten my room before Teresa gets here."

When I walk into the kitchen, Dad is fiddling with the napkin holder. He looks up and smiles. "Why don't you pour yourself some coffee and have a seat?"

I do as he tells me and join him at the table. "So what did you want to talk to me about, Dad?"

"Your mother is worried about you." He purses his lips, looks down at the table, then meets my gaze. "I just happen to be very proud of what you've become, so I'm not sure how to approach this."

I scoot my chair back from the table and fold my arms. "Approach what?"

"Do you really know what you're getting yourself into with that property?"

"Yes, I think so. I've been in business for a long time now, and I'm fully aware of how to buy property."

"You've been renting that space on Main Street, which is quite different . . . "

"Don't forget, I bought the land and built the salon and office in Jackson."

"But this is Piney Point."

"Yes." I tilt my head forward and hold his gaze. "Why does that make a difference?"

Dad frowns. "I'm afraid your mother thinks that if you fail . . . not saying I agree with her . . . you won't have a place to go."

"You mean I won't have a place to hide?"

He holds out his hands and bobs his head in the affirmative.

This is utterly ridiculous. I stand up. "If I fail, the last thing I have to worry about is having a place to go or hide. In spite of what you and Mother believe about me, I'm a very good businesswoman, and I take extremely calculated, well-thought-out risks before I make decisions. Y'all do not need to worry about me. Instead, I'd like to suggest getting some outside help with your marriage."

I hear a gasp behind me, so I turn around. Mother is standing there, her face red, her mouth open. "Priscilla!"

"Mother, you and Dad are worrying needlessly about something you can't control. I love both of you, and I see something going on with y'all that has me even more concerned than anything having to do with my salons."

"That's not—"

Dad clears his throat. "Suzanne, I think we've said enough now. Let's leave Priscilla to her business, and we can tend to ours."

"You're supposed to be with me on this, George."

I'm done with this conversation, so I hold up my hands. "If y'all want to argue about me, do it after I leave. I'm going to Jackson tomorrow."

"But you said . . . " Mother darts her gaze back and forth between Dad and me. "I thought you might want to stay the whole week."

"You obviously haven't been listening to me then. I've been very clear that I'm going up to New York to discuss my product line with the folks at TVNS."

"So you really are serious about hawking your stuff on that silly TV station?" Mother shudders. "How will your father and I explain that to our colleagues at the college?"

I shrug. "Maybe you can tell them to tune in and find out how to add volume to their limp locks?"

Dad snickers until Mother glares at him. He covers his mouth with his fist and pretends to cough.

"Why don't the two of you go out for dinner tonight?"

Without consulting Dad, Mother shakes her head. "We won't do any such thing, not with you going back to Jackson tomorrow."

"I have a date with Tim, so don't worry about me."

"You have a date on your last night here?"

"I'll be back after my trip to New York."

She starts to argue with me, when Dad clears his throat to get our attention. "I would love to take your mother out for supper if she'll do me the honors."

"George, that's just plain silly." In spite of Mother's reprimand, her cheeks are red, and she doesn't seem to know what to do with her hands.

I smile at his choice of words and her flustered reaction. It's almost like I'm watching him trying to court Mother, and she's too embarrassed to show she likes it.

When I arrive at the Piney Point salon an hour later, Sheila lifts her shears in greeting. I stop off at each station and chat with the hairdressers as they create their masterpieces. Pride swells inside me as I realize I couldn't have handpicked better people to associate with.

"We'll be prayin' for ya," Sheila says. "Go knock those TV executives over with your hair products. Got a name for the system yet?"

I shake my head. "I want to come up with something that'll stick in people's minds."

"How about *Priscilla's Fancy Hair System*?" she says.

Chester rolls his eyes. "That's way too old school."

Sheila stops cutting her client's hair, spins around to face Chester, and does her best to bob her head but looking more like she's lost her mind than anything. "Okay, Mr. Bigshot, if you're so smart what do you think she should call it?"

"Hmm." He glances down at his client before holding his comb like a scepter. "How about *Priscilla's Hair to the Sky*?"

"Oh that's just plain stup—"

"Wait a minute, Sheila." I hold my hand up to shush her while I turn to Chester. "That's actually pretty good, only just a tad off." I tap my chin with my index finger as I mentally try to tweak it. "Sky-High Hair?"

Chester slowly shakes his head. "I don't know. That name don't make me wanna pick up my phone and place an order for it."

"You two are silly." Sheila lifts the section of her client's hair that she'd dropped and starts whacking away with her shears. "What does a name really matter?"

Chester waves his comb in the air. "Oh, it matters, honey. The name is everything."

"Then think about your customer. Who do you think would wanna buy it?"

Her client lifts a finger. "I will. How much is it gonna cost?"

"Seriously?" I lean over, get a good look at the woman's face, and see that I'm talking to Trudy's mother. "Hey, Mrs. Shallowford. I didn't recognize you."

"That's 'cause I went red." She pats her half-cut hair. "Do you like it?"

I lean back and study the overall effect. "Yes, I actually do. So you'd consider buying something from TVNS if it promised to add volume to your hair?"

"Of course. After I hit the menopause, my hair started thinnin' out."

Sheila nods. "I told her not to brush her hair so much, but she still insists on doin' that hundred strokes thing every night."

"I've done that all my life. My mama always told me it made your hair shiny." She flinches as Sheila turns her head to get to a section on the other side.

"With all the color we put on your hair, it's brittle and damaged. Brushing it causes it to snap like a bunch of little twigs."

"Do you mind if I take a look?" I step up and inspect her hair before either of them has a chance to respond. "How about we get her started on the hair volumizing system right now?"

Sheila gives me a curious look. "Do we still have some?"

I nod, cup my hand, and whisper, "Not packaged yet. It's just my special conditioning shampoo, leave-in conditioner, root builder, and gizmo that lifts the hair at the crown. Once I'm sure what I'm gonna call it, I'll get new packaging."

"I'll be glad to work it into your hair," Sheila says.

"How much is it?" Mrs. Shallowford says.

I lean over. "How much would you be willing to pay for it?"

She says a sum that's way too high, so she's happy when I give her an amount that is much more affordable. Chester's customer asks if she should try it too. Chester nods his agreement and gives me a thumbs-up sign in the mirror.

"Hey Priscilla!"

The sound of Jackie's voice coming toward me grabs my attention. I motion for her to follow me as I head to the back room. Once we're in there, she squeals.

"What?"

She puts down her briefcase, puts her hands on my shoulders, and looks me in the eye as she nearly jumps out of her fancy suit. "I just heard from the sellers. They want to hurry up and make this deal, so they've decided to go back to your original offer."

"Why the change of heart?"

Jackie chuckles. "Do you know who has owned that place for the past six years?"

I shake my head. "I've been away so long I have no idea."

"Remember Mrs. McArthur?"

"Are you talking about the business teacher who retired right after I graduated?" I sink down in the chair at the table. "I thought the sellers were—"

Jackie interrupts me. "It's been in her husband's family for forty years. Until today, she was letting her son handle the transaction, but when she found out that you're about to make a deal on TVNS, she got all excited and said she can't risk losing this deal just for a little extra money."

I cringe at the mention of TVNS, knowing I shouldn't be surprised that word is out. "But why?"

Jackie shrugs. "She loves shopping on TVNS. Says she gets the best deals when they have their 'Today Only' sales."

"I still don't understand why that makes any difference."

"Wait 'til you hear what her new terms are. Once you're on TVNS, she says all she wants is a chance to meet her favorite show host, and she'll be happy for the rest of her life."

"What if I don't get on TVNS?"

Jackie shrugs. "I told her it's not a done deal yet, but she said she's willin' to take that chance if you'll agree to the terms."

This is such a strange request I don't know what to say. "Let me get a better feel for things when I go up there this week, and I'll let you know."

"Sounds fair. I'll tell her you'll get back with her by . . . " She turns her hands palms up. "When will you know?"

"Soon I hope. They want me to present my products to all the execs on Thursday. I'm up against two other strong contenders, and they can only choose one more new product line."

Jackie claps her hands and squeals again. "If anyone can do it, you can. And I can't wait to see you on TV."

"Tell you what. Let Mrs. McArthur know that if I get on TVNS, I'll take her with me on one of my trips."

"She'll be over-the-moon happy about that." Jackie pulls a stack of papers from her briefcase. "Why don't you go ahead and sign this so I can get the ball rolling."

I do as she asks. After she leaves, I say good-bye to all my Piney Point employees.

Chester waves. "Break a leg, Priscilla."

39
Tim

So good to see you, Tim." Aunt Tammy gives me a hug and a kiss on the cheek. "You're lookin' a tad tired."

Priscilla's reunion wore me out, but I don't reckon it's necessary to go on about that. As it is, Uncle Hugh and Aunt Tammy think I've wasted too much time trying to get Priscilla to fall in love with me. I admit they're probably right. I spent the first three years I knew the woman trying to show her why she needed me. But after her last reunion, I knew the spark just plain wasn't there for her. You might wonder why I went back to her fifteenth reunion, and I get it. I'm one of those guys who likes to feel needed, and, boy howdy, do those folks need me— especially Laura Moss. If it weren't for me, I don't know what they'd do. I suspect if I don't have a wife in five years, you're likely to find me at Priscilla's twenty-year reunion, doing the same thing I done for the other two.

Aunt Tammy leads the way to the room they let me stay in when I'm in New York City. Uncle Hugh's been wanting to buy a house on Long Island, but Aunt Tammy don't wanna sell their place in Mississippi. Besides, she puts up a good argument, saying what's the point in living in New York if you can't be close to everything? So they rent this big ol' house on Staten

Island. "I can walk anywhere I need to go," Aunt Tammy brags, "and when I wanna go to Manhattan, all I have to do is hop on the ferry."

Daddy and Uncle Hugh was born and raised in Pearl, a suburb of Jackson, which is as close to big-city livin' as you're gonna get in Mississippi. Aunt Tammy comes from Ellisville, a country town where folks often forget to lock their doors at night. Needless to say, moving to New York was rather traumatic for her.

"You got fresh sheets, Tim. Jerry should be home in about an hour, so why don't you put your things away and come on into the kitchen and keep me company while I cook supper?"

I find comfort in Aunt Tammy's relaxing voice and slow manner of speaking, but I often wonder how she manages to get around in the craziness of the big city. After putting my bags in the guest room, I head into the kitchen.

"Have a seat." She points to a chair. "I was just getting the spoon rolls ready for the oven. Want some tea?"

"Sounds good." No one makes sweet tea better'n Aunt Tammy . . . not even my own mama.

"So tell me all about why you're here." She sets the tea down on the table before sitting down in the chair next to me. "I hear Priscilla Slater is about to go national."

I fill Aunt Tammy in on what's going on with Priscilla, trying my hardest to downplay how excited I am for her. No point in acting like I think there's any hope for me and Priscilla in the romance department.

Aunt Tammy goes back and forth between the stove and the table as we catch up on each other's lives. When Uncle Hugh arrives, he comes at me with his arms open wide. He's still a southern boy deep down, but I can see the city's effects on his face. He's not quite so easy to read these days.

"I can't believe I sold her the rights on that product line." Uncle Hugh shakes his head. "But at least she's doin' somethin' with it, and she's still buying it from me."

Years ago, after Uncle Hugh failed to place a new line of products in the salons, he decided to discontinue it. At the same time, Priscilla was looking for something that would be exclusive to her shops, so she made Uncle Hugh an offer he couldn't turn down. Another thing I love about her is she never tried to cut him out of the deal, even though at the time he probably would've been okay with that. Now women all over the southeast go to the Cut 'n Curl to purchase the products, even if they get their hair done somewhere else. Uncle Hugh keeps saying that Priscilla Slater is a powerhouse in beauty, and she's a marketing genius.

After dinner, the three of us clean the kitchen, and Aunt Tammy excuses herself to go watch her TV shows. Uncle Hugh points to the chair. "Sit down, boy. We need to talk."

We start out discussing some of the products we sell, but I know what this is really all about. Finally, he gets to the point.

"When are you gonna stop chasin' after that woman?"

"Uncle Hugh, Priscilla and I are friends. I'm just tryin' to show my support." I pause. "Besides, you and Aunt Tammy tell me I don't get up to New York often enough."

"True, but we want you to settle down. Find yourself a good woman who loves everything about you, and your life will be as good as it can get."

"I know." I fiddle with the napkin holder. "I'll start workin' on it when I get back to Jackson. In the meantime, I plan to be there for Priscilla to celebrate if she's successful or listen to her if they turn her down."

The shield has faded from Uncle Hugh's face as he grins. "You're a good boy, Tim."

I go to my room and call Priscilla. "Can you meet me at the coffee shop on the corner at eight?" she asks. "I'm nervous, Tim."

"You'll do just fine." I'm nervous for her, but I don't let on. She needs to only hear my good thoughts. "I'll see you there at eight."

After a good night's sleep and only waking up once to the sound of sirens whizzing by, I follow the smell of bacon all the way to the kitchen. Aunt Tammy points to the coffeepot and instructs me to help myself. Uncle Hugh has already gone to the office, so it's just the two of us. She sits down with me while I eat.

"Tell Priscilla I said hi and to break a leg." She giggles. "That's supposed to be good luck before a performance."

"I'll tell her." I carry my plate to the sink. "I don't wanna be late, so I better run."

Not quite an hour later, I walk into the coffee shop and see Priscilla sitting in a booth near the door. She waves and motions me over. The table in front of her is covered with papers, and she has a frantic look in her eyes.

"Everything will turn out just fine, Priscilla." I pat her hand. She looks into my eyes. "Promise?"

I hate making promises, but I know she'll come out a winner, even if the TVNS executives don't choose her product. I rack my brain trying to find some comforting words, then I remember something important. "Why don't we say a prayer before you go in?"

Her eyebrows go up, a grin spreads over her lips, and she slowly nods. "Good idea, Tim. Who would have thought you'd be the one to remind me to pray?"

After we close our eyes, I start a prayer—awkward but heartfelt—and she finishes. I notice a much more peaceful look on her face after we say our *amens*.

"Thank you, Tim. You're the best." She stacks up all the papers, clips them together, and drops them into the big ol' fancy tote Uncle Hugh gave her. "Ready to go?"

I nod. "Ready as ever."

"It's show time."

As soon as we walk into the reception area of TVNS, I see two other groups of people waiting. Priscilla stiffens her back as she leads me to a corner.

"I wonder if they're my competitors," she whispers.

One of the groups has what looks like a kitchen gadget sitting on the table in front of 'em. A man is mouthing some words and practicing some gestures while a woman keeps interrupting him and giving him more instruction. The other group is doing the opposite—sitting all silent and appearing real nervous.

"Looks like they just might be. Do you wanna practice what you're gonna say?"

She shakes her head. "No, I don't have a canned presentation. I just have notes, and I want it to come across as natural as possible."

"Okay then." If it were me, I would have had my whole speech wrote out and made cue cards for myself. But Priscilla does things her own way, and it always works for her.

A woman comes up from the back. "Would the Kitchen Do-All group please follow me?"

Priscilla's hands get real still. I want to reach for them and hold onto her, but I don't. She knows what she needs, and if she wants me to hold her hand, she'll let me know.

We sit there waiting for nearly an hour before the Kitchen Do-All folks come out pumping their fists, looking all happy. I hold my breath to keep from saying anything. Priscilla smiles at the woman who gives her a possum-eatin' grin.

Priscilla is up next. "Want me in there with you?" I ask. She wasn't sure where I should be when we discussed it earlier.

"Yes, if you don't mind."

"Of course I don't mind. That's what I'm here for." My heart sings as I hop up and follow her down the long hall and into the boardroom, where about a dozen folks are sittin' around a big conference table.

As we take our places, I survey the people to try to get an idea of what we're facing. All the women are looking at Priscilla's bag, and I can tell they know the brand. They're smiling, but based on their expressions, I suspect they'd love to rough her up a bit. Uncle Hugh's generosity is nice, but it sure can backfire at times like this. The men are looking at her pretty face then at me, probably wondering what I'm doin' there.

A woman stands up at the other end of the table and introduces Priscilla. "Next on the slate is Priscilla Slater. She has a packaged system designed to add volume to hair." Without even cracking a smile, she turns to Priscilla. "So what is the name of your product, Ms. Slater?"

Priscilla swallows hard, and I feel something drop in the pit of my stomach. Last I heard, she didn't have a name picked out yet.

"Big Hair," she says softly before clearing her throat. "I'm calling my hair-volumizing system *Ms. Prissy Big Hair.*"

A few of the people around the table laugh, and I want to hop up and smack 'em. Didn't their mama's ever tell 'em it ain't polite to laugh in people's faces?

Instead of acting insulted, Priscilla surprises me and laughs along with 'em. "This is exactly the reaction I was hoping for," she says. "The beauty industry is a seriously lucrative business, but we can still have fun with it. My goal is to show women how to enjoy celebrating their beauty as they make the most with what they have."

From that moment on, I can tell that Priscilla has the entire group where she wants them. They hang on her every word, and she works 'em like puppets.

40
Priscilla

Adrenaline has flowed so fast and hard that the second we step out of the meeting room I'm limp as a rag. Tim is right there beside me as always, grinning like a proud parent.

He leans over and whispers, "You did great, Priscilla. I don't know how you did it, but you had them folks mesmerized."

"I did?" I flash back to the moment when I had to come up with a name for the system. I'd been toying with several ideas, and what I blurted surprised even me. The instant *Ms. Prissy Big Hair* tumbled out of my mouth, I knew there was no going back.

"Yeah, you did. What I can't believe is how you jumped right up and did that woman's hair. You didn't look nervous."

"Oh, but I was."

Tim laughs. "I thought that executive woman would have a coronary when the man beside her asked if you'd be able to do somethin' with her hair."

"I know. Did you see how his hair is thinning? I thought about asking him if he'd like me to work on his hair too."

"Good thing you didn't."

"You're so right, but the thought distracted me enough to keep my hands from shaking right off my arms."

"When you got done with that VP woman, she looked a-MA-zing."

Nodding, I agree. "She really did." I don't think I'll ever forget the way she studied her reflection in the handheld mirror I gave her. When she looked back at me, I knew she loved the way she looked.

"She knew it too." Tim places his hand in the small of my back. "Now all we can do is wait until they make their decision."

I glance at my watch. "We went over the allotted time, and I figure the next presentation will be at least an hour. Then they'll have to deliberate . . . " I make a face. "This could take weeks."

"I don't think so." He smiles down at me. "I think they'll make their decision very soon."

"So what do I do now?"

Tim shrugs. "We can go have lunch, or if you're not hungry, we can walk around the city and see the sights."

I'm glad Tim is with me. He's about the only person on earth who truly understands me, and he's so comfortable to be around—exactly what I need after that presentation.

As we walk around the city, going from one tourist trap to another, I get momentary giddy feelings that create tingling sensations from my head to the tips of my toes. And every time this happens, Tim smiles, letting me know he's aware of the tension crackling inside me.

"Would you like to have dinner with me tonight?" he asks as he walks me to the elevator of my hotel.

I'd really like to call down for room service, but after all Tim has done for me, I can't very well turn him down. "I'd love—."

My cell phone rings, interrupting me. It's Mandy.

"Hey, Priscilla." She lets out a loud squeal. "You did it! I am so happy for you I could spit!"

"I did what?"

"Oh, the people from TVNS just called and said they wanted to see you first thing in the morning. They love the product, and they want to discuss packaging."

I can tell she's jumping around in her seat, and the mental image makes me laugh. "Are you sure? They said they needed to discuss it at length."

"Positive. Mr. Waddell said after the miracle you worked during that meetin', they'd be foolish not to choose your products." She giggles. "Ms. Prissy Big Hair? How did you come up with that?"

"I don't know," I admit. "It just came to me while I was presenting. So what do I need to do now?"

Tim stands silently as I jot down the information. After I hang up with Mandy, he grins and opens his arms wide. "I knew you had 'em as soon as you opened your mouth."

"Thank you so much for believing in me, Tim." Tears spring to my eyes. "Why don't you hang out in the lobby while I go up to my room and get ready for dinner? It won't take me long."

"I have to run an errand, but I'll be right back. How long do you need?"

"Half hour?"

He nods. "That's fine. Call my cell phone when you're almost ready, and I'll be down here waitin' for you."

I go up to my room and call my parents. When Mother answers, I ask her to get Dad on the extension. "Hey, honey, we're really sorry about . . . well, you know, all that talk about wantin' you to follow our dreams, and . . . "

"Mother, don't worry about it. I understand. You only want what's best for me."

"Suzanne, I think our daughter has something to tell us. She called us, remember?"

"Oh, yes, sorry, honey."

"Mother," I pause. "Dad, I just heard that TVNS wants me to bring my new product, Ms. Prissy Big Hair, to their network. I'll be on air, selling this line to thousands, maybe even millions of women."

Silence falls over the line before Dad clears his throat. "Ms. Prissy Big Hair?"

"What in the world is that?" Mother asks. "Have you lost your mind?"

A laugh bubbles up from my throat. "Absolutely, and I'm gonna have a blast showing millions of women how to increase the volume of their hair."

Mother and Dad let out a collective sigh. "I suppose we should have expected something like this," Mother says. "At any rate, Priscilla, we're proud of you, no matter what career path you take. You've always had a mind of your own, even when you were a newborn. Did I ever tell you about—?"

"Mother, I have to run. Tim is picking me up in a few minutes, and we're going to dinner."

After I hang up with my parents, I call Sheila. "Yes, I know, I heard. Mandy just called with the news."

We talk about the name of the product, and unlike my parents, Sheila says she and Chester think the name Ms. Prissy Big Hair is brilliant. I hear Chester whooping in the background.

I don't have much time to get ready after we hang up, so I just freshen my makeup, fluff my hair, and swap my blazer for a sparkly sweater. Then I call Tim.

"I'll be waitin'," he says.

As I ride down in the elevator, I feel as though I'm hovering a few inches off the floor. We get to the lobby, and the door opens. There stands Tim, beaming from ear to ear, holding a bouquet of flowers toward me. The woman behind me whispers loudly to the man beside her. "I think he's about to propose." That makes me giggle.

"What's so funny?" Tim asks.

I take the flowers and kiss him on the cheek. "I'm the happiest girl in New York."

Tim extends his elbow, and I place my hand in the crook of his arm. "And you'll be the most successful girl in New York very soon. So where would you like to go for dinner?"

I let go of his arm, hand him the bouquet, and lift my hands over my head, palms up. "Somewhere really high in the sky!"

Tim laughs. "Looks like you're already there, Priscilla."

I give him a huge hug and back away, leaving him standing there with a dopey look on his face. "And I'll stay up there in the clouds until the next class reunion, when there's no doubt someone will yank me right back down."

"You're such a glutton for punishment for goin', but I totally get it."

"I know you do, and that's why you'll probably be there too."

Tim shrugs and takes my hand. "We'll just have to see about that."

Discussion Questions

1. After the events surrounding the ten-year reunion, why do you think Priscilla wanted to go back for the fifteenth? Would you have gone if you were in her shoes?

2. Why do you think Tim continues to have hope for a relationship with Priscilla?

3. Do you think there's hope for Laura and Pete's marriage? What advice would you give them?

4. Have you ever known a woman like Celeste, who goes from being dowdy to attractive after a makeover? Did anything change besides her appearance?

5. Do you think Trudy is changing? If so, is it for the good? What do you think Trudy is looking for in life? Will she find it?

6. How is Priscilla's relationship with her mother changing? Do you think she'll ever win her mother's full approval?

7. Why do you think it's so important for Laura to go to Pete's cousin's wedding? How does this tie in to other aspects of her life?

8. What are your thoughts about Celeste and Jimmy's relationship?

9. How do you see Priscilla's office manager, Mandy, developing? Would you put confidence in an assistant who has made the mistakes she has? Why do you think Priscilla has kept her?

10. Piney Point is a small town. Do you think it can support the new salon and day spa? Would you go there to get pampered?

11. Do you relate to any of the characters in this series? If so, who and why?

12. Laura's life is a whirlwind of chaos, so why does she constantly nitpick grammar with her kids and husband?

If you enjoyed *Bless Her Heart*, you will love all three books in Debby Mayne's Class Reunion series: *Pretty Is as Pretty Does*, *Bless Her Heart*, and *Tickled Pink*. Here's a bonus chapter from the final book of the series, *Tickled Pink*.

1
Priscilla Slater

Laura and Pete Moss are happy to announce
Piney Point High School's
Twenty-year Reunion
on June 15, 2013, at 7:00 PM
in the brand-new Piney Point Community Center
Multipurpose Room.
Attire: Casual
RSVP: Laura or Pete Moss 601-555-1515
Note: There will be no preparty.

As I hold onto the twenty-year reunion invitation I picked up before leaving Jackson, I look out over the Atlantic Ocean and reflect on the last two high school reunions. Things sure have changed for me in the five years that have passed. I not only have managed to become a household name among TV retail shoppers who desire to have the coveted southern-woman big hair but also own townhomes and condos in several places along the path of my chain of hair salons. I've put so much work into attaining my ultimate dream I sometimes forget to thank the Lord for all He's blessed me with. So I close my eyes and send up a quick prayer of gratitude before backing away from the view and heading toward the kitchen where my microwaved dinner is almost done. I might have hit my business success goal, but some things haven't changed—one of them being my lack of time to cook meals. Besides, what's the point? It'll take me an hour to cook a meal that I can eat in ten minutes, and then I'm left with a mess to clean up.

As soon as the microwave dings, I grab a potholder and pull out the plastic tray with steam rising from the corner where I've vented the cellophane. I place it on the counter, lean over it, and inhale, trying to imagine it being a nutritious, home-cooked meal. But that's impossible because all I smell is preservative-laced gravy. Maybe I should go back to my old nightly salad-from-a-bag.

Ten minutes later, the plastic tray is empty, and I'm left with a hollow feeling in my stomach and emptiness in my heart. You'd think that with all I've acquired over the past thirteen years I'd be on top of the world, kicking up my feet, celebrating my immense success. But I'm not. Most nights I sit in one of my townhouses or a hotel room, alone with my paperwork or one of my guilty-pleasure reality shows on TV. Or both.

Don't get me wrong. I'm grateful that I've managed to accomplish so much. But there are times when certain aspects of a simple life in my hometown of Piney Point, Mississippi, appeals to me. Then I come to my senses.

I've never been one of those girls whose dreams consisted of getting married, having children, and settling for whatever came my way. Instead, I went after whatever I wanted with the focus and tenacity of a shark, until I got it. Then I set my sights on something else. Besides, after experiencing the realization that my parents' marriage wasn't what it appeared to be, I know that my image of *home* is just window dressing that disguises harsh realities. But that doesn't stop some of the longing for a more normal life, whatever that is.

It takes me all of thirty seconds to clean my sparkling chrome-and-black kitchen before I pick up the class reunion invitation on my way back to the tone-on-tone white and ivory living room. A smile plays on my lips as a brief image of one of Pete and Laura's children in one of my homes flits through my mind, and then I grimace. No telling what they'd do to my perfectly ordered life. Thoughts like that should make me happy I don't have children, but lately . . . well, it's simply not happening, so what's the point of wondering what could've been. All the "what ifs" in the world won't change a thing. And besides, this is what I've wanted all my adult life, so I order myself to stop with those thoughts and get back to the task at hand. I have less than a week to list and send the features and benefits of my newly updated hair volumizing system that includes everything a girl needs to have the "Ms. Prissy Big Hair" style. The TV Network Shopping channel has me on their regular schedule now, so even that has become so routine I can turn most of the preliminary work over to my long-time assistant Mandy. But I need something relaxing to do right now, so I sit down with my laptop and tap out my list as I half-watch the second-most dysfunctional family I've ever seen holler at each other on TV. I wonder if they do that when the cameras aren't rolling. Too bad the network doesn't know about Laura and Pete Moss's family, or they'd likely be filming in Piney Point rather than L.A.

Five years ago, Bonnie Sue Moss, the third of Laura's four children, got busted shoplifting a skirt from La Boutique in Hattiesburg. When I offered to go back to the store with her, Laura accepted without a moment's hesitation, in spite of the fact that she's never even pretended to like me. On the way to the shop, we stopped off at the post office, where I was stunned by the fact that the preteen girl was embarrassed to be seen with me. However, her tune quickly changed when the manager of the store immediately forgave her because of my slight celebrity status. I'm not sure what lesson Bonnie Sue learned that day, but I'm afraid my plan might have backfired, and she came away with the idea that if someone is famous, she can get away with anything. Now she e-mails and texts me constantly, wanting advice on how to become a superstar. I've told her more than once to find her passion, set goals, and work hard. Too bad her passion is for people to be in awe of her existence. In the last text I got from her, she wanted to know whether she should go to L.A. or New York after she graduates and which place would make her more famous. I need to talk to her mother before giving her advice, so I still haven't gotten back with her.

The features and benefits of my product line are basically the same, only reworded to prevent sounding redundant. I'm about to click SEND when my phone rings. It's Laura.

"I was just thinking about you," I tell her.

"Why are you answering your own phone?"

"Huh?"

"I thought famous people hired folks to answer their phone."

I've heard that Laura Moss has grown into her own skin, but from what I can tell, that maturity ends when I'm involved. "So what do you need?"

"Just wanted to find out if you're coming to the reunion."

"Yes, I'll be there."

"Are you . . . will you be bringing Tim?"

I suspect that's the purpose of the call, since my good friend, former ardent admirer, and favorite beauty supply salesman, Tim Puckett, has not only attended the previous class reunions with me but also singlehandedly moved mountains to make sure things ran smoothly. I don't know what Laura would have done without Tim.

"I haven't spoken with him in a few weeks, but I can ask."

"Can you let me know what he says?" I detect a hint of desperation in her voice.

"Why don't you call him?" I say.

Laura snickers. "I don't have the same clout you have. In case you haven't figured it out, that boy will do anything you want him to."

"Seems he takes orders from you quite well, Laura." I have a hard time keeping the snarkiness from my voice. This woman brings out the worst in me, which is one excellent reason I don't need to stay on the phone with her any longer than necessary.

"Just let me know what he says, okay? Oh, and while you're at it, ask if he can come a week early."

"I'll see what I can do."

After I hang up, I have to take a couple of deep breaths to calm down. Ever since I started building my business empire, I've managed to stay calm enough to buy and open nearly a hundred hair salons, including a couple that are full-service day spas. I'm one of the regulars on TVNS with a line of products that sell out every single time I'm on air. But one short conversation with Laura sends me into a dither that takes hours to recover from.

I get up and go to the kitchen for a glass of water, and my phone rings again. This time it's Tim.

"Have you gotten your invitation yet?"

By now I'm used to the fact that Tim gets my class news before me. He's super connected through my Piney Point salon, which has turned into Prissy's Cut 'n Curl and Ice Factory Day Spa. After Sheila and Chester confronted me about how we'd outgrown our old location, I made it my mission to find a better place. The historic Ice Factory had potential, so when I had the electricity turned on for the inspection, rodent-chewed wires caused a fire. I wound up paying more for the vacant lot than I would have if the building had been salvageable.

But then I saved money on building from scratch rather than renovating to historical society regulations.

"Priscilla?" His voice has softened to practically a whisper. "Are you still there?"

"Um, yeah. I got the invitation. So do you want to go with me again? I mean, I can totally understand if you can't, considering how busy you are with your new position and all."

He laughs. "I've been regional sales manager for three years, so I can handle it. Besides, I'm due for some time off."

"If you don't mind wasting it on my class reunion, I'd love for you to attend as my guest."

"You sure know how to sweet talk a guy, Priscilla. I'd be delighted to escort you to your class reunion. And I'll get there a week early to help Laura."

"Good. That was my next question. I'll need to call her and let her know."

"Tell you what," he says. "I'll call her to save the extra step. No point in everything going through you . . . that is, unless you want to be the middleman, er, woman."

"No, that's fine. Please feel free to call her. I'm sure she'll have plenty for you to do."

Again, he laughs. "Yeah, I'd pretty much bet my next paycheck on that." He clears his throat. "Not that I'm a bettin' man or anything. I don't want you to think—"

"No, I know what you're saying. Thanks, Tim."

"Just makin' sure. Let me know if you need anything else. I'll be back in Jackson in a few days. Mind if I stop by and take you to breakfast?"

"Sounds good." My phone beeps, letting me know I have another call. "It was great talking to you, Tim. Gotta run."

I click over to the next call. It's my mother, and she doesn't even bother with a greeting.

"When are you arriving for your reunion?"

"I haven't had much of a chance to think about it, with the TV work and all."

I hear a low grunt, reminding me that my mother disapproves of my chosen career, in spite of my success. "You know you're welcome to stay here, but I'll need to know when to plan on your arrival."

"Probably a week or two, depending on what all Laura needs from me."

"You'll have to give me an exact date, or I can't guarantee your room will be ready."

Rather than ask why I have to worry about my old room being ready since I'm the only person who ever stays in it, I agree to let her know. "If it's not convenient, I can stay in a hotel. I really don't mind."

"Don't be ridiculous, Priscilla. How would it look for me to let my only child stay in a hotel?"

"I guess it wouldn't look good." I pause. "How's Dad? Have you spoken to him lately?"

"Don't go getting the notion that your father and I will ever get back together. Our divorce has been final a good two years, and we've been separated for six. There's—"

"No, Mother, I don't have any such notion. I was just asking a simple question."

"Are you getting smart with me, Priscilla? Because if you are, I want you to know that even though you're a big shot on that silly network, you're still my daughter."

My breath is ragged as I slowly inhale. "No, I just wondered if you've talked to Dad."

"My answer is no, and I don't intend to talk to him as long as he continues to see that bimbo he's been dating."

I shudder. The very thought of either of my parents dating other people seems so wrong. They're my parents. They made it through more than thirty years of marriage, so why couldn't they have worked things out? Of course I don't ask Mother that because now I realize it's not all her fault.

"Call as soon as you know when you're coming so I can have Teresa get your room ready."

After we hang up, I lift my laptop, but before I strike the first key, my phone rings again. I glance at the caller ID and see that it's Mandy.

"Yes, I know about the reunion, and no, I don't know when I'm going to Piney Point."

"Whoa. What's got you in such a snit? I was just calling to see if you needed help with the features and benefits."

"Sorry, Mandy. I just got off the phone with Mother."

"Oh, no wonder. Anything I can do?"

"Just keep things running smoothly like you always do."

"Oh, Vanessa just hired a new hairdresser. Will you be comin' back to Jackson before the reunion so you can meet her?"

I pull up the calendar on my computer. "Looks like I might have a little time, so yes, I can slip in for a day or two."

"Maybe while you're here you can do something with my hair. Ever since you let Rosemary transfer to Raleigh, my color hasn't been right."

"I'll see what I can do." I hang up and lean back on the couch and close my eyes. I've managed to get everything I thought I wanted, but now I don't have time to enjoy any of it.

Want to learn more about author
Debby Mayne and check out other great
fiction from Abingdon Press?

Sign up for our fiction newsletter at
www.AbingdonPress.com
to read interviews with your favorite authors, find tips
for starting a reading group, and stay posted on what
new titles are on the horizon. It's a place to connect
with other fiction readers or post a
comment about this book.

Be sure to visit Debby online!

www.debbymayne.com
http://debbymayne.blogspot.com

What They're Saying About...

The Glory of Green, by Judy Christie
"Once again, Christie draws her readers into the town, the life, the humor, and the drama in Green. *The Glory of Green* is a wonderful narrative of small-town America, pulling together in tragedy. A great read!"
—Ane Mulligan, editor of *Novel Journey*

Always the Baker, Never the Bride, by Sandra Bricker
"[It] had just the right touch of humor, and I loved the characters. Emma Rae is a character who will stay with me. Highly recommended!"
—Colleen Coble, author of *The Lightkeeper's Daughter* and the *Rock Harbor* series

Diagnosis Death, by Richard Mabry
"Realistic medical flavor graces a story rich with characters I loved and with enough twists and turns to keep the sleuth in me off-center. Keep 'em coming!"—Dr. Harry Krauss, author of *Salty Like Blood* and *The Six-Liter Club*

Sweet Baklava, by Debby Mayne
"A sweet romance, a feel-good ending, and a surprise cache of yummy Greek recipes at the book's end? I'm sold!"—Trish Perry, author of *Unforgettable* and *Tea for Two*

The Dead Saint, by Marilyn Brown Oden
"An intriguing story of international espionage with just the right amount of inspirational seasoning."—*Fresh Fiction*

Shrouded in Silence, by Robert L. Wise
"It's a story fraught with death, danger, and deception—of never knowing whom to trust, and with a twist of an ending I didn't see coming. Great read!"—Sharon Sala, author of *The Searcher's Trilogy: Blood Stains, Blood Ties,* and *Blood Trails.*

Delivered with Love, by Sherry Kyle
"Sherry Kyle has created an engaging story of forgiveness, sweet romance, and faith reawakened—and I looked forward to every page. A fun and charming debut!"—Julie Carobini, author of *A Shore Thing* and *Fade to Blue.*

Abingdon Press fiction
a novel approach to faith

AbingdonPress.com | 800.251.3320

Discover Fiction from Abingdon Press

BOOKLIST 2010

Top 10 Inspirational Fiction award

ROMANTIC TIMES 2010

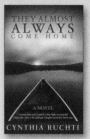

Reviewers Choice Awards
Book of the Year nominee

BLACK CHRISTIAN
BOOK LIST

#1 for two consecutive months,
2010 Black Christian Book
national bestseller list;
ACFW Book of the Month, Nov/Dec 2010

CAROL AWARDS 2010

(ACFW) Contemporary
Fiction nominee

INSPY AWARD NOMINEES

Suspense   General Fiction   Contemporary Fiction

Abingdon Press fiction
a novel approach to faith
AbingdonPress.com | 800.251.3320